About the Author

In 1994 Mark Robertson had his closest brush with fame when he 'became' the first drummer for legendary 'Girls Aloud' singer and X Factor judge Cheryl Cole. At the time Cheryl was eight years old and performing in The Whitley Bay Am-Dram Panto. Twelve years on Ms Cole was well on the way to amassing a multi-million pound fortune, pausing only to perform at venues like Wembley Stadium. Mark Robertson was still in the north-east, playing jazz gigs for food and/or petrol money. Stumbling on a set of cheap biros and some paper, he started an endeavour, the fruit of which you hold in your hands. It's a story about people who would struggle to find the entrance money to Wembley Stadium but they won't let a simple problem like being penniless stop them achieving their goal.

OFF KEY

Mark Robertson

Original cover art by Brian Gibson.
Cover photograph by permission of Jack Lowe © 2012 *jacklowestudio.co.uk*

Lyrics quoted in the text appear by permission of the copyright holders:
Devil May Care by Johnny Burke and Harry Warren
Lyrics © Warner/Chappell Music: Peer Music
Skylark by Johnny Mercer, Hoagy Carmichael
Lyrics © Warner/Chappell Music: Peer Music

Matador
9 Priory Business Park
Kibworth Beauchamp
Leicestershire LE8 0RX, UK
Tel: (+44) 116 279 2299
Fax: (+44) 116 279 2277
Email: books@troubador.co.uk
Web: www.troubador.co.uk/matador

ISBN 978-1784620-073

British Library Cataloguing in Publication Data.
A catalogue record for this book is available from the British Library.

Typeset in Aldine by Troubador Publishing Ltd
Printed and bound in the UK by TJ International, Padstow, Cornwall

Matador is an imprint of Troubador Publishing Ltd

Dedicated to Colin and Roma Carnegie, of Centre Stage, Northern Ireland.

To Ellie,

the Nerd who should be heard.

Love

Mark

The author would appreciate your thoughts!

markrobertson@offkeythenovel.com

offkeythenovel.com

My thanks to:
Denise Thubron, Barry Larking, Brian Gibson,
Jennifer Vigouroux, Northern Film and Media, Rea Cris,
Dr Jeremy Scratcherd MBBS DA, Elaine Connolly.

Prologue

She looked around the bedroom. Everything was ready. Her good navy suit, still in the cleaner's cover, hung on the wardrobe. Her shoes stood polished by the chest of drawers. Her makeup and jewellery were laid out on the dressing table. Undies on the chair. All she had to do was get eight hours of shut-eye and she could deal with anything the morning might bring. Her favourite nightie might be faded but it was warm and comfortable, she was moisturised to the nth degree. No stone left unturned, every foreseeable angle covered. She turned back the duvet and climbed into bed. If she got a decent night's sleep she could take the interview in her stride. She switched off the bedside lamp and snuggled down.

Chapter 1

"Of course he wasn't on a wage, you silly bastard."

"What did he live off then?"

"I don't know... what's the going rate for a homicidal maniac?"

"Search me... ask Kyle."

"You're seriously telling me that someone came round the Reichstag on a Friday afternoon, stopped at the Fuhrer's desk and said "Achtung, here's your wages."

"Ok. You tell me what he lived off then?"

Listening, Kyle bit his lip as he parked up the van. The vagaries of the Third Reich's pay structure had mesmerised them for over thirty minutes with little sign of it reaching a conclusion anytime soon. The sight of the battered notice board outside the pub's front door, as he alighted, did little for his morale either.

> "The Happy Man Public House
> resents jazz.
> With The Kyle Johnson Quartet"
> Admi sion £4, S udents / OAP's £2.

How had he, Kyle Johnson, ended up in a cultural desert like this? He'd practiced, he'd studied, he'd taken every jazz gig he could get his hands on. There'd been hours of solo noodling in his bedroom, sandwiched between football and half-hearted homework sessions. School bands, brass bands, quartets, quintets, be-bop, hard bop, post-bop, a veritable smorgasbord of styles. But somewhere along the line, the dream of performing in cities like New York, Chicago, and New Orleans had become, at thirty-four, the crushing reality of gigs in Sunderland, Hartlepool and Middlesbrough… physically and culturally about as far away from 'the home of jazz' as you could get. Which made what he was doing here now, in the sticks, when he could be at home with the woman he loved that much harder to bear.

He poked his head in the door of the pub and scanned the surroundings, hoping that perhaps something had changed since their last visit. It hadn't. They played there once a month in a venue that, he had to admit, had seen better days. Plaster from the distressed interior had sloughed off on to a carpet already heavily burdened with broken glass, dust and rancid pork scratchings. The windows, opaque with years of dirt and grime, allowed no looking in and no looking out. Everything in the place was on its last legs save for the 42 inch plasma screen television that dominated the room. Not surprisingly it was deserted. The band were now absorbed in the process of transferring their equipment from the van to the makeshift stage, all talk of Hitler forgotten. Kyle left them to it and set off to track down Alfie, the Landlord. This wasn't a difficult task. He was, not for the first time, asleep in the cellar, a copy of "TV Quick" rising and falling on his beer belly to the rhythm of his snoring. On balance, Kyle decided a sleeping Landlord was better than a grumpy one and left well alone.

When he returned he found the rest of the band were determinedly at loggerheads over which songs to play. A smattering of punters had trickled in which bestowed the mantle of a proper gig, as opposed to the glorified rehearsal it sometimes was. Which meant the set list took on some importance.

The most animated of the group was drummer Andy Valentine. He was a good looking boy, in a 'Lidl own brand champagne' sort of a way. A reasonable route map of his gigs could be gleaned from the "Little Valentines" that sprouted up around nine months after his musical engagements. This penchant for licentiousness had left

Andy with two ex-wives and many on/off girlfriends. His economic situation, femmer even before the closure of the local call centre, was now in free-fall and at this moment his rage, which had progressed to finger jabbing, was aimed in the direction of Barry. Barry was a different proposition. To be living with your divorced Mother, sleeping in a room that still had a poster of Man United's 1983 cup winning side blue-tacked on the wall, was not an ideal situation at any age... even more so at forty-two. He had only ever gone out with one girl, the daughter of one of his mother's friends. It had lasted a week and although it hadn't become a physical relationship he had still got himself thoroughly checked out by a doctor afterwards.

It was bass player, Ludo, who was the greatest enigma. Every band had a member like Ludo, an explosion of curly hair, crumpled cheese-cloth shirts and Rizla papers who could be as oil on troubled waters unless he was bored, when he became as incendiary as a petrol tanker doing handbrake turns in a timber yard.

Kyle watched as the situation escalated until the three of them were swearing and throwing sheets of music at each other. They were all claiming the mantle of band leader, an assertion which would last until the first sign of trouble, when it would transpire that he was the person in charge after all.

"Hardly worth you lot playing is it? Not to three people." Alfie had emerged from the cellar, rubbing sleep from his eyes. Kyle ignored him, opting instead to focus on the turmoil in front of him.

"Hardly worth you lot playing is it?" The Landlord was nothing if not persistent.

Kyle exhaled slowly and gazed at the visible condensation. If he could have played sax with his gloves on he would have done. The pub's heating system had given up the ghost in the December of 2003. It was, he had been assured, on the Publicans list of things to sort out... about half way down.

"I say, it's hardly worth you playing is it." Alfie had his teeth into it now.

But Kyle had had enough; he was not to be deterred any longer and made his way purposefully to the small stage. He had experienced poorly attended gigs like this a thousand times before; a simple absence of bodies wasn't going to stop him. The first note of his saxophone was bouncing off the far wall before the Landlord's comment was cold in the air. On occasions like this you were left with little option but to tear into the music like a man possessed in an attempt to fill the void. With the rest of the band in tow he laid into "Cherokee". Sometimes, if you closed your eyes for long enough, you could imagine the place was packed with cheering fans, standing room only. It was obviously going to be one of those nights where you had to keep your eyes shut so tight it hurt.

★

Harry caught sight of her, a blur of primary colours and a dirty blonde mop as she spun round the fitment. It happened occasionally. A small child would escape, bored with the endless rows of boxes, bottles, bags and bargains. He could relate to that, breaking free and running away. She moved with an abandonment that suggested freedom was a rare thing. He had used this supermarket before, understaffed, late evening and half asleep, as a source of topping up his alcoholic intake. They had usually stopped him way before this. Perhaps the security cameras were down. The little girl had seen him now and her mood changed abruptly. He must look quite threatening to someone that small, sprawled on the ground in his good herringbone coat and best fedora hat. She couldn't be more than five or six, thin legged and wild-eyed, like a new foal and clutching her tattered toy tiger for all she was worth. Kids were often like that, he thought, a bit wary. There was only one thing for it. He rushed to get his horn out of its case sharpish before she bolted. Postman Pat should do it… everybody liked Postman Pat. How, he thought as he placed the reed in his mouth, had he ended up here? Harry Crabb, "European jazz musician of the year" 1967 to 1968,

4

playing gratis to an audience of one in a Sunderland supermarket. With two choruses of the theme tune over, the little girl remained, wide eyed although he liked to think she was now more intrigued than scared. Ever the gentleman, he offered her a drink from the half empty bottle of champagne, rubbing the top with his sleeve.

"No that's dirty. Mammy says it's bad. It's a illness." Harry lowered his head in shame as the little girl held out her stuffed toy towards him in a gesture of apology.

"This is Mister Hobbes, he's a tiger."

"He's not hungry, I hope," said Harry.

"Yes, he is, very. He likes tuna fish."

"I thought tigers preferred cheese and onion crisps or, failing that, people."

"No, it's tuna fish."

"Do you think he might settle for a song instead? And you are?"

"My name's Trudy Rebecca and Hobbes would like a song very much, please."

A smile broke across the child's face, revealing a number of missing baby teeth.

"Very well, Trudy. This song is for you and your tiger." Harry beamed benignly as he began to sing, occasionally accompanying himself on the sax to the tune of 'Chinese laundry blues'.

"Oh! Mr Hobbs, no tears or sobs.
You've found yourself a girl
to call your own.
Now Mr Hobbs
no tears or sobs.
You've found that special girl
to call your own."

At the music's end Harry reached for another drink. Finishing the bottle he regarded her solemnly. "It's very late, Trudy, even for a grown up girl like you."

She nodded vigorously. "Mummy has to shop at night and work all the hours God sends because Daddy couldn't keep his prick in his trousers."

From the corner of his eye Harry saw a woman at the top of the aisle that he took to be the girl's mother. Even in his befuddled state he knew how people viewed solitary old men entertaining little girls but he was dammed if he was going to cut and run now, even if he could stand up, which he couldn't.

From the other end of the aisle two store security guards rushed towards him. They apprehended him just as the demented woman got hold of her daughter. Her judgment was swift "Pervert" she screamed. Groggy as he was, Harry thought this a poorly informed critique of his intentions as a performer. However that was the least of his problems.

Subduing someone who didn't look more than six years old wasn't a major problem; Harry knew from experience that he was a trickier prospect. Most of the guard's efforts were quite necessarily devoted to holding him upright, leaving very little over to propel him forward and out of the store. Trudy's face had fallen at their enforced parting but Harry, ever the pro, managed to free one arm and, taking off his hat, gave her the most dramatic bow he could manage. She waved back wildly before he was dragged out of her sight forever. This was not, he thought proudly, the first time the former European jazz musician of the year had made a female conquest during the course of a performance.

Returning his hat to its rightful place, he regarded his captors. "Please, sirs. I beseech you, a little more humanity and pray thee do not shake whilst full... I have been sampling your excellent selection of wines and spirits with a view to making a not inconsiderable purchase." The persuasiveness of this exposition was ruined once he started to vomit. "That'll be the Krug." he said, wiping his mouth on his sleeve. "It was very modestly priced."

Not for the first time in his life he found himself exiting one of his "gigs" head first.

★

The fact that they had managed to keep all three of the audience in situ for the duration of the performance was something of a comfort for Kyle. The gig drew to a sorry close with an incongruous rendition of "This joint is jumping" followed by a smattering of compassionate applause. All that remained was the real slog of the night, the breaking down and loading of their equipment. When you were setting up you had, in theory, something to look forward to. Once the gig was over it was work. The sheer bulk of gear needed for a small jazz quartet always staggered him, although once everything was up and running it didn't look like much. Over time and under a number of mentors, he had learned that there was a knack to packing a van. The trick was for everything to have its allotted place. Done properly it would end up as one solid piece of work and no road-works, cobbles or "sleeping policemen" could cause its disintegration. Doing it badly would necessitate removing everything and starting all over again... sometimes twice. The art was a cross between building a Ferrari engine and solving a Rubik's cube... in the dark.

As they worked it was difficult to ignore Andy's unintentional rumba as he dismantled his drum kit. It was a reasonable guess that his discomfiture was due to the germ warfare being conducted in his pants, as his latest STD tried to fight off the finest anti-biotics the NHS could provide. Kyle shook a rueful head and turned back to the packing. The landlord was fully engrossed in finding "Thongs of Praise" on the adult channel as a thought occurred to Kyle.

"Thirty years ago this place would have been heaving for a jazz gig; the older guys had it way too easy."

Barry grunted disagreement. "What publicity did you do for the gig?"

"I shouldn't have to do any publicity." The moment Kyle spoke he regretted it. He knew what was coming the minute he saw Barry reach for the log book in which he noted down the sorry state of the band's finances. This dog-eared inventory of failure always drove him crazy. Barry kept it, he claimed, so that "One day when our ship comes in I'll have a record of what I'm owed in terms both financial and emotional."

As Barry fingered his book he launched his attack. "If you'd got your arse off that high horse and done some spade work the audience members might have outnumbered the band members."

"So I'm our promoter now?" Kyle felt his anger rising as he spoke.

"It's your band and you've got loads more time than we have."

"You reckon?"

"Some of us have to make a living," Andy chipped in, unhelpfully.

"And I don't?" Andy gave him a look but Kyle continued undaunted. "For your information I have a busy teaching schedule."

This wasn't exactly a lie. "Busy" meant one or two afternoons a week teaching a local schoolboy to play the sax. These arguments with the band rarely led to any point, they just allowed everyone to vent off a little steam. Deep down they all knew they were stuck with each other. A wet Monday night in a deserted country pub wasn't the kind of gig for which other musicians would cut their throats.

Despite the friction the process of getting what seemed like one ton of equipment in a 1/2 ton truck drew to a close. Amplifiers were stashed, drums were cased, bass guitars and keyboards were sandwiched in between as Alfie hustled the band towards the back door, trying to minimise the disruption to his viewing as the faked orgasmic screams of the Adult Chanel filtered out into the night air.

"Right lads, that's you done then? Probably best leave next month's gig for now; I'll give you a ring."

Heads went down and seeing their obvious deflation, he continued. "You don't know any Neil Diamond songs do you? I've been dropped in it by Neville Emerald, Friday week... a proper gig, money upfront and everything... I've always got space for a decent tribute act. Take a tip from Welsh Tony's band; they go out now... Abba-rystwyth, I think they call themselves. They're cleaning up in the pubs and clubs round here."

"We play jazz." Kyle said defiantly.

"Well... if you ever fancy it... you only have to ask."

Kyle shook his head wearily and climbed into the driver's seat. Tribute band! As if! He coaxed the vehicle into life, trying hard not to dwell on the notion of making a living aping Sweden's most visible cultural export.

In the back of the van the autopsy on their evening continued but once they were packed in tight, their dynamic became one of unity against their trials and tribulations. Barry began the painful process of putting the night's business in writing. Even above the engine's noise, the scratching of the fountain pen got on Kyle's nerves.

"We made £9 in door money plus £12.52 in free beer. A profit of £21.52 pence, less VAT and capital gains tax, of course." This caused a number of groans and ironic cheers.

"That bloke in the corner got me a toasty," Andy said, attempting to raise their spirits.

"Well, why didn't you say so earlier?" Barry wasn't keen on making corrections. He had a crusty bottle of Tippex purchased in the 'Eighties' and he had sworn that the band would be successful before it ran out. There wasn't a great deal of it left.

"OK we've got £9 in door money, £12.52 in beer, how much was that toasty?"

Before Andy could answer, the minor growling that accompanied the van's general activity had progressed to a full-on grinding ker-chunk-a-chunk. The vehicle began to splutter and then over the course of fifty yards ground to a halt.

9

"Christ, this is all I bloody need." Kyle had had enough of the whole affair now.

The van's indoor light gave a weak gasp and snuffled out, leaving all four of them more than thirty miles from home in an over-laden and broken down rust bucket. He turned the engine over again and again but it was clearly impotent. In a last act of desperation he head butted the steering wheel, leading the horn to blare out continuously, which gave him some relief. He would've accepted anything in that moment, anything that would help blot out all thoughts of the days to come, days stretching on for ever, days destined to be spent in impoverished, unrecognised, unmitigated misery. Eventually, with a limp whine, the siren went the way of the light and the engine.

In the darkness, Andy broke the silence. "It cost £1.75… it was ham and cheese".

Chapter 2

It took Harry a while to re-orientate himself once he had climbed down from the industrial bins that had broken his fall. As ever, his foremost concern was for 'Baby' and at first sight everything seemed fine. They'd put her back in her case before they'd thrown him out, which was decent of them. He double-checked. There were no dents in the bodywork and the braces, key guards and springs were fine. He could relax, although, as the alcohol began to wear off, he realised that his own bodywork had not got off so lightly. His left foot had twisted rather badly and his elbow felt wet, as if it was bleeding through his good herringbone coat. Gingerly, he propped himself up and tried to place a little weight on his left foot but it wasn't pleasant. Tears welled up in his eyes at the second attempt. Steadying himself on his saxophone case he managed to get upright but it wasn't for long. The rapidly swelling ankle was incapable of giving him any real support so he lowered himself back to the ground on his good leg and reaching into the pocket of his coat gave thanks to St. Jude the patron saint of forward planning as he pulled out two Johnny walker miniatures and a triple pack of sandwiches, his favourite ham, cheese and pickle. He had been wise enough to stash away these emergency rations before his drinking escapade. The sandwiches were crushed and slightly warm from his body but they were utterly delicious and filled a gaping hole. Had the security men given him the opportunity to pay for the goods then he most certainly would have done. As they hadn't, he didn't feel any qualms about tucking in to them gratis. In fact, the method of appropriation only enhanced their already full-bodied flavour, almost enough to take his mind off his injuries. His leg and the grazed elbow were starting to throb. He knew from experience that it would only get worse as the alcohol left him. If he set off now it would be slow going but he should be able to make 'The Skinners' before what was always a generous interpretation of last orders and Dave wouldn't turn him away without at least one drink inside him. He'd probably need to play something on 'Baby' or the old piano if he was going to get anything else to drink but he didn't think it would be a problem. The last of the sandwiches gone, he steadied himself once more and tried to stand as the first of the night's downpours kicked in.

★

Kyle peered once more into the hot, dank recess of the engine. Twenty minutes had passed in a heated argument over strategy, with staring into the mechanical abyss as far as they had progressed. A root around in the undergrowth had provided Ludo with a stick which he used to prod at the engine, like a timid boy probing at a dangerous, but probably dead, creature.

"A friend of my Dad's bookie was scarred for life by an exploding van," he offered. Kyle didn't worry too much about this prospect. Ludo always seemed to have a friend of a friend who had come to a grim end from the most unthreatening of circumstances. A camping holiday, a visit to the library, the WRVS knitting circle… all of them posed their own cataclysmic threat.

He tried not to panic as Andy took the keys and turned the engine over again. What followed sounded like a chain smoker's rising cough. Storm clouds were gathering and the very real threat of being abandoned on the moors for a cold, wet night loomed closer. He could understand why the band looked to him for the solutions to their woes, but the answers he provided always entailed a greater degree of personal grief for him than for them. Soon, they would lean on him to call out Charlie, because, if a mechanic was what was called for it was a no-brainer... no one had Charlie's touch where ailing vehicles were concerned. But once it was sorted, the rest of them would be heading for home, he'd be heading for nowhere but the doghouse. He contemplated trying to load the equipment onto passing livestock and riding it all in to town like John Wayne but deep down he knew there was only one person who could get them out of this mess.

"Anyone seen my phone?"

He misplaced his mobile on an almost an hourly basis, a source of much ribbing from the band. Not for the first time it turned out he was the only person ignorant of where it was. There was a chorus of information and he retrieved it from the van's dashboard. At least it still had some power and he could get a signal... which was the most positive thing that had happened all night. He took a quick look at his watch. The night sky was hinting at rain any minute. Christ, it was cold; they could die here and not be found for days. He looked at his watch again hoping for a different result. It was late now, not musician-late but late none the less. He tapped out the number. The damage was done and it was simply a case of waiting for the inevitable fallout. The tired groan at the other end confirmed that the countdown to his personal Armageddon had begun.

"Hello Charlie, it's me... Yes, I know what time it is... yes, it is the van again... sure, if you want to lend me eight grand... yes I've tried that... and that." He hoped the darkness didn't reveal his blush. He thought it best to say as little as possible as the grief on the other end started to ferment.

"No, I didn't forget... you should have... please!"

He moved out of earshot of the band in an attempt to gain some privacy. There was no need for them to hear the 'dance' between him and Charlie again.

"Look, all I said was... look, you'll be fine... what else can we do... no, don't you worry... we'll just stay here and starve to bloody death. We've got to stay with the van... there's about five grand's worth of gear inside it... I'll get up in the morning and make you

13

breakfast, fried, the full bit, promise… we're about a mile from "The Happy Man" pub in Weardale. Yes… Ha! Ha! Very funny… see you soon… you're a star. You know I… " The call was terminated abruptly… not the most encouraging sign.

In his absence the band had progressed to rolling fags and swapping Miles Davis anecdotes.

"That's it sorted." he said reassuringly. For them maybe. His troubles were only just beginning. But then what else could he do when it involved spanners and tins of WD40.

Once the band had exhausted everyone's repertoire of Miles Davis stories they moved on to their other perennial topic, Andy's 'love' life… it was a rare night when there wasn't discussion on that front, principally because Andy's 'lovers' had a sell by date on them similar to a pint of milk or… if he was really smitten… a block of cheese. With the gentlest of coaxing, whilst rolling a fag, he went on to detail his adventures with the Head of the Pontypridd branch of the Abba fan club. A girl he referred to only as "the lovely Angharad"

"You know 92 million Chlamydia infections occurred worldwide in 2010." Barry tried to make the remark sound casual… no one was fooled.

"I know how to play safe." Andy said defensively.

Kyle listened passively, hoping it wouldn't come to blows. Barry had appointed himself Andy Valentine's conscience after coming to the conclusion that there was a vacancy in this position. He was in full flow now.

"If you're so careful, how come you've got the CSA on your tail?"

Kyle winced. What they needed now was harmony. There would be discord enough once Charlie arrived.

Receiving no answer Barry repeated his question. "I said how come you've got the CSA on your tail?" This time Andy had an answer.

"They're Guinness babies… they don't count."

Even by moonlight Andy's wide grin was evident as he removed the pitifully thin cigarette from his mouth.

"Guinness babies?" The band spoke in unison.

"Ever tried negotiating a Durex after half a dozen bottles of the black stuff?"

Ludo was sceptical. "If that was true then wouldn't the Holy Father pass out communion stout by the crate, soft lad?"

"Soft lad" was Ludo's least unpleasant moniker for Andy and, to Kyle's relief, before they could go any further down this route there was the sound of a car. Odds on it was Charlie, there in something under forty minutes. Kyle traced the headlights' rapid path through the pitch darkness before the battered Ford Fiesta screeched to a halt in front of them. If cars had possessed the ability to snort and sweat it would have done. Eventually, after what seemed like a lifetime, the door was swung open with a degree of force and Charlie emerged from the vehicle.

She looked like an unmade bed. Her hair was flattened down one side of her head and she was dressed in the not-exactly-cat-walk combination of pink nightie, leggings and a cardigan. Still in her slippers, she promptly sank into the cold thick mud around her. In other circumstances, that is to say with another girl, the band might have afforded themselves a little giggle, but this was Charlotte and they knew better. Kyle gave her his hand and guided her through the mire towards the van.

"I don't suppose you've looked under the bonnet." Her tone was ice.

Kyle looked down and mumbled, closely followed by the rest of the band.

Looking at them Charlotte felt some of her anger evaporate. "I thought you lot spent your youth hot-wiring cars?" She didn't expect an answer and none was forthcoming. It was no wonder. They only ever saw her yelling and raging at Kyle. Relationships apart, she was one of the planet's most placid human beings but with Kyle, and more usually with Kyle and his silly, bloody band, it was never long before her temper frayed.

Now she turned her attention to the stricken engine. It only

15

took one whiff of oil and petrol from under the bonnet of some stricken vehicle to conjure up memories, tinkering with Aston Martins with Mr Sykes as he performed miracles on her father's dilapidated classic veteran vehicles. Where were men like that nowadays? Certainly not standing in front of her right now.

She had a fairly good working knowledge of the van, born of previous call-outs to put it to rights. The A19 Washington turn off… slight drizzle. Easington services… dry but freezing. Stockton… so foggy it took an hour driving in circles to find them. Chester-le – street… total downpour and a gale force wind… what stellar memories to treasure of time spent with her boyfriend. Still, if she was to get any sleep at all she would need to coax the old girl back to life.

"Kyle, turn the ignition key… off… now try it again… hold on… and again."

She stretched to get to a far part of the engine. If she could just reach the distributor it might all end relatively happily and she could go back to bed. "What in the name of God" she thought "am I doing on the moors at two in the morning, guts deep in a clapped out Ford Transit mark two engine, covered in oil." The stuff was even on her bloody face now.

"Again," she demand of Kyle and he complied without question.

The van spluttered into life and the band gave a cheer, it was over. Kyle gazed admiringly at Charlie and hoped that just for once she might put it down to experience. It wasn't like he'd done it on purpose.

"Ludo can take the van and I'll come back with you if you want, Charlie," he said placatingly.

She hadn't so much as glanced at him since her arrival and he knew why. On the days that he had gigs he could forget things, important things, like Charlie's meeting with her new boss, which hopefully meant she would keep her job in spite of some kind of hoo-ha about being taken over by some multi-conglomerate. That was the problem with devoting yourself to the music of Miles and

Coltrane, they took you out of yourself and things happened in the real world while you were absent. With no answer forthcoming he spoke again.

"I'll get my horn. Are we all fixed for the rehearsal?"

He thought the best plan was to act like he hadn't done anything wrong. It was a high risk strategy bringing with it the possible additional accusation of thoughtlessness but it was his only tack.

"I can pick up Barry and we'll get Andy on the way" Ludo offered, getting into the van.

As they advanced towards the battered Ford, Kyle turned to Charlie. The timing of this wasn't great but he knew what he had to do. Only he'd need to do it quietly, he didn't want anyone else to know.

"I couldn't borrow a tenner could I? Only it was a door money gig and… "

She shrugged wearily and reached into the car for her purse, holding it gingerly in her oily hand.

"Go on. Take it, take it." He slunk back to the band and palmed the money to Andy as surreptitiously as possible; covering the deed with an excuse about making sure he had everything.

He returned to Charlie who was now revving the car impatiently. He clambered in beside her. Best to say nothing and sink deep into the seat. He had perfected the art of fading into the background while he was still a child; if he was really quiet as bedtime approached his Mother would forget the time, even if he was in the same room. Valuable minutes of television could be gained, especially on a school night, if you went into dormouse mode. Charlie still hadn't looked at him. Was he going to get away with it? The silence grew even heavier as the battered Ford hurtled forwards through the countryside. He realised, as the speedometer edged ever upwards, that far from being off the hook, the longer he waited the worse it was likely to be. A deeper silence settled… painfully deep, deeper still. Eventually, unable to handle any further tension, he snapped.

"Come on, I can't take much more of this. Let's get it over with. I'd rather you let me have both barrels now than you wrapped us both round some lamppost."

Charlie took a deep breath and held it. The length of time she could rant on with just one breath had always impressed him. She had the potential to make a half way decent sax player with that kind of lung capacity. He wisely decided to keep this observation to himself. He opted instead for the tactic of buttering her up before she could speak.

"You're good with things like that, cars and vans and… " Another high risk strategy but he was desperate. "I can't risk getting my hands hurt in an engine. No fingers, no gigs."

He trilled an imaginary saxophone as he said this, which he quickly realised wasn't doing him any favours.

Her voice was cold steel. "I think we'd cope with the financial blow somehow. You know what hit me as I drove through here? That if I hadn't had to support you, I'd be qualifying as a barrister about now.

"Hold on! You can't blame me for that, I was happy enough signing on once a fortnight but of course that would have made me an embarrassment when you introduced me to your hoity-toity bloody family. Now I understand, now we're getting to the truth of the matter."

"Kyle".

Oh God! It was that tone, the red button one! She was going to use the T word. He hated the T word more than anything.

"Look I really can't go on like this. We need to talk."

There it was, the God-awful 'T word'. And it was the way she said it. He always knew it was trouble when she started to sound calm and controlled. He was more at home with straight fury; he knew where he was with that. When she said they would talk it most decidedly meant she would talk. He took a deep breath; he might as well go hammer and tongs now in the hope that it would blow itself out like a bushfire.

"Yak! Yak! Yak! Every minor obstacle in our lives, "We need to talk". So you had to get out of your pit, I should be a qualified motor mechanic already. Oh no, too bloody late. "We need to bloody talk.""

"Well thanks, thanks a lot. I'm forgoing sleep, the night before an important day at work, to help my no-good, free-loading musician boyfriend and that's the thanks I get."

"You can leave anytime you want and anyway, I bet I cost you less than your clothes bill every month."

"You're thirty four, you shouldn't be costing me anything."

The plan was to egg Charlie on till she went over the top. Then she would feel guilty and he would be in the clear. Tonight it didn't seem to be working; he waited an appropriate length of time before breaking the silence with an act of contrition.

"You didn't mean it, did you?"

"What?"

"That bit about me being "a no good musician?""

"No. As a musician you're first rate. It's as a human being that you're a bit of a let-down."

Despite himself he found this last comment comforting after what had been yet another lousy gig.

Chapter 3

In the cold light of day Charlotte wasn't in the mood for tiptoeing around Kyle's sleeping form so she clashed her mug on to the drawers as loudly as she could. The degree of clutter the bedroom contained made her feel physically sick. Sheet music, compact discs, scribbled messages about gigs, set lists for gigs, directions for bloody gigs… how in God's name had she ended up here? At this point in her life she was meant to be waking up in a bedroom overlooking Hyde Park before preparing for a day spent as a humble yet courageous crusading lawyer. Instead she was in a pig-sty in Sunderland. The clock on the bedside table said 8.30 AM. Morning to most reasonable human beings but the middle of the night as far as the comatose creature still in her bed was concerned. Grouse over, she took a look in the mirror with a degree of satisfaction. Considering the night she'd had, she'd managed to scrub up quite well and the formal skirt and blouse looked business like. She turned to leave just as the prone figure stirred. He was blinking wildly and trying to focus on her face and, just for a fraction of a second, her heart melted.

"Well then, how do I look on four hours sleep?"

Kyle managed what he hoped was an appreciative grunt. He knew somewhere in the back of his head that he needed to be apologising for some transgression. That's why sleep was such a glorious state of being… you could hide from anything in the Land of Nod. He couldn't, however, hide from the note of sarcasm in Charlotte's voice as she thanked him for her cooked breakfast. Oh God, that was it. He roused himself on one elbow.

"Sorry I forgot, I… err… thanks for last night, the lift and all, sorry if I got a bit, you know, stroppy… it wasn't a great gig… can I make you some toast or something."

"It's a little late in the day for that. And while I'm on, have you rung your mother recently?"

"Not yet I've been… busy. I'll ring her today."

The memories of the previous night's debacle were slowly filtering into his head. He knew, even in this befuddled state, that pretending to make an effort now could save him untold grief when Charlie got back from work but, as the door closed behind her, the threat of "We'll talk this evening" hung in the air like a bad smell.

He rolled over and gave himself a good scratch. She was gone now so at least he had the rest of the day to marshal his arguments. A couple of hour's kip would help clear his mind so he could focus on what needed to be done. He stretched as wide as he physically could, yawned, rolled over and luxuriated in the warmth that Charlie's body had left behind. He would set the alarm for a reasonable time like midday and get to grips with things then. Tidying up the flat… that should get him some brownie points for starters.

★

Dave O' Driscoll surveyed his domain. "The Skinners arms" was a drinking man's pub for sure, without any of that neon signs, spritzers "happy hour" nonsense and, in his personal opinion, all the better for that. The giant clock above the bar said twenty past eleven. Seven and a half minutes out… which, for a clock that was over a hundred and twenty years old, wasn't bad going. The pub's owner, one Peter Cedric Callen, lived in Jersey and as long as they sent him a modest amount of cash at the end of each financial year they were free to carry on without recourse to modernisation of any kind.

Everything in the pub had been built to last, as long as a little spit and polish was used once in a while. The fixtures and fittings in the place looked old and distressed because they were old and distressed. This, he had come to realise after his fifteen years residency, could be applied to majority of the clientele.

The morning sun shone through the windows onto the cracked mosaic floor and he felt a warm glow at the sight. Donning his striped apron, he started taking the first steps towards shifting the pub into gear for the afternoon trade, carrying out his duties with a quasi-religious fervour. This was the one time of the day that any kind of order could be imposed on the place and he cherished every moment of it.

From out of the depths of a large green leather couch at the far end of the bar, oblivious to the graft going on behind him Harry Crabb, jazz musician and gentleman entertainer, slowly and shakily emerged… a little dishevelled even by his own basic standards. He ran through what he could remember of the previous night. It always set his mind at rest if he could remember why he was waking up where he was waking up. His arrangement with "The Skinners" had grown organically over his years of patronage. He could crash out there overnight, but no more than three times in any one four week period. That was their deal. This was time number three and it was still only the middle of the month. Fortunately, Dave O' Driscoll's mathematics could get charitably vague if he looked desperate. If he looked really, really desperate then he could leave Baby with Dave in exchange for the odd drink until he'd rustled up a few bob to get her back. Dave O Driscoll was the only other person in the world he trusted Baby with. Bang on cue, he caught sight of him and spoke. "The beast awakes." Harry gave a stretch as Publican drew nearer. "I'm glad you're up, Harry… five minutes more and I was away for to get the undertaker." With that Dave returned to his polishing and cleaning.

"I must have dozed off." Harry yawned as he stretched full length again then made a half-hearted attempt to make himself look decent. He knocked his hat into some kind of shape, scraped at the dry stains on his jacket and sniffed at the wet ones. None of these measures was particularly effective from a sartorial point of view but at least they served as some kind of inventory as to how he was. His foot was just a little stiff but his bloodied elbow hurt like buggery. Fortunately he was well practiced in a form of callisthenics which involved not only gentle exercise of the injured part but also the slow, pleasurable admission of an agreeable liquid analgesic.

"Continental breakfast, Sir?" Dave's timing couldn't have been any better.

Harry nodded his agreement. The Publican was certainly one of God's angels and knew better than to send a friend off into the World without something in his belly and certainly not a friend with Harry's comprehensive knowledge of the 'gee-gee's'. He savoured the aroma as Dave drew off two pints of bitter with the grace of a dancer. This was swiftly accompanied by a plate on the bar containing four pieces of hot buttered toast done just how he liked it, with the butter thick enough to see teeth marks in. The final touch was "The Racing Post", all pristine and virginal. What delights did it contain? Now they were ready to take on all comers... today was indisputably a day for picking winners.

★

Charlotte tried to make herself as comfortable as possible as they sat in the corridor. At least Dainty, as her closest friend, didn't require anything in the way of pleasantries. The plain truth of it was she was just too exhausted for small talk. Uptight suits hummed past as they sat side by side, static against the blur of activity fizzing around them. The way the world was geared these days, it was easy to end up obsessing about your work. Praying that you wouldn't lose a job you didn't like in the first place. The sad fact was that their small company had been devoured by a big company that had itself been consumed by an enormous one. A hundred new brooms had descended and every one of them fixated on changing everything they encountered. Charlotte knew she needed to keep her wits about her if she didn't want somebody else's promotion to be earned from handing out her P45. Meanwhile, her teeth gritted at the thought that lover boy would still be tucked up in bed trying to work out what TV programme he was going to eat his leisurely full English to. She wanted to scream at the thought but settled for yawning and swearing under her breath. Wanton howling outside the office of your new boss was probably not the wisest course of action for a girl who needed to hold down her position.

"You seem pretty laid back about this." Dainty whispered.

"I'm just exhausted."

"A night of passion?"

"Not these days."

"Couldn't sleep? You're not nervous are you… you'd be the last one they got shot of, you do know that, don't you?"

"I was filling in for the RAC at two in the morning for four grown men whose knowledge of car maintenance begins and ends with playing 'Grand theft Auto'. I got to bed at gone three-thirty."

Dainty tried her best not to scowl before she spoke. "He doesn't deserve you." She didn't expect a reply and she didn't get one. She wouldn't deny that divorce had coloured the notion of "true love" into which she had so readily bought as a young girl. 'Love'… that was a laugh… her friends had warned her and her family had warned her… even her hairdresser had warned her and still she hadn't listened. Now her Ex was road-testing the bed springs with her Chief Bridesmaid in their… that is to say her… marital home. Still, this wasn't the morning for bitter reminiscing. "I'm not overly fond of weekday mornings at the best of times," she said, looking sideways at her friend. At least Charlotte was there and that was a comfort. There were times when female solidarity was important… no… vital and this was one of them. Odd, in the circumstances, that they were so close really… Charlotte with all that old money in her family and going to a poncy school, which didn't sound like much fun for all the price tag. Not that her own home education at the hands of her dad had been an easy ride. By the time he had brought up her brothers and sisters there wasn't a single thing you could get past him. But, given the option, she was glad that she had been taught by someone who loved her. Charlotte was probably the first person since her Dad who understood how she ticked… no wonder they didn't take to her at public school.

"I miss Ken already" Charlotte said wistfully.

"I know what you mean. He was no alpha male but he was big and funny and human and I loved him… don't expect the office parties to be as much fun… I didn't think he was old enough to retire. Now what are we going to be stuck with? Someone who gets paid a lot more than we do will appear to tell us to 'push the envelope, till it's outside of the box facilitating transcendence in our core drives, it's all about how much bollocks you can speak these days. What they actually mean is "Hoy! You lot down there, work harder, our managing director's second yacht won't buy itself, you know."

Charlotte looked serious before she replied.

"When I was young the family money didn't register, it was just how things were. The only people I met who didn't have money were in our employ. Once I got to University it came as something of a shock to learn that the kind of privileges I'd grown up with weren't enjoyed by one and all. I spent the first two years at college wracked with guilt. Even went on some 'Socialist Workers' marches, I recognised most of the other protesters from the previous year's Tatler Ball."

Dainty shrugged. "Pressing as the class struggle is, I think we've got enough on our hands just at the moment, principally walking on egg shells while we try to work out who we should suck up to."

"I'm fine when I'm in there" Charlotte said, nodding towards the door "but when I come out I can't remember what I've said. I'm convinced I've confessed to either 'The Great Train Robbery' or to butchering my parents."

"I couldn't imagine you butchering a steak and kidney pie… the only good part for me is watching them sweat when they come to pronounce my name. They usually leave a gap. "You must be Dainty… " they say, hoping I'll supply the "Mukendi" for them. Management are always convinced that if they pronounce it wrongly I'm going to sue them for being racists. Silly bastards, that's the least of their crimes… you know that they'll want us to apply for our own jobs, don't you?"

"I suspected as much."

Dainty nodded. "I once had to buy my Dad's hub caps back from the thieving little sods who took them in the first place. So at least I know how it feels."

★

The toast had done wonders for Harry's constitution… he never tired of eating the stuff which was probably just as well. He was a connoisseur of the buttered delicacy and Dave had the touch of a Michelin chef as long as it involved bread, potatoes or Guinness. It was only fair that, lacking anything else about his person, he should give him a tune on the old Joanna, especially after Dave had rustled them up another couple of pints. He sat at the grubby piano and knocked out 'Devil May Care'. He'd known many pianos in his career but loved this one in particular, knew every battered inch of it. For years it had served as a drinks stand, an ashtray and, on occasion, an all-round litter bin. It wheezed debris into the air with every chord but to Harry's ears it still sounded as sweet as the concert grand in Carnegie Hall. The tune started off as something of a ballad but as his vital organs kicked into gear it began to take on a bit of steam. He played a solo with one hand while managing to finish his second pint of the day with the other. It was a particularly masculine piece of multi-tasking he thought as he congratulated himself. The sun was shining in on them and he smiled at the look of sheer bliss on the Barman's face. That would sharp go if the four nags he'd told him to back went down at the first, but for the moment all was well with the World.

★

"That's a weight lifted" Charlotte said as she and Dainty made their way through the building. She could relax. Nothing in the Bosses' office had suggested they were due for an early exit; still the minutiae of the conversations would need to be gone over with a fine tooth comb to make sure that no pointer, however subtle, had been missed. Still, she was breathing a little easier, there would be, at least for now, no fulfilment of her parent's dire warnings of boyfriend-inspired destitution.

"You can always tell from the opening salvo where you stand." Dainty said, pushing open the door to the loo. "As long as they're not pleasant you still have a job."

There was a spring in her step now. They were in the clear, salaries would be paid, which for Dainty meant holidays, shopping trips and nice meals out. For her it meant she could keep on subbing Kyle for a while longer. Try as she might, in the past few months she couldn't get a nagging thought out of her head. "Would she have put up with him so much had her parents not been so keen to write him off?"

"Fancy a drink?" said Dainty as she gently manoeuvred Charlotte towards the toilets. They were safe here. The bosses wouldn't be seen dead in anything other than their own rest room and she had meticulously planned for a livener after their ordeal. Reaching into her handbag she produced six vodka miniatures which she had wrapped in tissue paper to stop any obvious clinking. With a degree of practiced precision, she began to open them.

"Not only is the bar open it would also appear to be happy hour." Charlotte suggested dryly.

"You betcha. The thought of them was the only thing that kept me going in there. Did she ask if you were married?"

Charlotte nodded her head. "And if I had any children."

"Nosy bitch."

"I almost said yes."

"Well, let's not go there for now." Dainty said, clearly fighting a natural urge to do just that.

"She didn't seem that bad." Charlotte offered, her inclination always being to give the benefit of the doubt. But Dainty wasn't buying.

"They never do first off. After that it's iron fist in velvet glove and God did you see that make-up! Talk about laying it on thick. It looked like stone cladding."

Charlotte stifled a giggle. No doubt about it... Dainty was one of the few things that made "Peterson Partners" bearable.

"Of course, I've seen this before" Dainty continued. "Someone takes over from someone else and the old guard get squeezed out."

"I can't be old guard... I haven't lived yet. I haven't crossed America on a Greyhound bus or written a novel... I haven't had a baby."

So dangerous an admission was this that Charlotte almost whispered it. Their ticking biological clocks had been the 'elephant in the office' for some time. With every day that passed the proportion of colleagues who gave birth seemed to increase exponentially. Charlotte could just about stomach their daily moaning on and on about childcare and sleepless nights but it was the way they looked like they'd just performed lifesaving brain surgery on Nelson Mandela as they said it that rankled. But as long she and Dainty were both childless they wouldn't panic... not yet.

Chapter 4

Raising himself on his pillow, Kyle yawned as he surveyed the work in progress. CD's, sax tutors, old vinyl "Blue Note" albums, saxophone reeds and copious pages of written music were strewn across every surface. If he squinted he could just about manage to make out the titles on some of the sheet music on the dressing table. Some standards and some of his own tunes, he really needed to get them into some kind of order and sort out parts for the rest of the band. The few times they had played his tunes they had gone down pretty well. He would get on to it later that day. Charlie had spread his work to the four corners of the room looking for her make-up and stuff. Why couldn't she see that just because something was written on a scrap of paper didn't mean that it was scrap? Why couldn't she leave things alone? Some of that "doodling", as she sniffily called it, might change their fortunes one day.

It was heading for noon and nothing for it but to get up or at least begin to prepare for getting up. He'd read in some Sunday supplement that thirty-eight per cent of back injuries occurred getting out of bed… it could be bad for your health if you rushed it… it was thirty-eight wasn't it? It was certainly a lot, that much he knew. He turned on the radio and let the news of the day drift over him before he took on the world. He liked the *World at One*. Listening to it was one of the few occasions he felt connected to the rest of the planet. He groaned and wriggled a little in the bed as the twin desires to empty one end of himself and fill the other became unrelenting. Soon the battle to stay between the sheets would be lost and he would have to engage in real life. Like it or not, he knew that an hour spent tidying up the house would save him a lifetime of grief later. He imagined the look on Charlie's face when she walked in to a sparklingly clean and tidy house, that alone was worth the graft. He would start with the multitude of coffee cups that were lying around.

Once up, he gathered them together, which was a good start but before he could do anything with them the tune which had been running round his head for days began to form into something a little more substantial. He checked his memory banks, there was nothing worse than thinking you'd come up with a good hook for a song only to realise that it was a good hook… to somebody else's composition. But no… this didn't register as being part of anyone else's imagination but his own… this was good and too important to be left. If he forgot it, it would be lost forever. Best get it sorted now and then attack the housework. He sat at the piano and reached for a sheet of manuscript paper and a pencil. The verse and chorus came effortlessly but then came the void that was the middle eight. Writing music was like that. You got a spark and were in the thick of it, all guns blazing, and then you'd hit a wall. One tiny piece of the equation would be missing and wouldn't come no matter how hard you tried. The rest of the composition was strong; all he needed was eight bars in the middle that didn't suck. He chewed the end of his pencil to a pulp and still nothing. He was starving but he didn't want to leave the piano when he could be on the verge of writing something fantastic, a tune that might open some doors for him… well, possibly a door. The way things were at the minute he'd look gratefully on a cat-flap opening.

★

Sid Chase replaced the receiver and sat back in his chair. After a moment he shot his cuffs and regarded them… striped Egyptian cotton. You couldn't beat a bespoke shirt. All the same, if more work didn't come in he'd be back to polyester. He pursed his lips and thought about the phone call. On the positive side they had found Harry Crabb... a drunk with a future behind him. Some silly sod with more money than sense wanted to hire Harry to play at his golden wedding for no other reason than that, as a pimply youth, Harry had played at the original ceremony. He had at least four bloody good saxophonists on his books and he'd tried to push them but the buyer was having none of it. The conversation still rang in his ears.

'She wants everything exactly like it was then! Garage flowers, fish and chip supper, Harry Crabb, the lot.' And what 'she' wanted 'she' got, which is how women behaved when the barrow boy they married became Sir something or other and owned one of the country's biggest network of leisure complexes.

Still, Sir John had said expense no object and folding money was folding money. If he could get his foot in the door Sir John had a lot of venues and venues had weddings and parties and they'd be bound to need regular live music.

It hadn't taken long to find Harry, too many convictions for drunk and disorderly to be anonymous. But the rest of his band were long since gone, drink, drugs, an argument with a Spanish promoter over a bar bill, a couple of heart attacks and a drummer last heard of working for 'The Technicolor Children of Jesus' in the US. That was the problem with artistic types... too bloody unpredictable. The young lads fresh out of music college all drank Evian water and lived on mung beans but they'd run in terror from a presence like Harry Crabb. There was the option of the Scuttle Brothers, they were afraid of nothing but they'd also be liable to deck Harry if he gave them any grief and anyway all this was academic because the silly old bugger was living two hundred and fifty miles away. Sid sighed. He knew he was in schtuck. Harry was the last of a dying breed, his reputation spent. The few musicians who knew he still existed were wise enough to give him the widest of berths, Sid had put out a few feelers in the capital when the gig was first mooted, even though Harry hadn't played there for years. He'd got very few responses and those that did used the word "bargepole" an awful lot.

★

Harry drew up a chair and made himself at home in the bookies. It still smelled stale from before the smoking ban. He didn't really have enough cash for a punt but he thought it was a sign. "Kind of Brown" was a good name for a horse... a jazz man's horse. Miles Davis painted horses... lots of them, wild and free. He knew "Kind of Brown" was a cert the minute he clapped eyes on it in the "Racing Post". Dave O Driscoll had refused to jump at the odds but Dave didn't understand the meaning of Divine Providence, whereas he had put his all on it. Once it came through he'd have the best part of twenty quid on him and that would see him through the rest of the day in style. A new box of reeds, some manuscript paper for a bit of composing, a bit of grub from the Chippy and then back to "The Skinners" for an evening amongst friends... knockout. He might as well stay here now and watch the race. He was in no hurry. It was stunning how much joy one little piece of blue paper could give you.

★

'I've only had a cereal bar and a double shot of vodka' Dainty thought ruefully as they moved out of the cubicle. Booze on an empty stomach... that was the reason she felt so giddy. Still, she'd feel better once she sat down. There it was, that sweet spot, a warm glow where everything felt good. She assembled her papers in an attempt to occupy her hands and stop herself from giggling at her subterfuge; it wouldn't do to get the sack now after all she'd been through, especially as she relished, if not all then, at least ninety per cent of her job. All those clients needing her help, her love, her

32

nurturing and all of them pitifully grateful. Once before she had lavished that much care and attention on someone and the end result had been divorce and a less than harmonious legal fallout… one that still had to be resolved. Thank God they hadn't had children to complicate things… as long as she had a chance to be a mother with someone else, someone responsible… soon, soon like as in yesterday. She shook her head to try and clear it. She couldn't sit here all day thinking about babies.

★

Sid fiddled with his cuff again. Egyptian cotton or no Egyptian cotton it was starting to fray. It would have been a hard enough task to shepherd Harry through the job if he still lived in London… but Sunderland! In artistic terms it was Outer Mongolia and then some. He needed someone capable of coping with Harry on stage, who was able to play the music and desperate enough to want to do the job without being paid a king's ransom… and in Sunderland, or thereabouts, he'd have a thin field to choose from… a very thin field. He'd look in the Musicians Union directory… someone must play jazz up there. He could organise a couple of trial runs for them to make sure Harry Crabb was up to it. If it was going to be a balls up it would be best done in 'The Dog and Parrot' rather than in front of a catch like Sir John… and he could bill Sir John for the gigs as rehearsals. Magic! Everyone a winner.

★

Charlotte chewed absent-mindedly on her hair. She had broken one of the cardinal rules of the workplace. She'd finished everything in front of her. You were supposed to spin out your work to fill the time you had allotted it but she had wrapped it up in a couple of hours. God, she felt hungry. She needed something to fill up the hole in her stomach that the rushed slice of crisp bread and half cup of coffee hadn't. The chewing became a grinding when her thought turned to Kyle. The problem was he was an all or nothing sort of boyfriend. Today there had been nothing. It was nothing most days, if she was being honest, but when he did put himself out it was heart and soul stuff. At times she wondered if the effort was for his own sense of achievement rather than for her benefit but it was silly to let that detract from the heady pleasure of it.

On her last birthday, early in the year, he had made her breakfast in bed. Wearing nothing but a clean apron, he had announced grandly that it would be the most memorable breakfast of her life. He was not wrong. The term 'breakfast' hardly did it justice. Craster kippers, scrambled egg with smoked salmon, strawberries washed down with chilled champagne and not just any champagne... Armand de Brignac. She had only mentioned its delights to him once but he had remembered. It was hideously expensive but she thought it churlish to ask how he had come by it. Probably from Andy who could acquire most things at a sizable discount. Wherever it had come from, as thoughts go it was amongst the best.

She looked up at her co-workers. The office clock had barely moved a fraction during her reverie. The memory of 'room service' which had followed the breakfast still made her blush. But could a girl thrive on one all-dancing, Technicolor, spectacular gesture a year? Perhaps she should have two birthdays like the queen, an official one and an actual one. Although why stop at short measures. Why not half a dozen a month. She could feel the colour rising in her face as she recalled the afternoon they had spent in bed amid the empty plates and the ice bucket. Just the memory of it made her feel woozy. The breath control that was standard fare for a sax player was anything but standard in the right circumstances. His performance, including encore, necessitated a four hour nap for them both. When, later, the neighbours had enquired about the noise, Kyle had been forced into hastily blaming a horror film that had been on television.

Chapter 5

The voice on the other end was clipped and business like… which to Kyle meant officialdom, which usually meant trouble. Then again it couldn't be the SS. He hadn't signed on since Charlie had moved in. If it was the taxman he could barely owe them more than the cost of the phone call itself and if the person on the other end was trying to sell him something he hadn't got a bean. He listened to the preamble and tried not to give too much away as the voice on the end of the phone spelled out a proposition. Once he realised he wasn't in trouble he relaxed. Eventually he was passed on to a man calling himself Mr Sydney Chase and slowly Kyle realised he was being sounded out for a gig; someone had given his number to somebody when he'd played a one off gig in a big band.

He'd had this kind of phone call before; it was always wise to make it look like you were doing any agent or promoter a favour. Once the gig was over and done with you usually realised that you had. As his mind worked its way through "the pitch" he began to get an idea of what was going on. He was being offered four gigs for reasonable dosh with his band, backing another sax player. The last engagement was a fiftieth wedding anniversary in London. It was the name of the other sax player that threw him. "Buster Crabb". He had heard of Harry "Buster" Crabb, even had one or two of his albums somewhere. Sunderland hadn't turned out many jazz legends but Buster Crabb was one of them. Except that he was dead, wasn't he? It got even more mysterious when the agent couldn't give him a phone number for Mr Crabb. The phone call ended with an agreement to set up a rehearsal which the agent assured him Harry Crabb would attend. Four paid gigs coming in one day, normally he'd be over the moon but he wasn't at all sure what it was he had just agreed to and he never enjoyed being out of his comfort zone. He put the phone down slowly... why on earth would you want two sax players in a five piece band?

One thing was for sure, he was now officially awake. As he padded out to the loo it struck him that playing with someone of Harry Crabb's stature, even if he was a bit past it, might be a little bit daunting.

★

How could a horse with a name like that fall at the first hurdle? "Kind of Brown" had come in kind of last. Harry tore up his betting slip as he trudged out into the street. Not for the first time, bookies, those people with money to spare, had another slice more of him. Bastards! That was dinner up the Swanee for starters. He hadn't been hungry when he had placed the bet but the minute "Kind of Brown" hit the deck his craving for food, any kind of food, started to gnaw at his insides. When he'd first walked down the High Street all he'd had eyes for was the betting shop. Now, on his bankrupted return, all he could see were bakeries and take-aways but it wasn't the sight of them so much as the smell that hit hard. Fresh bread and pastries warm from the oven, Chinese takeaways, curry houses... it all hurt like buggery. 'The Chancellor' wouldn't be open for another few hours. He could go back to 'The Skinners' but of late he'd been welcomed too many times with empty pockets and you had to have some pride. All he had at home was a chocolate orange he'd been given by Sonny Rollins after a week-long residency at 'Ronnie Scott's'. He'd rather starve than eat that, that was a family heirloom and anyway it was a good thirty years past its sell-by date. It didn't bear thinking about. There were porridge oats somewhere, which were equally as old, but that stuff kept indefinitely and it had no sentimental value whatsoever. He had no milk whatsoever either. There was always the door-step challenge… except that he couldn't run like he used to.

★

Charlotte looked across at Dainty… she was, as ever, engrossed in her work. She envied Dainty's love of her job. 'I'm only here for the salary' she thought ruefully, not that money meant a great deal to her; her childhood had shown that it didn't equate to happiness. Her job allowed her to keep a roof over her head and food in her belly for Kyle and herself but the degree of satisfaction she got from it was zilch. She couldn't even pass it off as a mistake. She hadn't particularly wanted to work in PR but her closest friend in the world, Rebecca, had dragged her in to it. They were inseparable then, so why wouldn't she have followed her into the same profession? That was what she envied Kyle, his bull-headed devotion to a cause. Rebecca, bless her, had folded at the first work-related crisis, married her teenage sweetheart and shipped off to Hong Kong. The truth of it was that she, Charlotte, had ended up here while she was waiting for something else to happen in her life.

Then again she did have form in that department. That was how she had become engaged to Anthony. An education at Harrow and Oxford may have equipped him for a position in "shipping finance" but it hadn't taught him how not to behave like a shit. He had called off their engagement three weeks before they were due to set off for the States. No reason… just over. "Everything is a bit much" was the official excuse, relayed to her in a phone call from his mother. She'd never been sure if it was an emotional or financial appraisal. She'd run away then, from the pitying glances of her friends and her father's grumping about all the money he had expended on the wedding. Anthony had been her first big romance and his betrayal of her had left her devastated. That was how she'd wound up in Newcastle.

She looked up now to see Dainty's inquiring eyes on her. 'OK?' Dainty mouthed and she nodded. She was alright, really. She would never want for money... her family would see to that if there was a real crisis. But deep down she knew there was no pleasure in the world like making your own way. Too many girls from her background seemed to wither on the vine... public school, fashionable non-job, marriage, children, divorce, drink. After Anthony, she had resigned her job and taken a waitressing job in a Newcastle jazz club, 'The Rendezvous', while she weighed up the possibilities. The pay would have bought her a push bike rather than a Lamborghini but the club's clientele were, for the most part, interesting and passionate, the owner an eccentric character with a big heart, a colourful past and a large collection of hats. There were a few dreamers amongst the poets; they were occasionally argumentative and exasperating but never dull, and then Kyle and his saxophone had walked through the door.

★

There was something good about being home alone, Kyle reflected... you could sit around in your underpants and scratch yourself and there wasn't anyone around to give you a hard time. There were few upsides to being a jazz musician but this was definitely one of them. He still couldn't find the perfect middle eight, a quest that had occupied his waking hours so far. Before he could knock up a motivational cuppa a brainwave struck. He could kill two birds with one stone. Up in the loft there was an old record player and a bunch of vinyl LP's... he could set it up, find the recordings he had of Harry Crabb and listen to them now, get a feel for his music and, hopefully, get inspired to find the missing piece for his new composition.

The loft itself was a bit of a nightmare. It was principally the place where expired electrical goods lay in state. Charlie would have thrown most of it out but you needed to keep stuff close to you because one day it would be just the thing you were looking for.

Once he had located the albums he realised that in the two years since he'd bought them he'd never got round to playing them. It was in a job lot of LP's he'd got at South Shields market for a quid. Harry Crabb's "Manhattan Daytrip" was one but on closer inspection the other album "Live at the Manchester Free Trade Hall 1967" actually contained a well-worn recording of "Mrs Mills Knee's Up Party". Still one album was better than nothing. He checked the record player. It was all plumbed in, but no red light on the front... it didn't seem to want to play ball. He switched it off and on a few times and wiggled at the knobs... nothing was going to fire the ancient relic up, which was probably why it was in the attic in the first place. If he was going to find inspiration it was going to have to come from somewhere else. As he waited for his muse to strike he looked at the covers of the albums. Something had definitely been lost when packaging had been shrunk to CD size. The cover of "Manhattan Daytrip" showed a young, svelte Harry Crabb in a fedora hat and an immaculate black and red pinstripe suit, staring out at the world like he owned it and knew, for sure, that he did. On the live album, contrastingly, he was drenched in sweat and looking more than a little possessed by the music.

Looking at his watch Kyle realised that it was too late for playing "Musical Tricia", one of his favourite practice routines. You simply turned on Tricia, a programme where people who hadn't got much in the first place gave away their dignity for free. It didn't have to be Tricia, but Tricia was best. You turned down the sound and substituted any noise you could get out of your sax for dialogue. It was good both as entertainment and practice, although some guests could leave you more than a little breathless. Some exploded off set and a few well-chosen honks covered for that but more fun was to be had out of the participants that couldn't shut up. You could follow their emotional journey from their facial expressions, sadness, remorse, regret, schadenfreude, anger, the lot... it was a good way of filling in an hour. He'd have to settle for using Jeremy Kyle or something similar. At this time of day, it was never difficult to find a substitute.

★

Charlotte shifted the piles on her desk and moved them around as she scanned the rest of her workplace. It was important in the circumstances to at least look busy even if she was going to drift off into brooding about the new regime. You had to tread water until you'd fully sussed out the situation. You didn't want to plough full on with some client only to find that the new administration had drawn a polite veil over your graft because they didn't feel that your 'mark' was where the company's future lay. Kyle should be here; he should get out of his lazy pit and experience her working life just for twenty four hours. That would be enough for him to realise what the real world was like. In her darker moments she often wondered if Kyle had just been in the right place at the right time. If Anthony hadn't dumped her would Kyle have caught her eye at all? She sighed deeply then started to count how many staples the stapler actually contained. Was it too early to get lunch? From the corner of her eye she saw Dainty approaching her desk holding two fingers across the back of her other hand. Its meaning was clear… meeting… two minutes time.

The staff toilets at Peterson Partners, or the 'kharzi confessional', as Dainty had christened it, was a safe house where Charlotte and Dainty felt secure from the higher ups and could discuss anything they wished. Two minutes and thirty seconds later Charlotte headed towards the Ladies, leaving enough time not to arouse suspicion that she was following her friend. When she got in she could see from Dainty's face that she was excited.

"'Bite me-pinch-me-Susan' has dumped Gavin from accounts."

Dainty's expression showed how difficult it had been for her to keep this secret until they'd got behind closed doors. Charlotte wasn't quite as caught up in gossip as Dainty was but it was still nice to see her friend so animated. "Bite me" had worked at Peterson partners for longer than almost anyone else she knew. The origins of the name "Bite-me-pinch-me-Susan" were lost in the mists of time, although popular myth had it that it was earned after a liaison in a stockroom cupboard during an office party in 1997.

"Yes sir, no flies on that girl. Treat them mean, keep them… "

Before Dainty could finish the door was barged open, almost taking it off its hinges. With a great deal of ceremony the one person who had been there longer than "Bite me" entered the toilet, mop in hand. In real terms no one held more power at Peterson Partners than Lucy and, behind her bottle-rim glasses, she knew it. She was a woman of few words and seemed to be oblivious of their gossip, such was her concentration on her work. Charlotte knew their conversation would go no further. Lucy's whole reputation was based on an ability to keep schtum.

"Is Gavin the one with the facial hair thing going on?"

"No, that's Andy Peterson. He's a second cousin to the old boss or something." Dainty might have joined the company after Charlotte but she was infinitely more aware of the byzantine network of relationships that categorised it.

Lucy had finished her quick cleaning out of the toilet area but before she could exit Dainty accosted her.

"200?"

"They've gone up mind. It's twenty-five now… overheads." Dainty hesitated then nodded.

Lucy fished around in the hidden recesses of her trolley and produced 200 cigarettes wrapped in cellophane. Charlotte had heard about Lucy's dealings but never before witnessed them at first hand. Dainty grasped hold of the other end of the packet, keen to get her hands on the spoils but Lucy was too canny by half to let go before the financial part of the transaction was completed.

"Pay you Thursday?"

"Well, if you're not serious… " The illicit bounty headed back into the trolley's depths.

"Alright! Alright! Alright!"

It was clear Lucy had her over a barrel as Dainty started to fish around for money in her pockets. This gave Charlotte a chance to push her case.

"Treating Kyle mean doesn't seem to work. Still, I like to think of it like a sea voyage and yes, that means rocks and storms and such but I feel like we're on a journey... on our way to somewhere wonderful."

Dainty was frantically rummaging in the bottom of her handbag and was clearly more engaged in concluding the transaction than in hearing her friend's confidences.

"Can you lend me four quid thirty-five till I can get to a cash point?"

Charlotte started searching through her own handbag. Eventually Lucy got what she required, the money magically disappearing as she handed over the cigarettes and exited almost as swiftly as she had come.

"You don't approve, do you?" Charlotte asked.

"Will you just listen to yourself? Sea voyage? Wonderful journey? Someday you're going to wake up and find Kyle's made off for Fantasy Island in the last lifeboat. You'll be left with a basket full of dirty Y fronts and ovaries that look like walnuts."

The four quid thirty-five didn't seem to have bought her much in the way of a hearing from Dainty. And she wasn't finished.

"Seriously, Charlotte, if you keep on having to support him you're both going to end up resenting it and on top of all that the perfect answer is staring you right in the face. He's single, in line for promotion, he's clearly not short of a bob, he looks like Keanu Reeves and he follows you around the office like a lovesick puppy.

"The American? He does not."

Dainty raised an eyebrow and cast her a withering look.

"Oh God, he does, doesn't he?"

Dainty nodded smugly before gesturing to the door.

"Come on, let's get out of here. I'm starving."

Charlotte bit her lip and followed. She couldn't help but notice Ethan McCormack but she certainly wasn't going to acknowledge the fact in public.

★

As the programme's guests wept their last Kyle put down his sax and searched fruitlessly for his mobile. He patted both of his trouser pockets, nothing. He began a search around the house, the bathroom, the bedroom, down the back of the settee. In desperation he grabbed the land-line and rang his own mobile, round the house he walked dialling and listening. He looked incredulously at the fridge as the familiar ring tone did its best to be heard. Opening it he removed the phone and checked it… nothing. The fridge contained some unidentifiable food that Charlie would have thrown out given half the chance; she would occasionally have a blitz and bin his collection of progressing penicillin samples but there it was, on the bottom, the one that had got away. He reached for the plate. The substance reclining on it was soft and grey, possibly porridge, he sniffed at it before taking a dirty spoon from the washing and wiping it on his trousers. He started to eat. He still had some time to sort out the flat. It shouldn't be a problem, what he needed was a quick trip out to get a newspaper and a decent pen. You couldn't score out a decent middle eight with a biro. He licked his lips. It was porridge… well, a sort of eggy porridge.

★

Charlotte was hungry the minute she set eyes on the burger bar and it wasn't such a bad deal nutritionally, if you thought about it. The stodge would soak up the alcohol and it did come with salad… sort of. Outside the fast food outlet a man dressed as a clown was busily engaged in handing out promotional leaflets.

"Don't look now, but I think you've pulled."

Dainty might not have noticed the attention she was getting as they entered the building but Charlotte had. Dainty gave a snort of derision before blowing a sarcastic kiss to the clown as they made their way through the entrance.

43

They took a seat at the least messy of the free tables. It was clearly the busiest time of day as an army of hyperactive, ketchup-spattered children bounced off the walls, screaming in animated anticipation.

"What to eat? It's not quite the charge that choosing shoes or jewellery is but it'll do for now".

Charlotte agreed. She needed the hit that a burger and fries would give her.

Once served, they arranged the food and drink on the table in a way that allowed them to get down to the really important stuff. Reaching into her bag Dainty produced two women's magazines, one aimed at those with considerable disposable income, or at least those who aspired to such largesse, and one down market glossy which was more than averagely interested in who exactly was shagging who in the world of minor celebrity. This, thought Charlotte, was as good as it was going to get on a post bank holiday Tuesday.

Before they had managed to get through half their food, the models and their wares in the magazines were put under close scrutiny and found wanting, sometimes on the grounds of cost of clothing, sometimes on the grounds of physical imperfections. To aid herself in this task Dainty had cut out a photograph of her own head which she superimposed on the models. When it worked, thought Charlotte, it was really quite useful in seeing how something might look on you and when it didn't it was often pretty funny, usually because the photo was too big or small giving you that "Star Wars" extra look.

The sun had managed to poke out from behind the clouds and with their appetites sated and their morning's achievements taken into account, the whole world looked a little rosier as they left the burger bar. The sad Clown, who was still handing out the promotional leaflets, squirted a jet of water from his fake flower buttonhole, managing to make the action seem thoroughly obscene in the process.

"You can keep your cheesy quarter-pounder to yourself, Coco." was Dainty's solemn pronouncement.

As it turned out the lunch was, for Charlotte, the highlight of the day. The afternoon crawled by, with "Bite me, pinch me Susan's" asthma attack being the only thing to break the tedium. When she got home she had to make her own dinner. Kyle had managed to round up some dirty mugs but hadn't actually progressed as far as introducing them to soap and water. What did he do with himself all day? Now, he just kept going on about a middle eight. She hadn't got "a middle eight", she didn't even know what one was but if she ever did get one she would wrap it round his bloody neck.

Chapter 6

Harry Crabb propped himself up in bed. It had been a week since they'd thrown him out of the supermarket but parts of him still ached. Once he had got the sleep out of his eyes and pulled himself together, he surveyed his bed-sit. It was, as ever, a chaos of biblical proportions. The grey, nicotine stained walls were a pretty good match for the discarded Y-fronts on the floor. A lot of his financial affairs were filed there, amid the carpet of empty bottles, red bills and vinyl albums. In one corner there was a photo of his wedding day discarded on the ground, the glass on one corner cracked and the photo itself starting to yellow. She had worn a soft colour that day, primrose she'd called it. At the far end of the room sat his dusty television, a Rediffusion. A relic now but in its day it had been top of the range. It had stopped working properly in 1992, like he had. On top of the TV was a radio with the singular advantage that it was still functioning and tuned permanently to Radio 4; you had to take your civilisation where you could get it these days. He liked "The Archers" but it was as close up as he ever wanted to get to the countryside. This bed-sit was the place he'd called home for more than ten years. The only other living occupant had been a cat, Tabby Hoffman, dead a long while now. Run over in 2002 or three. He couldn't quite remember.

Atop the grubby Formica table at the other end of the room was Baby, his saxophone, awaiting its annual service check. It had been a year, hadn't it? It was getting harder to keep track. It was laid out like a body on a mortuary slab. He would check the pads, lubricate the keys and generally treat 'Baby' with tender loving care. Her overhaul was something he always found therapeutic. It would also take his mind off food. His recently sustained injuries were enough to put him off a return to the supermarket for a while. He'd been eating porridge for five days now, ever since that incident with the cross-eyed bow-legged horse that he'd backed on a hunch. He'd resisted the temptation to stick a piece of his chocolate orange in the porridge to give it a bit of flavour, but it hadn't been easy.

★

In twenty seven days he would be thirteen, Craig thought. It would be brilliant. That was two twelve's and three left over. He'd been promised a jumper for his birthday, a new one, not someone else's. It would be the best jumper anyone had ever had. The wall at the back of the house was easy; he had done things like this a thousand times before, which was why his knees were so scabby. Sometimes he did it for himself, but mostly to help other people. Occasionally they would give him money or sweets which was dead good. The wall was no trouble and the toilet window was just wide enough, not for bigger boys, but wide enough for him. With a quick look around he threw himself at the wall. Once he was up there it was, simple, one hand went easily into the partially open window, unlatching it to give him the extra, oh so important, couple of inches. An arm, then a shoulder, then the other shoulder, it was easy now to slither in like a snake. That was his favourite bit. He got up and shook himself down. He was hungry; no, it was worse than that, he was starving... he wanted something like a pie or a pasty; chips were a fiddly business but a pie... bang! Instant calmer, like his dad use to say, hot or cold, individual ones that were all yours, they were the best.

He made his way to the kitchen and opened the fridge. He'd known better stocked ones but it didn't matter. Lots of vegetables that were going off, jars of stuff, bacon, bits of cheese in water... what was that all about. There! A pie... magic. He ripped the cellophane off and tucked straight into the pastry case, steak and kidney, messy, rich and greasy. He took his time, savouring each

47

mouthful, before he set off through the rest of the house, stopping to look at the stuff that caught his attention on the way.

In the bedroom there was a saxophone and a piano. It was all dust and stuff inside. There was a mug of tea but it was cold, and underwear, girls' underwear. It smelled nice but why all the extra lacy bits? What was the point of that on underwear? He headed for the front door, plonking a few random notes on the piano as he went. At the door he stooped, lifting the letterbox to peer out.

"Twelve twelve's?"

"What?" Kyle sounded cross, which was strange as he'd just done him a favour.

"Twelve times twelve?"

"I don't know, a hundred and forty something... four, a hundred and forty four."

"Square root of twelve?"

"I don't know... Craig we haven't got time for this... OK twenty-four, forty-eight... five and a half, Sheffield Wednesday."

"Rubbish."

"Craig, we have to get on... why not just open the bloody door?"

Outside Kyle looked around, embarrassed. To any casual passer-by it looked for all the world as if he was deep in conversation with his own house.

"How many steps?"

Over time he had grown use to Craig's questions but this one had him. "What do you mean, Craig?"

"From my house, how many steps from here?"

"We're wasting time. I don't know, a hundred."

The eyes behind the letter box remained accusing.

"Loads more."

"A thousand, come on we have to get on... and what took you? You've been gone ages."

"It's 1,404 steps to your house from my house, that's one hundred and seventeen times twelve."

"Open the door Craig."

"You should put your house key on a bit of string round your neck. That's what my Mam makes me do, look!"

As he opened the door he proudly showed off the key around his neck on a bit of what looked like shoelace. Kyle struggled for composure. God, had it come to this, he was being given advice from a twelve year old. Perhaps he was as useless as Charlie said. Craig was still counting... it happened whenever he got excited and his saxophone lesson was the highlight of his week.

"The caretaker at the centre has thirty-seven keys. That's... "

"Three twelve's and one over, there's no time for a lecture Einstein... come on... "

Kyle had to admit that, if nothing else, his relationship with Craig had sharpened up his basic mathematical skills. They moved into the bedroom and he cleared some space so they could make a start. He handed Craig his saxophone case. It had been left with him at the front door with a firm instruction from his pupil that he was "Not to let anyone get it." If that instrument could only speak! Craig's 'horn' had been procured at a considerable discount on a "no questions asked" basis by Andy Valentine. Ordinarily Kyle wouldn't have approved of such an acquisition but in this instance the moral benefits far outweighed the probable criminality of the transaction.

"How about we play "Ricardo's rumba"? Page four?"

Craig could be hard work at times but Kyle knew it was worth the effort and he had the evening's concert to look forward to. One of his favourite sax players, Terry Bellis, working with one of his favourite singers, Jacqui Drinkwater... bliss. Yes, it was turning into a good day. Catching sight of Craig in the mirror he had to admit to himself that they were an odd pair but they looked right together... like family. He liked kids.

★

Once in gear, Harry took to polishing his sax. This always stirred up memories of what had drawn him to the blessed instrument in the first place… it was shiny, shiny bright. The name of the business on Sunderland's High St East had disappeared in the fog of years but he remembered the stuffed bison adorning the front of the building before it had disappeared to be replaced by a circular slab of grey epidermis stamped with the legend 'elephant hide' in inky black capital letters. He had entered the pawn shop looking for a Saturday job but had been beaten to it by squinty Leonard Watts, the laziest boy in his class. He was half way out of the shop door before the glint of bell metal caught his eye. A close inspection revealed, amongst the dusty furniture and jewellery, what he came to learn was a Selmer Mark VI tenor saxophone. The two months left on the ticket gave him half a chance to get the money together to purchase her. He walked into town every day after school checking on her availability because, at any point before her time was up, she could have been reclaimed by the owner. A scam that involved repeatedly returning the same crate of empty bottles to various public houses for a refund had netted him half the money before 'the Elephant man' as he became known locally, had given him a Saturday job to work off the rest. A stroke of luck after Squinty Watts had been caught red handed, leaving the premises wearing three more watches than he'd come in with.

Since then Baby, as he had soon christened her, had been the shimmering jewel in his world. They had been partners, lovers even, from the first time he felt her in his hands to the dizzy heights of his career, a time when the phone never stopped and his suitcase was plastered with stickers declaring gigs in New York, Chicago, and New Orleans, to the present day holed up in a dilapidated bed-sit in Sunderland. These days his luggage hadn't seen much action save for a guest house in Whitby in 2006, a week-long recuperation on 'medical advice'. Different location, different pubs, same problem.

★

"Eventually you'll understand that the more you study music the more you realise how little you know."

"Why don't we stop while we're ahead then?"

It had been Kyle's moment of towering insight and Craig had toppled it with eight words and a question mark. After an apprenticeship like this teaching anyone else would be a walk in the park. Kyle picked up his metronome and set it to a slow pulse.

He had met Craig in the supermarket eighteen months previously. Charlie was going to make something special that night and he'd been tasked with getting the ingredients. As he wandered up and down the shopping aisles looking for something improbably called "lemon grass" he became aware of a presence. Someone was following him. It had happened to him once before in the supermarket, somebody with an inordinate amount of tattoos and the breath of a pub dishcloth who, when he caught up with him, requested, somewhat impolitely, "the whereabouts of that fucker Valentine." Store Security had saved his bacon that time but this was different. Whatever was following him was small and more afraid of him than he was of it. He finally caught a glimpse of the tiny bespectacled face staring at him intently from an arrangement of corned beef tins as he headed for the 'Fruit and Vegetables'. Just as he thought he had shaken the spectre off he appeared again in the meat section and then again, a little closer, in 'Dairy'. He leant down to get at some cheese and when he straightened up there he was, a small, odd, thin boy, with a hand placed squarely on his saxophone case. The boy didn't say anything; he just stared at it, oblivious to Kyle and everything else around him before starting to stroke the case, feeling it, examining its lock and hinges and the colourful stickers upon it. Strangely enough, at no point did he feel that the boy wanted to make off with his horn... he just seemed captivated by it.

And then a woman's voice came from the end of the aisle. "He's alright." It was phrased as a reassurance to him but she needn't have worried... he didn't see any threat in the boy at all. The woman moved towards them at speed.

"Craig, Craig, we've talked about this."

She spoke slowly and patiently with a mixture of love and

51

weariness which eventually broke the spell that the case had cast.

"You have to speak… ask the man about the… " She looked up at him. "I'm sorry, but what is it?"

"It's a saxophone."

For a while no one said anything. The boy's hand was still on the case. It was clear that the only way to move on was to open the thing up.

"Look at that" said the boy's mother as Kyle took the gleaming Selmer Paris 54 Super Action 80 Series II Tenor Sax out of its case.

Once out it seemed a pretty small step to playing a few lines. It was a Wednesday afternoon and the place was practically empty. Kyle thought the hook from "A Love Supreme" might do the trick and it did. The boy looked on in wonder and then began to vibrate with joy before screaming in excitement at the top of his voice. It only crossed Kyle's mind for a minute, but nevertheless it did cross his mind, that he had wished the boy had been at the last rather sombre series of gigs he'd done.

Meeting Craig had been one of those events which stayed with you.

"Come on, lazy daisy." The barely broken voice shattered the silence. It was a phrase that Kyle had often used when teaching Craig but for once he was on the receiving end of it. Craig's grubby fingers had stayed the hypnotic to and fro of the metronome as Kyle realised he'd been caught out, lost in a world of his own. The two of them were probably more alike than he cared to admit. He looked at Craig now with what passed for almost parental affection. They had come quite a long way in their year and a half together but they wouldn't be going any further if they didn't get down to "Ricardo's Rumba".

★

With his mid-point cup of milk-free tea finished Harry returned to the needs of 'Baby' like an indulgent parent. During one particularly fiddly process with a small screwdriver he slipped and allowed himself a loud "bugger" which blended in quite well with the everyday story of country folk that followed the two o clock news on the radio. The small wound on his hand began to bleed. He stalled his labours to wrap a grimy handkerchief around the gash, confident that the germs on the rag were no match for the germs he already possessed. As the "Archers" drew to a close he joined in with the theme tune on his rejuvenated horn climaxing, with an impressive flurry of notes before taking the horn out of his mouth to produce a believably bovine "Moo". This one act of musical cross fertilisation made him happy for the rest of the day.

★

"You can play the first twelve bars; I'll play the second twelve, till the very end."

Over time Kyle had sussed out that if he broke things down into manageable chunks Craig was much more willing to take a crack at it. Once or twice in the early days Craig had thrown stuff across the room in a tantrum but it was always aimed at something that wasn't going to break. Only once had he had to run out of the house after the boy. From experience he knew that Craig was never good the day before an official assessment was made of his 'progress' by the authorities. At first he'd been taken aback when the boy bolted. Now he understood it, Craig worked on the principle that if he acted up, then he hadn't actually failed his assessment due to any lack of ability. He'd ballsed it up on purpose and that didn't count. There was a kind of logic in there that Kyle could relate to. When Craig had left the house he was a good half way down the street before Kyle had caught up with him. This left him with a dilemma, leave the boy to the danger of his own devices or grab hold of him in public. Craig's mother had told him to use his intuition when "a situation arose". She wasn't going to put up any sort of barriers to what he was doing with her son, she was just pitifully grateful that anyone would try to reach out to him. So he had got hold of Craig with something that was intended to be more avuncular bear hug than physical restraint and then he prayed to God that a mob wouldn't take him for a paedophile and beat him half to death. After a short struggle the boy calmed down… but only after an offer of a double dose of 'Hats'. Still, struggles like that were in the past now.

Teaching Craig had to be about the most rewarding thing he had ever undertaken. After eighteen months he had become quite proficient at managing to get him not only not to throw things, but to focus on the task in hand, even if it was for relatively brief periods.

Craig took his saxophone out of its battered case.

"The Porsche RT12 has a top speed of more than 219 mph. It's my best top trump. I won it off Doctor Jacobs."

"OK. Well we're going to start "Ricardo's Rumba" in twelve seconds. Twelve, eleven, ten, nine…

Kyle raised the sax to his lips.

"I'm twelve."

Craig had put down his horn and was now looking around the room, photographs, magazines, a collection of dinky classic model cars, socks, pants. He had the ability to be fascinated by everything. Generally Kyle thought that was no bad quality for an aspiring artist… just not during the rehearsal for a piece he needed to learn for his forthcoming grade three exam.

"I know, but if we don't play this piece soon you'll be thirteen and I'll be about one hundred and twelve."

Again he raised his horn to play, but Craig was having none of it.

"When you were twelve did you have a Mam?"

"Yes. Why don't we play this in twelve seconds time?"

"Did you have a Dad? A proper Dad… there all the time?"

"No, he died when I was small. But my Mam's nice, like your Mam."

"How small?"

"Come on, we've got to do this while we can. Twelve, eleven, ten, nine,"

Finally his persistence won out as they managed to reach "one" and Craig set off playing the short piece, falteringly at first and with a degree of support here and there from Kyle. Sometimes getting any work done at all was an achievement.

"Not bad. Let's try the bit from bar twelve to bar thirty-six. That's twelve twice."

"I know."

He'd learnt a little more about his pupil over the months. Though Craig had his problems, lack of intelligence wasn't one of them. As the session progressed Kyle played less as Craig grew stronger and more fluid with each repetition. It was funny, Kyle thought, how he himself had almost stopped registering the photographs that seemed to so pre-occupy Craig. They were literally part of the furniture... the formal portrait with his proud parents as a baby, as a young boy with his first saxophone and his recently widowed mother, his first college band, his graduation day and in pride of place a picture looking deliriously happy with Charlotte in the sunshine at Durham Cathedral. To Craig, they had been an endless source of wonder.

"I've been there, that's Durham. I do my assessments there with smelly Mrs Langford. I always want to go in the Cathedral but they always say there isn't time. Is that your mum? Is that you when you were little?"

Craig wanted to have an in-depth description of everything and everyone in the photos. Still, this was a lesson and Kyle attempted again to get Craig to knuckle down.

"OK. I think we can nail this; we're getting closer each time. Now if you close the whole tube we get a... "

Kyle waited.

"B...?" he prompted.

"Flat?"

"That's it. A b flat and from that we can get the... "

"Whole har... monic... series."

Craig's sense of achievement was palpable when he did manage to apply himself. He set off playing again with renewed vigour. It was now definitely recognizable as 'Ricardo's rumba'.

"That's the one, go for it."

The boy completed the tune with a small flourish.

"Brilliant."

★

Charlotte checked her email account for the third time that hour. Everyone else around the office seemed to be beavering away like their lives depended on it. She was already counting the hours down to the Jacqui Drinkwater gig in Durham that evening. A bit of live "music therapy" would lift her spirits later but it wasn't going to do anything for them now. In the week since the takeover Charlotte could see the way the wind was blowing. The bigger an organisation got the less it seemed she liked it. They'd spent most of the week filling in forms and surveys but she didn't think her opinions were going to be upper most in anyone's mind other than her own. Did she own a pet? Did she ever cry? Had she ever considered an act of physical violence against anyone in authority? Whilst this last question was the only one she'd made up it was by far and away the most gratifying one to answer. Her daydream of being a crusading lawyer had been fuelled by repeated viewings of Paul Newman in *The Verdict*. Could there be anything more rewarding than taking on abuses of power by those in charge. God what she wouldn't give to have a few cabinet ministers or ex-boyfriends in the dock for a bit of a grilling? For the first time since the morning she smiled to herself, savouring the notion of seeing a few community sentences dished out, involving a bucket of water, a toothbrush and a Glastonbury Festival latrine. Still she couldn't dwell on daydreams, sooner or later some new high-up at work would catch her idling in her reverie and that would be that. She returned to the questionnaire, question seventeen, part D (ii) 'Have you ever felt as though life is passing you by?'

"I'm hungry now." Kyle had ignored Craig's plea for food once but the boy was nothing if not persistent. Kyle had been forewarned by Craig's Mum that he probably wouldn't want to eat anything in front of him while he was there but if he ever did want to eat with him then it was best to make enough for a small to medium sized army. He'd had never cooked for Craig; he was barely able to cook for himself. The new economy drive meant that takeaways were off the menu. He rolled up his sleeves. He was after all a man of the World and he was sure he could do this.

The kitchen was small, clean and tidy and obviously not Kyle's natural habitat. He realised fairly quickly that he was going to have to dig deep to bring this one off. He opened cupboards took out packets, scanned their instructions and nutritional information. He would put them all back at the end of the operation. This was the planning stage.

Craig randomly sniffed and licked things then announced that he liked spaghetti and that was it. They had a plan and they were off. He didn't want to let Craig down after all the hard work they'd put in. Wanting to eat with him was a good sign, probably meant the boy trusted him. A voice whispered ever louder in his head "On no account give him food poisoning". It was Craig who recognised the pasta in the tall glass jar but there were no instructions as to how to cook the stuff. Boiling water, he knew that much, they could busk the rest.

★

The atmospheric forces that dragged at the hands of the office clock hadn't let up any as one painfully slow minute followed the next. She'd gone over her answers in the survey, twice now. It wasn't like there weren't things that she ought to be doing but the motivation to start them eluded her. Her attempt to rationalise her lack of activity had been wholly successful. What was the point of her job, food and shelter apart?

"It's not against the law is it?"

One of Dainty's best points was that if she asked you a question she brought you a coffee. Her timing was perfect.

"What?"

"Using one credit card to pay off another?"

"I don't know about illegal. It's probably not your wisest move financially."

"I know, but I comfort myself thinking of all the people I'm keeping in a job, bank workers, shop workers, finance companies, fashion designers."

"Bailiffs?"

"Killjoy."

All in all, she thought they were a good team. She was her friend's financial advisor and in return Dainty was her personal relationships expert. Though what she clearly needed now was a challenge. Not a Kyle shaped one but a career shaped one. If she was going to progress at all it had to be one problem at a time.

★

An hour and a half later he considered it "job done". He could relax as they entered the bedroom wiping their mouths clean. He'd managed it, he'd fed Craig and to bursting point partly due to the surprising increase in size of the pasta. They spent the rest of the afternoon listening to Coltrane, Bird, Lester Young and for light relief 'The "Bonzo Dog Doo Dah Band' which Craig liked to sing along with. A few more passes were made at "Ricardo's Rumba" which consolidated the progress they had made that morning, before the proceedings were brought to a close with 'Hats', Craig's favourite.

Kyle could still remember the first time he had seen it done, Stan

Laurel in 'Towed in a Hole' and it was more than suited to the saxophone. Taking hold of two proper hats, hats with brims, one an old bowler from a theatre show, the other Charlotte's, he put one on Craig then one on himself, leaning the brims against the wall, side by side as they looked at themselves in the mirror. They counted down to zero together before making low farting sounds on their 'horns' as they leaned back against the wall, making the hats lift off their heads in unison. This was always the signal for Craig to laugh until he was convulsed with hick-ups. They were both happy. It had been a good day, Kyle thought, as he waved him off with an admonition to practice for his forthcoming exam. Craig was smiling like a lottery winner as he set off on the 1,404 steps back to his home.

Chapter 7

Charlotte's afternoon stretched out uninvitingly before her, an endless stream of products to be placed in various niches, each screaming it's superiority over the last. As the clock staggered towards mid-afternoon the idea of somebody picking up the bill while she chased her dream became more appealing by the minute. But deep down she knew Kyle would wither and die without his music. He had been breathless with excitement about some gigs which had come in the previous week with some old relic from the sixties. Whatever else you could throw at him you could hardly accuse him of having his head turned by the glamour... his devotion to his career despite all the odds impressed and infuriated her in turns. He might have found his calling but she had to finance it. When was someone going to be her fairy godmother?

She really needed tonight's gig to forget her troubles. She wasn't always taken with Kyle's kind of music. Quite frankly, some of it sounded like it was being awkward for awkward's sake. She would hear them finish a tune only to find them still trying to wrestle the life out of it a quarter of an hour later... but she did like Jacqui Drinkwater. Proper songs and not too much of the noodling around nonsense.

Dainty and Ethan seemed full of enthusiasm but she was beginning to wonder if she could really do the 'Public Relations' thing anymore. When a career didn't fulfil you it was the start of losing your way; she knew from experience she could never excel at something she wasn't inspired by. Sighing, she glanced at the clock again. Kyle couldn't even get ahead in a career that did inspire him.

She glanced up to see Ethan navigating his way through the office.

He certainly qualified as 'eye candy', charming everyone who crossed his path. It didn't seem to matter if it was the power-dressed boss with her pneumatic chest or the cleaner, curlers still welded to her head under a scarf. They were all equally deserving of his time. He'd appeared out of nowhere and clearly had enough money not to need to bother. He was a genuine, twenty-four carat enigma. Perhaps he was running up the World's biggest debt this side of... well, these days too many other groups and individuals to mention. No, on reflection Ethan had the sort of class that only came with long exposure to hard currency. It wasn't difficult to spot the genuine article. She looked down at the file in front of her. Daydreaming wasn't doing anyone any favours. That was Kyle's modus operandi but it wasn't going to be hers.

★

Kyle felt a spring in his step as he navigated his way through the upmarket cafés and converted cottage shops, packed to bursting with costume jewellery, crocheted clothes and ironic postcards about modern life. A concert by Jacqui Drinkwater in a venue he had really fallen for... perfect. The concert hall's capacity was roughly a thousand, maybe a little more, big enough to attract the acts that could deliver and small enough that you could feel part of the entertainment rather than just a distant voyeur. It had been there for as long as he could remember. He'd seen some household names there on their ascent and a few major acts on their way downwards to oblivion. He placed his hand on one of the solid stone pillars at the entrance. It would feel good to play here. You wouldn't have to explain to people that this <u>was</u> your day job if you were working in places like this. Meanwhile in the real world he needed a drink. That would get him chilled before the main event.

★

It had been a long, hard day, thought Charlotte as she headed for home. She would have to make herself a decent sandwich before the gig but she needed time to relax first, she had enough time to have a long soak and drink at least a gallon of tea. She picked up the mail as she entered the flat but before she could open the letters she walked into the kitchen. THE KITCHEN... OH! MY GOD!!!! It was a nightmare. They'd obviously been burgled. She looked around the rest of the flat. No, the few things of any value they possessed were all undisturbed and in their rightful places. The culprits, there was too much damage to be one person alone, had made their way in, had fought violently with each other using a number of foodstuffs and fled which, after she had considered the actual evidence, only left one person in the frame. Actually, it was two people, one child one adult... it was the day Kyle gave his sax lesson, she remembered now. At least, technically it was one child and one adult. The damage from their cooking adventure was spread across every single work surface. How many people had they fed? It had to be around twelve, minimum, and they'd all had twenty cups of tea each to help sustain them through it. It was meant to be a music lesson not a chimp's tea party. There were pieces of 'sheet music' and CD's strewn around the floor, open packets and jars, a piece of paper with a game of hangman on it; the answer, when she studied it, inevitably being some bloody Miles Davis album. Someone had attempted to write a treble clef with a piece of cooked spaghetti which had now adhered itself to the table. Finally amongst the chaos were two hats. Why were they in the kitchen? And why were they curled up flat at the back? She knew where his saxophone was... all she needed was a bloody hammer. She counted to ten, then another ten. By the time she had got to thirty seven she had resolved to sell the fucking saxophone and use the proceeds to take a trip to the other side of the World. Sod it, she would leave the chaos and run her bath... it was barely a quarter full when she realised she couldn't leave the place in that sort of state. They would be too tired when they got back after the concert and she would die before she'd have her breakfast in that bedlam. No, she would establish a bit of order, enough to make the place habitable then she would deal with his saxophone. She could certainly ring him and tell him what she thought of him. She pressed at the buttons on her mobile as if she was trying to snap the thing in half. She had a mouthful prepared for the moment he picked up and if he didn't she would leave a message that would curdle his blood. It was a full twenty seconds before she realised that the idiot had left his phone in the clutter not ten feet from her.

She set to, fuelled by rage. At the half way point of restoring some kind of order she allotted herself five minutes for a sit and a cup of tea, or at least she would have done had there been any milk. Well, that was it, that was what she needed to push her over the limit. She had been considering it all day but this was the final straw. Dainty had talked a lot of sense in the toilets and something had to change if the pair of them were to have any sort of future together. Kyle might not like it but he would come round eventually… and if he didn't… tough.

★

Kyle made his way through the auditorium, patting himself down as he went, looking for his phone. He had planned to meet Charlie at the entrance but he could send her a text and just see her inside if he could find his phone… if not, he could use Ludo's. The sign outside had said "sold out" which was no surprise; Jacqui Drinkwater had learnt her craft and built her reputation by playing every venue she could, every time she could. Inside the audience was much as he had expected… a mix of mature couples, music students there for the fireworks and a few old timers keeping the faith with Terri Bellis, a sax player from Teesside, a region close enough for him to be embraced as one of their own.

He found his seat, four rows from the front. Barry and Ludo were already there. Kyle greeted them briefly. He could see that they, like him, were in that pre-gig zone of breathless anticipation. He would have borrowed Ludo's phone but he didn't know Charlotte's number… he had it stored on his own phone so he never needed to know it. She had her ticket and she knew where they were. If she was going to be late because she was faffing on, that was no reason for him to miss out. Andy was missing out, that was bad enough. In the call he had made that afternoon, Andy had explained, in mortified tones, how 'the girlfriend' had threatened him with castration if he missed his eldest's performance as "Skater dude 2#" in her year's production of "High School Musical." At least, Kyle thought, he could update Ludo and Barry. "I heard from Andy. He's fine for the gigs with Harry." Ludo nodded without ever taking his eyes from the stage, although as yet there was no meaningful activity there. "When you listen to these artists on C.D it's easy to forget that they're just flesh and blood, human beings like us."

Kyle wasn't entirely convinced. "You're sure? The sax workshop Terri Bellis did in Sunderland last year marked him out as super human. I've spent the last ten months working my way through the stuff he gave us to do over the course of just one day. Still, tonight should be a good kick up the backside for us before we start working with Harry. I'm starting to get pretty excited about it. It could be the start of something big. Contrary to popular belief Harold 'Buster' Crabb is still very much in the land of the living."

"Preserved in alcohol from what I've heard" added Ludo.

Kyle was pleased he would have his regular line up for the gigs with Harry. If half of the stories about Harry were true the band were going to need their comradeship to get through it all. You didn't always get to work with your regular band members. Sometimes they would be unavailable and would call in someone else to deputise for them. On the whole the system worked pretty well, it allowed everyone to have a life or to take up a better offer if it came their way, which few people resented. Occasionally you would find yourself in a band where everyone was a "Dep"… all Indians, no Chiefs. That could be pretty hairy but if you knew your job you could cope. There was an art to picking your 'Dep' too. If they weren't up to the job you got a hard time on your return but if they were too good you could find that there wasn't a job to come back to.

He ceased his ruminating as Barry held forth. "You know that Harry Crabb was the highest selling English jazz artist in Sweden from 1966 through to 1972, excluding 1969" Having laid this on them Barry then proceeded to go through the rest of the list up to 1983 and had to be physically restrained from doing the runners up. Kyle suspected that there was more than a whiff of the autistic about Barry. But it was Ludo who really nailed Harry's persona.

"Harry Crabb. Some people find love, some find God and some find the off-licence at the bottom of the street."

★

Once Charlotte had established a basic order in the kitchen she had ten minutes left to get ready. She was, however going to leave herself just a moment to retrieve a letter from her bed-side cabinet. She had written it and stuck a stamp on it two months earlier, after another ding-dong about leaving towels on the floor. She had been bought off with an apology and a foot massage and had never posted it… but she would now. There it was, already addressed under a pile of old utility bills. It just needed sticking in a post box. She checked the address and crossed her fingers.

Faculty of Business and Law
Edinburgh Building
City Campus
Chester Road
Sunderland
SR1 3SD.

Whatever their future held, Kyle had brought this on himself she thought, as she slammed the door behind her.

★

An expectant hush fell across the audience as the house lights dimmed. Kyle loved this moment more than any other. You could close your eyes and drink it all in and just for a second imagine it was all for you, that it was you who was waiting in the wings with an audience of people desperate to devour your every note. The band appeared in the half light and moved purposefully towards their instruments as Jacqui Drinkwater, a mass of auburn curls and crimson silk, took her place centre stage. Silence… just for a second. The audience held its breath. When she opened her mouth it filled the whole room. It wasn't bombast, it was full and round and complete, like something that had grown to its rightful size. The Quartet locked in right behind her, one direction, one cause, one entity, one emotion as the swinging up-tempo opener began to dig in. It was absolute heaven.

★

Charlotte had missed the first twenty minutes, which in the circumstances wasn't bad going. She made her way down the aisle, apologising for the disturbance to the seated punters who had all managed to get there on time. Kyle kissed her on the cheek without bothering to take his eyes from the stage. Only her self-control stopped her from slapping him round the face in front of both his band and the entire bloody audience. She had hoped at least for a little more interest from him in light of the day she had endured. Dainty was right, as long as the money came in and he got to do his thing he wasn't going to change. Did he care about anything at all other than himself? Clearly not when Terri Bellis was taking a solo. Kyle's rapture at his fellow musician managed the unique feet of enraging her and beguiling her at the same time… it was clear who he was in love with in the here and now and it wasn't her. The soloist, centre stage, eyes shut in fierce concentration, told his story. She studied Kyle's face, lit up like a five year olds on Christmas Day, as lost to the sound of the tenor horn as if he was playing it himself. It was hard to accept that Kyle's undiluted passion for music was one of the things that made her love him. Try as she might she couldn't stay angry with him for long. That was not to say she was about to let him get away with things any longer. She had vowed that, standing in the vandalised kitchen. Should she have posted the letter? On balance yes and anyway it was done now and he would have to live with the consequences.

★

As the night progressed the cascade of sound emanating from the stage made Kyle realise how much work he still had to do. He practised regularly and took every gig he could but he had to admit he could be doing more. That's what it was going to take if he was going to play at this level. After the interval, Singer and Sax Player performed a slow duet, the notes entwining languorously around each other like snakes in a pit. He wanted it to go on for ever. Singers could get in the way of a jazz tune but Jacqui Drinkwater was a musician who sang. There was a difference. He knew now, more than ever, there was no other path he could follow.

At the song's end the audience roared their approval before Ms Drinkwater draped herself over the microphone and addressed them. She thanked band and audience before lamenting, as so often was the case with sidemen, that Terri Bellis was moving on to pastures new which drew a sympathetic 'ahhh' from the crowd. You'd have to be pretty sure of yourself to leave her company, Kyle thought as he caught the glance between Sax player and Singer. A look that suggested there was a lot more to this abdication than met the eye. The band struck up again as some people danced as best they could between the aisles. It felt good to be alive. Nobody here was likely to start a riot so they were left by the security staff to get on with it, as couples, not in the first flush of youth, broke into a sweat "cutting a rug". After an embarrassment of encores, that was it. They were gone, on to another town, another city, even another country to seduce and enrapture all over again. The house lights went up; their short vacation from the real world was over. He could never understand why people were so eager to leave after a gig. After the transportation of delight that good music afforded you, you needed to lower yourself back into the real world slowly in case you gave yourself 'the bends'. Even Charlie, as he contemplated her, seemed like she was in another place.

Once the cleaning staff started to operate between the aisles, there was nothing for it but to pick up his coat and join the others as they moved towards the exit.

"Well that's given us something to chew on." said Kyle as he fumbled for the van keys to hand back to Ludo. "I'll go back with Charlie and see everyone tomorrow."

"I'm going home to burn my bass." Kyle knew Ludo was joking but he guessed they all felt a little overwhelmed by what they'd just witnessed.

"Let's see what tomorrow brings." He was trying his best to gee them up. Far from discouraging him, the nights music had made him all the more keen to get down to working with Harry Crabb.

Chapter 8

Charlotte's anger had abated during the gig but she found herself turning down the offer to link arms as they exited into the damp night and headed for her car. They walked down the street in silence as the noise of the throng dissipated behind them. She knew she was going to have to tell him sooner or later and striking while the iron was hot and he was in a good mood was, she reckoned, her best option. As if he read her thoughts, he spoke.

"Do you fancy another drink?" She nodded and they headed towards the nearest pub.

Once inside, Charlotte glanced around. If there was going to be a ding-dong between her and Kyle the fewer spectators the better. The pub was warm and inviting with a decent open fire and in any other circumstances she would have enjoyed staying for a drink or two. Now it was quiet and practically deserted, save for the jukebox pumping out innocuous dance music at a level you could barely hear. Kyle was at least trying to look contrite as he took a fiver from her and went to the bar. That gave her a chance to marshal her arguments before battle commenced. The little knot of guilt that was forming in her gut needed to be pushed right down if it wasn't going to stop her in her tracks. What was it Dainty had said to her? "If you keep on having to support him you'll both end up resenting it." It would be easier if she capitulated as she had done so many times before but she steeled herself to the task. Once she was qualified she'd be in a much better position to help him and his dreams, all she had to do was get through tonight. She would be calm, she would glide delicately onto the subject and, like a nurse giving a five year old an injection, it would be over before Kyle realised.

He presented her with her drink and change and sat down.

"Kyle, during the interval, when we were in the bar… the tenner I lent you last night, how come you're still broke?"

"I… er… "

"They don't all go to CSA, do they?" He looked puzzled at this.

"CSA, Cash Strapped Andy. I might as well send a fortnightly cheque to his ex-wife."

"Wives! He is trying, he's signed up with a temp agency but if it's not cash in hand he might as well not bother… he can't afford to be recognized by anyone from the Social. He's paranoid enough about the Child Support Agency as it is."

Charlie shook her head in disbelief and Kyle's heart sank. He knew where this was heading, "Armageddon". Past skirmishes had taught him that this was just the start, the opening move in a war that had raged between them for far too long. She continued.

"Last week I said we were going to talk."

Here it came. He braced himself. "Fire away."

"Kyle, I want to do a bar vocational course… I am going to do a bar vocational course."

"You want to work in a bar."

"The Bar". To work in court… you know, be a lawyer or barrister. I've posted the application to Sunderland Uni. I can start in September if they'll accept me."

"Part-time?"

"Full time."

Oh God! He started to panic as the details of what she was saying sank in. The three years Charlie had supported him financially had gone in the twinkling of an eye. True, he'd always said he would return the favour if ever she wanted a break from work. He'd just never expected her to call it in. She was still speaking, the words bouncing off him as he tried to assess just how much trouble he was in. Despite everything going on he still had half an ear on the jukebox… there was something familiar about the tune but he could barely hear it over Charlie.

"I haven't been happy at work for a while now."

Kyle scanned her face, looking for the tiniest hint that she wasn't being serious. Her eyes remained resolutely focused on the floor which pretty much suggested that she was. What did this mean for him? What was he going to have to do to keep his career on track? Christ, how would he cope getting up at 8AM?

"If it wasn't for Dainty I would already have walked from Peterson Partners."

Jesus, she wasn't going to cry was she? He really couldn't handle that right now. He thought rapidly. His best chance was to agree to all demands immediately, surrender completely and then try and negotiate better terms for himself during the drawing up of the treaty.

"Ok, if that's what you want. I'll need to keep my hand in… you know, a couple of gigs a week."

"That's what you're doing now."

"Yes, but if I had more gigs coming in then I'd do less of them."

Charlotte watched him, marvelling at his internal logic. She couldn't work out if this was the smartest or the dumbest thing she had ever heard. This was probably her last chance in terms of age to make such a big upheaval. She'd seen a few late career changers at work and they always had that haunted look as they scrambled to get up a ladder they hadn't set foot on till their late thirties. It would be so much better for them both in the long run if she struck out now. It just involved a bit of short term suffering. She had to keep telling herself this. No… she had to keep telling him this.

There followed a pregnant pause. Kyle stared at his pint and then at the loudspeakers surrounding the pub. He knew the first one to break would lose valuable ground. Usually, Charlie was the first one to crack but for once it seemed she was determined not to concede.

"I could get a bar job or something." Kyle hoped the "or something" left him plenty of wriggle room.

"Are you sure we could live on that? I suppose if I got a part time job as well... what about some peripatetic teaching?"

"Going into schools? It's just not me."

"Talking of which, what's happened to the money from your teaching?"

God! She was opening up on two fronts now and he could barely defend himself on one.

"Good point. Well... "

"It's Andy again isn't it? You're funding that one-man population wave. Kyle! There's a crèche named after him at the bottom of his street!"

"It's not Andy."

"Well what is it?" There was a pause before she struck.

"You are charging Craig for his lessons?"

"I am, or at least I was. He said he would have to stop coming because his Mum's lost her job. She hadn't got the money. It's only temporary."

"Kyle!"

"She's a single mother and Craig's got a grade three exam to pass. I can't just turn him away... not after all we've been through."

"So he has an hour long lesson which... you've told me yourself... goes on for three or four hours, for which he doesn't pay a penny?"

"I guess that pretty much sums it up."

He assessed his position. Should he mount an all-out attack or hunker down for the night, leaving a final push for later in the campaign?

Charlotte was warming to her assault. "And we're feeding him now? I saw the kitchen. You get to play Mother Theresa and I'm left to clear up the mess. For Christ's sake, Kyle... you're not a charity. When are you going to start living in the real world?"

Things were starting to get a bit close to the bone now. Somehow he needed to extricate himself from the nine to five rat-race future she had planned for him. While he was ordering the drinks he had tried to gather his arguments but his head was still full of Jacqui Drinkwater's music. How could Charlie do this to him after all that divine music?

Charlotte could tell from the look on his face what he was thinking. He might be caught up in the romance of the evening's concert but she wasn't... she couldn't afford to be. Someone had to have their feet on the ground in this relationship and it was clearly going to have to be her.

"There will be two years when I won't be earning anything, but it'll be over in a flash. It's going to be so much better for both of us, you'll see. We might be able to get a mortgage once I'm earning a bit more."

He could see her lips moving but to him it felt like he was submerged in a swimming pool. He kept on trying to think what his next move should be but the damn tune on the jukebox kept on nagging away at him, as it had since they had entered the pub. What the hell was it?

"Then there's a two-year training contract with a firm of solicitors but they put me on a salary."

Eventually it clicked into place. It was "Giant Steps. That chord sequence... the jukebox... it was definitely Coltrane's "Giant Steps" with somebody warbling some inane lyric over the top. He wondered if he should note the name of the song down so he could inform the Coltrane estate. He was sure that whoever had lifted the tune wouldn't have gone out of their way to credit the original composer. Really it was daylight robbery; slap some vocals on and run it through a sequencer and there it was like a stolen car with a re-spray.

"It's what I really want to do with my life." Charlotte waited for a response but none came. "Kyle! Hello... Kyle, are you at home?"

"Sorry?"

He had started jotting down the lyrics on a beer mat so he could trace the song and the 'guilty parties'. It was, he later came to realise, a major tactical error.

"KYLE! Have you listened to a word I've said? Oh, forget it!"

As she stood up, Charlotte realised she had been wasting her time. She unclenched her fists. It was either get another drink or slap him round the face there and then. It was the second time she'd wanted to do it that evening, one more provocation and she might actually go for it. God in heaven, how did she end up in these situations? She didn't deserve this, she was a good person, she was trying her best. Couldn't he see she'd had enough? She turned on her heel and approached the bar.

As she neared it a well-dressed man, crouched over paperwork caught her eye. He was quite attractive, if a little older than her. No one else was waiting to be served. She tried to make herself look visible and thirsty but the Barman was wrapped up with a televised football match. The man with the paper work looked up and saw her predicament. One word from him and the Barman snapped to attention as if on an army inspection. The drinks were swiftly provided, but before she could pay the stranger intervened.

"I've got these."

"There's no need, really… I… you've already done enough."

"Think nothing of it. It's no hardship… I own the place."

"This is yours?"

"Guilty."

"And doing paperwork, in your own bar? Isn't that something of a busman's holiday?"

"If only it was that simple. I'm bogged down in trying to set up a charitable scheme whereby our pubs are twinned with watering holes in the less salubrious parts of the World."

"When you say "watering holes" you mean pubs, right?"

"No, sometimes they literally are holes with water but the hoops you have to go through to try and help a little could actually drive you to drink."

He gave her that wide smile again and she felt her knees go a little.

"Well, if it's any consolation, I think it's very admirable."

"You should see these places… I've been across twice now… on my own… it definitely makes you count your blessings."

At first she wasn't sure but then he shot her that smile again, warm and broad and confident. Here she was in the middle of this to-do about her future existence and she was being hit on by a stranger. She stole a quick glance at Kyle. Any danger that he was witnessing this attractive man chatting her up? Not a chance. He was rooting through his pockets, probably looking for his bloody phone. Anthony, her Ex, had been prone to fits of jealousy which she had always detested. It didn't take much… a look, a conversation going on longer than he might like, too much décolletage. He must have thought she was up for anyone from fourteen to fifty. Kyle had never knowingly succumbed to the little green eyed monster, although she thought just for once it might have been nice if he had.

"Thank-you you've been very kind… sorry, but I should be getting back, my… friend will be… "

She motioned towards Kyle and made her apologies, took the drinks and made her exit. She deposited them on the table. Kyle was now involved in jotting down something on a piece of beermat. He grunted a "thanks" without bothering to look up. She sat and proceeded to sip at her drink. Surely that wasn't it? That wasn't his reaction to her attempt to turn their lives around? Eventually, after what seemed like an age, he spoke.

"I just want to say, I'm going to do it. I said I would, so, if that's what it takes, I'll flip burgers or get a factory job or something, if that's what you want me to do with my life."

So that was going to be his tack was it? Her heart sank. For once in his life why couldn't he stand foursquare behind her? She'd been carrying him on her back for more than three years and she was sick of it. Just for once, couldn't he step up to the plate and be the man.

"I might not be at it for long; it's a rather competitive profession. The exams are pretty tough and the higher up you go the more serious the competition gets. There can be as many as a hundred candidates for one post as a barrister."

"Oh! You'll get through it alright. Your sort always does."

Your sort!!! She knew she was being baited now but she wasn't going to bite. She'd rehearsed this in her head too much to blow it now in a fit of anger. Calm, calm, calm.

"The past few months haven't been great for either of us and I know I can get a bit snappy at times," She said it as placatingly as she could.

"File under 'Understatement!'"

Charlotte let this go. If she lost her temper she knew it would just end up another shouting match and nothing would get resolved.

"It doesn't have to be like this. Really, with the minimum of fuss we could both get what we want. And don't get your hopes up but, I might have a solution. And for once in your life just hear me out first. Jacqui Drinkwater, the singer, she must pay good money, regular gigs, that place was chock-a-block."

"Go on."

"She needs a sax player… you heard."

"Probably got someone already lined up. Anyway, I wouldn't suit her."

"Shouldn't you let her be the judge of that?"

"She's never heard of me."

"There was a moment in time when no one had heard of Miles Davis."

"He was a trumpet player."

"Yes I know. That's not the point. I could get her number. What have you got to lose by calling her?"

"My dignity."

"Your dignity? Kyle on Thursday you played a gig for three people, you made £2.50 less your drinks and a share of the petrol."

"So I'm not good enough?"

"Of course you're good enough but you have to get out there and prove it. She's not very likely to come knocking on doors down our street just on the off chance. The difference between you and me is that I'm getting off my backside to try and make a go of my life."

76

"So am I. Playing gigs to three people at a time isn't the picnic you think it is."

"And coming home to a kitchen's that looks like a bomb site and finding I can't have a cup of tea because you've used up all the bloody milk isn't my… "

She hesitated, trying to avoid saying "cup of tea", not only because it was nonsense but also because she knew that if Kyle laughed at that point then she really would swing for him.

"So that's what this has all been about… a pint of bloody milk. I was going to sort it out later."

"Of course it's not about the milk. I'm trying to sort out our lives. Do you really want to be living like this in ten years' time?"

"Yes. What's wrong with how we live? Is it not up to your standards, your Ladyship?"

"It makes me feel like I'm your mother."

"Oh! Just fuck off!"

"Don't swear. I've told you not to swear at me. You want the truth? You're so scared of failing you're not even going to try. You're a coward. Stand up and be a man, for God's sake."

"Typical bloody woman! You pick up a copy of "Hello" or whatever and all of a sudden you're dissatisfied with your "lifestyle.""

Kyle drew a set of quotation marks around "lifestyle" which only stoked her fury. But he wasn't finished. "You can always try your family for a few bob, it's not like they're short."

"Do you know how many times I've seen my family since I moved in with you, Kyle? Twice! Twice, that's right… one wedding, one funeral."

"And tell me, in all honesty, could you tell the two apart?"

"I gave up my family for you and you can't give up an hour to audition for a band."

"I've had enough of this. Your family will take you back as long as you hook up with some rich, chinless, inbred."

"That's right walk away" She was shouting now, despite herself. "… and it's all very well you playing a cross between Mother

Theresa and Bob Geldoff but you're not paying for Craig's saxophone lessons, I am."

"I'm leaving. Unlike you, I don't believe everybody in the World has a price on their head."

"If you walk away from me now Kyle, don't bother to come back."

A weight the size of a bowling ball hit Kyle in the stomach. He wanted to return, wanted to tell Charlotte how much he loved her, wanted to be the man, wanted to do his bit, but she was right, he was terrified. If he had a proper job he couldn't practice, if he couldn't practice he'd get left behind and if he got left behind any chance that he could play his way into a successful music career would be lost. The one person he had desired in his whole life and he was letting her go. Without knowing where he was going or what he was going to do, he slammed the door as he exited the pub.

The man at the bar, to his credit, pretended not to notice.

Chapter 9

The cacophony that awoke him that morning sounded like the collective works of the Sex Pistols performed by the Band of the Scots Guard. Kyle struggled to make sense of this new hell, which ultimately turned out to be nothing more than Andy's alarm clock. As he slowly re-orientated himself to his surroundings he realised he had spent the night on the couch of his long suffering drummer. He felt as though someone had put a gun to his head and fired it... more than once. What was less certain to him was why. Slowly he moved towards the toilet, a limb at a time, as small episodes from the previous night filtered into his brain.

He had meant to go home but he had called in on Andy on the way and they had broken out some of the home brew which Andy had managed to bring to fruition at a cost of thirteen pence a pint.

Kyle didn't mention his argument with Charlotte. Andy's desire to hear about Jacqui Drinkwater erased all memory of "High School Musical" from his mind... which led to them leaving the Government's recommended four units of alcohol benchmark a speck in the distance.

Having successfully negotiated the toilet he returned to the sanctuary of the couch. Why Andy had set the alarm for 8 AM escaped him altogether at first, although, as more of his addled brain kicked in, the significance of this day began to register. Jesus! How could he have forgotten their first rehearsal with Harry Crabb? It was important enough for Andy to have skipped work. There was no way they could cancel it now, so no matter how bad he felt, he was just going to have to get on with it.

Andy appeared, looking fresh as a daisy, brandishing a very welcome cup of tea. If he could keep the tea and a bit of toast down he might be able to function. This just left the Charlotte problem. She would be bound to come round sooner or later, she wasn't one for grudges. Still, one step at a time. The tea was sickly sweet and carried a fair belt which, Andy later revealed, was due to lacing it with a small shot of rum. Whatever else, it did the trick. Less than thirty minutes later they were heading for the rehearsal. Ludo had volunteered to pick up Barry and Sid Chase had phoned, informing them that Mr Crabb would be making his own arrangements. After a minimum of coaxing they got the van up and running and were soon navigating the seedier parts of Sunderland.

Kyle had heard of the rehearsal room by reputation, a bad reputation but it was about all they could afford in their current circumstances. Eventually, the boarded up shops and houses gave way to 67-68 Greek Lane, home of "Acropolis Rehearsal Studios". Once they had trooped inside with the equipment Kyle, head still throbbing, took a minute out to survey the place. The room was shabby and probably structurally unsound. There was a deep fug hanging in the air, foetid enough to require him to clear his throat. The din of various aggressive rock bands in the surrounding rooms permeated the walls, rattling his teeth as a shower of dust fell to the floor dislodged by the heavy metal onslaught.

Was Charlotte right? Did he really want to be plying his trade in dumps like this in ten years' time? Then again, at his age what else could he do? It might be all well and good for Charlotte to change careers mid-stream but a CV that consisted solely of badly paid pub gigs wasn't a C.V at all, it was a confession. As far as he could see, his only way out of the mire was to practice hard and cross his fingers, though obviously not at the same time.

Once Ludo and Barry had arrived and the equipment was set up there was little else to do but await the arrival of "sax legend" Harold "Buster" Crabb. They did this in what passed for silence in room number seven. The gear was tinkered with, a few tunes mulled over, sinews and synapses warmed up, coffee consumed… nothing… more coffee… fags smoked… nothing. They remained resolutely a quartet. Kyle looked at his watch for the enth time. It didn't alter the situation nor did it make the time go any quicker. Next door to them one of the heavy metal bands ran repeatedly, at mind warping volume, through a tune that, he eventually gleaned from the screamed vocal, was called "Wargasm." This didn't help matters.

Eventually Ludo broached the subject.

"I've met his sort before, washed up and living off their past."

With that, and much to Kyle's dismay, the floodgates opened on the subject of their absent 'star'.

"An hour and fifteen minutes, that's eleven quid twenty-five of our money he's washed down the drain." Barry reached for his well-worn ledger and proceeded to scribble furiously as Andy spoke up.

"I heard he passed out at a gig at the "Rendezvous" in Newcastle donkey's years ago and almost got himself a good hiding. Don't be surprised if he doesn't show… or if he does, don't expect him to have it together enough to have his saxophone and if he does show and he has got his sax, don't bank on him being straight enough to find his mouth."

Andy's grim assessment had probably been gleaned from the other acts he worked with. He was usually pretty well informed. Sometimes Kyle wondered if he was the only one who had any faith in their venture. He still wasn't ready to accept that the musician he'd seen on the cover of "Manhattan Daytrip" looking so in command of himself, could be so un-together now, so much a shadow of the player he had been in the sixties and seventies that he could contemplate not showing up in a fit state.

But as time passed, even he fell to doubt. The whole point of the rehearsal was that a little graft together would allow the band to sound like they had some sort of working relationship with Harry on the forthcoming gigs. At a lot of jazz gigs you met whoever you were working with on the night. Sometimes you got away with it and sometimes…

Harry had been up and down a dozen streets and didn't seem any closer to his destination. At this rate he reasoned it would be another fifty years before he got there. Half a ton since the gig… gone in a puff of smoke before you could say "When are we getting paid." The 13th Dec 1961. He could remember it like it was yesterday. Actually, he could remember it a lot better than yesterday, he couldn't remember yesterday at all. Thank God he still had the letter telling him about the gigs and the rehearsal tucked safely in his pocket.

It was his first job in London as a band leader, a wedding… wearing a stiff seven shilling tux that carved a welt in his neck he could still feel. He had liked the groom. A Yorkshire man, a no nonsense sort of bloke. The band were paid twenty pounds or at least they should have been. The groom did his best but weddings always had unexpected costs. He was a millionaire now or something. He certainly wasn't when he got married. Still, on the night they'd all sat down and had fish and chips together. Not everybody felt obliged to feed the band on wedding gigs and a bit of grub was much appreciated. All that time gone in the twinkling of an eye… most of the band had passed on. Drink and drugs did for Beech Chapman, an argument with a Spanish promoter and his sons over a bar bill saw off Gianni and as for 'Bobby two bits'… he wasn't quite sure if Bobby was alive or dead. Drummers were always a bit wayward… rumour had it that he'd jumped ship in the States, joined "The Technicolor Children of the New Jesus" and never been seen again. Who would have thought that he, Harry Crabb, would be the last one standing? His reputation wasn't much these days, which was a shame. He still felt he had it inside of him… deep down he was still the same player. Some musicians had pretty much said their piece before they shuffled of this mortal coil. If the good Lord was keeping him around then it must be for some purpose.

★

From her car Charlotte stared across at the office block that contained Peterson Partners. The staff were trickling back. She hadn't been able to face work first off but she knew if she didn't make it in for the afternoon she was liable to spend the following month wallowing in a sea of gin and wet tissues. She shook her head, barely able to comprehend the amount of time she had spent working there wishing she was somewhere else, all for the sake of that bastard Kyle Johnson.

Life with Kyle had been pitch perfect in the early days even though their first few dates consisted of little more than her going on and on about her Ex. She had vacillated between swearing vengeance and crying until she was incomprehensible and Kyle had simply held her when she wanted him to and listened thoughtfully to her self-pitying litany. She'd read the articles in "Cosmo" and "Marie Claire" and was well aware that harping on about your previous love while on a date was a valid enough reason for any man to run in the opposite direction. But he had stayed.

It wasn't her first experience of being given a shoulder to cry on but it was the first time the other party hadn't been thinking it was the surest way to get her into bed. Kyle had been so reticent of the physical that she had wondered at first if he was a virgin or gay, or even both. He had mentioned short flings with singers and dancers but none of them sounded long term, serious or sane. Once he had taken her car keys, to stop her driving whilst she was full of vodka and, without any attempt at all to psychoanalyse her, he had simply helped her to do what, in her misery, she felt was necessary. He had driven her to her Ex's house in the band's van, had left her alone with her thoughts and a mobile phone and then had quietly driven her home two hours later when she had punished herself enough for being dumped. He had then spent the rest of the night cleaning her up, after the reappearance of most of the vodka. She never felt

83

the need to repeat the exercise again and he never mentioned it. OK, so perhaps 'bastard' was a bit much but she couldn't excuse his behaviour now, however many brownie points he had clocked up in the past.

No, back then he hadn't put a note out of place whereas she'd been as discordant as a hen-night Karaoke. In the end, even before the worst of her hangover kicked in, she had realised the absurdity of being alone outside the house of someone who didn't love her as opposed to being inside her own home with Kyle, who did.

The trickle of employees had increased to a steady flow now, as she looked towards her workplace. She had come through being dumped by Anthony and she would come through this. Picking up her handbag she checked her face one last time for any sign of tears before she exited her car and headed towards the office.

★

"We'll give it another few minutes." What harm was there, thought Kyle, in waiting a couple more minutes after fifty years?

"I could be putting in a shift" said a clearly aggrieved Andy. "Nappies don't buy themselves you know."

"You might find spending the money on birth control a more financially sound investment."

Kyle groaned inwardly, he'd worried that if boredom overcame them it wouldn't be long before some smart-aleck comment from someone like Barry would light the blue touch-paper. Andy didn't hold back.

"Like I need a lecture on sex from Mother fucking Theresa here and if you think I'm wasting any more time waiting for some senile old 'has been' to show his face you've got… "

At that moment the door swung open, almost coming off its hinges as Harry Crabb burst into the room. His left hand bloody, his hat askew, his distended stomach sticking out through layers of clothing which had clearly been slept in more than once, Harry Crabb had arrived. Kyle looked at him, awestruck. There was little that resembled the young man from the album covers.

Harry raked them with a glance. "Well you're too young to be the Rolling Stones and too old to be pop stars so I guess I'm in the right place."

He stuck out his good hand and, with all the bonhomie he could muster, introduced himself. Kyle and the band couldn't quite comprehend the ramshackle whirlwind of activity that had entered their lives as he proceeded to get his sax out of its case.

"B.flat Blues to get the old engine running?"

He didn't wait for an answer; there was no time like the present as far as he was concerned. In the reviews Kyle had read, someone had compared Harry Crabb to an ocean liner. Once he'd set off it took a lot in the way of time and effort to change his course. Hesitantly the band joined in, first the drums but soon the whole outfit pitched in gaining in strength and confidence as Harry weaved his magic through a selection of standards from "The Great American Song Book".

By God, this was blowing away the cobwebs, Harry thought. It had been a few years since he'd played with anyone and he'd forgotten quite how intoxicating it was. They weren't the greatest band in the world but they certainly weren't the worst. It was like putting on a favourite old coat you'd forgotten about. By the third tune they were starting to get the measure of him and how he liked to work. He had always taken pride in his ability to sound at home where ever he was, which always put bands at their ease. As the songs progressed he could feel them relax and really start to play with him despite the god-awful racket that was coming from the other rooms. The rest of the session was spent tearing up Stella by Starlight, All Blues, Desafinado, Summer Wind and a welter of other classic tunes. After a particularly furious rendition of "Cherokee" he suggested a break and a coffee and they all headed into the communal area of the rehearsal rooms.

Behind the desk in the foyer sat a painfully thin and serious looking boy. In between extracting money from the bands that trooped in and out of the rehearsal rooms he appeared to be working his way through what looked like a comic book. Harry tried not to stare. The boy seemed little more than a child and his white face and black make-up made him look like one of the un-dead. He managed to raise his head a little as the band moved towards the drinks dispenser but, odd assortment that they were, they still failed to get any reaction out of him. Then Harry realised what it was he was looking at... the youth was... a Goth, he'd heard about it on Radio 4 one Saturday morning, and had seen a few in Whitby. Apparently they liked sad music and they all wished they were dead... he could relate to that. Perhaps if he'd been born later he could have been a Goth, although he wasn't sure about all that eyeliner.

As they worked their way through the tepid coffee, the questions from the band came thick and fast. Who had he liked the most, who was the best musician he'd worked with, what was the most he'd ever been paid? He answered them with as much honesty and wit as he could muster. Some things had naturally become a little sketchy with age, which led to some embroidery, but only a very little.

"Shall we get stuck back in then?" he suggested as they drained the last of the lukewarm liquid.

"How about "Cry me a river"?" Andy asked as they got up to leave, winking at a girl with fluorescent hair, who was heading for the room with the 'Wargasm' band in it. "I quite fancy a ballad."

"Do you mind if we skip the heartbreak tunes just for once?" Kyle's tone was heartfelt.

Harry found this a little odd from a fellow sax player; tunes of loss and passion were usually meat and drink for them, still each to his own. Eventually they settled, with a minimum of fuss, on playing 'Footprints'.

Once back in again the tunes came thick and fast. Soon they

progressed to making some minor arrangements to the tunes to make them a little more interesting. All in all, Kyle considered, it was turning into quite a productive day. It was just as they were building to a crescendo in "Softly as in a Morning Sunrise" that without any warning blackness hit... not just their room but the entire building. The electricity had obviously cut out; it was black, pitch black, a room without windows in a basement, 'twelve inch, box set vinyl black'. Eventually, even the drummers throughout the building stopped pounding.

"What's all this about," Harry exclaimed through the darkness.

The black-out at least allowed Kyle to keep his disappointment to himself. Why was it, he pondered, that nothing in his life could ever go right for longer than five minutes. Still, it was up to him to explain to Harry.

"This is the most competitively priced rehearsal room in town. It's half the price of Metal Mickey's place. That means that it's a little more prone to the occasional absence of things like electricity."

Before Harry could register his disbelief, a crash sent a shiver up their collective spines as a cymbal hit the concrete floor.

"Do you know how much they cost, you arsehole?" Andy was clearly not pleased.

"Cymbals, especially decent cymbals, aren't cheap so if you fancy explaining to the woman in my life my need to spend money on them instead of nappies and dummies, step right up or, alternatively, just stay still, you pillock. It'll be back on in a minute."

"I am not a pillock."

"I think you'll find that you are, Barry." Andy's bitterness was evident, even in the darkness.

"And anyway how did you know it was my fault?"

"Call it an inspired guess."

For a moment silence reigned as everyone took stock of the situation.

"This reminds me of being inside." Harry said eventually.

During the coffee break it was the one question he had expected them to ask. Then again, perhaps these young lads didn't know as much about his background as the musicians of his own age did.

"Yes, it's exactly like being locked up," he repeated. "You'd just be about to read who'd won the 2.30 at Chepstow and bang, that's it, lights out, without a by-your-leave."

"You were inside?" In the darkness Kyle sat down before Harry spoke.

"Pentonville, fourteen days, theft of medical ephemera and breaking Section five, sub-section two of the Criminal Law Act 1967 " causing any wasteful employment of the police by knowingly making, to any person, a false report". I even set up a prison band while I was there, "The Behind Bars All Stars". Harry started to laugh at the memory.

"It started with me and Johnny Drinkwater. We were playing one of those fancy medical balls with a big band. Huge great teaching hospital it was, in Battersea, Victorian thing. We went for a bit of a poke around in between sets and just as we were about to go back on, there it was, large as life, or not… in this case. Hanging from a frame, a human skeleton, full whack the whole thing, nothing missing."

Andy flicked on his lighter and the single flame cut into the dense, damp black of the rehearsal room with an eerie glow.

"Well, we didn't know when we'd get an opportunity like that again, so in between the second and third set we took him to "The Prince of Wales" in Tooting. We had to spend an age convincing the Landlord he was over eighteen but after that we were sorted. Left him behind the bar with a decent tab to keep him occupied and then we went back to the gig. There was disco dancing on after us so we got away early enough to spend some quality time with him.

"So your new friend wasn't legless by then?" suggested Ludo, which rather tickled Harry.

"No, and we thought after the pub he might like a night on the town, like that musical, you know the sailors, Gene Kelly, Frank Sinatra and that other one. If we were really going to do the sights then he needed kitting out. We got him a jacket and pants from 'lost property' in the pub and then we got him a fag and another pint in. Some of the regulars included him in their rounds but he didn't seem all that thirsty, so by the time me and Johnny had helped him put a good face on it we were in a right old state. By then the devil himself was in us and the cream of London's nightlife awaited. We fancied Stringfellow's but not surprisingly we struggled to get a taxi. You should have seen the rubbernecking. 'John the Greek' stopped to ask us what we were doing with his mother in law which didn't go down so well, what with his wife sitting next to him. Anyway, in the end, we just started walking towards the West-end, more in hope than expectation. Then as we passed the municipal cemetery on the Kings Road we looked at each other and all at once we thought "Well, we'd be fools not to." We found a bit of rope and tied it round the hook in his head and then shinned up one of the trees by the graveyard wall.

We heard the first victim before we saw him. He was singing "The Old Rugged Cross" at the top of his voice. He could barely walk but by God he could belt out a tune. Big fella, big beard and a belly full of beer. Once we spotted him it still took him twenty minutes to get up to us, two steps forward one step back. We almost fell out of the tree twice. He was about to sing an umpteenth chorus of "The Cross" when we launched Mr Bones out of his tree. By Christ, you should have seen his face. He was sober in a second, had invoked the entire Holy Trinity before two and broke the land speed record before a third one had elapsed. We pulled it off twice more but in the end one of 'Mr Bones' legs fell off which made me quite sad. I thought that we'd already had the evening's highlight but Johnny was always one to push the boat out that little bit further. He turns to me all serious and says.

"Let's get him his ride home". So we laid him in the middle of the road and... "

Wiping away a tear, Harry started to laugh again.

"And then we phoned for an ambulance. It was there in a flash, coming round the corner all bells ringing like it was 'The Great Train Robbery' and the 'Fire of London' all rolled into one. And there we were 'the devastated family' crouched over him, holding his thin little hand all concerned like, his other leg on the opposite side of the road and Johnny turns to the Uniform and says "Sorry mate, I think he's already gone, he's cold, you're too late, we've lost him… "

We were pretty easy meat for the Met, to stick us in the Black Maria when it showed up. I couldn't run for the tears in me eyes and the booze in me legs."

The band laughed fit to burst before Andy's lighter gave its last gasp.

"Do you think we'll get our money back?" Barry asked scrabbling around in the darkness for his ledger book.

Chapter 10

Having managed to get into work, Charlotte realised that remaining there for the rest of the afternoon would take some perseverance. She was resigned to being dignified and magnificent and stoic and lots of other positive things. That had been the plan. Now she was in, it didn't seem so easy but it had to be done. She would take herself off to the restroom and make a fortifying cup of coffee for herself before figuring out the rest of her life. Her plan worked until the moment Dainty came in. With Kyle out of the picture, Dainty was all she had in the world, the one person with whom she could afford to come apart at the seams without shame. Dainty was too decent and wise to play the "I told you so card" immediately, but Charlotte knew she was going to get it sooner or later. She saw her reflection in the mirror. God… she looked a fright… she was going to have to patch herself up before she went anywhere else in the building but, at the moment, that was the least of her worries.

The hug from Dainty came the minute she could see her friend's distress. The pursed lips followed when she heard the news. "Not that it's any of my business, but I think you made the right decision… give it a few weeks, you'll see."

"I just couldn't… he left and I couldn't take… "

The sobs came quickly now as she lost her capacity for coherent sentences. With uncharacteristic bad timing, Ethan McCormick entered the room. He wasn't quite prepared for what he saw but he was smart enough to know that his best option was to make his excuses and to get out as quickly as he could.

"Ok! I was just after a coffee… it can wait… you alright?… Sorry."

Dainty watched him go. She had always thought that Ethan McCormick was where Charlotte's future lay. She had no desire to see her friend look so miserable but if, in the long run, she ended up with Mr Right as opposed to "Mr Right Up His Own Arse With Only A Saxophone For Company", then it would be worth it. She went into her handbag and took out a few items to fix Charlotte's face.

"Look, if you'll cheer up I'll show you how I got through my break-up. Not a word though, you'll be the only person I've ever allowed to see this. It's my memento-mori album dedicated to Michael 'commitment issues' Fuller... currently shacked up with my bandy-legged Chief bridesmaid. You might not be one for revenge but by Christ, I am! Just stay put, I'll go and get it."

Dainty returned with a very grand looking photo album. The title on the front said 'Silly M.F' in gold embossed letters.

"I keep this under lock and key and I look at it if I'm having a bad day... if you tell anyone I'll have to kill you... understand?"

She handed it to Charlotte who tried to smile as, with a degree of trepidation, she opened it. Wedding photos were the last thing she wanted to see at that moment.

On the first page there was a picture of the bride and groom. Dainty had never looked lovelier or happier but it was the absence of the groom's head that really caught the eye. The head of Mr Michael "commitment issues" Fuller, the groom, had been cut out, which perhaps should have served as a warning for what was about to follow. The decapitation was merely the start. Charlotte turned the pages slowly and deliberately. Dainty's marriage had been quite a sacred thing to her and since its sticky end Charlotte had always trodden warily. The groom's head formed a fundamental part of all the other pages that followed in the book. On each page there was an unflattering picture with the groom's severed head superimposed at appropriate and not so appropriate places. There was a baby wearing a nappy, a sumo wrestler, an impressive one with Hitler, with a second photo included which she took to be the Chief Bridesmaid and, rather worryingly, a still from "Carry on Doctor"... a man swathed in bandages with four broken limbs in traction above a hospital bed. Had she not had first-hand experience of Dainty's good heart, she might have considered the photo album to be the work of a psychopath.

"So what do you think?" Dainty looked unbelievably well pleased with herself.

"Well, whatever gets you through the night, if it helps you to come to terms with things."

"Come to terms with things? Bollocks to that. What you've got in your hands there is a blueprint. By the time I'm finished with him he'll wish he'd never been born… listen, why don't you stay with me for a few days while you get your head around things and please promise me you're not going to chicken out and rush back to him?"

"No. I've taken all I can. God! Why are they so… juvenile? All we want is a decent man and all that's on offer are boys, hopelessly lost little boys."

"I might skip the last page if I was you." The tone of the warning made it practically irresistible. Charlotte turned to the back page of her friend's bizarre tome. She could barely believe the depravity her eyes alighted on. Dainty's laugh was loud enough to scare off the dead.

"Oh, My Lord!" Charlotte said.

"Well, he went on, and on and on about how he wanted to do that to me, so I thought I could do with an image of someone doing it to him. I got the photo from one of his "adult magazines". I would have preferred his eyes to be watering but that will have to do… for now!

Dainty gave her a hug and Charlotte managed a smile. She was going to be fine. They looked at each other for a moment before they both shuddered at the memory of the last twisted image.

★

Even in his delicate state, the rehearsal with Harry Crabb had provided Kyle with something to occupy himself. The following day, however, dragged interminably. He hadn't expected to find Charlotte at home when he returned. She had walked out before and stayed with friends for a couple of days. This, though, seemed a bit more serious. His attempts to practice with his sax had lasted no more than five minutes; he was even too listless to get through a session of 'Musical Trisha.' In the late afternoon he finally resorted to fresh air. It started off as an invigorating walk round town. However, at an early stage it became a walk to the pub, where he remained as the deserted bar filled with evening revellers. A cheque from a function gig had arrived that morning and was more than enough to pay for his debauchery. After a couple of hours it dawned on him that it was getting increasingly hard to remain upright. He had arrived early enough to have a choice of barstools. That had been easy. His louche demeanour earned him a bit of breathing space as it got busier. He was trying to focus on the television set above the bar; some kind of award ceremony or something. There was an endless succession of the beautiful and the bizarre celebrating their successes. How did they do it, what was it that decreed that he, Kyle Johnson, was a failure whereas someone whose commitment to playing music stretched to one hyped up album, three autobiographies and a career designing pants and eating bugs in the jungle, was a success.

He hadn't slept a wink that night, experiencing what was to become, a recurring nightmare. He was running down the High Street looking for his gig, he could hear the rest of the band, he knew this was his big chance but he just couldn't find the venue and he couldn't play or even ask anyone for help because he had no mouth, nothing, nothing at all, just scar tissue where his mouth once was. All he could do was rage impotently at the world while grappling with the over-sized post-boxes in his path that turned into hysterical, scarlet-faced pub landlords.

To take his mind of the television he tried to engage a group of girls with some opening gambits about "the legacy of Miles Davis" and "the place of the pentatonic scale in western music". These had not proved to be the magnetic opening lines he had expected. He could feel the liquor sinking into his legs, its weight pulling him down by degrees like a swirling sea. He was forcing the stuff down his throat now out of sheer bloody mindedness, glancing up at the screen again as the paparazzi's flashbulbs exposed another minor celebrity traipsing down to collect an award.

"The award for the best music video in the dubstep dance genre goes to… "

Who made these decisions? If Coltrane had been around now they'd probably have been nominating him for "most drug dependent artistic performance in a 'neo-urban setting'. Coltrane's use of drink and drugs at least had the whiff of romance about them. A troubled musical genius out of step with the world, a degree of romance that he couldn't compete with, not as a thirty four year-old unemployed part time music teacher drinking cheap house doubles in a Sunderland city centre pub. At this point the notion entered his head that if he sang a song, a ballad, a torch song of love lost, then someone, somewhere, perhaps a woman would see the depth and beauty of his tortured soul and would take him home. Half way through the second verse, someone, he wasn't sure if it was a man or a woman, threw a roast potato at him.

★

Harry had managed to clear a space on the floor. He lay down and stretched out as far as he could before staring at the ceiling and attempting to focus his thoughts. He would try deep breathing exercises. He needed to remain calm that was the key to it all. Inner serenity would bear fruit and would enable him to access the furthest recesses of his mind in order that he might find the half bottle of scotch he knew was somewhere on the floor. When you lay on the floor and you weren't drunk you could never get comfortable but then again why would you lie on the floor unless you were drunk, which he was and if you were drunk then the floor was more than comfortable enough, thank-you. You saw all manner of things once you were down there, old newspapers, photographs, spiders, mouse droppings, odd socks, CD's although as he hadn't got a CD player they were a bit immaterial. Every so often a CD of an old album he'd done years ago would find its way to him. It would be nice to hear that stuff again one day.

★

At the behest of the Manageress, Kyle left the bar. She was clearly not a fan of the songs of George Gershwin. He had just enough of the sober in him, he thought, to get himself back home. The streets were practically deserted now and briefly he thought how nice it would be to stumble in to the house and have Charlotte shout at him. He was still singing in a genre somewhere between crooning and baby talk, a style unlikely ever to win him an award of any kind, ever. All that awaited him at home now was a hangover and a cold bed. On he trudged, fighting the urge to vomit, pushing it down inside him, daring to contain it. Sometimes he would get on top of the compulsion and think he had conquered it but a few sad sorry steps later on it would rear its ugly head. He could tell the few people who were out were staring at him as he reeled towards home. Usually he enjoyed attracting people's attention but not now, not like this. It was no longer a question of if, it was simply a matter of when he was going to be sick. A back lane would be best. Somewhere no one could see his shame.

★

Charlotte hung up. She had left two messages, she was not about to leave a third. All she wanted was a little peace of mind. She was free now and no matter how much she loved Kyle it did feel like a burden had been lifted from her. Still, she would sleep easier if she knew he was safe at home or with his friends.

She left the bathroom and padded towards the bedroom. It

didn't do for Dainty to know that she'd rung him; she hadn't been lectured yet but she could feel it was coming if she showed any sign of backtracking. She entered the bedroom and clambered on to the camp bed. Dainty was engrossed in one of her magazines, trying to read it whilst not spreading the inch-thick face lotion she was wearing all over the duvet. On sight of her friend, Dainty put the magazine down and looked seriously through the gloop.

"You know those endless interviews with career girls in the colour supplements and what not? I always think 'poor girl she's in for a shock when she finds out you won't get a mother's day card from your company car'. And then as I read on I realise it's me. I'm the girl in the picture. It wasn't meant to be, I woke up one morning and my "twenties" had vanished, just like that. Being twenty-one lasted about three years but twenty-nine was gone in a month."

Charlotte had faced this demon down before and she wasn't about to let Dainty succumb to it now.

"I wouldn't worry, there's a woman in Barcelona just given birth to twins, she's in her sixties."

"She's sixty-seven. Maria del Carmen Bousada de Lara. I have a photograph of her in my bedside drawer… I pray to her most nights."

"So there's hope for us yet?"

"Yes, but can you imagine it. I mean one incontinent member of the family at a time would be grief enough… Never mind, I dare say the new regime at Peterson's will give us our cards soon so I can get pregnant and you can go and study law to your heart's content." There was a pause and then she spoke nonchalantly, too nonchalantly.

"Did you see Ethan's new car. It's your life savings in red chrome. You'd look perfect getting out of it."

"You mean the Mercedes Benz SLR McLaren Roadster, based on the Mercedes-Benz 300 SLR of the fifties."

"Er!… Possibly, I knew you were keen on fancy cars but I didn't think you were that oiled up."

"Most of my friends at school went home to nannies in the summer holidays; I went home to a mechanic called Sykes. He worked for Daddy and I've known him all my life. I cried for weeks when he retired. I was only fifteen but, God, he was a miss. He dreamed of getting his hands on an SLR, had a little jar in his house with spare change in it just for that. Don't ask what they cost, it would curdle your face cream. Whatever else I do this month I must go and see him. I've neglected him since I fell out with the rest of my family."

Charlotte sighed and looked a little wistful before she continued.

"Not that anything is going to happen, because it isn't, but I did think Ethan was sweet today."

"What? Sweet as in "bless" or sweet as in "shag me till my fillings drop out?""

"Don't push it."

"Shall we pray?"

Dainty reached into her bedside draw and withdrew the photograph of Maria Del Carmen Bousada de Lara and then crossed herself, Catholic style, before placing her lotioned hands together. Charlotte wondered how she would ever live without her work mate now that she had made her mind up to leave Petersons, but she couldn't resist a cautioning remark.

"Dainty love, in all honesty, I think you actually have to have sex for all that to work."

*

Kyle sat down and attempted to clean himself up a bit before girding his loins for the final push home. If he could just get the key in to the door and could get into bed he would be alright. He had hoped that throwing up would have improved his general wellbeing, alas it had not. The expelling of his demons would not come from the bottom of a glass. The contents of his stomach had been turned inside out but the "bowling ball" of despair stayed right in place, deep in his guts. As he searched vainly for some mints to take away the acid taste in his mouth he took in his immediate surroundings, almost walking into a lamppost as he recognised the street he was on as one they had passed when they had given Harry a lift home after the rehearsal. Not, it had to be said, the most salubrious part of town. Harry had invited them in but the whole band had thought better of it and declined as politely as possible.

Harry understood the legacy of Miles Davis and pentatonic scales… who needed women? Harry and he were kindred spirits, artists, passionate, wild eyed loners, beyond the constraints of being tied to just one woman. He struggled to his feet and set off as best he could towards Harry's home, avoiding stepping in the acrid pool he had left behind.

★

Harry had started singing. That often helped. He was desperate now. In the future, when he was sober, he would put his emergency supplies somewhere safe and in clear view. He rolled off his back and stopped half way through a chorus of "My Mans Gone Now" and there it was, like a glint of gold in the prospector's eye, looking right at him… the bottle he so badly wanted… no needed. Under a pile of half used manuscript paper past the far side of his bed. If he could just stretch out the arm that didn't have pins and needles, it would be his.

★

A constant stream of kids running a succession of what Kyle imagined were nefarious errands, meant gaining access to Harry's block of flats had been relatively easy. He had a vague notion that it was on the third floor and once the din of "drum and bass" from the second floor was out of earshot, it was Harry's singing that dominated the stairways.

He tried to gather his thoughts before making his entrance but this was entirely thwarted by his specific gravity as he fell through the front door of Harry's bed-sit onto a heap on the floor.

Harry, it turned out, seldom felt the need to lock his own front door. There was nothing worth stealing except "Baby "and "Baby" pretty much went wherever he did. He would die before he would give up "Baby".

He was clutching the saxophone now as he glanced up at his visitor.

"It's Kyle isn't it? How nice of you to drop by, Sir."

He gave Kyle a wink and a grin as if his entrance was the most natural thing in the world, as he pulled up a cushion for him. Kyle joined him on the floor. Harry hadn't been expecting company but now that Kyle was here they could have a little celebration.

Kyle spoke. "S'not right, is it?"

Harry shook his head. Now that he had found his beautiful bottle he was in a particularly agreeable mood.

Kyle continued. "Miles Davis's wife, Mrs Davis... Mrs Davis, she wouldn't say "Miles, you've finished recordin "Kind of blue" the bestselling jazz album ever, now do the washin up". And if she did say "do the washin up" he would say "Hey quit me, woman. I gotta write 'Sketches of Spain' before the 1960s happen."

Harry nodded "Oh no! No she'd never say that... he wasn't good to her though... she was a nice girl, she danced."

"Sorry, Mr Head of Columbia Records. I haven't got Concierto de Aran... juez recorded but I've tidied up the living room an made the bed."

Harry offered his guest a drink but Kyle didn't seem keen. Still, that left more for him which was nice. You had to offer though... it was good manners. He contemplated his young guest. It would have been strange if he'd had kids. Still, he was too long in the tooth for all that nonsense now. Kyle had fallen asleep or passed out, he wasn't really sure which. He stuck a pillow underneath the boy's head. He didn't smell so good but he seemed, at least for the time being, to be at peace.

Chapter 11

The cafe was clean enough to reassure Charlotte but downmarket enough that they could both pig out for less than a fiver. If she and Dainty were going to make it through to the weekend then a full English breakfast was a must. The little spray of flowers on each table turned out to be real rather than plastic which was a nice touch and there was a copy of 'The Independent' as well as 'The Sun' put out for the patrons. After years of making breakfast for two, including the occasion that she returned home from work to find it uneaten and Kyle still in bed, it was a nice change to have the first meal of the day made for her. Even in her thirties having breakfast like this, with a friend or work colleague, made her feel grown up. Diets were off the menu for now and so was economising. Today was a time to enjoy a little personal quantitative easing. First thing tomorrow she would start restructuring her debt in preparation for the austerity that returning to education would bring.

"Penny for them."

Dainty's offer brought Charlotte back down to earth. "Sorry I got a little taken up with micro economics… extremely micro."

Before Dainty could make sense of this a young mother staggered into the café pushing a pram complete with a grubby baby, a small boy dragging furiously on her hand in every direction but the one she wanted to go. The woman appeared to be in possession of what looked like a lifetime's supply of nappies. Charlotte could see how fraught, harassed and utterly washed out the woman looked, as she tried to squeeze past them, excusing herself as the nappies caught Dainty full in the face. There was a moral here but she wasn't sure whether she wanted to see it stated quite so baldly so the arrival of the substantial breakfasts was a relief as the baby's gurgling turned into a thick wall of noise. When Dainty spoke it was clear she was trying to reassure them both.

"It's not always like that."

As the wailing subsided briefly the small boy, who had temporarily given up his attempt to permanently elongate his mother's arm, turned to Dainty.

"That lady's wearing knickers." he said, aiming a grimy finger at her to emphasise his point.

"Yes, yes I am" said Dainty who, to Charlotte's amusement, was clearly determined not to let this wanton child get the better of her.

"Ha! Knickers" said the small boy triumphantly.

"I'm sorry… he's at that age" his mother said, attempting to gain control of him.

"Don't worry" said Dainty "I think you'll find boys are always at that age."

On this point the three of them agreed.

★

It was easier now, thought Kyle. He could hear it loud and clear in his head. The music flowed from his tenor sax in an endless stream of consciousness. He understood his horn like never before. It was genuinely effortless. He could play anything he wanted, new lines and melodies flew from his fingertips as if he was at one removed from the world and floating up above it. The pulsating thud of the drums played a wild counterpoint to the rhythm of his all empowering solo. Only a thick ache in his head that throbbed ever stronger with the beat threatened his refrain, as he reached new musical pinnacles time and time again. He never wanted this to end. He had finally become the musician he'd always dreamed he'd be. The audience were shouting, yelling, screaming passionately in full voice, yelling, over and over again…

"Shut up, you mad fucking bastard, shut up, you mad fucking bastard."

Slowly he managed to open one eye. It was morning and he was prostrate on the floor. OK, the old man who they'd had the rehearsal with was at the other end of the room playing his saxophone. OK. The thin walls were shuddering in and out as someone pounded on them and cried out as if in pain...

"Shut up, you mad fucking bastard, shut up, you mad fucking bastard."

Harry Crabb seemed oblivious to his next door neighbour's desires and continued his musical reverie.

Kyle felt as if his head had been used as a football in a particularly bad tempered Derby match. He was going to throw up but he reckoned he could handle it. He had only a vague idea of where he was going but he stumbled out on unsteady legs and managed to find the communal toilet for Harry's floor.

Once inside he hung over the "great white telephone" and called for God, hugging the porcelain bowl with both arms. This clearly was the bottom layer of Hell. As a communal toilet in a particularly run down block of bed-sits, nobody had the specific duty of keeping it clean... so no one did. This, he could now see, was the sight and smell of a Charlotte-free World. It was not a good World by any standard. As soon as he was able, he removed his head from the foetid toilet and tried to stand up. He was caught in the unpleasantly contradictory state of sweating and shivering with cold and thirstier than he had ever been in his life. He winced his way to the sink and turned on the tap; it spluttered and gasped before letting loose some fairly off-coloured water. Steadying himself on the basin he took a mouthful from the tap, spitting out most of it. It actually had lumps in it, real lumps. He settled for dowsing his head in its stream before staggering back towards Harry's room and slumping on the floor. He had made it back; it would get easier from here. He tried to piece together the preceding hours whilst, with the one eye he had the strength to keep open, he surveyed the bed-sit that Harry called home.

It was a chaos that put even his own dwelling to shame. A prehistoric TV, endless utility bills, pictures of Harry from gigs long since gone, some autographed by big jazz stars from the past, all lying in various stages of decay on the floor. Some of the photos involved Harry and his band and liberal supplies of drink. At this point he couldn't even bear to look at pictures of alcohol. Eventually his gaze fell on a battered photo of what looked like Harry on his wedding day, well-scrubbed and looking supremely happy in a three piece suit with his wild hair Brylcreamed to within an inch of its life. It was a very much more lived in creature in front of him now. Harry's early morning practice session eventually drew to a close, his neighbours having long given up the struggle to silence him. They were both still in the clothes they had slept in, making them look, he thought, like a particularly plaintive poster from Christian Aid Week.

"Breakfast?" Harry offered, taking a grubby spoon and rubbing it on his leg before offering him the tin of cold beans he had opened for the occasion. Kyle wasn't quite sure what had been transferred to where during the rubbing but he was sure he didn't want cold baked beans. He hadn't got the stomach for it, or anything else for that matter, not even for Alka Seltzer, but he needed re-hydrating desperately. As Harry attacked the beans Kyle picked up a photo of Harry with Cannonball Adderley, featuring two of the biggest smiles he'd ever seen.

"You've got to know the lyrics," said Harry pointing at the picture with the spoon "especially for the ballads. If you don't know that its boy meets girl, boy loses girl, it could just as well be boy meets goat... you don't want to be blowing a lot of nonsense, all 'sound and fury', over the top; you've got to tell them a story... Cannonball knew that more than most."

Harry drifted off for a moment, lost to the past, before snapping out of it and warming to his theme.

"Don't just take them round and round in circles, it should be a journey, you need to have a destination. It's not about the saxophone; it's just about your head and your heart. It's who you truly are. Once you can genuinely express that, then you're getting somewhere."

In between these pearls of wisdom Harry chewed slowly on the beans like a cow with cud as Kyle moved back to the wedding picture.

"She's very pretty... still around?"

"Left me twelve years and eight months ago. "Had enough!" she said. We didn't have kids so there wasn't anything else much to consider."

"Why did she leave?"

"I forgot her birthday."

"Seems like something of an overreaction."

"Do you want a cuppa?" was Harry's only response.

"Well to be honest your water supply looks a bit iffy."

"Nah! I know this little place. Get your coat."

Harry reached into a pile of dirty clothes and pulled out an off white shirt with a tie still round the neck and after something of a wrestling match with getting his coat off his sizeable frame he managed to get it on. After another rummage in the pile of clothes he produced a large seventies style kipper tie of a size and colour Kyle hadn't experienced before, a kind of florescent mauve.

These uniforms donned, they headed for the door.

"I said I forgot her Birthday... actually it was a bit more complex than that."

Outside Kyle winced as the daylight hit his eyes. Thank God the sun wasn't shining. Harry was clearly made of sterner stuff and proceeded to take him, at pace, through several back streets and underpasses in what was not, it has to be said, the most wholesome part of town.

"She was born in India, the daughter of a schoolteacher and a serving army officer from Aberdeen. That's a fiery bloody mix I can tell you. In the early days she was crazier than I was but she was smart enough to call a halt to the madness before it took her down."

Harry smiled as he slowed his pace to let Kyle catch up.

"It was her birthday, a big one with a zero in it. So she loaned me the money to take her out to dinner. She went off to the West End to get herself all kitted out. I couldn't see the point myself. I mean all that money on clothes, you got dressed up like that if you were on the pull, but she was a grown woman and she already had me at home... sort of. We were booked in at "L'Etoile" for eight o-clock. She was coming straight there from shopping. She'd said she wanted us to "eat, drink and celebrate like civilised human beings". I was just putting my best clobber on when the phone went... Johnny Drinkwater. He'd just been dropped in it for a big band gig at the Hackney Empire. I mean, we hadn't seen each other for months, how could I refuse?"

During their long walk, dressed in his florescent mauve kipper tie, Kyle began to question Harry's sanity. Was this, he thought, how he would end his days, wandering through the rough parts of some city dressed like an inpatient of a long-term institution, all for the want of a cup of tea. It was, in every sense of the word, a sobering thought.

"I thought "I'll phone her from the gig and join her later" then I could pay for the meal with my own money. I got to the gig sharpish and me and Johnny had a few liveners and the stories started coming out, we had a lot of catching up to do. I remembered about phoning the restaurant about half way through the second set and by then... "

It was at this point Harry raised his hat in greeting to the two police officers that were heading towards them.

"Good afternoon, Gentlemen."

To Kyle's surprise they both tipped their caps back towards Harry before they made their way down the street.

"You know them?"

"Yes, certainly the little one. After a while you get to know most of them. You see, I'm always very agreeable when they arrest me. They're not a bad lot up here, not like the Met. Wouldn't want any more run-ins with them if I can help it."

Harry gave a shudder before turning on a sixpence and into a large building at the top of a row of rundown shops. The neon sign said 'The Chancellor Casino.' It was big, modern and brightly lit, making even Harry wince a bit now. Reaching into his herringbone coat he produced a battered looking membership card.

"One guest with you, Mr Crabb?" said the girl behind the desk as she looked Kyle up and down.

"Yeah! He's kosher… "

They took a photograph of him, despite Harry's reassurance, making him feel even more like someone on the wrong side of the law.

"So anyway, Louise… when I got home there was a note on the kitchen table, the phrase "the straw that broke the camel's back" was mentioned a few times" and "You totally selfish bastard", got a couple of look-ins. I haven't seen her since."

They weaved their way slowly up the stairs ending up on a balcony overlooking the rest of the club. Harry was moving with a sense of purpose now and seemed to know exactly where he was going.

"Did you love her?" Kyle felt odd asking the question at all, but it felt necessary.

Harry shrugged what was probably a "yes" but it was open to a myriad of interpretations.

In the casino a few tired punters were doggedly trying to break the bank but it was understandably quiet for the time of day. The staff all seemed to know Harry and before they could approach the bar an attractive Chinese waitress came up to them.

"Two teas this time, Mr Crabb?"

"God bless you, pet. I'm parched." croaked Harry

"I'll bring them across."

Just the thought of the tea was making Kyle feel high, his mouth now as dry as a sand trap. They gazed down on the activity on the casino floor. It was a lot less glamorous than he had imagined.

"I mean look at me."

Harry was something to behold, standing in his raggy coat, sporting an equally raggy beard flecked with tomato sauce.

"That's why I behaved so badly. I wasn't good enough for her and I knew it and ultimately that was her fault, wasn't it?"

Harry's logic was something Kyle readily comprehended.

"I don't understand women." he said eventually "Whenever they say "We need to talk" they mean "I need to rant.""

Harry nodded sagely before his considered reply.

"I like listening to music, don't know how my ears work, the little bones, bits of skin and such but I still like listening to the music."

The Waitress sashayed over to them carrying a tray.

"There you go Harry, there's some bacon sandwiches left over, you might as well have them, they won't go now."

"You're a Pearl of the Orient, pet… Leyton Orient."

The Waitress swatted Harry playfully as he set about the refreshments. The ache in Kyle's head had subsided to a manageable dull throb as he attempted to pay for the drinks.

"It's all free, son. Never underestimate the benefits of friends in low places."

As the Waitress left she glanced over her shoulder at Kyle and suppressed a giggle as he quizzed Harry further.

"Why don't you track her down?"

"Louise? After we broke up I went on a bit of a bender… a big one… even by my standards ended up back here. I don't think I'm much of a catch for her these days."

"Don't you think she should be the judge of that?"

Harry shrugged again. "I think she fancies you."

"Who?" said Kyle.

"Tiger Lily, there. You could do a lot worse."

Harry nodded towards the waitress. Kyle looked at the floor abashed.

"I'm not really interested in anyone… not anymore."

"Oh dear, you've got it bad. She's left you, hasn't she… your one and only love."

Kyle shrugged and gripped on to his tea. He didn't want to talk about it.

For a while they just sat and watched the money change hands as the casino got richer and the punters got poorer.

"I remember you now." said Kyle after they had been there the best part of an hour and had got through several more cups of tea. "I wasn't sure at first but now I am."

Harry looked a little blankly at him.

"You were there at the Black Bull in Sunderland city centre, about four years ago. There were only seven people there, you stood out like a sore thumb."

Harry nodded.

"You didn't say anything and I didn't recognise you from your album covers."

"Yes, I've had something of a makeunder since the 'Sixties.'"

The more Kyle thought about it the more vivid his recollection became.

They had been playing a jazz gig in Sunderland, a previous incarnation of his current quartet. Harry had stumbled in and sat through both sets in silence, he had offered nothing in the way of applause but had listened with the kind of fierce concentration Kyle recognised as that of a fellow musician. He had wondered when they had first met in the rehearsal room why it was he looked familiar; now it had all become clear.

"You didn't think much of us, did you?" he offered.

"I thought there was room for growth." It was clear that Harry was being as diplomatic as he could.

"And now?"

"Your closer, you're not quite the finished article yet... but you are closer."

It wasn't the answer he wanted to hear but he knew deep down that Harry was right. For a while they concentrated on the punters. A large man in a gaudy striped suit was clearly on a winning streak and was keen to let the world around him know about it. His joy stretched to buying champagne in industrial quantities for those around him, but neither he nor even Harry felt inclined to wander down the staircase to the free booty.

"You wouldn't know how I could get hold of Jacqui Drinkwater, would you?" Kyle asked over the sound of another cork popping the air.

"The singer? Yeah! Doddle, through her Dad, bit of a jazz dynasty, her Family, Father, Mother, Brother, all at it. One of the best alto's this country ever produced. I've still got his number somewhere. We played together for years. We can sort it out back at my place."

Kyle knew he could probably find a contact number for her agent on the internet but he'd worked for agents before and knew that any message that didn't directly involve them getting a cut in the near future would probably end up in a waste paper bin. He also felt, hangover apart, as though he'd emerged from a grey fug for the first time in months. He wanted to put things right with Charlotte and he wanted to do it now.

★

Charlotte hated to admit it but she was relieved to find that Kyle wasn't in. She would collect another car load of her things, including some important work stuff, leave a short note and be gone. She only had her lunch hour so there wasn't time to dwell. She would have to work quickly, she really wasn't in the right frame of mind for a confrontation and if she set to, it would help her to forget why she was there in the first place. But every now and then a small memento stopped her in her tracks, a wooden frog bought at Tynemouth market, a compilation CD of the silliest music imaginable made for her by Kyle when he'd been working away in Scotland and a DVD of an old black and white movie. It was funny how something as simple as a little virus could change the path of your life. How would her life be now if she hadn't had a head cold that day? She smiled and wrinkled her nose at the memory. The month before she met Kyle, absent from work, with nose streaming and head blocked, she turned for some light relief to the afternoon movie. She'd never been much of one for the goggle box but she didn't feel capable of making it back to her bedroom let alone the outside world. The two hours she spent alone with lawyer "Atticus Finch", the hero of "To Kill a Mockingbird", all but chased her infection away and settled her on a career in the law. She felt she could do so much good representing the broken and the dispossessed, it was the nearest thing she'd ever felt to a "calling". Before she could get anywhere she had met Kyle who had the air of the broken and dispossessed himself. Within four months she had moved in to his squalid flat, the beguiling version of "What's New" he had played in the Rendezvous jazz club removing the doubts she should have had... all thoughts of studying for the bar put on the back burner. She should have known he was trouble when she'd first seen the inside of his fridge; it had looked like "The Black Museum."

Putting the wooden frog into one of the carrier bags, she collected up what she most urgently needed, relieved that she had avoided a confrontation with Kyle. This was tempered by her concern for where he actually was. She'd half expected him to be in bed, rotting in his own filth; perhaps her absence had spurred him into activity... or propelled him towards another pretty shoulder to cry on. As she closed the door she knew she mustn't look back. This was a Rubicon, one glance over her shoulder and her resolve would disappear. She squeezed the last of the boxes into her car and only when it was in motion, did she allow herself a half glance backwards... and a tear.

Chapter 12

Harry rummaged through the piles of debris and anything which didn't come under the heading of "what we're looking for" was cast aside with vigour. The warm tea and cold bacon sandwich had been utterly rejuvenating but he could see the boy was still looking a little wan. They didn't make musicians like they did in his day. All the same Kyle was soon pitching in. The boy's excitement at looking for the buried treasure of the notebook was quite infectious… as was much of the aged debris in the bedsit itself in all probability. They toiled on without much profit for what seemed like hours before Kyle spoke.

"What exactly are we looking for?"

"A black notebook with a red trim."

"Perhaps I should have asked earlier on."

The decade of accumulated dust in his bedsit was starting to get up Harry's nose. He found another half bottle of scotch which, as he hadn't been looking for it, gave him an inordinate amount of pleasure.

"That's lunch taken care of" he said, patting the bottle affectionately.

Eventually, just when he was beginning to doubt the existence of the damn book at all, the chaos gave it up. He held the book aloft in triumph before starting to thumb through it.

"OK… Drinkwater J. De-da-de-da-de-da… Chelsea."

Kyle routed around and found his mobile phone. Things were looking up.

"Chelsea?"

"Yes, Four… eight… six, three yes, Chelsea, four, eight, six, three."

"That's it?"

They looked at each other blankly.

"It has been a while since I last saw him. There's a slight chance that it's a little bit out of date."

★

Dainty was pretty sure that Charlotte would be on her way back from collecting more of her possessions. She had a fairly good inkling of what would be going through Charlotte's head. She knew from experience that returning to a place you used to call home to retrieve your belongings was never likely to get a name check in "My Favourite Things". She had offered to help but it more than served her purposes that Charlotte had politely refused. From here on in, it was all about timing. That gave her at best fifteen minutes. She could grab a sandwich later and eat it at her desk if needs be. This was important… no vital… if her closest friend was to be emancipated from "the dark little cloud" that was Kyle Johnson. She quite fancied the idea of being a matchmaker. If her own Mr Right never came along she would fix up her friends and end up being "Aunty Dainty" to hundreds of adoring Godchildren. It wasn't like she didn't have the brothers and sisters to provide them. All she was doing was just helping things along like Jane Austin's Emma. Buoyed up by this notion she headed off to track down Ethan McCormack.

★

"Do you know where he lives?"

Harry looked at Kyle, who seemed crestfallen, now that this avenue to his salvation had turned out to be a dead end. "To be honest I don't even know where he lived when I did."

The boy just looked confused now. Harry shook his head and tried to make things clearer.

"I went to Johnny Drinkwater's place more than enough times but more often than not I was carried in and usually staggered out a day or two later so my memories of the place are a little vague."

This explanation didn't seem to do anything to alleviate Kyle's despondency. They sat side by side as they pondered their predicament while the full bottle of scotch became the empty bottle of scotch. He offered the boy 'a sniff' but it only seemed to make the poor chap look greyer still. When he did speak he sounded deflated.

"So it was in Chelsea?"

"Sorry?"

"The house, Johnny Drinkwater's house! Was it a bungalow, a high-rise, a palace, a tent?"

"It was a house boat. I remember that alright! I tell you from experience, never get a hangover on unstable terrain like a bloody houseboat." He was motioning swaying from side to side and throwing up when it clicked. He leapt off the floor, sending his hat flying. He remembered now, he'd seen the name half a dozen times when he'd been sick over the side.

"It began with an L... Low something or other. Johnny wrote a tune, he wrote a song dedicated to his boat. Start looking for his albums."

Harry was on a roll now. He hadn't felt this good in years. The boy was definitely good company to have around. The two of them started working their way through the renewed chaos of his flat, pausing only to examine the 40 years' worth of vinyl albums scattered across the floor. During the process Kyle held aloft a Patsy Cline LP with a quizzical look on his face. The "Queen of Country Music" sticking out like a sore thumb.

"Louise's".

Another ten minutes of trawling threw up a dusty 'Womble's Christmas' album, which also stopped Kyle in his tracks.

"See the third Womble on the left, the one with the saxophone?" Harry said, buffing up his nails on his lapel. "Don't look like that... it got me a Ford Mustang and two weeks in Mustique."

They searched on as the small piles of debris became one giant central pile in the middle of the room before, eventually, the 'film noire' cover of "This We Dig." by the "The Johnny Drinkwater Septet." gave itself up to them. Harry scanned down the track listing.

"Here it is track three "The Lorelei"... "Lorelei". Just hearing it gives me the D.T.'s again. Lord, the mischief we got up to on that leaky tub."

He sifted through the rubble, this time for books. The boy's fervour was getting to him. A few cowboy novels, some Raymond Chandler and a few tattered phone directories, most of them, though not all, for the North-East region. Just when it seemed that the whole exercise had ground to a halt he caught sight of a dog-eared copy of the Musicians Union phone directory. True it was for the year 1998 but it was probably their best hope. It wasn't bang up to date but it was bound to be a damn sight closer than "Chelsea four, eight, six, three."

Blowing the dust off he worked through the directory.

"Drinkwater... Lorelei? Lorelei... ?

At last his eyes alighted on the entry.

"The bad news is he's moved, the good news is that it says here Drinkwater A, "The Lorelei", that's probably his son, little Alex. Actually it's got to be him, it's not like its Smith or Brown is it. This calls for a celebration... you?"

He offered Kyle another shot of something from a cough syrup bottle, pouring himself a generous measure. The boy not surprisingly refused again. They were all lightweights these young lads.

"Little Alex?"

"Well I say 'little Alex', he'll be about... forty seven now."

Kyle contemplated the possibility that by now a tearful message of apology from Charlotte, awaited him. He could wallow in it without any guilt at all because, well he was about to do the right thing and everything was going to be ok. He'd sorted it all out, off his own bat. There was something to be said for going out and getting completely wasted sometimes. Occasionally you could drink yourself through to a solution. He, Kyle Johnson, had proved that. His phone, however, was in less of a celebratory mood and, however much he wanted it to be otherwise, his mobile was as flat as the AGM of the Gary Glitter fan club. Harry, witnessing this latest obstacle, raked around in the debris one last time.

"Don't worry its round here somewhere."

After some scrabbling through the dust Harry passed him a phone from one of the piles of rubbish they had created; it looked for all the world like a museum piece.

"That's how I ended up taking a piss in front of 15 million people."

Kyle looked nonplussed. He lifted the receiver but couldn't get any signal.

"Sorry… you did what?"

★

"Oh! Hello." Dainty spoke with as much nonchalance as she could muster having run twice round the entire building in her pursuit of Ethan. She had finally caught up with him coming out of the one room in the building that was off limits to her. Boys and toilets! It was like they had some kind of radar. If you really needed them, as in really, really needed them, they disappeared off the face of the map only to emerge an hour later after reading "Auto trader" or "Nuts" in its entirety. Having tracked him down she could certainly skip the gym tonight that was her workout done for the day.

"Mr American, good, I'm glad I bumped into you."

The human heart was a funny thing. Ethan versus Kyle? They were light years apart. A little time alone together and it would be obvious to Charlotte that she and Ethan were made for each other.

However she had to get this just right if her plan was going to come off. Nothing too full on, just nice and vague.

"Charlotte said something or other about would you look in on her before you left work. At least I think it was you she was after, but best go anyway."

Ethan nodded, his twenty-four carat dental work lighting up his face. How could Charlotte not fall for that? She had covered her tracks. Not "she wants to see you" but "I think she wants to see you". Genius! In time she would be the best boss Peterson's had ever had.

★

"Sorry... you did what?" Kyle repeated incredulously.

"I took a piss in front of 15 million people... must have been nineteen seventy something or other. Christmas "Top of the Pops", a nice little earner from a friendly Music Director. Me and Johnny spent all day in "The Tavern" in White City waiting to do "Remember you're a Womble". So after "you're on in an hour" ended up being "you're on in five hours" we were a bit lairey. Didn't think it was a problem, on with the gear, nip down the corridor, quick leak and run up and down the set with a sax sticking out of me costume but just before we were due on I goes to the toilet and before I can get any relief from what had been an impressive day of refreshment, the zip on the cossie busts."

Harry reached for his little bag of sax tools which were one of the few things that he had tucked safely away. He knew from experience they were perfect for repairing phones. He laid them out like a surgeon about to perform a heart by-pass. This wasn't the kind of thing you could rush, no matter how impatient Kyle was.

"Give it here, it was fine at Christmas. Probably explains why I haven't been getting too many calls."

Kyle handed over the phone as if it was some priceless family heirloom.

"So I'd already had a coronary getting the damn costume thing on, there was no way I could get out of it before our spot. We waited for another 20 minutes while they messed about with green crepe bloody paper trying to make the set look like Wimbledon Common. So on we go and by now I'm close to passing out. Johnny keeps on asking me if I'd seen "That Niagara Falls film with Marilyn Monroe", the evil bastard. "Water, water pouring off everywhere mate… splash, splash, splash." I would have mauled him with my paws if I could have seen straight."

Harry poured himself another measure from the bottle of cough syrup.

"Eventually I just had to let go. They're quite absorbent, your Womble, so I got away with it. But it meant I also pissed away my chances of chatting up that blonde bird in Abba, Agatha something. Very easy on the eye."

Despite his best efforts he was getting nowhere with the phone. He picked it up and shook it.

"Now, I come to think of it, I haven't paid a phone bill in a while. Bit of a non-starter really, very clean living people your Swedes, and there I was furry, sweaty and smelling like the gents in "The King's Head.""

Kyle shook his head in disbelief as he jotted down the number for Alex Drinkwater on a scrap of paper.

"Look, Harry, its ok. I've got the number now, you're a lifesaver. I'd better be off. I've got some serious bridge building to do… you are going to be alright on these gigs, aren't you?"

"Son, you can depend on it."

Kyle had seen how Harry drank and he didn't fancy the responsibility of keeping him sober for the duration of four gigs but how could you sack a man who'd been responsible for the largest single act of public urination in the history of mankind?

Chapter 13

It was funny, thought Kyle, as he made his way back home, how in twenty-four hours the World could look like a much sweeter place. All it had taken was a drink, a chat with a friend and a piece of paper with a phone number on it. OK, so he wouldn't get the gig with Jacqui Drinkwater but Charlotte would see that he'd tried and they could finally put all of this nonsense behind them. Just thinking of Charlotte gave him a satisfying glow. Tonight they would have the best "kiss and make-up sex" of their lives. He would cook his signature spaghetti dish. He didn't want to wait a second more than was necessary for their reconciliation. He hadn't run down the street like a child for years but the desire to tear headlong into the breeze out of sheer joy overtook him. He would get home, charge his phone up, tidy the flat, get cleaned up a bit and then make the call that would propel him back into Charlotte's good books. And his mother, he must phone his mother. Charlotte would be sure to ask him if he had. He had barely raised a sweat before a phone-box loomed into view. Why not strike while the iron was hot?

He hadn't been in a phone box since he'd got his first mobile; they were pretty much redundant these days, functional only as an occasional toilet for drunks on a Saturday night. Their importance now was not lost on him. As he drew closer he realised it was occupied by a pensioner, but surely this could only be a temporary brake on his master plan. Once he'd caught his breath, he made sure that she saw him as he started to dramatically look for change through his pockets. The woman talked on oblivious to the urgency of his quest. He looked at his watch; he looked at her, he looked at his watch again. No, this one was here for the duration. He set off at speed; there would surely be at least one more phone box before he got home.

It was much more than a jog he broke into now, he was putting some real effort in and going for the burn and he felt completely and utterly alive. The spattering of rain that had been with him since he'd left Harry's was heavier now. It was refreshing and cooling. Another phone box came into view at the end of Princess Road. He put on a final sprint and got there just too late to stop a painfully thin teenage girl entering it. To add insult to injury, once in she proceeded to get her own phone out of her pocket; she was clearly less enamoured of the weather than he was. He went through the rigmarole of making himself highly visible again, starring at his watch, going through his pockets... but the girl looked straight through him.

Standing still in the rain was less cathartic than charging through it and was well on its way to becoming something of a pain. Eventually, he could take no more and set off down the street towards home again. He could feel the excess alcohol pouring out in his sweat now, the endorphins rushing round his body. The next phone box would be his. Eventually he saw it at the end of the main road, an empty phone box with his name written all over it. He dived in, claiming his prize and was met with the familiar male lavatorial odour that had haunted him all day. He didn't care. He would take a bath with Charlotte and then cook pasta and then they would shag like long stay prisoners on a conjugal visit. The dirtier and sweatier he was now, the better it would be later.

He picked up the clammy receiver... silence... he listened again... not a sound, not even a recorded message... it wasn't working... dead... stone dead... shit! He left the phone box and squatted on the ground while he caught his breath, staring at his distorted reflection in a pool of rain; he wasn't going to give up now. No, not now... he stared at the impression of the grey brick buildings in the dirty water as the precipitation distorted the reflection… my God, he had it, staring at him right in the face. There was an answer to all of this, a solid gold, diamond-encrusted genius of an answer. He would run over to Charlotte's office and phone from there. He'd be hot and sweaty and she would see him make the call. He would be like that bloke in 'An Officer and A Gentleman'. He felt fantastic. He definitely should get fit. He'd look better on stage. He'd be a better lover for Charlotte and his sax playing could only benefit from an increased lung capacity. Who knows, he might even get the damn job with the Drinkwater band. How good would that be? Anything, anything was possible. Picking himself up from the ground he started to run again.

★

It had been nice having the boy there, Harry thought, nursing a cup of black tea, as stillness returned to his bed-sit. He could remember the days of having that sort of passion, for his music, for his band mates… his lovers. Then there was Skylark! How could he forget Skylark? He winced at the memory and the scars it had left behind. He'd only ever proposed to one woman, well, only one whilst sober. His first instinct had been to do it half-cut, but ultimately fear of death won out over fear of heights. You didn't want to be messing around with the drink if you were swinging 200 foot up in the air, even he knew that. It had been the fifteenth of October, a full week after her birthday and a full moon. They had been seeing each other for over a year and he had never been happier. Louise could have had anyone and here she was involved with someone like him, a jazz musician living a hand to mouth existence from gig to gig, holed up in a tiny squat in North London. If his proposal was going to be successful then he needed it to be not just a big gesture but a huge one, something that befitted a girl of her quality. Just playing one of her favourite tunes and then popping the question over a drink was never going to cut it. What he'd needed was a touch of Hollywood. He rubbed at his crotch now, remembering the pain of the makeshift harness thirty years on. It had almost cut him in two. It had also helped him reach notes hitherto incapable of being produced by the Human Species.

'*Skylark, have you anything to say to me? Won't you tell me where my love can be?*'

On the night he had stood, saxophone in hand, a view over the whole of the city to contemplate and then she arrived far below him. He didn't know if it was the sight of her, the occasion or the two hundred foot drop that had made his heart set off like Buddy Rich and Gene Krupa settling a wager.

'*Is there a meadow in the mist where someone's waiting to be kissed?*'

Ultimately he had brought it off, she had said yes and he hadn't ended up breaking every bone in his body. Keeping up that level of stardust in their relationship?... No man could have done. It was inevitable that she would leave eventually. He counted himself lucky to have had as much of her as he did.

★

In little more than five minutes he was inside the anonymous, building where Charlotte worked. He recognised the big bloke at reception on account of the shambolic dancing he had inflicted on everyone at their last Christmas party. It was the third floor he wanted so he vaulted the stairs three at a time. He meant business. He could explain everything at reception on his way out with Charlotte. His legs had done their job but he really couldn't have gone much further, he was going to need a breather before he talked to anyone on the phone. The last flight of stairs was particularly hard work. He was on the right floor now and he could see Dainty. She was ok. He quite liked her. She had the balls that everyone else in the place seemed to lack. But now she was standing in his way, barring his progress to Charlotte and her phone, and the answer, and his job, and the sex. Admittedly he knew he looked a bit deranged and probably smelled like a tramp's mattress but, of all the people here, he thought Dainty would understand the most. He smiled at her but there was no welcome in her voice as she addressed him.

"If you're lost, Kyle and I assure you, you are, I can show you the way out, right now."

"I wanted… to use… Charlotte's… phone. I'm going to ring… the… "

"It being the only phone in the vicinity, I suppose?"

He could hear her tone loud and clear and it wasn't good. Apart from that, the physical exertions of the past thirty minutes were beginning to catch up with him. Things weren't being made any easier by the sweat pouring in to his eyes.

"… don't be like… that… it's… Dainty isn't it?" She didn't smile at the mention of her name.

"I've seen the girl I call my best friend run herself ragged, solely to save you the bother of growing up. Well guess what… it's over now, finito, finished with, done, curtains! Welcome to the real world."

"You don't… understand… it's urgent… I have to ring… about… a… gig… and… and a… "

"A gig? Urgent? Please.! Robbie Williams? Kings of Leon? The Band of the Coldstream Guards? No, I didn't think so."

It was so damn hot in here, why didn't they turn the heating down, hadn't they heard of global warming… Jesus. The sweat was stinging his eyes now. God, he hoped she didn't think he was crying.

She was continuing, her voice ice cold.

"I'm not going to have you spoil things again. Charlotte's my closest friend in the world and I'm not going to have her brought down by you anymore."

She was practically propelling him to the small window in the door of an office. There was Charlotte, looking even lovelier than he remembered and someone was talking to her, helping her on with her coat. He was at least six foot four and looked like Bill or Ted; he couldn't remember which one was which, from the "Bill and Ted" movies. He couldn't get his breath, so damn hot, couldn't breathe. He could hear his heart beating like it was going to rip through his chest. He was… he was going to be sick. He swallowed hard and looked at Dainty. She continued, her demeanour unchanged, as he wilted before her.

"I'm sure you're a great guy and I'm sure all your musician chums think you're a knock-out, but come on, you're not in his class and for the record he's absolutely loaded. You've had a good run for your money but Charlotte needs someone who's in her own league.

Was he really that bad a prospect? This wasn't fair. He just hadn't had the right breaks yet. He should have realised that just giving the impression that he was after the job wouldn't be enough. Christ, why didn't he bite Charlotte's hand off the first time she suggested it. Because he was a loser, that's why. Dainty was right. Charlotte deserved something better and it looked like she had found it. He looked up at Dainty, wanting to speak but the words wouldn't come.

"Come on, I'll let you out the back way." Her voice had softened now. "There's no need for security if you leave quickly. This can be our little secret."

She guided him down the fire escape stairs. She was in complete control of the situation and she knew it. So did he.

"Goodbye Kyle. You really ought to go home, get cleaned up and sort yourself out."

She sounded sympathetic now, which hurt even more than the earlier outright hostility had done.

He was back on the street, wet, dishevelled and exhausted. When he reached the flat he was unsure of why it had taken so long to get home. But he knew it had involved running and crying, talking to kids and feeding ducks in a park.

★

Dainty could scarcely believe how well her plan had worked as she observed her protégés heading for the staff car park. They hadn't exactly fallen into each other's arms but it was early days, no need to rush. Now that she'd got what she wanted, she could afford to feel a little guilty. She'd expected a lot more cockiness from Kyle. He'd folded like a pack of cards at her first gust of anger. Still if he wasn't man enough to fight for Charlotte then he wasn't up to much.

As Dainty watched, Ethan escorted Charlotte to her car like a gentleman. The contrast in their two vehicles rather shattered the illusion of them as social equals, the more so because it appeared that Charlotte's car was incapable of movement. For a magical moment, she hoped that Ethan was going to give her a lift home… she couldn't remember what kind of car Charlotte had said it was but she knew that, to all intents and purposes, it was made of solid gold and ran on champagne. But Charlotte's gentle coaxing of the engine of her own banger finally paid off as it sprung to life. Never mind. Now that she had tasted matchmaking success she really had a taste for it… this was just the start. But she couldn't forget the look on Kyle face. She'd never seen a man cry in public like that before.

Chapter14

Entering the flat, Kyle realised that it wasn't just an empty house. It was a deserted house, a place someone had left, the only presence an absence. He looked around for Charlotte, realising, as he went forlornly from room to room, that a little more of her stuff was missing. He searched on with the knowledge that somewhere in the flat there would be something waiting for him. He found the note on the kitchen table and steadied himself to read it. The message was conciliatory and mature and wished him well. He would have been happier if it had contained some comments about straw, camels and "being a totally selfish bastard". No, this letter was devoid of passion, the kind of letter you sent if you were putting paid to something, like winding up a business venture. Its tone was very matter of factly "this is over". She had wanted to tell him goodbye to his face but he hadn't been there for her, which was typical really. He went to the cupboard and poured himself a drink, a large one. He was on his third shot when he was interrupted by a knock at the door. He knew it wasn't Charlotte but there was a degree of pleasure in pretending to himself that perhaps it was. In the haze of the last 24 hours he had forgotten that Ludo was going to drop by and help him plan for the gigs with Harry Crabb.

"Jesus… What happened to you, you look like shit."

Despite Ludo's opening gambit Kyle was glad of company but even genial Ludo couldn't shift the object, the size and weight of a bowling ball, in his guts. A weight that had grown even heavier since his ejection from Charlotte's workplace. Ludo was wearing his 'special operations jacket' an oily green thing with around two or three hundred pockets crammed with pens, pencils, paper, puncture repair kits, super glue and glucose tablets. If Kyle was caught unprepared for their "mission", Ludo certainly wasn't. In the circumstances it was just as well that Ludo was up for the task. He really needed someone to jolly him up and at times like this his bass player's enthusiasm was vital.

★

Dainty sniffed the night air as she moved down the high street. She loved late night Thursday shopping. If she had her own way then every night would be 'late night shopping.' But for once there was something more important than banners saying 'Sale Now On'. She took out her mobile. She could hardly wait for Charlotte to pick up. When she did Dainty couldn't stop the flurry of words from her mouth.

"So, what happened, what did he say, what did he do, did he offer you a lift in his Mercedes Bends Roadrunner thing, when are you seeing him again, should I be buying a hat?"

"Wooooahhhh. Steady on, first of all who are we talking about?"

"Come on don't play dumb with me, Charlotte Wendingham. You know exactly who I'm on about. Looks like a film star, talks like a film star, walks like...

"No I haven't the foggiest."

"You are the world's biggest tease. There's a special place reserved in hell for your sort."

"Ok. I give up. I assume you mean the American."

"Obviously."

"He walked me to my car, we exchanged some pleasantries, we went our separate ways."

"That was it... really? You've ruined my day."

"You'll get over it when you see what's for supper when you get back."

"Forgiven... almost. I'll be back in a couple of hours."

Dainty sighed and put the phone back into her bag. OK, so it was going to take a little more work than she had anticipated but she was more than equal to the task.

★

Try as he might Kyle found it difficult to concentrate on the matter in hand but Ludo was even more chipper than usual.

"Rubber gloves check, water bowl check, time check, beer check, not beer check, marbles check."

"You're not taking this too seriously are you?"

Kyle spoke more in sorrow than anger as Ludo carried the washing up bowl across the kitchen to where they were working. The "washing up" itself had been preying on Kyle's mind for a few days now, although not enough to motivate him to do anything about it. It now took up the sink, either side of the sink, most of the kitchen table and two of the kitchen chairs. What was more pressing, though, was keeping Ludo right as they prepared their subterfuge.

"You've got the crate of "Cholmondley's Olde Strange" 5.00 ABV here and I've got the more liver friendly "Drivers Friend", which has an ABV of 0.2. For Christ's sake make sure we don't get them mixed up... shall we begin?"

"It's got to be illegal" said Ludo, immersing the first bottle into the hot soapy water in the washing up bowl.

"It probably is but I don't know quite what the charge would be. False pretences, fraud, impersonating Alfie from "The Happy Man?""

"So Harry's going to drink the soft stuff and think it's the hard stuff and be quite content?"

"That's the plan; one bottle of Cholmondley's has the same amount of alcohol as twenty five bottles of "Driver's Friend.""

"And we'll be left with a crate of label-less real ale."

"And we'll be left with a crate of label-less evidence, which one way or another we'll have to dispose of."

"Pete Docherty eat your heart out. The label says hot but the contents say not."

It was getting easier now to slide the labels off the bottles as they emerged from the hot foam. Ludo was finding the whole process hilarious. Every band needed 'a Ludo' thought Kyle, for those times when you had to laugh or you'd reach for a hand gun and cash in your chips.

"Even if he downs the lot in one" Kyle said, as they peeled off the last label, "It's still only like a pints worth of alcohol. I'll pay you back after the London gig."

He had thought about solutions to Harry's drinking since their first rehearsal but hadn't managed to come up with anything better than outright deception. Quite how he was going to pay Ludo back for the beer he wasn't sure either. The London gig paid well enough, the other three less so, but he was going to have to get used to buying his own food and paying his own rent and quickly. It wasn't so easy to sign on anymore and he couldn't run the risk of being forced into some job he didn't want, not after all he'd been through. He had till the end of the month to come up with something substantial but that was a worry that had to be put aside, at least for now.

"This lot should get him through the first gig" he said, as he attached the last fake label to the anaemic bottle of 'Driver's Friend.'

"And when this runs out?" Ludo was sceptical "I've shared digs with alcoholics before and they can be a pretty devious lot in order to get their fix. You might fob him off with this stuff once but I doubt he'll be so easily conned a second time."

"I know but we've got to keep Harry on the straight and narrow. These four gigs might be a springboard for the band but not if Harry's the worse for wear and makes a prick of himself... and by implication us."

Ludo didn't often look serious but he did now. "I've done more than enough gigs with someone pissed in the band, you always feel like it's your fault that it makes you suck. Mind you these days with the music colleges knocking out decent young players left, right and centre, all living on bean sprouts and Red Bull. It's becoming an ever more dangerous luxury to be drunk on stage. On top of that there are fewer venues than ever to play in. Karaoke has a lot to answer for... bloody amateurs. Everyone who can, is teaching to make ends meet, which creates even more players chasing even fewer gigs and so on and so on... "

Kyle nodded his agreement. "Do you want a beer, they are going begging." Drinking wasn't a permanent solution to his mood but it would at least see him through till tomorrow when he would start coming up with a more permanent solution to his woes. Ludo pulled a CD from one of his jacket pockets. It was Harry playing at the Manchester Free Trade Hall in 1967, the album he'd had the cover for but not the actual disc. Music filled the room as they sat back and enjoyed a last beer while a younger, care-free and more boisterous "Harold Arthur Crabb" expressed himself. It was the sound of unadulterated joy, an artist pouring himself into his saxophone like a man possessed.

"So how much did they sting you for that piece of history?" Ludo had a knack of obtaining CD's on the cheap so the answer came as something of a shock.

"I got it on EBay, £19 plus postage and packaging."

"Do you reckon any of that money will find its way into Harry's pocket any time soon?"

"Can't see it myself."

"Someone's making money from him, it just isn't Harry."

They sat in silence for a while and drank in what was a stellar performance by the whole band. Eventually Ludo looked up from his beer.

"Where's Charlie?"

The question, which came at the night's close, was something of a surprise. Kyle hadn't mentioned Charlotte all night, which was probably what had made Ludo so suspicious.

"We've... er... split up. She couldn't handle my... lifestyle."

"Oh! Right… OK… that's sad. I thought you two were a good… you know… together."

"I'm past all that nonsense now. You can crash here if you like. I'm beginning to wilt."

"No, I really should be getting back. We're having a late bite of supper."

Kyle felt a twinge of jealousy as he saw the twinkle in Ludo's eye. But it was a small, sad twinge. He could see his friend was keen to get home to Carol, the primary school teacher he'd met on one of their gigs. She had taken issue with one of the slogans on his T shirts and love had blossomed. It had been on the go for two months now and Kyle could recognise what was on his friend's mind.

"You want to borrow this tonight?" Ludo handed him the CD on the doorstep. They both knew it was a consolation prize. Still, as Ludo departed he could at last drop the happy façade he'd had to maintain all night.

He looked around his flat as he prepared to turn in; it was becoming a bit worrying. Charlotte had a word for it when she had first moved in, SMOC, Single Male Occupancy Chaos. Yes, it was a little untidy but it could wait until tomorrow. What he needed to do right now was crawl into bed and draw the covers over his head, no need to wash or clean his teeth just climb in and fall asleep… no bath, no spaghetti and no sex.

Thirty minutes in and he was no closer to dropping off. The digital clock's glow illuminated the pillow next to him enough to see the impression where Charlotte's head had lain just days earlier. An hour crawled past, still sleep wouldn't come to set him free regardless of how much he desired it. In a desperate bid to fill the absence that was Charlotte's breathing he decided to listen to the CD of Harry. It would help blow away her ghost. He padded out to the living room and back to the bedroom managing to stand on another CD, a CD case and one conker that Craig had given him. "A twenty four-er" he was reliably informed.

With the album on and the light killed he got back under the sheets. He'd given up everything for his music now, even Charlotte. From here on in, he would play sax all day and be wild and free like Harry… perhaps a small drink would help him to sleep.

★

Charlotte had got used to the creaking of the camp bed and Dainty could, it seemed, kip comfortably through the apocalypse but it was difficult to sleep that night. What had disturbed her piece of mind was the phone call she'd got from her mother, that afternoon. She had always known it would come, it was just a lot sooner than she had expected it. Whether the cause was the 'work grapevine' or just her mother's intuition she didn't know. A part of her had hoped it might be Kyle but it was not. She recalled the voice on the phone with a shiver.

"Really, it's been quite long enough, and there's no reason not to meet up is there?"

She needed an excuse but she couldn't think of one that would get her off the hook.

"It'll have to be the weekend. There's been a lot of upheavals at work and now's not really the time to be taking a day off."

She knew the temptation that Saturday held for her; she would have to steel herself against weakening and deciding to return to the fold, however tempting it was. She had tasted a degree of freedom and she wasn't about to give it up easily, attractive as it was to sink back into her old ways.

★

Kyle lay motionless on his bed, staring into the darkness as the voice of Harry Crabb on the stage of the "Manchester Free Trade Hall" drifted out of the speakers. He couldn't have been that much younger than Kyle himself when it was recorded. It was the end of the evening, specifically the end of August 22nd 1967. It was quite a raw recording and it wasn't difficult to imagine Harry on stage lean and wiry, sweating like a thoroughbred convinced of his own immortality. A hush fell on the exuberant audience and for a minute Kyle wondered if the concert was finished. If it was, it seemed a bit half cock. Then the voice came again, higher pitched than the husk that had stumbled into their rehearsal, sax in bandaged hand, a voice unblemished by the life of debauchery that was to come.

"Ladies and Gentlemen we'd like to slow proceedings down a little now to allow the rhythm section to get the essential medical attention precipitated by that last number. This is a tune I wrote last night, just before the Landlady took all the bulbs out of the lights, and it's dedicated to… well let's just say I know who it's for and she knows who it's for; this is called "All I Ask of You."

The heartfelt ballad that smoked out of the speakers and across the floor was at once the very best and very worst thing for Kyle to hear. He turned to look at the vacant pillow next to him, as the bowling ball gave another sickening lurch.

Chapter 15

The sound of tyres on the driveway signalled Charlotte had reached her destination. The journey to her parental home had passed with nothing more than a vast emptiness occupying the space where her emotions should have been. She still wasn't sure if the estrangement from her parents, while she had been with Kyle, fell into the plus or minus column of her life. Her father had been characteristically blunt. So long as Kyle was a feature in her life she wasn't welcome in her family home. Now that Kyle had left… at a time when she needed him most… the impediment to her returning to the bosom of her family was gone. But was that what she wanted?

The crunching sound at least covered the sound of the radio. She had been glued to the on-air discussion, despite the fury it had caused in her, as a group of right-wing pundits berated a university lecturer for having the temerity to donate part of his salary to help the starving in Africa. One of them was from Durham and had been Head Girl at her school, though you would never have guessed it so thoroughly had she reinvented her accent to fit in with her Neo-Con friends. Charlotte realised it had possibly not been the wisest decision to have listened to it just before she addressed how she was going to play her family reunion. Perhaps she could just not bring up the subject of Kyle and their failed love affair. How could you mention it and not have it sound like abject defeat? How could she not swing for her father if he uttered some barely camouflaged variation on the theme of "I told you so?" Then again could you blame them? Kyle had more than lived up to their poor expectations. She wanted to scream at him for letting her down and then scream at her parents for thinking he could do such a thing.

As a child it had been the noise of the tyres on their gravel driveway that alerted her, when she was barely old enough to see out of the Bentley's windows, that she was home. The sound still aroused painful memories. If studying Law turned out to be a blind alley, she would write a self-help book for those adults who knew the awesome distress of being shipped off from the family home once they were old enough to feed themselves. Long before 'Harry Potter' had made the notion of boarding school 'cool' she had been subjected to its cold embrace, a custodial sentence for the crime of reaching pre-pubescence. She shivered at the memory of it all. During the holidays the excitement of being home usually wore off pretty quickly but then came the painful wrench back to do the rest of your time, just when you'd managed to put down some roots.

As the house came into view, she couldn't deny that it was an impressive pile. To her great relief no other motor vehicles were parked outside as she brought her battered Ford to rest. There was the option of hiding it at the back in the family garage. She knew it well enough, it was where she had spent most of her time during the school holidays, year in year out, but ultimately she was not in the mood to hide the antiquated 1.1 litre Fiesta from sight. In the light of day you could see that it was two parts blue to one part rust, but hadn't it got her everywhere she needed for three years. She had grown to love its alternative colour scheme; it was like a weather beaten face with lots of experience and character.

She hesitated as she got out of the car. She wasn't sure whether to knock or just go in. She still had a key but it had been so long now both options seemed a little uncomfortable.

If she turned back no one would ever know that she'd been there at all and it seemed, at that moment, like a pretty attractive option. She tapped at the door so lightly she knew no one would hear, which bought her a little time. She knocked a little louder… nothing. They were expecting her so what was going on? After a third knock, more forceful still, she opted for opening the door to find what appeared to be an empty house. She hadn't expected a welcoming committee but perhaps somebody might have been there to greet her. The hall was much as it had ever been… a monument of sub-zero splendour and oak flooring. Should she call out? This wasn't going awfully well.

"Hello. Anyone home?"

There was a shriek from within. Judging from her gardening gloves, her mother, when she appeared, was engaged in the daily ritual of tending to her plants, but she looked the same as ever… twin set and pearls, a vivid bow in the now completely white mane of hair.

"Oh Lord! You gave me such a start."

Charlotte strode briskly across the hall and hugged her mother. "Hi, Mum".

"Come in, come in, and me looking such a state."

She was already well inside the building and her mother, as ever, didn't have a hair out of place but it was still nice to hear the welcome and give way to her mother's embrace. She had been prepared for her Mother to look somewhat older but she was pleasantly surprised. It had been over a year and a half since they had last met and even then that had been briefly and behind her father's back.

"Is Daddy… ?"

Her mother shook her head. "He's out on a shoot, some kind of corporate thing… it's the bloody Chinese now, if you please; it's been in the book for months. He'll be back late tonight if you're going to be around?"

"I have to get back; I'm snowed under with work."

She was surprised at how easy an excuse it was to make.

★

Kyle woke up with a start as the empty beer bottle that had nestled in his lap hit the floor. He tried to focus on the wall clock, which only exacerbated the problem. That was the trouble with falling asleep mid-day… it left you feeling completely disorientated. Jesus… he'd been out for the count for over three hours. He'd have to get into gear and bloody quickly. He had just about enough time to get scrubbed up for their first gig with the legendary or at least previously legendary Harold 'Buster' Crabb. Any kind of warm up on his sax would have to wait till he got to the venue.

Forty minutes later, his hair still wet, he was loading the crate of hooky beer and his saxophone on to the band van. He gave a slight shudder at his surroundings as he clambered into the driver's seat. In daylight you could fully savour the wretched state of the vehicle. Take-away cartons, empty cans of WD40, an A to Z, a well-thumbed copy of "Loaded", a copy of the Bhagavad-Gita next to it, various social security forms and STD pamphlets including the seminal "So You Think You Have Crabs", all spattered with spots of oil, beer and curry sauce.

★

"We'll just have to make the best use of the time we have. I wish you could stay longer." her mother said, as she kissed her again, whispering "Welcome home, I'm so glad your back." Her mother had spent her life making the best of things so Charlotte resolved, at least for now, to do likewise. It had come as something of a relief not to have to meet her Father; one step at a time was probably a good dictum. That was the problem with her family. Old wounds needed to be healed at a snail's pace, bring anything out into the open too overtly and you risked "frightening the horses" and that would never do. There were still members of her extended 'clan' that were moving slowly towards reconciliation from grudges started before the Norman invasion.

The long afternoon was spent pleasurably enough drinking tea in the conservatory and getting up to date with the flora and fauna her Mother had so lovingly cultivated throughout the entire building.

"Yes, you couldn't fathom the contentment I get out of the green fingered thing. I can scarcely believe it myself. Can you see the anthurium next to the geraniums? That's a life's work in itself. It would be easier in a greenhouse but I want a little colour indoors. It's like nursing a small infant.

"How is Daddy?"

"Fit as a butcher's dog dear. He'll see me off, that's for sure."

"Don't say that… you're not… ?"

"Heavens, no, I haven't any complaints. The eyes aren't quite as 20/20 as they have been and the daily struggle with horticulture takes it out of one's back but I can still give a good account of myself if needs be. I've given up riding, I bruise too easily now."

Charlotte wondered when the subject of her failed romance was going to surface. By the time the second pot of tea was brought in she realised that it wasn't going to surface at all unless she raised it. As she scoffed her third amaretti, she couldn't decide whether she was relieved or disturbed by her Mother's ability to pretend that nothing had happened and that Kyle had never existed. She should have known better. One of her second cousins had got pregnant as a teenager, ended up taking a "gap year" in Australia and was never spoken of again.

"How's Sykes? Do you still hear anything from him?"

Her mother looked abject.

"Didn't we tell you… Oh I'm sure I meant to? I am so sorry, he passed on… March… or April, a thrombosis I think they said. I'm quite sure it was sudden. We were busy, away in Nice and missed the funeral… at least I think we were. I know we sent something or other. More tea?"

Charlotte tried desperately hard not to show any emotion. She'd been back less than two hours engaging in small talk and now she actually wanted to scream at her mother and then herself. Sykes was gone and she was bereft but she was dammed if she was going to let it show.

★

Harry was waiting when he got there. "I've had a couple of beers but that was a few hours ago. I'm sure I'm OK to drive," Kyle said clambering into the driver's seat. If he was driving that would cut down on the possibility of arguments.

Harry shook Kyle's hand warmly; Ludo and Barry were in place. There was only one omission.

"Where's Andy"

It was always Andy.

"Hidden within the bowels of the "black economy" Ludo said, as he manoeuvred for a space to sit. "But don't worry, he gave me directions for picking him up... sort of... I'll ride up front with you and navigate." He pulled a sheet of crumpled paper Andy had given him out of his back pocket as he headed for the front of the van. "The girlfriends have taken to calling him "The Scarlet Pimpernel." Ludo was straightening out the piece of paper as he spoke.

Kyle struggled to stay patient. His dilemma was that Barry was a much more effective co-pilot than Ludo but he was also an infinitely more annoying one. He finally got the van into gear and with a shudder they were off.

"Technically this place doesn't have an address, being as its only half built." said Ludo, surveying the now flattened piece of paper.

Kyle could already feel himself getting stressed and they hadn't yet managed to get to the bottom of the street. He had thought that the driving would calm him down but nothing could have been further from the truth.

"He's working cash in hand." said Ludo, staring intently at the scrawled directions. "Apparently they get clobbered if the building work isn't completed on time and on budget, so they're taking on all comers, no names, no pack drill, no health or safety."

They had been driving fruitlessly for thirty minutes before Barry, who had been engrossed in his "Daily Telegraph" opened his mouth. To Kyle's annoyance, he could see through the rear view mirror that Barry hadn't even bothered to put down his paper but it didn't stop him giving an opinion.

"Yeah... there it is again, we've passed that three times already." How could the bugger see if he never looked out of the window?

That was Barry all over, he didn't even specify what landmark it was they had passed in triplicate. He just let them know they were in it up to their necks whilst giving the impression that not only would he not have allowed the situation to occur but that he was also the only person with a solution to their problems.

"You should have brought SatNev along," said Ludo as it began to dawn on everyone that they were thoroughly lost.

"I don't have a bloody satnav."

"Sat-Nev" I said Sat-Nev! Welsh Tony's van driver, Neville Hopkirk. He can find anywhere in the UK or Europe after looking at a map once… they think he might be a bit autistic."

"Well, I happen to know that Neville Hopkirk gets paid more than twice as much as anyone else in Tony's band and we are skint. Any more bright ideas?" Kyle could feel the vein in his head start to throb.

"Going by our last few gigs we'd get him for about four quid a night then." Barry's intervention merely added fuel to the flames.

"Even so we still can't afford him." Kyle hoped this was an end to the matter. It wasn't.

"Yes, but think how much extra petrol you're wasting going round and round." Barry punctuated this comment by putting down his paper and reaching for his ledger book.

"Start working that out and you're dead." Kyle said, through clenched teeth.

★

As the evening drew in they reached a point where it was impossible to contemplate any more tea. The mixture of guilt and sorrow she felt had rendered her numb to the rest of the afternoon's proceedings. If nothing else, her time with Kyle had given her a chance to see how most people lived and at that moment in time she felt her family might as well have been from another planet. "I must be going, I'm afraid."

"Daddy doesn't know I'm doing this but just consider it an update on birthdays and Christmases missed," her Mother said, as she reached into her handbag.

Charlotte didn't bother to look at the cheque when it was written.

"No, really it's not necessary; I've been promoted at work... the stuffs coming in faster than I can spend it."

"Good Heavens, really? I do wish you'd have a word with the rest of your generation, they go through the stuff like water."

Chapter 16

"Round and round and bloody round, like a farmer on the pull at a country dance." Kyle could do little but concede that Ludo had a point as they circled the city for the umpteenth time.

"This is all wrong you know". Barry spoke with a degree of bitterness. "That pub's been there for over two hundred years and what in the name of God is that they've built next to it. Of course it could be me, perhaps the architect was four years old and had a job lot of Lego."

"I like it. Everything can't look ancient. You wouldn't want a new car to look like a 70's Ford Anglia."

Kyle sighed. All he needed now was Ludo and Barry going at each other.

"I might… I like fins on cars." Kyle was pretty sure that Barry didn't like fins on cars, what Barry liked was stirring it. As for himself, he was living on his nerve ends as he tried to look for clues to their destination through the van's grimey windows.

"Far be it from me to try and save us money and gets us to our gig on time… " Barry said, still smarting from the jibe at his bookkeeping. "… but we might as well follow those two wagons with the name of a building company on the side of them because we've run out of any other meaningful plan."

It proved to be an inspired suggestion, which meant it was something of a double edged sword. They arrived at their destination within little more than ten minutes of his suggestion but Barry, they knew to their cost, would be regaling them with his moment of inspired 'genius' for at least the rest of the week. Kyle surveyed the landscape as they pulled up at the half completed building where dozens of labourers scurried around like ants. He couldn't see Andy and it was getting late, very late.

"Where is he, we're running out of time… Christ, they're all in disguise."

Everyone bar the Foreman wore overalls and the majority a facemask; even from a distance the amount of dust the building work was causing was evident.

"Stands to reason" said Ludo "The masks make a pretty good disguise, most of them will be on the social. I reckon that if anyone with a clipboard looking faintly official appeared from round the corner there'd be an exodus like a fire drill at the Olympic village."

When, after a process of elimination, they did work out which one was Andy, he appeared, for no particular reason, to be turning a big piece of rock into a small piece of rock. Absorbed as he seemed in this task, the unmistakable din of the band van turning over eventually got his attention. He gave them a wave as he motioned to the Gaffer his desire to leave.

The foreman shook his head, clearly intent on having his pound of flesh.

"Why won't he let him go, he can see we're in a bloody hurry."

Kyle, who was by and large a peaceful sort, was now on the verge of sizing up Andy's boss. Every man had his limit but his were fast being exceeded.

"You may not have experienced this personally" Barry's tone was nonchalant. "But it is customary in the regular world of employment to OK the boss before you leg it out of work."

On reflection, Kyle decided the Foreman looked like a bit of a bruiser but if Barry opened his mouth with another wise crack like that he would definitely lamp him.

Andy tried his best 'exasperation face', to see if the Foreman would cut them some slack. But the man simply gesticulated at his watch, dramatically tapping it and sorrowfully shaking his head in refusal. He looked at The Foreman again. The Band looked at Andy then the Foreman, the Foreman looked at the Band then Andy. The whole thing started to take on the air of a spaghetti western shoot out. Eventually the Foreman relented and their drummer was set free with a regal wave of the hand. Without any more ado he legged it to the van and dived in through the open side door.

★

Dainty let out a deep sigh of contentment. Whilst it might not be, literally by definition, very "street" there was something deeply satisfying about a girl's night in, no one to impress, the freedom of shapeless old nightwear and the bliss of consuming industrial sized portions of Chinese food from the local take-away. As if that wasn't pleasure enough they had wine, they had face packs, they had a television… nirvana. The mugging and gurning that followed, once they had plastered on the "self-heating" face packs, was inevitable. It was definitely more fun with a friend.

She stretched the white goo on to her face before it set. This done, she perused her ashen face in the mirror.

"It's not all it's made up to be."

"Sorry." Charlotte broke off from her thoughts.

"Being white, distinctly underwhelming."

"You won't be able to dance but your bum will be smaller."

"Two negatives."

"Sweaty Gareth from Accounts certainly thinks so."

"No?"

"He follows your backside round the office like an umpire glued to a tennis ball."

"Two tennis balls, thank-you."

"Quite."

"Have you seen Mrs Sweaty Gareth?"

"No, never."

"She picked him up from work last week; she could fit in his pocket."

"He probably thinks of you when… "

"Sooo don't go there."

"Poor Sweaty Gareth."

"Come on I need a decent sized drink. I'm emotionally scarred by the thought."

The cork gave a satisfying pop as it left the bottle.

"How were your parents?"

"I left feeling pretty low."

"It'll pass."

"I'm not so sure."

She gave Charlotte a reassuring hug. She knew enough about her friend to know that now wasn't the time to probe. A change of subject was in every ones interest.

"Can we watch 'Modern Law'?" Charlotte simply had to let her. It was her newest vice.

"Well, I think it gives a rather warped view of the legal profession."

Even before Charlotte had set the wheels in motion to study law Dainty had become addicted to "Modern Law", a TV series set in a New York law firm, and it was going to take more than Charlotte's mock opprobrium to stop her indulging herself in it.

"I'm sure it's very accurate and impeccably researched" she countered as Charlotte handed her the remote. "Consider it homework."

★

"Jesus, how much dust have you brought in with you. I had a bath for this gig. I might as well not have bothered." Barry was off again and they were still a long way from their destination.

"Nobody said anything to me about doing gigs with the 'Village People'," Ludo said, in contemplation of Andy's attire.

"Ha! Bloody Ha! If you want we can go back to my place, I'll get a bath and get changed and we can all be an hour or two late."

For once Kyle could sympathise. Andy had just finished a hard day's graft and was in no mood to be the butt of someone else's joke, especially Ludo's.

"Technically, it should be in the singular, he's a" Village Person."

"Barry, are you saying I'm gay?" Andy sounded outraged.

"Well I don't know what you get up to when we're not here."

"I'm not gay, right."

"Yes we know. I've met some of the witnesses… and their kids," countered Ludo as Andy snarled at him.

"I wonder if they had solo careers?" Barry said as he reacquainted himself with his broadsheet.

"Who?" Kyle asked in desperation, hoping it might move the topic away from Andy's sexuality and Ludo's snipping.

"Ladies and Gentleman will you please welcome on stage "The Village Person." Ludo was so entertained by this notion that he said this a few times more for effect although it went largely ignored.

Kyle knew that somewhere in the van was a half full bottle of herbal sedatives. At the first opportunity they would be his… all of them.

★

This, thought Charlotte, was exactly what the doctor ordered. A night in, with her best friend, with some serious pampering and takeaway consumption to boot. This was as likely to put the thought of her visit to her Mother behind her as anything. But it was specifically the goggle box that eventually got her off the hook. She stretched out and contemplated the screen as the credits to "Modern Law" rolled.

"It should be terrifying really."

Dainty looked at her friend in surprise.

"Really? It was only a television programme… unless you mean the bottles, two bottles between two of us, it's not exactly "party hard"… is it?"

"No, "Modern Law"… a kid who's planning to blow up an entire school and, what's more, with the wherewithal to do it. The worst thing they ever found at my school was a couple of gay sex magazines and a still containing ginger beer… I say ginger beer… it was a packet of ginger snaps swimming in a jar of ethyl alcohol stolen from the chemistry lab but, let's face it, it's small potatoes compared to teenagers these days with stocks of rifles and semtex!

"It's just a TV drama."

"You think it wasn't based on real life?"

There was another full bottle sitting enticingly in front of them but the corkscrew had become lost in the pile of take away boxes.

"I'm glad I was educated here." Dainty said wistfully as she attempted to all but wring a glass out of what remained of the second bottle.

"Never mind, at least the little sod got his comeuppance."

"Would you do it, though? Like Jenny Brown." Dainty, after another sortie, found the corkscrew. "Would you defend someone you knew was guilty?"

"I think the trick is not to ask. God, I'd think twice before I took a job in the US. I don't much fancy a job where if you had an off day someone ends up going to the electric chair… Still I should worry, if I qualify I think most of my bread and butter cases will be people with early onset Alzheimer's forgetting to pay for a tin of dog food as they potter out of Tesco's."

"Wait a minute if I'm going to have to put up with working at Peterson Partners without you I at least want know that you're battling District Attorneys and saving people from judicial execution."

"You appear to have swallowed the boxed set of "Modern Law" whole."

Dainty's stuck out her tongue before smiling as she uncorked their last bottle of supermarket plonk.

★

They were on the A19 before it struck Kyle how subdued Harry Crabb had been, preferring it seemed, to concentrate on the case of beer, which he had been nursing paternalistically since the start of the journey.

"Anyone else, while I'm on?"

There was a chorus of polite refusals as Harry liberated his fourth bottle.

"Oh! Right, just me then, I'm not a great one for drinking alone. Andy, you'll have a beer you must be gasping."

Again Harry was knocked back. Only the look between Kyle and Andy gave any indication of subterfuge. Harry was half way down the bottle before he paused.

"You're not all… Mormons are you?"

He was assured they were not.

"Christ I thought I was off to a gig with the jazz section of a Tabernacle Choir." With that Harry relaxed and set about tackling the rest of the crate.

They were past Scotch Corner before Barry found anything worth mentioning in the paper.

"It says here that if the rate of Elvis impersonators increases at the same pace that it has done in the last thirty years that by 2062 everyone on the planet will be Elvis Presley."

"So long as they don't all want their burger and fries at the same time," Ludo said, whilst still keeping an eye open for any road signs to their destination.

"Shut up about food, all that building graft makes you hungry." said Andy

"There's only one thing you're ever hungry for, mate." Ludo was, as ever, pushing his luck.

"I have my needs; you sound like a bloke who's not getting any."

Kyle gripped at the steering wheel till his knuckles went white… when would they give him a break? Andy gave his rhythm section partner a two fingered gesture which looked like it was all he had the strength for at the end of his shift. Barry, being himself no slouch at winding people up and most specifically his band mates, decided this was the moment to pour himself a tea from his flask and tuck into the sandwiches his Mother usually made for him. Not for the first time when they were off to a gig, he didn't feel particularly obliged to offer them round. Eyebrows were raised. Nothing was said.

Harry was by now onto his sixth bottle and Kyle could see, in the rear view mirror, that the aged sax player was examining the label, somewhat suspiciously. Suddenly he spoke.

"Sorry, we're going to have to stop, this stuff's going straight through me."

Kyle bit his lip. They were out in open countryside now but barely a third of the way through the journey. If Harry was going to arrive in any fit state at the gig it was essential he didn't twig just yet what it was he was consuming.

'It's not off is it?' Kyle hoped his nonchalance sounded more convincing out loud than it did in his head. He pulled the van in at the next service station and the band spilled out on to the forecourt, glad of the stretch and the break from the atmosphere of cement and asbestos that orbited Andy Valentine.

"You know statistically you're more likely to be involved in a fatal accident on a petrol forecourt than on the motorway."

"Barry, at this moment in time you have no idea how close to the unvarnished truth you actually are." Andy Valentine rarely got through a band journey without some form of not so covert death threat to the group's pianist.

"Right, if we're not going to balls this up we have to be back here in ten minutes tops!"

Kyle knew he needed to keep an eye on Harry if he wasn't to find that he'd bought himself something a little stronger to top himself up for the rest of the journey. After a joint bathroom stop, they headed together towards the main shopping area. To his relief the single till in the shop had a sizable queue behind it.

"Fraid we haven't got time to queue," he pointed out with faux disappointment.

"Actually, I was just following you; I'm a bit short of readies at the minute."

"Well, it's a cash gig so I can give you something on the way back."

Sad though this exchange was he still felt a degree of relief at Harry's lack of money as they returned to the van. They were, thankfully, all back bar Andy.

"Ten minutes? We're probably leaving a pregnant waitress behind… maybe two" was Barry's take on Andy's absence just before the drummer turned up with a small army of pasties and scotch eggs, which he proceeded to demolish with relish in front of the sour faced keyboard player.

As the aged van geared itself up to its pitiful maximum speed, Harry examined another of the bottles

"This beer's like making love in a canoe." he declared finally.

The business of travelling in the back of a darkened van has a natural soporific effect but this caused all heads to turn. He had their full attention now.

"Sorry… it's like what?" Even Kyle was mystified.

"It's like making love in a canoe… It's fucking close to water."

Chapter 17

Charlotte frowned as she waited for the kettle to come to the boil. For the first time in her life she was in a situation she couldn't do anything about and she hated it. The fact that she only had herself to blame just added to her misery. Dainty had popped out to the local twenty-four hour supermarket, which was just about walking distance, for one 'definitely last' bottle of wine and, if she was honest, Charlotte was glad of the solitude. She had told Dainty about Sykes's death but it hadn't given her any kind of respite, comforting as Dainty had been. It really didn't take a huge leap of the imagination to see Dainty running Peterson Partners in a few years' time. She, on the other hand, wasn't fit to run a whelk stall. It wasn't that she had forgotten Sykes, it was just that there had seemed so many things pressing on her time. Somehow, not calling in on him at Christmas one year had morphed into three in the blink of an eye. All the things that had seemed so pressing then seemed like nothing more than a series of pointless exercises now. Running around buying clothes she didn't really need and meeting acquaintances for lunch once a week and all the while there was Sykes, bereaved and alone. All she could do was pray that he'd had friends more steadfast and decent than her. At least she could punish herself with memories of the two of them driving round in the wonderfully restored cars with the wind blowing through their hair. Unlike her father, Sykes had never failed to see her off and wish her a safe journey on the days she had joylessly returned to school. He had always been there for her. Why had she not been there for him?

★

As they left Durham Services behind Kyle relaxed a little, although he still thought the gig seemed a bit out of the way for a warm-up. Paying barely more than their expenses, it would have been just as easy to do a few more rehearsals instead. But try as he might to keep business uppermost in his mind, he couldn't help thinking about Charlotte and all that had passed between them. It was easy to see now where he had screwed up but that only made it harder to bear. Eventually the "bowling ball" became too much and he made a concerted effort to dwell on other matters. They were just past Scotch Corner when it came to him. Sid Chase wasn't daft. He had booked three gigs before the main event just to make sure that Harry wasn't going to blow it on the big day. John Lindhope was, in all probability, paying for some rehearsals and a gig so Chase, the crafty bastard, with an eye on 'the bottom line', was being paid for public rehearsals that weren't costing him a penny. Through the mirror Harry beamed at him from within the dark recess of the van, a jazz legend in a threadbare coat and dog eared hat. It was Sid Chase and a thousand other shameless scammers like him that had left Harry all but destitute in the autumn of his years. Still, this might be the moment for the former European Jazz Musician of the Year to reclaim some of his former glory.

Within the hour they swung into the car park of the "The Fatted Ox" in a small village on the outskirts of Harrogate. It looked nice, one of those "hub of the community" sort of places with ivy on the exterior walls and a menu that ran to little more than, "Ye Roaste Chicken" but with portions that were on the generous side. The band were at home in a places like this. They might not have been here before but they had worked in identical venues around the country a thousand times. Mostly it was a pub but once a month they declared themselves a "Jazz Club".

The keys were barely out of the ignition before the van doors burst open with an audible degree of enthusiasm, everyone keen to get on with setting up the gear and sussing out their new workplace.

Ludo patted the van. "There, there, girl, job done… rest now."

Kyle looked with incredulity at this display of affection. There was always a sense of relief when they managed to arrive anywhere in the van. It should have been sold off for scrap years ago but until they had the wherewithal to replace it, this wasn't a serious option. Perhaps he was being too cynical, he thought, and Ludo's love was keeping the old dear on the road. As it stood it was a love affair that was going to have to last longer than his own had.

Andy worked out the best entrance for the equipment and set about conveying the stuff in to the venue as swiftly as he could, followed by the rest of the band.

It had been obvious to them all since they first met Harry that he wasn't physically capable of lugging around heavy musical equipment. Nevertheless, he still offered to help as Barry struggled manfully with his not insubstantial keyboard.

"He hasn't really got the strength to move it on his own without rupturing himself and he won't let us touch it because we haven't washed our hands" said Andy, as the last of his own equipment went inside. If Barry had a riposte then he kept it to himself.

"Sorry I can't do more." said Harry apologetically "I rather buggered up my ankle and elbow late night shopping."

"I wouldn't worry" said Andy kindly, as he made his fully laden way into the pub "If you can bring in the pad of tunes it'll be help enough."

Andy could have his moments but Kyle knew that for the most part he was one of the good guys… as long as you weren't in possession of ovaries.

Once they had completed the task of setting up their equipment Kyle caught sight of a man, stick thin, plastic carrier bag in hand, probably in his mid-sixties with hair Brylcreamed into a soggy trifle topping on the front of his head. The carrier bag was the biggest give away. Nobody running a jazz club really cared about how they transported the accoutrements of their trade, they just grabbed the easiest thing to hand, which nine times out of ten had Asda or Tesco's written on it. They were an odd bunch, the men who ran jazz clubs, and it was always a man. They were sometimes the most wonderfully warm human beings on the planet and sometimes not quite the full shilling. Occasionally they were both. To run a jazz club required a combination of steely business acumen, saintliness and insanity. It wasn't a coincidence that they often resembled the selfless human beings that cropped up on the nightly news, running refugee camps.

"Hullo, I'm Derek." he said as he shook Kyle's hand. "We spoke on the phone. No problems are there? Lovely, you're cutting it fine mind. You're on in about fifteen minutes. There are two sockets behind the big tables and another one below the stag's head. Someone will need to sign for the money before you go, don't forget."

He took a sup of his pint "We've had them all here you know… Old Ronnie Scott, Tubby Hayes, Dudley, Humph, both the Kennys… oh yes."

"You've obviously had a busy week then" said Ludo straight faced. But Derek was oblivious. He had already zoned in on Harry. Fortunately, it appeared Derek's finances didn't run to getting Harry a beer in. Kyle had managed to keep an 'eagle eye' on Harry thus far although he hadn't expected him to try to get a drink while they were setting up, but now… who could tell? With the equipment finally in place, he promptly got Harry a pint that was half beer and half "Driver's Friend"… which he thought was probably a good stop gap. Harry himself seemed quite content, deep as he was, in conversation with Derek. Kyle reckoned that if he could keep Harry straight till the end of the first set he couldn't do too much damage to himself in the short break in-between… that was the plan. If Harry cut a bit loose in the second half it probably wouldn't be too much of a problem and even if there had been a plan B it was too late to try anything else now.

With the room relatively quiet, the best place to be was by the bar. That way he could see anything Harry attempted to do and, if necessary, intervene but then again Harry was a grown man. He could hardly forbid him from getting a drink in, could he? The best thing about Harry being skint was that it meant he couldn't get drunk under his own steam. All Kyle could hope was that if any of his fans turned up they were stingy types.

His attention was diverted from chaperoning as two of the early arrivals approached the bar. They were clearly of Harry's generation but, unlike him, didn't bear any of the scars of a life lived in extremis. One, in a pristine trilby, his regimental tie forming an affixiatingly tight grip on his neck, the other, a shorter, balding man a pink, podgy sea of beige. Kyle was close enough to them to hear them address each other as Albert and Clem and he gathered from his eavesdropping that they had been awaiting the re-emergence of "Harold Arthur Crabb" for some time. He leaned in closer.

"I see you've escaped" Albert, the taller and more distinguished of the two, was polishing his bi-focals to a fine sheen with a small piece of yellow cloth as he spoke.

"I told her it was the police on the phone... said someone had broken into the allotment again."

"That's the fourth time they've got in this month isn't it?"

"Third. Remind me on to rub a bit of muck on me boots before I go home. I've left my overalls there as well. It's like being a member of the SAS. "I mustn't get under her feet" she says but if I go anywhere it's always the Spanish Inquisition when I get back."

The mirror at the back of the bar afforded Kyle a glimpse of Clem as he grasped at the heavy wooden bar in what Kyle supposed was an attempt to control his marital frustration.

"Yes, it's a fine line you have to tread with the fair sex and every morning you wake up to discover the fine line has been drawn somewhere else." Albert said, with a sorry shake of his head.

Kyle tried to look nonchalant as he became more engrossed in their discussion. If he was honest he even felt something of a pang of regret. He'd rather fancied the idea of being wizened and grumpy around Charlotte once they were both a thousand years old. The two men talked on, oblivious to his prying.

"Buster looks like he's got a bunch of young lads with him." said Albert, wiping foam from his moustache.

"Young lads? I hope it's not all going to be crash, bang, wallop."

"Another pint?"

"Lovely… you'll want to get some polo mints in for your trip home unless you fancy convincing your good lady that your allotment is now a licensed premises."

"All prepared, I've got some in my jacket pocket… you didn't happen to hear how Durham got on did you? They were 116 for three when I last looked… I daren't use the teletext once Corrie's on and she's got her feet up."

With that the two men ambled off to take a couple of seats at the back of the pub. Kyle looked around the room. He'd always been fascinated by the ritual every musician had before the off. Barry trying to finish the crossword in his newspaper, Ludo perfecting some pub trick, balancing a fork on the edge of a pint glass with a matchstick, Andy fielding phone calls from a succession of either smitten or enraged women. Only Harry warmed up, standing alone in a corner trilling quietly on his sax, which for reasons known only to himself he referred to as "Baby". They could have waited in a backroom but there didn't seem much point, this being "The Fatted Ox" and not Wembley Stadium.

*

Charlotte was glad when eventually she heard the sound of Dainty's key in the door. She looked down at her fingernails, chewed to pieces and for what? She was no further forward, how could she be. The man was dead. How could she possibly make amends to someone who was dead? And it wasn't like there was family left behind either.

Dainty's head appeared around the door beaming but she was too smart not to realise that all was not well.

"Still beating yourself up over Mr Sykes."

Charlotte nodded. She couldn't even bear to hear the sound of her own voice.

"Look, we all make mistakes, it's not like you did it deliberately. Do you think Hitler lost sleep over anything, let alone the things he did by accident. You might be a skinny bitch despite guzzling two cream cakes a day and with more good looks than anyone has any right to deserve in this world but you're not Hitler... don't you forget that."

She gave Dainty the smile that she knew her friend wanted to see. If Dainty had been a man she would have married her in a flash.

Dainty produced a paper bag from behind her back as she spoke.

"I forgot to tell you I got some free samples at work for something we're doing a number on. What are the two most wonderful words in the world, especially when placed side by side?"

Charlotte shook her head. She was in no fit state to work out riddles. Dainty held out the bag towards her.

"Continental and... Chocolate."

"No? For free?"

"Utterly gratis... they want some puff pieces on their centenary."

It was only after the wine was gone and Charlotte was putting the box and paper bag in the bin that she saw the receipt. Dainty had known how upset she was and had gone to the trouble of faking free chocolates to cheer her up. That was how good friends behaved. She had let down Sykes but she swore she would never let a good friend down again, it hurt too much.

★

Kyle had checked the backroom but no one had fancied shifting out the tables and chairs that currently occupied it. A few more punters had started to drift in. There was an advantage to playing in a small village. You were invariably the only show in town and so you often got quite a good showing. Albert and Clem returned to the bar, Clem's frantic attempts to get the barman's attention a clear expression of his desire to make the most of his freedom. The din from the extra punters meant it was necessary to move closer if he was going to pick up the thread again.

"He owes me 15 shillings."

"Sorry?" Albert was clearly lost in a moment.

"Him, Harry Crabb, the sax player, he owes me fifteen shillings… Wallsend memorial hall 1967."

"So that's about seventy five pence then. Look, they're kicking off."

He had become so lost in the gent's conversation that he hadn't realised his restless band had taken to the stage and were picking up their instruments in readiness to play. With a minimum of fuss and nothing even approaching an introduction, Andy was laying down a muscular swing groove that he looked incapable of an hour earlier. Kyle stared for a second as clouds of dust emanated from Andy's work clothes as he began to get into his stride. Albert peered at the band.

"They're alright this lot… look! The drummer's on fire."

Chapter 18

The first few songs passed in something of a blur. Harry moistened his lips and surveyed the room. He'd played in better venues but then again he'd played in worse and it was certainly a half way decent crowd. He'd been all but washed up a few weeks ago, now he was back where he belonged although, if he was being honest, not feeling too grand. Still, "Doctor Stage" would rescue him, he certainly had in the past. He'd broken his leg falling into the theatre pit half way through a gig in an Oslo theatre in October 1969, but he'd managed to finish the show and the 'knees up' that followed it. It was only the following day, after he'd been nagged into visiting outpatients, he found out why his leg was still numb.

Barry took the first solo of the night during the opening number. It was 'Skylark', Harry smiled to himself, recalling how much Louise had liked the song. He instinctively stroked his cheek, remembering the almighty crack it had received. Louise had slapped him good and proper across the face when the Swedish doctor had told him his leg was fractured. "Running the risk of a thrombosis like a bloody idiot" she'd said. It was odd. He didn't feel like he'd had that much to drink that night either. The sight of Kyle's frantic nodding brought him back to the present. The boy was flapping about, motioning for him to solo. Harry drew a deep breath and brought the sax to his lips but before he'd made a sound the boy had jumped in and started to play. Just as well really, he didn't feel quite himself at all. It had got steadily worse during the journey there. Slowly it dawned on him that the booze the band had provided him with in the van was suspiciously weak fare. He'd been playing jazz on stage all his life, usually he felt completely invigorated as his moment came to shine… but this time… he couldn't deny it, he didn't feel so good.

He patted his leg. He was still here so it hadn't turned out too badly. They were playing 'Dolphin Dance' now. Had he soloed in the last number… he really wasn't sure? Thinking about a thrombosis wasn't good for him. His whole body felt like it weighed a ton. He didn't feel half as inspired as he had at the rehearsal. When they were getting ready to go on he'd felt a little twinge. He hadn't done a proper gig for a year or two now, if you discounted busking. Had he simply forgotten how much hard work performing was? Or was he just getting too old for it? The thing was, he'd felt like this before, a guest house in Whitby in 2003 was the last time. Yes, he recognised his symptoms for what they were now. He'd had the DT's before, there was no mistaking them. He'd had his doubts about that beer in the van, at first he thought perhaps he was coming down with the flu, but the more he thought about it… nobody else drinking it… the stuff going straight through him… two of the labels sliding off in his hands… the nausea came at him again as his nerve ends jangled and his head spun. Those fucking 'college boys' had stitched him up good and proper. They clearly didn't trust him. Wherever he looked now there was alcohol… pints, halves, shorts, cocktails, everywhere except inside of him. He needed a drink, a decent sized scotch, ideally. They were playing "All The Things You Are" now. He ought to lamp the bastards, he would have twenty years ago but now he knew he couldn't, too old, too weak and too dis… ori… ent… ated. He gripped on to Baby. Mustn't shake, not in front of his public, mustn't shake. Constantly fluctuating images raced through his brain, melting in front of his eyes. He was sweating heavily but his hands felt cold and clammy against the sax. On the Waltzer at Seaburn funfair thirteen years old, round and round, the man with the dirty fingernails and the cheap tattoos spinning him and his Mam round and round, trying it on with Mam in front of him, round and round, being sick round and round on Mam and everything round and round.

He steadied himself on the mic stand next to him and took a deep breath. Deep down there was still a part of him that was 'Harry Crabb, European Jazz Musician of the Year'. He wasn't going to let the side down if he could help it, especially not in front of these cocky young lads. So they thought the "old man" would embarrass himself and get too pissed up to play? He wasn't going to let this slip by without a fight, not after all this time. He was blinking and twitching as he started his solo in "I got rhythm" and the sweat stung his eyes as he reached for the notes. He didn't "have rhythm". What he had was "cold turkey".

Ultimately the solo at the end of the first set wasn't one of his best but he knew it probably counted as one of his most remarkable in the circumstances, though few people outside his nearest and dearest would have guessed it. He felt a damn sight older than he had done on arrival when he returned "Baby" to her case at the end of their first spot.

Kyle had become more concerned about Harry as the gig had gone on; it was, after all, his head on the block if his plan didn't work. My God… what if it killed him? At the end of the set he could see just how great a toll the lack of alcohol was on Harry, as the aged horn player steadied himself on the nearest chair before he helped him down from the small stage. He couldn't do this to him on the rest of the gigs that was for sure.

"Ludo, get me a double scotch and a pint double fast."

Ludo didn't move. Instead he spoke softly in Kyle's ear. "He's not looking too good is he? You know if he dies before the end of the gig Barry will want to deduct something off his wages."

"Just go!" Thankfully Ludo did.

Harry could barely focus; he didn't feel at all well. The audience ranged around him like so many amorphous blobs. This was more like being pissed than being pissed was. One of the blobs came closer and practically filled his field of vision, all beige and tweed. It was quite tall, grey faced and audible, though his ears felt all fuzzy like he'd just got out of the bath.

"You owe me fifteen shillings… "

He felt utterly bewildered as Kyle handed him a large scotch. He downed it in one. The shape spoke again.

"You owe me fifteen shillings… Wallsend memorial hall, 1967."

He still felt somewhat adrift as Andy handed him a pint of bitter which he took without a word. As he worked his way down the glass he began to get a grip.

"You wanted to get a bottle of Champagne and a hotel room." said the figure, which now at least had some kind of face, even if it wasn't one he recognised. "She was blonde, about so high, black and white mini dress. Nice legs."

There was a sharp intake of breath as Harry gasped at the recollection before he broke out into a large smile.

"Good Lord… Karen!"

"Kathy," it corrected.

"Kathy. Good God! That was it. Cor! She was a tremendous girl, very easy on the eye and terribly keen on things physical… fifteen shillings, you say. Tell you what, you get me a double scotch, no, make it a couple of them and we'll call it a fiver."

★

Charlotte lay in bed waiting for sleep. After all the grief of the day she had opted for a comparatively early night. The final bottle of wine had helped the chocolate go down a treat. If only sleep would come to stop the swimming in her head. It was a readily available cure, a little anaesthesia from the bottom of a glass, but it didn't appear to be working very well. How did people cope with guilt? There were men and women walking the streets fulfilled and happy, who had killed people or ruined their lives. You didn't have to look far… opening a newspaper usually did it. Drunk drivers, fraudsters, rapists, bankers, hedge fund managers, Michael Gove. She took a deep breath; if she was simply going to swap sorrow for anger then she wouldn't be getting off to sleep anytime soon. It was at times like this that she missed a presence beside her, something warm with a heartbeat, even if he had cold feet and was rubbish at housework. It was no good, she was going to have to get up again.

★

As he wiped the sweat off his brow, Kyle reasoned that they had managed one set and they would just have to take their chances with the second. That had been the original plan and nothing so far had completely scuppered it. The Harry situation was under control and he could relax. That was when it came to him, like a slap in the face. The glimpse across the melee of what was now quite a well packed pub. The familiar bob to her hair and that unmistakeable red jacket, the one from Tynemouth market, it was her. Whatever the nature of this vision one thing was for sure she was there for one reason alone… him; she had tracked him down and come all this way. He could feel himself start to perspire and pant as the 'bowling ball' bounced from his guts to his head and back. She was still there at the far end of the room and nothing was as important to him now as getting to her.

The faster he tried to carve a way for himself past the punters the harder it seemed to get through. Everyone seemed to be carrying a tray of drinks. Charlotte had stopped briefly to talk to someone. Perhaps she wasn't leaving. Why had she come? Because she still loved him, that's why, even if she was going to slope off in secret. Why, wouldn't she at least turn around and speak to him? Perhaps she was being mysterious… all that romancey bollocks. She was going to get away. He was panicking now and sweating profusely in the pub's heat. Just when he thought he was going to pass out with the need to reach her, a little voice in the back of his head popped up. "Stay cool dimbleweed, remember she's come back to you; you can afford to be a little aloof." He steadied himself and took several deep breaths, the kind befitting a horn player. That was it, he was 'The Man', he was in control, he was good. Charlotte had just seen him playing to a packed house of appreciative punters, even if Harry Crabb hadn't been at his best. He caught up with her just as she opened the pub door, putting a gentle hand on her shoulder and turning on his best smile.

"Couldn't stay away?"

She looked round at him, a little startled. She looked a lot less like Charlotte than she had done from the back of the packed room.

"Sorry... I thought you were... someone else, sorry. She's my... was... we've just... "

The woman smiled politely and left, looking more bewildered than he was. He had got this one very wrong. Charlotte wasn't here, she hadn't seen him playing to a packed house, she hadn't come crawling back to him, she hadn't gone out of her way to find him and so it must logically follow, in that case, that she didn't love him.

He returned to the bar to see that Clem was at Harry's table with a number of empty glasses before them and Albert in tow. Harry was speaking. "Lovely leggy Kathy, I wonder where she is now?" Harry was beaming as another tray of drinks was placed in front of him.

Clem pursed his lips and paused for a second

"She's at home watching Inspector Morse."

★

True, it had all been a bit touch and go but in the end all the planning and subterfuge had been worth it, thought Kyle as the van trundled its way back home towards Sunderland. Harry had perked up in the second set, the alcohol almost magically rejuvenating him. The band had dug in behind him and the audience had gone home cheered and contented. But he knew he was going to have to come up with a better solution for the other gigs if they were going to get through them unscathed. The poser was how to keep Harry on the wagon or at least close enough to it to keep himself upright for the rest of the duration, they couldn't run the risk of him ending up in either casualty or the morgue ever again.

The mood in the van was very up, in marked contrast to their last gig, Kyle realised as they hit the A19. "We weren't half bad" was the general consensus although Harry didn't say too much on the subject. Forty minutes in, Ludo produced his harmonica as they crossed the border into County Durham. Kyle liked the mournful howl that seemed to give the van an air of a First World War post.

Half-heartedly at first, but growing stronger as it progressed, the whole band joined in for several choruses of "When This Bloody War Is Over." It was an apt song for what he was going through, what with Charlotte and work and everything. He looked out at the endless road before them before chiding himself for comparing his situation to that of some poor bugger in Afghanistan, not yet twenty and with his limbs blown off. Christ, some of those boys were musicians... it didn't bear thinking about.

"Why don't we stop at Lee's? We got paid in cash didn't we?"

Before Ludo had got to the end of his sentence Barry's little black book had been produced. The band was democratic. If the people wanting to take time out to eat outnumbered those that wanted to continue straight home, they stopped off.

"Those scotch eggs were hours ago, Andy, you must want some proper grub now. They'll stick gravy on your fried rice if you ask."

"I'd love to but I have kids to support... I should get extra for playing gigs. I've got responsibilities."

"You want us to subsidise your shagging about?" Barry pressed so hard into his ledger book as he said this that his pencil snapped.

"Kyle, you'll eat something with me." Ludo was clearly going to try and pick them off one by one.

"I should save up. I'm going to be out in the streets if I'm not careful."

It wasn't an excuse. He was truly beginning to panic about how he would keep body and soul together.

"Harry, you must fancy a bit of the old take-away? Lee's Chop Suey House, Chester-le Street... it's good". Ludo wasn't going to be dissuaded easily. Eventually Harry shrugged.

"So it's agreed then… ' Ludo's relief was short lived as he looked at his watch.

"Bugger… we're twenty minutes away and it shuts in five."

Andy stroked his chin before he offered a suggestion.

"Ring up Lee, tell him there's fifteen of us, we're starving and we'll be there in ten."

Thirty minutes later Kyle realised nothing tasted as good as Singapore noodles in a rusty transit van after a gig. Even more so as it was the first decent meal he'd had since Charlotte left. Harry bought some chips but he didn't seem to do much with them save push them round the polystyrene tray.

Chapter 19

A week had passed since their first gig with Harry and Kyle's mistaken belief that Charlotte had come back to him. But, despite having gone to bed at 3AM, he woke at 7.30, still pinned to the bed by the bowling ball. It wasn't difficult to work out why he woke so early; this was the time Charlotte had risen for work. When they had been together he had always slept straight through her alarm, now its absence was more rousing than its presence had ever been. Wandering through to the kitchen he managed to rustle up some porridge, although he wasn't hungry, truth be told. He'd had to use water instead of milk but it filled a dull ache. The cuppa was better, Earl Grey, her favourite. He'd always called it "snob tea" but actually it kind of hit the spot and gave him a little bit of 'get up and go'. By 8 AM he was ready for action… how many brownie points would that have got him when they'd been together… 8A.M!

Fortunately Charlotte had left her computer behind, possibly on purpose. After work she had rarely wanted to come into contact with one and he was sure it could be pressed into promoting their next gig. After twenty minutes of surfing, twenty-five if you included a sneak look at "The World's ten biggest vegetables", he alighted upon a site called:-

"PROMOTE MY GIG. COM"

It was a simple enough business to go to the jazz and blues section and input the details of their next gig. Once Harry's list of accomplishments and awards were included it really did look impressive and there was a degree of pleasure in seeing it appear on the screen in front of him. There was a review section that allowed for comments on previous gigs which unsurprisingly looked like they had been filled in by the bands themselves rather than their audiences. A shiver ran down his spine as he envisaged a review containing the words "saxophonist, alcoholic, pandemonium and arrest warrant". He looked up to see a picture of Charlotte on the mantelpiece, looking down on him benignly. He could remember the day it was taken, her brother's wedding. She'd looked fantastic whereas he looked like someone who'd only had three hours sleep, principally because he'd just come back from a gig in Oxford and had. He'd fallen asleep during the ceremony, which hadn't exactly made him the hit of the month with her parents. That was him marked down as a drug addict for starters and the "For Fox Sake Hunt Sab now" badge he'd worn to wind them up did just that. Try as he might to concentrate, his gaze kept returning to the photo. There would be no peace for him till he packed it away or at least turned it to face the wall; she was looking straight through him.

The photo of Charlotte reminded him of the dog eared photo that he'd seen at Harry's. Why, he wondered, would he still have a photo of Louise in his bed-sit after all this time? Harry didn't strike him as overly sentimental, probably just never got round to getting rid of it… how long was it those two had been apart? That the day had been a glorious one was clear from the picture itself, the pair of them looking as happy as it was humanly possible to be. He looked back at Charlotte's photo as the "bowling ball" in him lurched again, despite the damn picture being faced to the wall. Eventually he relented and turned it the right way round again. He would have to learn to live with it and try not to think of her beady eye on him, making sure he pulled his finger out and made something of himself. What if he never met Charlotte again, or not till he was Harry's age? For a minute he gave in to daydreaming. He would eventually make a breakthrough with an album of his own compositions. By then he would have lived in Paris, Milan and obviously New York. They would meet and she'd tell him how awful her life was and what a dreadful mistake she'd made deserting him whilst he would be wise and comforting and worldly but would eventually be dragged away by which-ever former Playboy model had latched on to him that month. Try as he might he couldn't end the dream without a blissful reconciliation with his Ex.

★

Charlotte had set off not long after breakfast. What little sunshine there was soon gave way to a sky the colour of a Turner seascape and a wind serious enough to trouble the trees. She would cope with whatever the day threw at her but it would be nice not to get a soaking. Her ancient car did its best with the antiquated road system but it clearly lived in mortal dread of cobbles. She didn't think it would be difficult to find the cemetery in a village that size. One was enough to cover the local population and as Sykes had, as far as she knew, lived there all his life he was hardly going to be laid to rest anywhere else.

Once she arrived in the village it was a simple case of asking anyone who worked there for the exact location. Walking through the wrought iron gate she scanned the horizon. It was Sunday so the staff were non-existent, she couldn't even see any other visitors. Just as she was beginning to think her only option was to go through the whole place plot by plot she spotted someone whom she assumed was a gardener. He was wearing overalls and carrying a pair of secateurs and didn't seem to be visiting anyone in particular. He was stooped and thick set, with more hair sprouting out of his ears than on his head. It struck her with a shiver that, as a man in advanced age, he was working in the place where he would soon enough end up himself but despite that, once she had approached him, he seemed the most serene human being she'd ever met.

"No, love. I did work here but that was… twenty or so years ago

I suppose, I still like to pop in from time to time, I do most of me thinking here. I wish I could help, I have no trouble locating the ones that were laid to rest thirty or forty years ago, but the recent ones I couldn't place at all, sorry I can't be more of a help to you. All told, you might take a look by the greenhouse; most of the recent activity is up there… recent activity… ha! There's a thought if you gets me drift."

★

It dawned on Kyle as he waited for the kettle to boil, that you read about that sort of thing every day, lovers who were reunited after years, even decades, apart split by family feuds or warfare, couples who never quite got over each other even after moving on, even after being married to other people and having kids. Eventually he realised he'd been stirring the jam in his Earl Grey for over a minute, the sugar having long since run out. That was it… that's how he'd get Harry through the next gig, he'd find Louise. It was a great idea. Even if there hadn't been a gig in the offing it was great idea. The thought of making Harry happy was the nearest thing to joy he'd had in months.

He reached into his pockets and after some searching finally produced his phone and laid it down by the computer. He had some information to go on but whether it was enough to track her down he was about to find out. If it wasn't there was no plan B. He didn't fancy being onstage again with someone going through withdrawal symptoms. He typed the words 'Louise, poetry, actress', added Harry Crabb's name in inverted commas and began working his way round cyberspace. Google typically gave him either three hits in Japanese or thirty thousand hits from around the globe and rarely anything in between. Painstakingly he edged towards his goal. It was baffling trying to work out why the words "Louise", "poetry" and "Harry Crabb" should lead to so many offers of penile enlargement but within an hour he had a maiden name. This was the "in" that he needed… it would get easier from here. A further trawl using the name "Louise Campbell" led to the name of her publisher, a book of poetry produced by a radical feminist group in the late seventies. He took a deep breath as he made the first speculative phone call.

"Hello you don't know me but… "

It was a phrase he got used to using during the long afternoon.

"I'm sorry but I've lived here for more than five years now and I've never heard of her" was, with a few variations, a refrain he heard repeatedly and "I didn't really know her but… " accounted for quite a few more, inevitably they had either no idea of who she was or, if they did, where she was currently living. But by far the most common thing was an answering machine. By the end of it Kyle had begun to worry that the messages he had left sounded as mechanical as the instructions he'd just heard.

★

Charlotte worked her way around the area near the greenhouse where the old man had suggested and found the spot as the clouds, which had been threatening for so long, finally spattered into rain. It was a simple stone.

Rosalind Sykes
born 1st August 1931 died December 14th 2008.
Beloved wife of
Belvedere Sykes
Born 3rd August 1927 died 6th December 2010
Blessed are the pure in heart, for they shall see God.
Matthew 5:8.

She had gone over at Christmas every year after Sykes's retirement with a small hamper, but having left the family pile for Kyle's flat, she'd missed the last three years of his life, the years when he had been alone in the world. She had not been there when it mattered most and now there wasn't a damn thing she could do about it. Yes, she could clean up the grave but what use was that. She placed the simple bunch of flowers by the headstone and then started to clean up the neglected space, binning the crisp packets and bindweed that covered the plot. Finally she arranged the bunch of freesias in a stone pot and added some water. That morning she'd considered bringing a small can of "Three in one Oil" to put on the grave in remembrance of their time together. It's aroma of citronella and spindle oil always brought the memories flooding back but she worried that people would think it was litter or the latest legal "high" for the local tearaways. There was no one, as far as she knew, she could explain or make amends to and she was stricken. As she gazed at the rain spattered headstone, she would gladly have given a year of her own time for an hour of his.

There had been a second cousin in New Zealand but not, as far as she knew, anyone else. Her stiff upper lip began to falter and, if she was honest with herself they were, when they came, tears of shame that she cried.

★

It was a few hours before any of the people he had left messages for got back to him. The majority of them were, as before, absolutely clueless as to the whereabouts of "Louise Campbell". He was in the middle of another restorative cup of Earl Grey when the phone went again. He listened more in hope than expectation of anything positive.

"You reckon you're looking for Louise Campbell... looking for that bastard Crabb more like, two panes of glass and a brand new trouser press. I ought to ring his fucking neck. If you find him there's a cash reward... bastard."

Kyle wasn't sure if, in this instance, he was the "bastard" or Harry was. He had barely finished his tea before the phone went again.

"She was never the same again."

"Sorry?" He was a little taken aback by the elderly female voice.

"Hildegard, never the same, mother blamed them for causing her angina till the day she died, the two of them in the bath like a couple of animals when they had a perfectly good bed for that sort of thing. I don't know where they are but if I did I'd give them a piece of my mind."

"Oh!" was all he got to say before another phone call was terminated abruptly. They must have been quite a pair to generate this much fury this long after they'd parted. This set off a steady stream of callers who clearly knew the pair just not their whereabouts and by the end of the afternoon his best efforts had done very little other than increase his rude word power.

Eventually even the abuse dried up. The last decent lead found him talking to a bookseller in Aberdeen who was keen to get rid of several hundred anthologies of Scottish poetry. The day did have one thing to teach him. The only way to stop the "bowling ball" weighing him down was to stay busy. Trying to locate Louise Campbell had worked for a while but once the calls dried up he was left just staring at the phone with a dull ache in his guts. A quick revisiting of "The Worlds ten biggest vegetables" revealed no change, with a pumpkin from Massachusetts still comfortably beating Lloyd Bright's watermelon. Not long after, he fell asleep.

Chapter 20

In the gloom of the bedroom Charlotte poked an exploratory toe out of her bed. It was freezing. Perhaps she could get Dainty's boiler put right as recompense for her extended stay. It had been, at best, a fitful night's sleep. There was nothing worse than remorse. She was increasingly desperate to make up for her neglect of the one person she could remember bringing her any real joy as a child. All she could do now was replay things in her head and grieve over how she had got it so wrong. A quick peek out of the curtains confirmed her fears that it was raining heavily; below her, in the street, her poor, exhausted Ford Fiesta faced the elements, getting rustier by the minute. Sykes could have sorted out the decaying bodywork and healed its stray growls. She had loved watching him work. The trials of not fitting in at school would melt away in the summer holidays. For a young girl lacking in confidence, helping him in the garage was far and away the best form of therapy. Her father would buy some broken down husk of a classic car at auction, one that some twit had either written off or neglected and Sykes would labour away for months till the thing looked like it had just been driven out of the showroom. She shivered again. Damn… if the light had gone out on the boiler then not only was there no heating there was no hot water either. That left her the choice of a cold shower or armouring herself with deodorant. The day's trajectory already seemed to be one way… downward. She snuggled down again.

She had once suggested at school that they should have the option of car maintenance lessons. She was roundly informed by her head of year that it was nonsense to even consider such a thing.

Her classmates christened her Diesel Dyke for the rest of the term and she never brought up the subject in class again. As the years wore on her father acquired a serious collection of classic cars but rarely, if ever, got round to driving them. It was Bel Sykes who lived and breathed them.

She shifted in the bed. It was going to have to be a cold shower. She could never do "confident career girl in her own right" if she felt the least bit unwashed. She would gear herself up to it by counting down from sixty… or possibly a hundred and sixty… before she left the warmth of her bed. She allowed herself to daydream again.

When everything in the garage was in working order Sykes would go around the estate repairing things but the garage was always his natural home. When still at prep school she had presumed he slept there at night, next to the vehicles like some kind of oil-flecked shepherd. Did men like that exist anymore or had they been killed off in the stampede towards metrosexuality? Certainly, Kyle would never trouble himself to get his hands dirty in an engine's workings. Perhaps it was the notion of being up to your elbows in engine grease that did it but she was out of bed and in the shower before her countdown had reached double figures.

How, she wondered as she moved into the kitchen, hair still wet, could she be up and ready in good time for work on ten minutes sleep and Dainty still be in her pit and, furthermore, how could Dainty get up twenty minutes after her and still be ready to leave at the same time. Actually, that was easy enough to deduce… Dainty managed to get the extra time in bed because she put her face on as Charlotte drove them both into work, including painting her toenails… staggering really. She had got the knack of doing her nails and face while travelling into work down to a fine art. She knew which stretches of road were the straightest and afforded her the longest amount of "steady time."

With the clock ticking Dainty appeared as a whirlwind, a piece of toast jammed in her mouth and clutching a handbag the size of a small child. They clambered into the battered Fiesta as Dainty began the process of organising herself for the coming day.

"One doesn't want to arrive at work looking like one is auditioning for the "Big Top", does one, and one doesn't want to plaster it on like one's boss who one thinks looks like a cheap tart, does one not."

"We are, in light of the overwhelming evidence, inclined to concur with the prosecution." Charlotte said, straight faced. Perhaps they could buy somewhere together... Dainty might not suit everybody but she definitely suited her.

★

Kyle flipped his legs out of the bed and drew the bed sheets around him for their warmth. No doubt about it, winter was on its way and there was no way he could afford to put the heating on the way things were going. The silent curse of Charlotte's absent alarm clock had got him again, it was barely eight o clock. After managing to cobble a breakfast together out of what was left in the cupboards he occupied himself constructing a poster for the forthcoming gig in Norham. He typed in the basic details to Charlotte's computer and then messed around with various fonts before arriving at something which was eye catching without being likely to scare off the elderly and infirm.

On its completion he managed to coax the aged printer into running off a few copies. He could put some up locally, which would help get their name known and the rest he could send up to the gig itself.

THE LEGENDARY HARRY CRABB.
(European Jazz Musician of the Year 1967)
And his quintet.
LIVE AT
THE BLACK RABBI JAZZ CLUB.
NORHAM
Friday16th Nov 8.30PM
£5/4 concessions.

If push came to shove after the gig was over he could retrieve them and burn them to keep warm… at least for a bit.

★

"Wakey, wakey."

As a general rule Charlotte, like most people, didn't care for being roused from a doze although as it was gone eleven am and she was at work she could appreciate the necessity of it.

"If that had been anyone else or if you hadn't been bearing coffee there might have been words."

Dainty smiled as she passed the steaming mug over.

"I've made it double strength. It's my own recipe. They're promoting it in hospital trusts as a means of bringing people out of comas. You're not sneaking out in the middle of the night and putting in a shift somewhere are you?"

"No, I've got a lot on my mind"

"Go on."

"It's complicated"

"Do you want to have a decent night's sleep again?"

"How do you make amends to someone who's dead?"

"If you've killed your Ex, I'll be a character witness, if you'll return the favour."

"Not yet… it's probably less likely to happen now that I don't have to repair vans in the pouring rain."

"Is this about the car fella, what's his name? What about doing something for his kids"

"They couldn't have them, which made me finally realise why we were so close when I was young but it only goes to make what I did all the more ghastly. I'm afraid there isn't anyone left in his family that I could really do anything for. A second cousin he barely knew on the other side of the World… no it's hopeless."

Dainty took a sip of her coffee before she spoke.

"When my Uncle's baby died prematurely they organised a fundraiser for the hospital."

Charlotte ventured her own sip and tried not to gurn at the taste. It was, after all a quasi-medicinal concoction.

"And… ?"

"Why not qualify at the Bar and then fund a bursary in his name in mechanical engineering somewhere."

"And give someone who couldn't afford it the chance to get a decent start. Dainty, you're a genius. All I have to do is get accepted to study, fund my studies, pass the exams and find somewhere to live… easy! I thought I was never going to sleep again."

"Nothing you're not capable of. Another coffee?"

"No, my hair's starting to vibrate."

"You haven't forgotten Saturday, have you?" Dainty asked, a gleam in her eye that could only mean fun and trouble in equal amounts.

She could hardly have forgotten the oncoming celebration of Dainty's 'Decree Absolute'… her friend had talked of little else. Much as she loved Dainty she could see they were very different creatures. The end of her relationship with Kyle was something that had made her want to hide under the bedclothes for a month. Dainty on the other hand wanted to celebrate her official singledom with the mother of all blowouts.

★

As the rather fetching posters began to churn out of the printer his phone went and after a quick search he retrieved it from the back of the sofa. At the other end a grim tone enquired of the whereabouts of "that scoundrel Crabb." He didn't think that anyone talked of 'scoundrels' anymore, outside of costume drama. He went through his, by now, familiar process of trying to get the maximum amount of information out of the caller whilst returning the minimum amount of information back, specifically in relation to the whereabouts of the "Scoundrel Crabb."

"No, she doesn't owe me money… I know her husband, her ex-husband now I suppose."

The caller did not take kindly to Kyle's association with "The Scoundrel" and not for the first time Kyle found his eye wandering around the room and finally down towards the printer as it now happily churned out copies of the poster. He had pretty much screened out the rant on the other end of the phone as his eyes alighted on a typographical error.

"Shit! Shit! Shit!" It was a disaster.

"No! No, not you. It's the po… "

After a further ticking off about his bad language the line went dead… It was all going wrong. He attempted in vain to stop the printer making more copies of the unusable poster. At first he tried to use the decrepit mouse and keyboard but having been slow to start there was now no stopping it, as one after another of the useless declarations spewed out. Eventually he tried to rive the paper from the machine; it was an uneven struggle that ended badly in a ball of paper and ink. He stared at the already printed pile of neat posters fit for little use but to start a race riot.

"THE BLACK RABBI JAZZ CLUB."

How did he miss that?

It seemed the perfect moment to retreat and knock up a broth from whatever had been left over from breakfast. If it got much worse he'd have to go busking again. Before Charlotte he'd managed to keep body and soul together on occasion by busking in nearby metro stations. But this wasn't busking weather, people were too cold to stop and listen and they rarely felt inclined to pay you for the ten seconds worth they heard in passing. The rest of the afternoon was spent trading the kosher for the secular as he added a letter "T" to the posters, so that it read 'LIVE AT THE BLACK RABBIT JAZZ CLUB.'

He spun the task out as much as he could but with its eventual completion the low feeling that had haunted him since his split with Charlotte returned with a vengeance. He sat on the bed with a mug of coffee, the seeds from the jam rising to the surface, and stared out at the silent street. He could call her and say sorry but there didn't seem much point. Charlotte wanted someone to provide for her; he was barely managing to provide for himself. He could try and get a regular job but, with his C.V. in this economic climate, he'd have more chance at coming up trumps on the national lottery. He had seen other musicians buckle under pressure from a partner and get' a nine to five job' and he'd seen what it did to them. The first sign was usually spending obscene amounts of money on holidays and clothes to try and compensate for how miserable they felt. Then they'd get stressed, then they'd get on each other's nerves, then they'd have fights and finally they'd end up splitting anyway. It wasn't like he'd turned fifty, dumped his family and decided to pack in his job at the bank to be a pop star. He hadn't changed at all, she had and there was nothing he could do about that. His only chance with Charlotte was to turn his music career around and that would take a deal more graft. It was at this point that he remembered the crate of label-less beer left over from the last gig and he could think of nothing he wanted to do more than sample a generous amount of the stuff.

Perhaps he was being hasty, he thought, as he stared at the fourth empty bottle. He could have created the World's first Kosher Afro jazz club. 'THE BLACK RABBI'. It had a ring to it and, surely, if jazz was about anything it was all about mixing it up.

★

It was unquestionably the most expensive department store in town and certainly a place of myriad delights for Charlotte, even if it was only for an hour before heading back to work. The prices were high but not to the extent that you couldn't give in a little if the right thing caught your eye. But she knew deep in her heart that most of her income was going to have to be dragooned into furthering her education, even more so now that you were expected to pick up the entire tab yourself, so much for the country investing in its future. If the only people qualifying in professions like the law were the sort of people she'd been at public school with then they'd soon be transporting people back to the Australia for buying their own furniture and using the wrong knife at dinner.

"Do the assistants here remind you of anyone?" Dainty asked as they made their way through the Cosmetics Department. Her hushed tone suggested the comparison would not be a favourable one.

"Too much make up, the need to lecture the riffraff and a belief that they know it all?"

"I'm sure one day, in good time, the name Dainty Mukendi will adorn the boss's door and you can herald in a new era of advancement and recognition for the poor workers below you. Until then, don't get caught out bad mouthing her."

"No, you're right I need to conserve all my energy to concentrate on a new outfit that will dignify one's 'Absolute Party'."

"To be honest, any cash I've got left at the minute should be going to you for giving me houseroom, so I'm a little wary of spending a three figure sum on clothes." But she spoke too late. Dainty had already left skid marks heading towards the women's fashion section.

"Nonsense, I'm paying so don't stint yourself… I'm never getting married again so we're going to celebrate in style. High fashion, cocktails, debauchery… the lot!"

Charlotte could feel herself weaken as she caught sight of the department's colourful stock. Perhaps there might be something on sale.

"I could try a few things on I suppose, as I'm here."

"That's the spirit" Dainty said, wading through a sea of fabric before holding a blouse up against herself.

"What do you think? Ascot or Gerry Cottles's Circus?"

Her actual thought was, that there had never been an outfit made that equalled the fun of just trying lots of them on for the hell of it. Dainty, however was clearly made of sterner stuff and she wasn't going to take 'no comment' for an answer.

"It's good if you're going for that Queen Mother vibe." she eventually offered as tactfully as she could before a fit of the giggles gave her away.

"OK Then. What do you think of this?" Dainty tried on a jacket that could best be described as "high visibility".

Now it was Charlotte's turn to whisper.

"Dainty, the assistants are looking at us like my Mother used to… and not in a good way."

"Don't worry… they'll get their commission."

Eventually Dainty settled on an animal print dress and Charlotte decided on a classic two piece. She realised as she took hold of her purchases that it would be unlikely to ever come into contact with bolognaise sauce in a messy flat, courtesy of a something purporting to be a music lesson. It took her longer than she would have liked to decide that this was an entirely good thing.

★

When, sometime later, the phone rang again it jolted Kyle from his temporary slumber. With his neck in a major crick and still half asleep he had to take a few seconds out to re-orientate himself. Where was he? What time of day was it? Where was Charlotte? Why did he feel so low? He answered the phone still not quite compos mentis. A middle aged woman with an Edinburgh accent was babbling on the other end of the line.

"Hello, I'm replying to your inquiry about Miss Campbell. I could be wrong here but if it's Louise Campbell you're looking for I work with her. I won't give you her personal number but I'll pass on a message to her. From my experience either you'll hear from her pronto or not at all."

Kyle could do little but thank her profusely, as he tried to get up to speed with himself. He needed to be sure he got this right.

"Miss Campbell's Ex… her Ex-husband is playing a gig this Saturday, that's the 16th of November, Friday the sixteenth at the Black Rabbit Jazz Club in Norham, Norham near Berwick… on November… the sixteenth… that's this Friday in Norham."

Kyle repeated everything again as the woman on the other end wrote it down but he could feel from the other end of the phone that she wasn't entirely convinced of the venture.

"Her Ex? To be honest, I think you're more likely to get a call from Bill Gates trying to scrounge a tenner. Are you sure you want me to pass it on?"

Kyle assured her that he did. This was as good a break as he was going to get. So many people had been so guarded about Louise he wondered what had gone on between her and Harry. All he could do now was wait while a few more beers helped him pass the time. They would also help him sleep. Whatever he was getting himself into it was too late to back out now.

Chapter 21

Louise Campbell stubbed out her cigarette and darted back inside to get away from the rain. God in heaven, if the lung cancer didn't get her first then getting soaked to the skin for the sake of a fag would see her off. She had, she reckoned, just enough time to pick up a coffee from the machine and then get to her next assessment. She gave the ancient machine a nudge of encouragement as it spattered out the scalding, vaguely coffee-flavoured water. She had the case notes, she had her drink, she had forty-seven seconds. She set off at a lick for the treatment room, through the endless corridors of the centre, swearing under her breath. She had made her usual mistake. Yes, she could do the journey to the treatment centre in under two minutes but not whilst holding her own weight in case notes and a polystyrene cup full of boiling liquid. She swore under her breath a couple of times more for good measure as the liquid sloshed about ominously. She arrived only three minutes late with a good half a cup of coffee and three sticky, scarlet fingers. The porter stood outside of the room, his charge next to him in a wheelchair. The pointing at the watch and tutting was to be expected, but as it was Nick and he had, in the four years he had worked there, bummed enough fags off her to kill the both of them she could consider herself off the hook.

"Sorry I'm late… "

"Don't tell me, you got held up saving an orphan child from a pack of wolves in the Botanic Gardens."

God bless Nick, he could never fake being pissed off for any length of time.

"Hello Mr… Chapple. My name's Louise Campbell and I'm a Speech and Language Therapist. I'm going to bring you into this room so we can have a chat."

Nick gave her a wink as he pushed the chair into the treatment room before exiting for his next job. She took in the man in front of her for a moment… pale, dishevelled and almost bald, dressed in a shirt that might have been white when he'd still been a young man and a pair of black track suit bottoms. The notes said he was in his late sixties although sometimes it was difficult to tell. Despite herself, she often compared the clients she saw to celebrities of a similar age like Cliff Richard or Tom Jones. The patient rarely came out of it well.

He remained slumped in the wheelchair, staring out of the main window, his breathing heavy enough to affect her own. A traumatic brain injury. It was a familiar story… he drank, he fell over, he hit his head, something she witnessed all too often. It was rarely the first tumble that got them but after the sixth or seventh fall there was no going back. Each fresh accident took out a few more brain cells and in the end it was difficult to know what inside their heads was old and what was new. It was bad enough to suffer that sort of trauma naturally or from an accident but to bring it on yourself from the drink… how in God's name did you reconcile doing that to yourself. Then again, it wasn't as though she had been drug and alcohol free herself in the past. But unlike some of her contemporaries she'd been smart enough to call time on it before something else had called it for her.

"Now, Mr Chapple, I'm here to talk about your condition. How are you getting on?"

"Very well, are you sure you've got the right person?"

The pitiful monotone of his voice and the vacant stare made it a reasonable bet that she had.

"Do you remember what happened to you?"

"No, nothing wrong with me, I'm fine. Are you sure you've got the right person?"

Despite her best efforts she couldn't arrest his attention from the willow tree in the centre's grounds. Even at this time of year it was beautiful.

"Just imagine you're looking in a mirror at an image of yourself a month ago, how are you different now to how you were then?"

"There isn't a mirror here. Do I need to get one... you know there's nothing wrong with me, I'm fine, pet. Are you sure you've got the right person?"

It was going to be an afternoon long on problems and short on fags and she hadn't even begun to think about her ex-husband. She looked at the husk in front of her. He was, give or take a year or two, the same age as Harry. Harry's problem had always been that he was too full of life; it literally spilled out of him, uncontrollably and onto everything around him. And now, after all this time, the old devil pops up again out of nowhere. Not in person, no just a message delivered third hand about some silly gig.

Mr Chapple remained resolutely focused on his willow tree as a small trickle of drool fell from his bottom lip. Perhaps it was a legal matter. Perhaps Harry was about to drop dead... one thing she knew for sure, any involvement she had with Harry A Crabb would be sure to leave her more out of pocket than simply the price of an off-peak phone call. If her Ex-Husband was doing a gig in the Borders then he was at least in the land of the living... but why contact her now after so much water under the bridge? He must have done a thousand gigs since they split up and who the hell was Kyle Johnson? She would call again from the phone box on the Dalkeith road and if it smelled the remotest bit fishy she'd just walk away. She looked for any sign of life in Mr Chapple's eyes. Men! Why did they always have to go one step too far? The smartest thing would be to leave it and not ring back at all. You could guarantee that it would be nothing but trouble. God, she needed a fag, she needed a whole box of them and a decent sized scotch. The only way she'd get a cigarette was if she took Mr Chapple into the grounds, which was highly unethical even before you took into account the way the weather was... and what bloody business was it of Kyle Johnson's to rake through her private life and jangle her around. No... she'd just pretend the whole thing had never happened and that was an end to it.

"Do you have any close relatives who live locally?"

The question passed him by.

"Mr Chapple... Mr Chapple, do you have any close relatives in the area?"

It was a good sixty miles to Norham, a taxi back to Edinburgh was out of the question. She could stay overnight with her sister nearby in Berwick but that was by the by, she wasn't going to go running at Harry Crabb's beck and call. He could go swing... he hadn't even had the bottle to call her himself. He was like some spotty teenage boy trying to get a date.

"Mr Chapple, I think we might make a little more progress if we went out in the grounds."

★

There was something magical about getting into the flat and slobbing out in T shirt, leggings and slippers Charlotte thought, as she and Dainty flopped in front of the telly for the night. She had succumbed to taking another peek at her new clothes. This time the usual shot of pleasure was replaced by a wave of melancholy. She had occasionally splashed out on an item of clothing when Kyle was being at his most obnoxious. Now she didn't need an excuse it seemed a bit pointless. Dainty had made a pot of tea for them both in return for her lift home.

"You haven't got any tampons have you, sis? I meant to get some today but what with the clothes and all it went right out of my head."

Charlotte smiled before replying. It was a very Dainty-like mistake.

"There's some in my handbag, help yourself. It doesn't get any easier does it? God I hate the curse."

"Don't. I remember the first time, middle of the night it was.

My bed looked like a sacrificial altar. Still, I had been forewarned, one of the few benefits of being the youngest of four sisters. I didn't feel like I could just lie in it so I tried to clean it up with a bar of scented soap. In the end it still looked like someone had been murdered but smelled like the culprit was an Avon lady."

Dainty poured the tea and Charlotte felt the weight of the day leave her. Tea was wonderful like that. Now they could get down to the serious stuff… gossip was a pejorative term but she was yet to come up with a better name for it.

"The word is she's been botoxed." Charlotte had heard the rumour in Admin and had sworn a vow to herself not to pass it on, present company excepted.

"The crafty cow, so that explains her poker face," Dainty said as she eeny, meeny, miny, moed her way through a box of cream cakes.

"Yes. She's injecting one of the most poisonous substances known to man into her face."

"It probably feels right at home. You must have noticed that recently she's been coming in dressed to kill. I don't know how Ethan feels about it but she scares the life out of me. There's no doubting it, she wants him. Have you seen the looks she gives him? Poor boy, like a lamb to the slaughter… you could save him." Dainty punctuated the suggestion with a very deliberate nudge.

"Ethan? I don't think so… anyway, I'm more than sure he can take care of himself."

Charlotte stared purposefully at a Peach Melba. She wasn't going to have anyone badger her into a relationship… not even her closest friend.

"Are you sure you're not just a little bit keen?" Dainty was not easily put off.

"What's the point in taking up with someone who's moving back to the other side of the world in a few months' time?"

"So that's your only reason then?"

"No… God, you're a sly one. I need to give you some money for those clothes we bought."

"I told you it's my shout; after all it's my party… think of it as that bastard's money."

"You give me food and shelter, you're certainly not going to start paying for my outfits."

"This is my "Absolute Party" I make the rules and anyway, you buy most of the groceries."

"On one condition, before the end of this month we discuss me paying you some rent."

"Agreed."

"An "Absolute Party"… it's a bit unusual isn't it?"

"Trust me, when your husband runs off with your chief bridesmaid, a whole new plane of "unusual" opens up, whether or not you like it.

★

Louise looked out across the estate, warming the teapot in her hands as the young professionals living in the surrounding flats made their way home. All in all, for someone who hadn't really started her career until her late forties she had done ok. She'd led too bohemian a life to ever get on the housing ladder but the place she had now was pleasant enough. The rent took a big chunk out of her salary every month but she had laid her head to rest in much seedier places when she was with Harry. Some of the rooms in London had been rank, although the places Harry had lived in when they first met were infinitely worse. He fell on his feet just once with a place that really was a tiny North London Shangri-La. Whatever else she felt about Harry she had to admit she had some fond memories of the flat near Summers Town, not least his roof top rendition of 'Skylark'.

It was the kind of moment you remembered as you took your final gasp. Even now the recollection almost brought tears to her eyes. It had been the fifteenth of October, a week after her birthday and a full moon. They were living on either side of north London and it was getting serious but she had never thought of him as one for the epic gesture. Harry's approach to life seemed flotsam and jetsam. When he had somewhat cryptically asked her to meet him outside his block of flats she didn't suspect anything special. The thought that he might be about to tell her he was moving abroad for work or that he'd got involved with someone else crossed her mind, but only fleetingly. Technically, it was a squat but it was a comparatively civilised place with a child-minding service for the locals, which they would have called a crèche if they'd been posh enough, and shrubs and flower beds everywhere. Harry was viewed as a welcome bit of colour in the neighbourhood and he seemed very happy to be there, always available for some youngster if they expressed an interest in "that trumpet thing round your neck." That October night she was on time, as per usual. Harry was nowhere to be seen, as per usual. She had stared at her watch and tutted as the minute hand headed out of 'slightly miffed' and towards 'thoroughly pissed off'. To while away the time and lower her blood pressure she found herself singing a Hoagy Carmichael song under her breath.

"Skylark, have you anything to say to me?
Won't you tell me where my love can be?"

She was half way through the first verse when she got the distinct feeling that what she was engaged in wasn't a solo performance. She closed her mouth and listened hard... there it was, she could definitely hear it now, couldn't make out where it was coming from, someone's flat? Or a radio? A passing car?

"Skylark, I don't know if you can find these things
but my heart is riding on your wings."

And then she caught sight of him, silhouetted against the moonlight on the adjacent block of flats. The madman Crabb himself, complete with wings, his tenor horn louder and fuller, now percolating throughout the whole complex, two hundred feet up at least. She held her breath as he appeared to step off the top of the building only to start a slow-motion descent, flight by flight with only the slight sound of grinding gears betraying the winch he was attached to. He was wearing his best herringbone coat and a halo fashioned from tinsel and a coat hanger. She stood in wonderment as one of the homemade wings plummeted to earth, coming to an abrupt stop with a distinctly none too angelic crunch. She was half entranced and half terrified by the spectacle. What in the name of God was he doing? He was past the halfway mark and she still didn't know whether to laugh or cry. And then Harry had stopped moving altogether before going into a reverse and returning towards the Heavens. The celestial vision had suddenly cried "Not yet, you silly fucker, not yet." There had been a pause and then, with some more grinding of the gears, his downward spiral resumed. His juddering progress did nothing to alter the fullness of the tone of his sax. She had never heard him sound more magnificent, reaching notes she had not thought humanly possible.

As his feet touched the ground she had moved towards him. The absence of one wing had left him looking a little lopsided. "Louise will you make me the happiest man in the WOOOOOOOOooooooooooooooooooooooooooooooooooooo" was all that escaped Harry's lips as he was whisked back up to the roof at double speed, the force of it putting paid to his one remaining wing.

Had she answered him? She couldn't remember. She'd shouted something but it might have been a warning rather than a yes. How could any other proposal compare to that. There had been a few men after their separation but what were they other than a series of paler and paler cover versions of the original?

They had married in the winter, a thick carpet of snow all around, with his bass player, Pete 'Winch Operator' Stuart, as the Best Man. Silly sod, she would have said yes if he'd just popped the question over a pint in the pub. He hadn't needed to hit the roof.

Chapter 22

Kyle had a lot on his mind as he closed the door to his flat and got into the van. Once again everyone was there bar Andy. Harry was lost to the world, sleeping peacefully in the back, having been picked up from "The Skinner's Arms".

"Where's Andy?" Kyle asked as he took over from Ludo in the driver's seat.

"Doing the job he hates the most. He'll be like a bear with a sore head when we pick him up."

Knowing that Ludo was probably right didn't make the prospect any sweeter to contemplate.

"That's what happens when you spend all your days proving you're the most fertile man in show-business. You wind up dressed as a clown pimping fast food to feed your kids. You don't need to be Einstein to see the irony. Still, he's only got himself to blame."

Barry tried hard to keep the note of glee out of his voice.

"I think you'll find that outcome is specific to Andy, rather than an inevitable consequence."

Kyle thought that someone had better stick up for Andy before Barry's condemnation picked up any steam with the rest of the band. If Barry brought this up with Andy then Andy would certainly lamp him. Worse still, he could see a similar destitution beckoning him if he wasn't careful; there was no Charlotte now, he was on his own and his funds were running out fast. A couple of weeks wielding a sledgehammer or flipping burgers and he might as well play sax in woollen mittens.

Andy was only a short distance away and Norham was easy

enough to find, the only thing he didn't fancy about the trip was that their route passed by Charlotte's work place and the less he was reminded about what had gone on there the better.

As they turned the corner and headed towards the burger bar he could see there were no half measures in Andy's get up, red nose, big boots, and a wig sporting two large sprouts of ginger hair on an otherwise bald pate.

"Now we've got one gig under our belt let's not screw things up by antagonising our hard-grafting drummer, I know it's tempting but best not go there just because he has to dress a little unconventionally for work."

After this admonition they appeared on their best behaviour as they urged Andy to get in.

"I'll just get changed" he said, backing off.

"We haven't got time, we need to be in Norham in less than two hours" Kyle said, shouting above the din of the engine.

"But… "

"Come on, you can get changed in the van."

"Don't say a word, not one." The tone of Andy's voice was serious as he clambered inside. Despite Kyle's exaltations and prayers Ludo managed to contain himself for all of thirty seconds as he surveyed the fast food joint through the back windows of the van.

"There's a lot of kids back there in tears; they think you've been kidnapped. They're not all yours, are they?"

"Go claim your free milk-shake, tosser."

Andy thrust the remaining leaflets at Ludo. 'It's all very well taking the piss but as well as your basic you get £1.50 on top.'

Ludo was clearly fighting the urge to follow this up but to Kyle's great relief his desire not to get thumped won out. Andy however was off.

"Bloody CSA, you can't escape them… they're like cash seeking missiles. I've got them after me for the twins in Newcastle and for little Jen in Sunderland. Bloody vultures. Her mother's got her playing the piano now, eight years old… playing the piano, wanted an extra tenner a week from me for the lessons. I said "Don't worry I can teach her the drums for free."… She said nothing for a bit and then she told me to "fuck off"."

That the band hadn't come to blows was a plus, the night would be difficult enough without a dust up between the artistes making things worse. Louise Campbell had left him a message detailing why she shouldn't be there, which, over the course of its fifteen minutes, sounded more like a therapy session than anything else. He had spent the rest of the week hoping for another call saying she had relented. He had considered ringing her again and begging but she didn't sound that biddable. So it was down to him. Hopefully he could put Harry off till the end of the gig, when they could all get steaming and Barry, who never drank, could take them all home.

It was the growling of the engine after a particularly acute corner leaving the A1 which Harry first registered. His alcohol induced slumber was wearing off. It took him a while to orientate himself. It had been a nice afternoon in "The Skinners" he'd caught up with some old friends and seen some of the 3.30 from Haydock on the box. Now he was in a van and off to a gig, just like the old days. He regarded the band a few times, then focused on Andy and tried to make sense of the apparition in front of him. Andy started to struggle out of his costume as they reached the A1, thinking the straight Roman road provided him his best chance of getting undressed without tipping over. In the cramped situation of the van his contortions resembled someone having a fit. Eventually he gave it up as a bad lot and sat down.

"Never mind son." said Harry eventually "It won't be the first gig I've done with a clown on drums."

★

As it was early evening, Charlotte and Dainty had their pick of tables at Monet's, a fashionable wine bar in town and a favourite haunt for them when times were good. Just walking in was enough to make Charlotte feel all was right with the world. Everything in it looked modern and fabulous even if the furniture was more fashionable than comfortable. The few people there had come straight from work, giving the whole place an air of 'schools out.'

Charlotte felt a little thrill from her new outfit. Dainty herself was clearly in the mood to celebrate.

"You need to let your hair down for once; you'll feel more at ease after a few drinks. One way and another you've had quite an eventful month. This 'Absolute party' is a celebration of my, no our, freedom and it is most certainly not a wake, although the thought of killing my now officially ex-husband is still worth due consideration. Come on, let's get the party started. Pass the cocktail list."

Charlotte briefly scanned the drinks "menu". The names all seemed ridiculously pornographic but ultimately she knew Dainty was right. After the month they'd had they were entitled to some mindless hedonism. She looked at her friend and smiled.

"Yes, I have earned it and anyway, I'm helping you in an official capacity as the Master of Something or other… this being a bone fide civil occasion."

"You can be Mistress of Ceremonies… now for God's sake let's get some drinks in."

With the bar still thinly populated, it wasn't difficult to grab a waiter and get a drink. They were off. Charlotte proposed a toast.

"To freedom… we're both young, free and single and we have the right to use men just as we wish. By the way, who else are we waiting for?"

"There's no one else."

She had always supposed that Dainty would have had the world and his ex-wife out with them on her big night.

"No one. I said everyone that mattered would be here and you are. You never know, we might pick someone up along the way."

★

"Blimey are you sure you've got the right place, it's not the usual kind of dump." Andy, who had eventually managed to get changed, eyed the club dubiously as he spoke.

Kyle had to admit it wasn't the kind of thing you expected in a small village perched on the Scottish Border. The place did look a cut above with an impressive neon sign that announced the venue as:-

'"THE BLACK RABBIT" JAZZ CLUB'.

"No, this is it alright; I heard mention it was a bit flash." Kyle said this with a degree of satisfaction.

He led them from the van as they stared in wonder at the building in front of them.

"Look, they've got a proper poster advertising the gig."

"Don't get any ideas about taking it at the end of the night, Bazz… it's mine." Ludo was adamant.

"Don't see your name on it."

"There it is. Look… Lewis Donkin – bass."

"Bloody hell, so is mine. You don't think the Social will see these do you? Andy sounded worried.

"I'm sure they've got more than one poster and I doubt very much whether South Tyneside Social Security office keeps tabs on the activity of Jazz Clubs in the Borders." Kyle assured him.

Just for once he wanted them to enjoy the situation. It wasn't like they usually had such sweet surroundings to work in. The stylish brick building was sandwiched between an organic food shop and a clothes shop that seemed to have cornered the market in tweed and tartan. Looking a little over-awed, the band entered the club cautiously.

"It's like your first visit to Santa's Grotto." Ludo said as he gazed in wonder at the design features in the hallway before they turned into the main concert room. There wasn't a soul around.

"Smell that… new-baked bread and freshly ground coffee beans. Our gigs usually smell of piss and stale beer." Andy was right. The whole venue reeked of ciabatta and Observer colour supplements.

"I can't handle this. Perhaps we've died and gone to heaven"

Ludo said, running his hand along the marble-topped bar than ran the length of one wall.

★

The first drinks, attractive as they were, did not stay on show for long. As the second drinks were delivered complete with foliage, umbrellas and sparklers, Dainty had a surprise to spring.

"As you've decided to desert me I might as well get something out of it. I'm thinking of applying for your job." Dainty looked at her hopefully.

Charlotte smiled. "I love the idea but don't let on its up for grabs yet. It's all a bit hush-hush. I'll tell them once I get the nod from Uni. It'll give me a chance to store up a little cash."

"My only fear is that I'll end up watching you raking through the bins at head office for your next meal... so you don't mind?"

"Of course I don't. I remember you on your first day. I thought there's one to watch... she's obviously going to take everything in her stride."

It was true; she had immediately noticed a steeliness in Dainty when she had first started at Petersons.

"I always was a cocky bitch." The laugh that emerged from Dainty's frame was loud enough to stop the blood.

"I worked out within the first five minutes of walking in that you were the lynch pin at Peterson's. I never go by peoples titles; they've usually been gained by brown-nosing the boss. Every organisation has one, a lynch pin or the enterprise goes belly up, one person who really understands how the whole thing works and who can get things done for you. It's never the boss... never, never at all."

"God, I always felt like I was flailing around without a clue."

"Trust me, you didn't hear some of the advice I was given by the 'higher ups' before I worked out who had the measure of the place. When they thought they'd lost the Hetherington-Gore contract who did they send to charm the pants off them? Haven't you twigged that, when the shit hits the fan, little Ms Maybelline comes over to you to sort it out?"

"No I've always lived in fear that the fan's shittyness was down to me."

Dainty slapped her head in exaggerated exasperation and sighed. "If only sister, if only."

★

Just when Kyle was beginning to wonder if the whole place was deserted, a well-kept man in his early sixties dressed in loafers and a Pringle jumper wandered in to the concert room and headed towards them, shaking hands as he went.

"Noel Catchesides, I suppose you'd call me the general manager round here. Now which one of you is Kyle and of course I recognise Harry from way back… Mr Crabb Sir, a pleasure to meet you. Let me give you a hand with your equipment. We've invested in a bunch of trolleys to make life a little easier for the musicians."

Noel broke into a broad smile as this announcement led to an actual whoop of delight from the band. There was only one logical explanation for this, thought Kyle, but Noel Catchesides had to be the least likely front for a criminal organisation that had ever lived. It was pretty much a given that Jazz clubs only ever ran at a loss and people like Noel would count themselves lucky if they didn't have to regularly make up the short fall at the end of the night by dipping into their own pockets.

"Now if we can have the first set at half eight and the second at ten… we've sold out you'll be glad to hear.

"This is alright. I could get use to this." said Ludo as he propelled their largest amplifier on one of the well-oiled trolleys with little more than the finger of one hand.

"Alright? We're unique" said Noel with a degree of pride. "The Gentleman taking the door tonight, Crombie, this is his place. He dropped 17 million quid on the lottery, last February… it was in the papers and everything. Before that we use to put on a gig once a month in the old wooden scout hut by the church hall. Crombie got a bloke from London to draw up the plans and build the place. The whole venue is ergonomically designed and we brought in an acousticologist from Sweden during the early phases so everything sounds superb on stage. We've got enough cash now to last us till 2136 then we'll probably go back to raffling bottles of wine to help cover the running costs." Noel's grin was now about a mile wide. He looked, thought Kyle, like the happiest man who ever lived.

Kyle had maintained his vigil on Harry throughout this, although, on the face of it, their most experienced member seemed quite well balanced and composed as the afternoons alcoholic intake filtered through his system but Kyle knew a lot of tonight's success relied on how he coped with Harry during the show.

★

As they talked the drinks began to arrive and disappear at pace, brought by a succession of waiters, most of whom Dainty considered fit enough to pull her "sex face" at.

"Oops! Nothing spared… bottoms up. What do you fancy now?" Dainty urged, she was clearly having the time of her life.

"I'm going to have a Cuban breeze… it's as close to the Caribbean as I'll get for the next couple of years."

"Just wait till you're a barrister then you can buy yourself an island… or two. You'll be minted… You sorted things out with the folks at home?"

Charlotte frowned. "I'm not sure I can make sense of my return visit even now. Everything is just as it was, my mother looks well enough. My parents are quite ready to pretend that Kyle never existed but I'm not. Given half the chance they'd be back to setting me up at dinner parties with dreadfully pale, bullish boys who do something in the 'City'. To be honest I don't want to rely on anyone else anymore. I've worked it all out I can start my course if I live like a field mouse and I get a part time job… "

"Field mouse? Look you've got a little black dress? You've got a bank manager! Turn up looking like you mean business and they'll give you the where with all. Trust me."

"I've never done debt before."

"Then they'll love you, it's not like you're about to do a class A drug."

"I think that's exactly what I'm about to do. The big high followed by the big downer with a spiralling addiction that finally destroys you."

"Steady on love, it's Lloyds not the Mafia."

"There's a difference these days? You think I'd be good for a loan? What about the financial crisis?"

"You might not appreciate me saying this, but if someone with your accent asks a bank manager for something you'll get it with nobs on, whereas I get clobbered for £50 if I go over my limit by a fiver. You think bloody Cameron would be running the country if he sounded like Jim Royale… My arse he would! And anyway if your job is going involve convincing a jury that the man in the dock is a cross between Mother Theresa and Bob Geldoff when he's got "National Front 4 eva" tattooed on his forehead then you should be able to crow-bar a few grand out of your bank manager for a year or two. You only have to take care of yourself now. No wed date, I mean dead weight."

"Don't say that."

At this point Dainty thought about mentioning Kyle's little interlude at their workplace but she managed to resist the urge to tell, thinking of the distress it might cause. And on top of that, this was as serious as she wanted the night to get. From here on in it should be an endless parade of fun. They needed more drinks.

"Come on, fancy a couple of slippery nipples?"

"I've already had a bit too much. I need the loo."

As Charlotte headed off to the toilet, Dainty reflected that her friend was something of a lightweight in affairs of the liver. She looked around the bar. She liked Charlotte, no… she loved Charlotte but much as she did, the two of them did not a party make; something was needed to get the thing going. Staring down at the table in front of her she saw that Charlotte had left her phone and after taking point five of a second to assure herself that what she was doing was ethical, she took out her own mobile. It was a simple matter of getting Ethan's number from hers and then sending him a message via Charlotte's phone. That she achieved this feat whilst also managing to order two more cocktails and flirting with the waiter was a source of immeasurable pleasure to her. Crisis management at 'Peterson Partners' would be a cinch.

I'm on a jolly in
Monet's with Dainty
why not come down.
CHARLOTTE X".

That was all it took to start the ball rolling.

Chapter 23

With everyone in such high spirits the business of setting up and sound-checking was completed with the minimum of fuss. The band even began to behave civilly towards each other. Taking his eye from Harry for a second, Kyle scanned the punters as they began to enter the venue; it was a veritable flood and a joy to behold. Just as he was about to recommence his probation work with Harry he caught sight of her. She was a striking figure, certainly attractive but it was her general air that made her stand out. She was older now but still recognisably the woman from the wedding photograph, with a mane of jet black hair and a look that suggested she was the queen of Bohemia. Seeing Kyle, saxophone slung round his neck, she stopped and gave him a nod. She had, against his expectations, arrived and he could relax a little. Harry, thankfully, was deep in conversation with Andy and blissfully unaware of what the evening had in store for him.

★

Dainty had scanned everywhere from the main entrance to the futuristic spiral staircase at the opposite end of the room and almost given up hope of her plan coming off when she saw him enter the bar. She knew Ethan wasn't one for spontaneity but she also knew that two attractive single girls and a drink was too good an invitation for any single man to turn down. She let him trawl the bar, briefly savouring her scheme. The place was busier now and just at the point he was about to give up she waved at him wildly, like a child looking out of a bus window.

"Well, there's a turn up for the books. Guess who's just walked in the door" she said nonchalantly as Ethan threaded his way through the throng.

"I'd just put the Stapleton file to bed and before I could follow it, I got your message, Charlotte."

Understandably Charlotte looked a little puzzled at this but before she could be rumbled Dainty dragged Ethan out of harm's way and over to the bar.

"Come on, let me get you a drink. You're the token man here so you'd best get a couple of stiff ones down you to cushion the blows. Driving? No, good, you're in for a bumpy enough ride as it is. Have you ever been to an 'Absolute' party before? Hold on, I've forgotten what we're drinking is called, what we're drinking is called? Yes what we're drinking is called... all I know is I'm buying and it involves sex and gin".

He was easily the best looking guy in the place and loaded and American. Dainty could feel numerous glances heading their way as she ordered the next round of drinks and she loved every minute of it. Ethan was not the boy for her but it wouldn't do any harm to let people think that he was. Seizing her chance, she brushed an imaginary piece of lint from his shoulder. If some girls wanted to think that bestowed ownership on her let it be. She was now officially single. Ethan was way too much the metro-sexual for her tastes. Nevertheless, in the fullness of time, she would be rubbing Michael Fuller's nose in the dirt with someone new, see if she didn't.

★

Noel crossed the floor to introduce Kyle to Crombie, the owner. For a rich man Kyle couldn't help but wonder why he was dressed in the most threadbare clothes he'd ever seen.

"Hello... It's a great club you have here."

"Thanks." The voice was a thick, though not unpleasant, growl.

"All built on one lucky ticket."

"Yes."

"Like all your Christmases come at once."

"Aye."

It seemed to all intents and purposes that Crombie was still in shock from his good fortune. Kyle was about to make an excuse and turn away when he spoke.

"It brings a degree of class to the neighbourhood."

"Sorry?"

"It brings something, some class, some culture. Ever seen a punch up in a jazz club?

… no, me neither. Right, I'm off to the cellar. There's enough heads in here to drink the bloody place dry."

And with that he left, leaving Kyle to head back to the band and mobilize them for their performance. As yet Louise Campbell hadn't thought it necessary to reacquaint herself with her Ex. Kyle wasn't sure if that was a good thing or not. The club was packed to the gills and it was no mean task to get to the stage. Whatever the night had in store it was going to be witnessed by quite a crowd.

"Right, it's a similar set to the last gig but I've picked a couple of things we can stretch out on."

For once in his life he felt he had everything under control. Ludo had got Harry a beer and a chaser which Kyle seemed to think would be enough to oil the wheels without them coming off the cart. Louise had taken a seat a little way off the stage. She seemed blissfully unaware that she might be in Harry's eye line. Looking at her, Kyle reflected it didn't take much to realise what Harry had seen in her.

Noel introduced the band and with a count in from Harry they were up and running with "Softly as in a Morning Sunrise." The audience were rapt as the band hit their stride. The solos performed by the other band members, as the night progressed allowed Kyle to keep an eye on Harry. The chaser was gone in the blink of an eye but two numbers in, he was still to make any impact on his pint. So far, so good. Then a thought struck him. What if inviting Louise was a tragic mistake? What if the sight of her tipped Harry over the edge and into a bender? Was he about to grasp defeat from out of the jaws of victory? They might even get into a spat. It was clear that their time together had been a very volatile state of affairs. He sought out the former lovers with his eyes. Harry beamed seraphically at the audience, oblivious to Kyle's concern or indeed to Louise. Harry was blindingly, blissfully ignorant to the situation... her eye's, however, never strayed from Harry's face. Still, it was too late now; all he could do was cross his fingers and hope for the best.

As Kyle gave himself up to the music he realised that these were the kind of gigs he'd always dreamed of doing. The audience were attentive, sometimes it was their silence that spoke loudest of all, their focus shifting from player to player with most of the solos getting decent applause. It was so much easier to excel at your art when the place was full and the punters were keen. Kyle could feel it. With the first gig out of the way the band were more relaxed and, himself apart, more focused. He hadn't told anyone else about Louise. He was never sure if Harry had twigged what they had done to his beer at the previous gig but it was safest to assume he had and to work on the principle that he was going to be a little suspicious about anything out of the ordinary that happened on this gig so the fewer people who knew the better. Perhaps she would just slip away at the end and no one would ever know. The whole point of her being here was to act as a restraining influence on Harry's wilder impulses, well that and the tiny possibly that their meeting might just effect a reconciliation.

Between solos Harry sipped at his pint, just ticking over. He was actually enjoying playing in a way he hadn't in ages. He'd get a few liveners in after the first set... that should see him through to the conclusion of the gig. All he'd need after that was a good bottle of something to see him home... wouldn't be a problem, they'd filled the place hadn't they and it was a cash gig. Actually, this band wasn't half bad now that he had a chance to hear them without feeling so rough. During the piano solo in "Body and Soul" he looked out at the punters in the hope of possibly seeing an old familiar face. Most of them were about his age. And then it happened. At first he wasn't quite sure if it was her until she stared back at him. That "look" wasn't one you forgot in a hurry, but surely not here, not after all this time. After what seemed like an eternity she smiled at him… Christ! It was the genuine article, it was Louise Campbell… she hadn't changed a bit… if anything she was more beautiful than he remembered. First his mouth went dry, then he thought his legs would give way. He took a dirty hanky out of his pocket to wipe away the sweat on his brow. After all this time, there she was as if it was the most natural thing in the world. Jesus, Mary and Joseph the things that happened with this band! It was the second time he'd ended up with his legs all but buckling under him on stage. He expressed himself the only way he knew how, by pouring himself into his sax. The audience responded with unbridled delight. If this was the return of the love of his life then she wasn't going to witness anything other than him at his absolute peak. At the end of their last song he managed to get off stage himself, scorning any help from the band. He wasn't some old codger who needed a hand.

He couldn't get anywhere near her at first. Too many "old hands" who'd come out of the woodwork. They had come to see him from a sense of nostalgia and hadn't expected to be blown away by someone who was, like them, old enough to draw a pension but it was clear to them that he still had the magic in spades. It was when she started to walk towards him that his composure, which he had managed to keep on stage, really went. As she got closer he could see her look was softer now but no less divine and it played almighty conkers with his heart.

"Hello, stranger."

She gave him that look, the one which had always left him feeling completely exposed.

"Don't worry; it's a bit late in the day for me to be claiming alimony," she offered as he planted a kiss on her cheek.

"Louise… I… er… you look well."

He led her to a seat at the bar which Barry grudgingly vacated. Louise looked him up and down before she spoke.

"Still drinking tomorrow's beer today, Buster?"

Just to hear her say his name made him want to cry.

"Just the occasional sherry after supper." Harry mumbled, still at something of a loss

She smiled at him, that killer hundred watt job that shone a light onto every dark recess of his grubby existence.

"How someone so close to pond life makes that thing sound so good is still beyond my comprehension, even after all these years. You put your lips up to it and blow and I lose all sense of reason… still it's hardly what you'd call breaking news, we've always known that, haven't we? I just thought I might have grown out of it by now."

Harry caught the barmaid's eye and thought about a couple of doubles to steady himself but he was as surprised as Louise herself when he heard his own voice.

"A… a lime and soda for me please and… " He looked enquiringly to his ex-wife.

"Well this is an experience; I'll have a scotch and water."

Harry reached into his pockets and pulled out several dirty, crumpled notes which, bar 'Baby', pretty much represented his worldly possessions.

Kyle kept his distance as the rest of the band were glad handed by punters keen to converse. That was the thing about older jazz fans, they were just piteously grateful that someone from the younger generation was looking to keep the music alive. The whole place exuded bonhomie. Noel sat at the back of the room with Crombie, the pair of them looking like Cheshire cats. Ludo looked up from his pint as he handed Kyle his beer and caught Harry and Louise's tender reunion. "He hasn't pulled has he? Dirty old sod."

"No. That's his ex-wife. She's just turned up out of the blue," Kyle said, as nonchalantly as he could manage. He knew that, with the pair's history, their bonhomie could disappear within seconds so no point in making a big thing of it to the band. But looking at them, he couldn't help feeling optimistic. Perhaps age or experience had mellowed them and now that Harry was over the shock it could be the start of a whole new life for both of them. He felt a degree of satisfaction in having re-united them but he couldn't tell the one person in the world who mattered to him most what he had accomplished. The "bowling ball" gave a shuffle in his guts but this was not a moment for despair. One day, in the distant future, after all this was done, he would meet Charlotte on a different street and it would all be good. No more demons.

Chapter 24

Left alone in the increasingly noisy bar, Charlotte took in the gleaming chrome and neon of her surroundings. She'd never have managed to get Kyle across the threshold of somewhere as upmarket as this. He had always been happiest frequenting dank 'boozers' with sawdust on the floor and toilets you could smell halfway down the street, which seemed daft when that was where he was forced to ply his trade. Now she could see just a little something in their warm earthiness set against the anti-septic coolness of the wine bar. On a whim she picked up her phone and scrolled through the contacts till his name came up, staring at the entry for longer than was strictly necessary, even contemplating a quick call, just to see how he was for old time's sake. It was all over now, their affair. She knew it, but that didn't preclude her from being interested in his life and how he was getting on, nothing wrong with that. Drink had a way of doing that to you, she thought, the haze of the evening's alcohol consumption, coating everything with a light fuzz that made it easier to forget quite how awful things had been. Glancing up for a second, she saw Dainty and Ethan heading back from the bar. The phone call could wait, she was meant to be having fun and Dainty would go down her neck if she found out. She would handle it better if she rang in the morning and she could tell him all about Dainty's 'Absolute party'… actually on second thoughts that would probably be a bit tactless.

Dainty was clutching something that looked like a scale model of a desert island. Somewhere in the middle of it there was a drink. She was so deep in animated conversation with Ethan on a subject that had exercised them both that she didn't even bother to sit down.

"So you think that's fair?" Dainty said as she chased the straws in her cocktail around the foliage.

"I didn't say it was fair. I just said there isn't a man alive who wouldn't accept earning 12.6% less a year for being multi orgasmic."

"You think you're good at winding me up, Mr American."

"Yeah! I think I'm pretty good at it."

Charlotte looked on a little wistfully. She missed that sort of banter. For a boy who had managed to succeed at nothing Kyle had held lofty opinions on everything. She didn't know how he did it. The whole world was telling him that he should lay down his arms and fall in step with everyone else and no matter how much they said it he refused point blank to listen to them. On a good day they would discuss the world and everything in it but towards the end of their relationship all of Kyle's conversations had dripped with the growing bitterness he felt at his "lot". Her reminiscence was stalled by Dainty shouting above the din of the now increasingly noisy bar.

"Right, we're all going clubbing. My treat, so drink up!

Charlotte glanced at her mobile again. She was trying to join in but the last thing she needed to be doing now was playing gooseberry. Dainty had taken to arranging the umbrellas from their cocktails in Ethan's hair.

"Come on, legal girl… take a photo with my phone for posterity. Oh! No. That's no good at all, that's all wrong for you, American. We need something to bring out your lovely eyes."

"Like absinthe?" Ethan was mugging like crazy. Dainty cackled like this was the funniest thing she'd ever heard as she steadied herself with the table. There was no stopping the newly emancipated Ms Mukendi in her pursuit of fun, fun, fun and you could say what you liked about Ethan but, for a good looking boy, he wasn't afraid to play the clown. Charlotte smiled at him as she began to scan the bar, looking for a friendly face, someone, anyone, to balance things up. But Ethan wasn't finished. "While we're on the subject, little Ms Equality, women get cheaper car insurance although your driving sucks." Ethan ducked as Dainty swatted at him.

"Come on! Drink up, hurry. Feet say dance. Get a move on, you're about twelve drinks behind… lightweight. It's just like the Second World War all over again… the bloody Yanks turning up late in the day to claim all the glory when most of the graft has already been done. "

"And, in both cases, here to save your sorry ass."

At this point Dainty dropped her phone again in a fit of giggles. Even in this state Charlotte knew that if anyone else had said that they would have been flayed alive, but Ethan could get away with it, especially when he looked so… well… try as she might, she could come up with no other word for it… hot!

★

Craig knew from the number of street lights that he was half way to Kyle's. He thought thirteen was the best, it was the sixth prime number and it was one hundred and eight steps times thirteen's to Kyle's house with nothing untidy left over. He'd told his teacher that thirteen was the smallest emirp number, a Fibonacci number and a Wilson Prime but she had just got all cross and said she already knew. Mam's new job in the supermarket meant he was on his own at nights which was dead good! He watched loads of television; there was loads of great stuff on late at night, stuff about Albert Einstein, about matter and energy with loads of explosions in it. He had promised to stay in and he had been good for three weeks but now he'd come out to see Kyle. He'd forgotten to put his coat on but the running was keeping him warm. Their last lesson had been five days ago and he had his exam in eleven and a half hours and there was loads of stuff he still didn't understand. A whole har… monic… something came from a B something. All of the stuff was in his head but sometimes he couldn't get it to come out right. It was freezing and pitch-black now. He had to admit it was a bit scary as he turned up Kyle's street. He had sprinted some of the way and his shirt was sticking to him because it was all wet. The saxophone case kept on hitting his legs and he had a big stitch. All the running had upset his counting of the steps as well so it wasn't one hundred and eight times thirteen's to Kyle's house it was ninety three with two left over, he hated that more than anything, even more than Ms Langford at the Centre.

★

The punters in the "Black Rabbit" had made good use of the interval to get fed and watered and were now, as one, eagerly anticipating the next set.

"I thought he was good but I didn't realise he was that good." For once in his life Ludo was being deadly serious.

Kyle was experienced enough to accept that on certain nights all you could do was acknowledge you were getting your backside kicked. There was no shame in admitting that Harry was a cut above him as a sax player. All he could do was keep his mind and his ears open and hope that some of Harry's genius rubbed off on him.

Harry appeared in front of them and as far as Kyle could see the appearance of Louise had knocked about twenty years off him. Now he could see the man from the covers of his sixties albums.

"Come on then, it's probably time we were back on, we can kick off with 'Cherokee'. That should get the blood coursing through everyone's veins." Harry said as he all but vaulted the chairs back towards the stage.

Once the second set started Kyle could hear the years of dedication in Harry's playing. Graft from an endless succession of sweaty clubs coming through every note and phrase. He could see now that it was true, it wasn't how many notes you got through, it was what they actually meant that mattered and it was plain tonight that Harry meant every single one of them.

In the middle of the set they cooled things down a little with "My One and Only Love" Harry took his solo centre stage and it was clear to everyone whom it was meant for and, to her credit, Louise didn't flinch although Kyle could see the colour start to rise in her cheeks.

The second set went down a storm and the band revelled in the adulation. The more the audience liked them, the better they played.

At its conclusion with two encores and calls for a third, Harry signed off just as he had done at the 'Free Trade Hall' in '67'.

"I'd just like to say, me and the boys in the band, we love you madly." They screamed for more. For an audience whose average age was comfortably pensionable they sounded more like a bunch of teenagers in the dance tent at Glastonbury Festival.

Harry was clearly back where he belonged, playing at his best with his band and no one was happier about that than Kyle.

★

He had knocked on the door thirty-nine times. Someone across the street had shouted at him to stop but he didn't. Nobody answered because nobody was at home. He didn't want to break in when there wasn't anybody there because Kyle had told him it was wrong... he would think about it, if it started to rain though. Now that he wasn't running he could feel the cold, especially with his shirt all wet. He had sat on the wall for ninety one minutes, during which there had been four police sirens and two barking dogs or possibly one dog barking twice. There were some gangs of people coming back from the pub, shouting and laughing... he didn't like people who went to the pub. He held on to his saxophone tight in case anyone tried to get it. No one had showed up, no one at all. If he lost his saxophone he wouldn't be able to do his exam. Dr Jacobs had sent him to do an assessment in a big building in Durham that smelled of Domestos but he had hidden in the toilets because he didn't like tests. In the end they had promised him a sticker with DURHAM printed on it to put on his saxophone case. He was worried about his saxophone exam. Perhaps when he came home Kyle would have a pizza or a Chinese with him. He was cold. It was ninety four minutes now.

★

"Don't worry there's no rush." Noel still looked like a man who had bathed leisurely in sunshine as a few of the punters stayed to chat. "Just relax, you've earned it, Mr Crombie wants to buy the band a drink."

Crombie, the owner, kept to himself, head down in a book about the Second World War, occasionally sipping at what looked like lemonade. Periodically, he looked up and a smile would break out across the expanse of his beard.

"Do you have any recordings I can buy?" The first time Kyle was asked this it was quite flattering; by the twentieth time it was becoming annoying. Of course they didn't have any recordings. As he made the most of the drink that Keith had provided it hit him. 'Live at the Manchester Free Trade Hall £19 plus postage and packaging.' Why give someone else money to listen to old CD's of Harry? They could record something with him and it could make a few bob for all of them, and be a marker for them, perhaps something to leave for posterity. It was a brilliant idea… why had he not thought of it before? He was soon lost in picturing album sleeves and track listings as Noel appeared to thank everyone for the night's entertainment as the last of the punters headed for home.

Even Andy seemed blissfully content as he shifted the drums out of the Concert room. "It's easy on a night like this, dismantling the gear; it just sort of takes itself down and floats into the van."

Kyle knew he could relax the surveillance on Harry, now that the gig was over and anyway he had been deep in conversation with Louise for some time and neither Kyle nor anyone else in the band was going to disturb them. The ex-lovers leant in close towards each other. Whatever had happened in their past, they certainly looked much taken with each other now. Only a monumental dig in the ribs from Kyle stopped Ludo shouting "Get a room".

Chapter 25

Charlotte fell for Golightly's nightclub the minute she set eyes on its interior decor. It was painstakingly 70's, from the male bar staff's facial hair right down to the female staff's hot-pants. As they struggled to get served at the crowded bar she tried to recall her night's intake but the spinning lights of the glitter ball only added to her disorientation. She couldn't remember how much she'd had. There were two cocktails before Ethan showed up then there was one more or was it two or thereabouts and then… she could vaguely recall the sequence of drinks early on but as she traced her steps forward she got increasingly hazy. With their new drinks in hand they made their way over to a table near the dance floor before plonking down on one of the few faux-leopard skin seats that were un-occupied. Before she could draw breath, a squealing Dainty had dragged them all on to the dance floor. No bad thing. Sweating out some of that alcohol would help.

It was good to get lost in the crowd, dancing to ever more overpowering music on a packed floor. She had never been one to do her thing stone cold sober; it had always taken a few liveners for her to lose her inhibitions. It was definitely less than ten units she'd had or was that ten drinks? Ok maybe a bit more than ten units but not more than a dozen, anyway how could you tell with cocktails? Too much thinking… not enough boogie. If that wasn't the title of a song it ought to be. They danced together like friends, with no one taking it very seriously. "We are Family" made her feel light headed but very, very happy and "I'm Every Woman" had her singing her heart out. One song merged into the next, getting progressively wilder as the night wore on. During "Disco Inferno" she caught a brief sight of herself in a mirror over the bar… the UV lighting was doing nothing for her complexion.

A few men tentatively tried to boogie their way into her orbit, the lasers and strobe lights making every face mysterious, but she blanked them all. It would be a long time before she put a toe in the water where that was concerned. Still it was nice to know she could still attract someone. Some of them were quite dashing when you got a decent look at them, but she certainly wasn't going to allow herself to be pulled whilst pissed in a nightclub, especially one with leopard skin seats! What would Mama say! Despite her best efforts, in a room full of strangers, she laughed out loud. Thank God it was so noisy in here.

She reached a peak of frantic activity with 'Play That Funky Music', the end of which left her feeling exhausted. She hadn't danced like that for years. Given the option of being in a 'disco inferno' or a real one, Kyle would have undoubtedly opted for the later. She'd had a gym membership but it had been gathering dust for the last six months. She would have to start going religiously if a little bit of activity like this had left her this shattered. Getting in another round of drinks would at least give her a breather, although the scrum at the bar meant it wasn't that much of a respite.

When she returned with the drinks, Dainty and Ethan were still hard at it. Dainty was clearly in her element but she could see Ethan was starting to flag a little and took the arrival of the drinks as an excuse to leave the floor. Dainty wasn't perturbed by this and immediately directed her attentions to the attractive, Afro-Caribbean boy next to her.

Standing at the bar for ages had left Charlotte feeling more semi-detached from the proceedings. She forced the last of her old drink down in the end and the sickly sweet taste stuck in her throat. Ethan, bless him, tried to make conversation over the pounding music as he wiped the sweat out of his eyes.

"You seem a little down… still a bit raw?"

"SORRY? It's a… a bit… " She really was finding it hard to hear.

"LOUD? I said "STILL A BIT RAW" You know… YOU SPLITTING UP… WITH YOUR EX."

By now she was beyond making the effort to understand so she did the only thing she felt she could do, considering what she'd drunk and the loneliness she felt… and anyway they were old friends. It seemed perfectly natural for her head to flop down on to his perfectly formed shoulder. She was tired, she was drunk, she was lonely, he was there.

"I don't… I… I want to go home."

As K.C and the Sunshine Band's 'Don't Go' came to a close, Dainty pitched up at the table with her new man firmly in hand. Charlotte was keen to bow out as quickly as she could now and this seemed the perfect excuse.

"Sorry… I'm flagging… NO FLAGGING… I DON'T WANT TO SPOIL YOUR NIGHT… NO, YOUR NIGHT. YOU STAY HERE."

Dainty was shouting now. "I can get a TAXI with LINFORD here and text you when I get in… DON'T WORRY I'LL GET A TAXI… I'LL CALL YOU WHEN I LEAVE."

The man was speaking now. "Listen, to be honest, Linford is just my stage name; call me Warren… NO, WARREN… LINFORD IS MY STAGE… DON'T WORRY. IT'S NOTHING."

'Stage name Linford' seemed nice and Dainty seemed, not unnaturally, very taken with him.

"ETHAN WILL TAKE CARE OF YOU… WON'T YOU?" As Dainty said this she nodded her head in Ethan's direction, suggesting that if any harm came to her friend he would be garrotted. Charlotte decided she loved Dainty… if only she were a boy.

Ethan nodded and Dainty allowed herself a big smile before heading back to the dance floor, 'Stage Name Linford' in tow.

They exited Golightly's and the cold air struck her like a slap in the face but Ethan was there to hold on to her… which was nice. It was relatively early, thank God and there wasn't any queue for taxis and soon they were speeding their way through the city streets as she clung on to him for dear life. Ethan had bought her two drinks, or was it three? Whatever it was, it was more than Kyle had ever done for her.

She heard her own voice but didn't know where the words were coming from. "What's he know 'bout dignity? I could marry you; you've got a chin… OK magazine, ha! It'll be Tatler or they can all bugger off and we won't let him in with his silly band… see that scar on my leg I got it at a gymkhana when I was twelve… I want to sit down now."

"You are sitting down." said Ethan, as she nuzzled into him.

The garish street lights made her feel giddy as the taxi picked up pace. She tried once more to work out how many drinks she'd had but by now she wasn't even sure what day of the week it was. Yet even in this state she could still register the neon glow of the city giving way to of the gentler atmosphere of the village where Ethan lived, with flower tubs and hanging baskets bedecking the streets. Lovely, this was living alright… oh dear, she didn't feel too steady on her feet.

Ethan paid the driver. She really must settle up with him when she could, she hadn't thrown up in the cab… that was something. Her legs were all jelly, which was funny and everything was bendy, bendy rubber. She giggled as Ethan tried to shush her, silly boy, the house was really, really big… bigger than it looked from the inside… outside. He was a very good looking boy, the American. If all the boys in the world were stars there would be lots of them.

In his bedroom, she rallied briefly enough to give Ethan the best kiss ever and promptly passed out.

★

It was quiet now, just the odd taxi going by. The street lights had been switched off, which wasn't very nice. He had to make a decision; he hated that, deciding stuff. He needed to talk to Kyle but what if Kyle was away all night? His Mam would be back from her shift at the supermarket in twenty minutes and he always made her a cup-a-soup when she came in. She would be worried if he wasn't there and she would shout at him and then cry and say he was going to turn out like his dad. A boy sped past him on a bike, shouting something rude, but he didn't pay him any attention and the bike was out of sight in seconds. He was really cold now; his hands were practically frozen to his case. But he needed to know about harmonic series and B flat and stuff. He would count to one hundred and thirty but if the dog barked again he would go straight away. He blew on his hands and rubbed them together to warm them up and then got his horn out. He liked the way the moon bounced off it, deflecting the light like a shield. Gazing at his sax made him lose count. The dog hadn't made a sound but Kyle had warned him that the most important thing before the exam was a good night's sleep. Kyle had told him four times at their last lesson that the hard work had been done, all he had to do was turn up, be awake and do his best. He shut the case carefully after giving the sax a quick polish with his sleeve; he needed it looking its best for his exam. He'd made his decision. If he was quick he could be home before mam. He set off as fast as he could. There wasn't even time to count.

★

As final proceedings were wrapped up for the night, Noel appeared to pay the band.

"We generally do quite well here but I reckon that extra bit of publicity you sent out and the stuff on the "Net" made all the difference. You know, so many bands come up here and expect me to provide a big turn out; it's nice to see someone who's prepared to put in the spade work. That's the first time I've had to turn people away since the opening night, not even standing room left. You will come back here soon, won't you"? Kyle had the unusual experience of feeling both pride and shame at Noel's effusive praise. Perhaps the band had been right after the "Happy Man" gig. It hadn't taken the greatest of efforts to get a reasonable crowd to show up. He was manoeuvring the last of the equipment out of the door when Noel called back to him.

"We've got that Robbie Williams on next week."

Noel, having been the perfect host, Kyle wanted to be polite.

"Well, that'll be nice for you."

"I'll say. We've hired him to collect the empties."

Kyle flicked Louise a glance and she smiled at him benignly. She was now the sole punter left in the place. She kissed Harry as she got ready to take her leave. Kyle tried not to stare at the re-united lovers but it was touching as they tried to make up for the past years of estrangement with the few minutes they had left. It was clear that Louise was off but before their goodbye she broke away from Harry and made a bee line for him.

"Miss, Mrs... Crabb... Campbell? What do I owe you? The train fare, petrol or what not." He said it at a whisper so no one heard.

"It's Kyle, Isn't it? The Emma Woodhouse of jazz. Forget the money, it wasn't far to come, well not in terms of miles anyway. Off the wagon he may be but he can still charm the birds from the trees. It was good to catch up with the old bastard. He's shorter and frailer than I remember him, but then again, aren't we all. You know, looking at that stage tonight you reminded me of him in his younger days."

Kyle wasn't quite sure who Emma Woodhouse was but the latter comparison gave him goosebumps. She offered him a cigarette, as she rooted around for the mobile ringing in her bag.

"No, thanks. I need all the lung power I can get to manage the sax."

"I didn't think you would, you're a chip off the old block. It was the one vice Harry disdained. God... what happened to the years...

I have an awful feeling you're going to be seeing a lot more of me in the near future. Goodnight. Keep an eye on the old devil will you?"

Louise kissed him on the cheek before returning to Harry, who escorted her outside as if she was the Queen of Sheba.

When he re-entered the venue, Harry was proudly brandishing a piece of paper with Louise's phone number on it.

"Jesus, how about that and I did a set straight, stone cold sober. Get me a pint and a chaser will you, I'm gasping. I told you she was a belter."

"I guess you've earned a drink". In the circumstances Kyle thought they both had.

Chapter 26

Dainty had undoubtedly drunk more in her time but this was a new low. The pint of water she had downed before bed and the two aspirins she had forced down herself at first light had been woefully ineffective. Still, she had one trick up her sleeve, the "Jamaican Surprise", her father's old hangover remedy. A single measure of rum, one teaspoon of honey and a teaspoon of double cream. From experience she knew that if you could manage to prepare it and then manage to keep it down, it worked… a bit. No sign at all of Charlotte, so she had stayed out all night with Ethan… well, well, well. It was nice that celebrating the end of her own relationship could be the start of someone else's, yin and yang, opening and closing of doors and all that positive stuff. She looked at the clock, it was still early. Comforting as her bed was, the desire for warm sugary tea was becoming impossible to ignore. She would have one last indulgence before hauling herself out of bed. Taking her mobile, she flicked through to the latest addition in her address book. There it was… Linford (Warren)… and it was his landline number not just a mobile, so he was single as well. No married man would take that sort of risk. Life was sweet, despite the aching head. Tea first, "Jamaican Surprise" second… it was a plan of sorts.

She manoeuvred herself upright and sat on the bed, still a bit groggy. She would count down to ten and then she'd stand up. She got as far as seven before her mobile rang. She didn't recognise the number so it could be easily ignored. Her Dad's remedy could wait; she needed that tea as quickly as her state of health would allow. Slowly, and with the odd wince, she managed to complete the task without being ill or pouring boiling water on herself. Mug in hand and back in bed she sipped the warm, sweet nectar as she listened to the answer phone message. The voice was hesitant and unsure.

"Hello, hello… my name's Geoff… Geoff Harris. I play football with your Mick. Sorry, your ex… it is ex now, isn't it? He never really said… we just wondered if anyone had told you about the accident. He's in Sunderland General… a car crash. I forget the ward… but it's… you know… the one when it's serious".

★

Kyle gave a yawn and went for the biggest stretch he could manage. Early morning starts were becoming his habit now. This was, he assumed, Charlotte's dig from beyond the grave of their relationship. The deep satisfaction in rolling over and giving in to a blissful half-sleep till mid-day was a lot less of a pleasure when it wasn't set in stark contrast to your girlfriend's early rising. He had tried for more than a month to fight it, trying to doze to sounds of "Woman's Hour" on radio 4 or counting backwards through the Miles Davis's discography till sleep returned. Nothing worked. Charlotte had cursed him forever to wake at the same time as the rest of the working population. Actually, it was even worse than that. Saturdays and Sundays were no exception for him, waking again and again at the same bloody time. Even people in regular jobs got to lie in at the weekend.

There was nothing for it, he might as well give in to fate, get up and make some use of the time. There were some things Harry had shown him before the last gig that he wanted to get to grips with. There was no promotion to do for the next venue. 'Already a sell-out' was the missive that had come back from the organiser, which was nice. Word was getting around. He would get up, have breakfast, practice a little and then start looking for other gigs. That way there'd be no agent to pay, and while he was on, he could look at that website where you could offer your services as a peripatetic teacher. He'd been doing pretty well on that front. It was Craig's exam today and if there was any justice in the world he would sail through. But there was still the nagging doubt that once again the boy might decide that he didn't fancy being judged and that he would throw it rather than tackle it. He'd done all he could for Craig, all he could do now was hope and pray. The idea of peripatetic teaching was growing on him. The pay wasn't bad, certainly much better per hour than jazz gigs. Somehow or other, he had to cobble the money together to get the band in the studio. A couple of days a week teaching and he'd be able to do it... eventually. There was no spur now like the idea of holding a CD case with a photo of his band standing next to Harry Crabb. They could all wear black and red pinstripe suits like the "Manhattan Daytrip" cover... blinding!

Looking down at the bed sheets he realised how grubby they'd become. Charlotte had taken care of all that nonsense. He had always loved it when there were crisp, clean sheets on the bed. He would have to change them now, they really were beyond disgusting. He knew there was at least one clean set put away somewhere. He bundled up the bedding and was about to dump them in the overflowing wash basket but when it actually came to it he bottled it. He stood holding the sheets for a while, building up to it. There it was again, the bowling ball swinging low in his guts. He just couldn't finish the job. These were the last sheets that they had slept on together. If he washed them she was gone from his bed and his life, for ever. He would have to face that it was over. He put the sheets back. He would change them tomorrow. He sat on the crumpled bed, just him and the overwhelming ache in his guts. At first the sensation felt like a purely an emotional thing, although a major part of it turned out to be the phone in his front trouser pocket. Removing it, he instinctively turned to Charlotte's number.

★

She took in her surroundings one eye at a time. The pain on opening both at once had been way too great. She tried to orientate herself. Ethan lay beside her fast asleep. She felt like she'd been hit with a club rather than having been inside one. The clock on the bedside said 12.30pm.

Ethan's bedroom was like something from a "House Beautiful" photo shoot. Actually, it was better than that… it was the centre page spread from "House Beautiful Pick of the Year", colourful, orderly and with a great deal of attention to detail, a large number of well-tended plants giving it an airy feel. She winced as she focused on the framed photographs that ran along the shelves, showing Ethan's sporting prowess in high school and his popularity with his classmates. The daylight streamed in through the window and hit her between the eyes. It was a low blow.

"Oh God! Oh God! Oh God!"

She knew she was going to have to find a toilet and quickly but she didn't know where, in Christ's name, it was. Staggering out of the bedroom without waking Ethan was hard enough. This house had a lot of rooms. She ricocheted from wall to wall, trying various door handles. Either she was still drunk or Ethan lived on a houseboat. Just when she thought it was hopeless and she would have to give in she found the toilet and salvation.

"Oh God! Oh God! Oh God." She caught sight of herself in the mirror.

A girl like her shouldn't get caught out like this, looking like a scene from 'the director's cut' of 'The Exorcist'. She would never, ever drink alcohol again.

When it was over she crawled back into Ethan's bed and hugged a pillow to herself… never again, no really, never, never again.

★

Serious! What did that mean? Dainty sat up straight and tried to make sense of the phone call. It was alright, she could stay calm. It was probably the hospital being cautious… obviously, that was it. She reached for her phone. These days, what with lawyers and

225

solicitors getting in on the act, the whole medical profession was terrified about things turning out worse than they'd implied and anyway, as they were no longer man and wife, this was a courtesy call, that was all. She hadn't even left the confines of her bed.

The voice on the other end was apprehensive. "Can you tell me who's speaking?"

"Yes, I'm his… wife."

She started to say it out of habit but before she got to the W word she knew that it was now a lie. It didn't really matter, it was a small "white with a hint of beige" lie and it was the only way she was going to get any information out of them. But the price to be paid was hearing the nurse's change of tone on the other end. It must seem pretty despicable, what sort of wife would leave her husband in intensive care for days without even an inquiring phone call?

"I'm afraid he's been in a road traffic accident and has suffered a serious head injury. You might want to come in so we can explain what's happened."

One thing Dainty knew for sure, there would be no visiting Michael "commitment issues" Fuller and anyway he would only think she'd come to gloat. This would be her secret. She would tell nobody, not even Charlotte. No, ill or not, she couldn't visit him and that was an end to the matter, regardless of how cold or selfish it sounded to the stranger on the other end of the phone.

*

Kyle had lost track of time whilst sat on the bed but he knew if he stared at the number any longer he was simply going to blow it. He pressed 'call' and crossed himself. It rang… and rang… and rang. Eventually the answer phone kicked in, that was good. Best just say your piece and be gone.

"Hello… I've been meaning to ring you for a while now, I'm not very good at this… sorry. I know this might sound strange and you might not realise it yet but you need me. I'm your man. I've had my doubts in the past and I know there's every chance you've made plans with someone else but all I'm asking for is a chance to prove myself. I've been sitting on my hands for way too long and it's time that I did the right thing. I got your number from your brother, I'm down in London doing a gig with a friend of your father's, Harry, Harry Crabb, if you're around on the 13th of December and you want to hear me play just call me back on this number. I'm not as old as your dad... not that being as old as your dad is a bad thing... sorry, my name is Kyle... Kyle Johnson and I'm a sax player... sorry, I probably should have said that first... yeah... OK... well if you want to call me fine. Good... yeah... thanks... sorry."

In the end it had been easier to ring Jacqui Drinkwater than Charlotte. At some point he would speak to his Ex but now was not the time.

★

The door swung back almost off its hinges as Ethan manoeuvred his way into the bedroom bearing a large breakfast tray with fruit and cereal, tea and toast.

Charlotte squinted at the alarm clock. My God! It was two in the afternoon.

"So how is the unacceptable face of British Laddette culture this afternoon?"

Ethan put the tray on the bed and threw back the curtains. She was feeling marginally better than she had done but still several evolutions away from anything vaguely human.

"The fizzy stuff is Resolve, that'll give you the strength to get some grits inside of you. The black stuff is tea sweetened with honey. We should be able to have you back in the pub by three-o-clock without too much trouble." Charlotte offered little more than a groan.

Ethan buttered a piece of toast and poured himself a cup of

coffee. Even in her fragile state, she could see that he had laid on a particularly good spread and she was now terribly thirsty. This would be perfect if it wasn't for the agony in her head, the sweating and the nausea. However, one thought was uppermost in her mind.

"Ethan, last night, did we… you know… you and I… ?"

"No, you were a tad inert. Not that the thought didn't cross my mind. But I googled it and it was a definite prison sentence and, lovely as you are, I wasn't prepared to slop out for the next five years."

"Oh my word, thank God!"

She clutched her chest dramatically.

"Steady on. Back home I'm considered something of a catch."

"I'm sorry… I didn't mean… it's just… well… "

"Relax, I'm just yanking your chain. You English girls really need to lighten up a bit. Now drink your Resolve and try not to think of good old British cuisine too much, you know cold tripe, jellied eels, calves foot jelly that sort of thing."

This was too much for Charlotte and she made a lunge for the bathroom. It was happening again, Oh lord! She could still hear the laughter as her head descended into the toilet bowl.

She returned feeling sheepish but sure that she was now over the worst.

"Come on, Ms Rehab, you need some re-hydration. You haven't done much in the way of partying recently, have you? From what I hear you haven't had any kind of fun for quite a while."

"You could say that."

"Perhaps that's about to change."

"Not if this is the price you end up paying."

"Perhaps you'd be happier taking things more slowly."

They sat on the bed, drank coffee, chatted about the small stuff and gave the night's events a fairly wide berth and by the time she was ready to take her leave she was feeling a little more like herself.

As they made their way to the door she got a better look at Ethan's house. Thank God he'd never seen her flat. The 'objets d'art' and the décor were all impeccably chosen and displayed, as one perfectly laid out room led through to the next. If you were going to spend time recovering from a hangover then there were worse places to do it in.

"Perhaps you might need a couple of days drying out. I've got some contacts if you need them."

"Seriously, I'm not like that I'm… "

"AL-Anon, The Priory, The Betty Ford clinic… "

"You're kidding again aren't you?" Ethan nodded sagely, a grin spreading across his handsome face.

"I hope Dainty's OK. She seemed quite ensconced." It was the first serious thing he had said.

"I dare say she sent him home with his tail between his legs. She's never knowingly undersold that one."

"You really wouldn't want the lasting memory of our one date together to be of you being ill?"

"God no, but then I didn't know it was a date."

"OK. Well get yourself put back together and I'll take you out for dinner Thursday night."

"I don't know. I'm only just… getting over… "

"No strings, just something a little more civilised, help to draw a veil over last night's atrocities."

Charlotte bit her lip as she considered the proposal though it didn't take her long to accept. In those circumstances how could a girl refuse?

Ethan's concern for Dainty impressed Charlotte as she stepped into the taxi and made her way back home. It wasn't as if her flat mate gave the impression of not being able to stand up for herself. As the car wound its way back through tree lined streets she looked out at the landscape and realised she had no idea where she'd spent the night. What would her family have thought? What had she been thinking last night? Thank goodness Ethan was a gentleman, although, if she could admit it, a small dark part of her wondered if it would have been the worst thing in the world had he been less gallant.

Chapter 27

Dainty looked at her watch as she moved into the Lingerie department. She'd been shopping for seven hours and still didn't want to go home. Home made her miserable and she couldn't face a club. It had been three days since their blow-out at Golightly's but she still didn't feel up to a night on the town. She hadn't yet managed to meet up with Stage Name Linford, who seemed to work most nights, but they had pencilled in Sunday. Charlotte was off on a date with Ethan that night so everything in that particular garden was rosy. All she needed was as many retail outlets as her feet would take her to. She was owed four days from work and they all had to be taken by the end of the year.

She had paid off most of the debt on her credit card… down from £879 to £246. That gave her about seven hundred quid to play with. The poor card itself was beginning to look translucent from overuse. Question was what did she need at the minute? Certainly not a winter coat, unless it was in a sale. There was something about seeing the words '50% off' that gave her a thrill bordering on the orgasmic. She moved quickly through the rows of new arrivals and headed for the cosmetics. Her sister Rose was one for the salsa clubs there would be bound to be something she could get for sis to shimmer in on the dance floor. She hadn't bought anything for her sisters in ages, one of the casualties of her divorce. Her sisters had warned her about Michael and whenever they met now he was the elephant dung in the room.

To be off again with the band was a good feeling, Kyle thought, as he found himself behind the wheel of the van. They were really shaping up together and the notion of a recording session gave him a warm glow. It was a comparatively short drive to the venue, a large concrete 60's-built workingmen's club, just off the A19 in a semi-rural part of Teesside. He'd played there more than a decade ago with a jazz rock band and it felt odd to return older, wiser but still as skint. The journey had been a good humoured affair. It wasn't just that they could do a good job; it was that they now knew they could do a good job. They were becoming, in the words of Noel, "quite a turn." Still, the smell of stale beer and disappointment that greeted them on arrival was enough to remind them that the 'Black Rabbit' lovely as it was, was the exception rather than the rule.

Kyle got into the swing of things as they began the process of dragging the equipment up the fire escape and into the back of the club. He was quite chuffed at how efficient they were becoming, executing their tasks with as much military precision as a jazz quintet could have. The concert room was a sea of empty chairs, not a table in the place. They were clearly expecting a lot of punters. Sid Chase didn't exactly have the best of reputations as an agent. A quick trawl round the internet had uncovered that. Double bookings, late payments, an ability to avoid his phone if you were stuck in Wales with a Social Secretary who'd never heard of you, but as far as 'The Harry Crabb Quintet' was concerned their "Mr 17.5%" had excelled himself.

"Here they are, come on in, lambs to the slaughter." The barmaid winked at him as she tossed this comment into the ether, which he thought a little strange. Still it wouldn't be the first time someone in a venue had tried to spook them out. What she didn't know was that she was about to witness a band of seasoned professionals whose days of playing in small clubs would soon be behind them.

"You're expecting a lot of punters." He pointed at the rows of seats.

"Absolutely, sold out in September… it's not difficult, love… just give them what they want." There was that bloody wink again.

Somehow or other they had fallen into a vortex where jazz gigs sold out months in advance. His heart gave a little summersault of joy. God bless Sid Chase. Perhaps this was the beginning of the upsurge in audiences; the upsurge that everyone had been predicting for jazz since Louis Armstrong first broke sweat.

★

Charlotte pulled into the car park of Delamere Hall, a two hundred year old edifice overlooking the North Sea. She was painfully aware that her car stuck out like a sore thumb amongst the top-of-the-range vehicles parked beside it, not least Ethan McCormack's Mercedes Benz SLR McLaren Roadster. Perhaps they would think that she waitressed there… in the future she might need to. She tried not to dwell on the previous visits she had made with her parents. At the moment, any thought of her family was grief she could do without. She knew from memory that the food here was good, actually it was exceptional, and she also knew that it was fearfully expensive. It had Michelin stars, a rare thing this far from the south-east, but try as she might she could still only ever think of "Michelin" in relation to car tyres.

Back at Dainty's, the outfits on the camp bed were a testament to the trouble she had taken getting dressed. Perhaps being restricted to two car loads of belongings, retrieved since she had left Kyle, had been a blessing in disguise. In the end she had slunk back to the comparative safety of the little black dress. At least it was Roberto Cavalli and never failed to make her feel glamorous.

Seeing Ethan, she decided the chaos she had left behind was well worth it. Attired in his finery, booted and suited, he came out of the pillared entrance to greet her, umbrella in hand, looking like he had just left the set of a fashion shoot for 'Bulgari'. His kiss on her cheek lingered perfectly between 'just friends' and 'Oh! La! La!' Try as she might she couldn't recall what kissing Kyle had been like but it had, towards the end of their relationship, been such an infrequent occurrence that it was little surprise she'd forgotten. It was also lovely just to be hugged by someone who made her feel protected. One of her mother's criteria in a beau was that "He should be big enough to carry you out of a burning building." Well, no problem on that score. Side by side, they entered the restaurant. Ethan held out her chair as the whole thing began to take on the air of a Scott Fitzgerald novel. "What can I get you to drink? The Chablis Grand Cru is very palatable."

"That's fine… that would be lovely." She looked around her.

This place had always given her an illicit thrill. The restaurant part of the building had been converted from a chapel. This added to the decadence of what was a fairly debauched experience in the first place. Here and there small ecclesiastical features had been left in the architecture and décor. Even if you watched the calories, and avoided the veal and pate de foie gras on moral grounds, the implication was clear… eat here and you were going straight to hell… but what a way to go. The Devil, it seemed, not only possessed the best tunes, he also had double chocolate ganache. It was perfect… the whole thing was utterly perfect as long as she could rid herself of the notion that people's funerals had been conducted there. Weddings yes… fine… bring it on, but you didn't want to think your table had been the resting place for somebody's mortal remains, not if you were having the pork or the chicken.

★

Kyle looked around the club as the band completed their set up before fine tuning their instruments. No one had appeared claiming to be in charge, as animated punters started to stream in through the doors. Why, he wondered, were they exclusively female?

Hundreds of them young, old and everything in-between, and why were they in such a state of dizzy excitement? He was perplexed. These were not the typical bearded, middle aged, down at heel jazz punters he had expected. Still, he was leading a band of pro musicians. All they needed to do was pick a couple of sets that reflected the make-up of their audience and they'd would soon have them eating out of the palms of their hands.

"Something's not right here." Barry had not wasted much time reverting to his default position of gloom and pessimism.

Andy was short and to the point. "If you're getting paid and the place is full I wouldn't grumble."

Andy was talking sense, Kyle thought, as the ceaseless flow of women continued. They'd had enough of playing to cold, empty rooms.

The stage set, they trooped off to the dressing room in order to thrash over what would keep this specific audience happy. Kyle was guessing that meant a lot of syrupy ballads. The dressing room itself was small, shabby and starkly lit, adorned with a collection of old paint tins, which, from the messy state of their surroundings, looked like relics from the last re-fit. The walls were peppered with posters and glossy stage photographs from past decades of performers who had worked at the club, some low rent, some simply past their prime. The Visiting "Artistes" had mercilessly graffitied each other's pictures. Everyone who had worked there was accusing everyone else of being engaged in every sordid carnal act known to man, occasionally with basic diagrams to aid explanation.

Just at the point when Kyle wondered if anyone was going to step up and claim to be running the show, an enormous man bustled into the room. His suit, a sort of mauve tartan, was even louder than he was and not the most becoming thing for a man of his age and stature to be wearing.

"Well gentleman, they can't say we haven't tried. Bob... Bobby, call me Bobby. I'm your Compere for tonight."

Bobby had a microphone case in his hand but if the volume of his natural voice was anything to go by he could stick the mic on EBay now.

"We've had rock bands, country and western, funk, punk, a string quartet and two lads from Rhyl who played rap songs on spoons and washboard. They went down a bloody storm but they got themselves a summer season in Grand Canaria and never came back. Can't take the heat, me... brings me out, got so bad now the wife has to go off on holiday with her bloody sister instead of me. Still swings and roundabouts, son, swings and roundabouts, eh!"

As Bobby talked, apparently without needing to breathe in, he valiantly battled with a stray tuft of hair as it refused to stay plastered to his otherwise bald pate. Kyle gave a shake of his head to Ludo, who was trying hard not to giggle.

"Not one of them got through to their second set, mind. You're our last chance, then its extra bingo and sod the union. Now, have you left enough room for the boys?"

They stared at the Compere... boys? No one had told them about any support band. At that exact moment a head popped round the dressing room door. It was evidently the first of the "Boys". Shaven headed, he was by Kyle's estimation, at least six foot six and as camp as the gift list at Elton John's civil ceremony.

"Hey, ho, girls. Factory's open. Hello, Big Bob, don't tell me... you've been working out."

"Ha Bloody Ha, Gloria" said Bobby. As the six foot plus of Gloria made to kiss him, he ducked in barely concealed terror.

"You'll be sharing the dressing room with Glen Miller here; the other's got the chairman's new kitchen unit in it."

Kyle assumed that in this instance he was the "Glen Miller" in question. At this point another of the "boys" stuck his head round the dressing room door and gave the place the once over.

"It was never like this in Vegas."

"Bugger Vegas! A lot of fat cowboys pissing their wages down the sink" said Bobby, backing towards a wall.

The rest of the "Boys" were soon attempting to get in, clutching their costumes. It was quite a struggle as PVC waistcoats, leather chaps, police helmets and handcuffs went by. The band started to look uneasily towards Kyle. Barry in particular looked mortified. What the hell was he meant to do, Kyle thought, as he followed the Compere out? His nearest exposure to male strippers was flicking past Chanel 5 with the remote control. He hadn't arranged this gig! He had just taken the phone call from Sid and would hopefully be paid the money at the end of the night. Backstage, he sneaked a look through the curtains. The concert room was now filled to overflowing.

"What in god's name have we got ourselves into?" he asked under his breath.

★

"Hello." Charlotte looked up. Ethan was regarding her quizzically across the table.

"Sorry?"

"You seem a little preoccupied."

God, what was she thinking? Here was Ethan looking twenty-four carat and she was dreaming about dessert. She looked up and smiled, realising, she didn't have a thing in her head to say. Damn that ganache.

"The Chablis is lovely." she said lamely and reached for her glass.

Alcohol would oil the wheels although, after the last time, pray God not too much. She smiled wryly as she realised that the last time Kyle had bought her a drink it had been a half of cider at "The Black Horse" in West Boldon. She thought about the meal they they were about to order. If you dwelt on how much it cost per mouthful it could stick in your throat. And what price chocolate ganache if that was half her student heating allowance for next winter? But after her recent upheavals she might as well be wholeheartedly sinful for old time's sake.

No sooner had she absolved herself of any culinary guilt than she thought about the mess she had left behind at Dainty's. Much as Dainty obviously enjoyed her company she needed to get her own place and soon. They rubbed along together quite contentedly and it was good to be able to chat at any time but even with just a few of her possessions in place things were bursting out at the seams. And though she was prepared to admit it might just be her imagination she couldn't help but feel that Dainty had been a little withdrawn of late. Ever since the absolute party, come to that.

"I'll just order for both of us shall I?"

"God, yes… sorry, I'm not quite with it."

She must try and concentrate on her companion… Ethan did look stunning in his suit. His outfit didn't scream money, it just casually pointed it out in passing. That, she decided, was the epitome of class.

★

Despite health and safety, the clubs and his own, Bobby was treating himself to a sly fag before battle commenced.

"Er… what's the set-up here?" Kyle asked, hoping for reassurance.

"You go on first, take most of the flak, the girls get a bit pissed up, then we unleash "Brokeback Duncan and his Chaps"… you do another 25 minutes to settle them down before they hit the streets and each other. We rake it in with the door money and the booze which keeps us in touching distance of solvency for another month. We all go home happy."

Bobby took a last drag on his cigarette. Kyle could appreciate now in a way he couldn't have in the past about doing whatever was necessary to keep yourself afloat. He nodded. It seemed like the perfect set up. At that moment from the corner of his eye he caught sight of Harry, who was heading towards the bar, fighting his way through a swathe of thirsty women. Like a shot Kyle tagged after him. He couldn't afford to let Harry have free reign at the bar but getting through the women was akin to swimming through treacle. He kicked himself for not inviting Louise. She could have worked her magic again. He managed to get behind Harry just as he got to the front. Of all the gigs where Harry needed to have his wits about him, it was this one. Before he could get served Kyle caught the eye of the barmaid and with a desperate combination… part mime, part semaphore… indicated that Harry was not to be served on any account. Fortunately, the barmaid understood the situation in a twinkling. She didn't even bother to look at Harry as she spoke.

"Sorry love, we're only licensed to serve women on a Thursday… it's them EEC."

"But, but, but… " Harry looked bewildered. One of his few avenues of pleasure had been abruptly closed off to him. The other barmaids were more than a match for him as he feebly waved a fiver at them, a limp flag of surrender. Eventually Kyle managed to shepherd him into the dressing room where Ludo was dispatched to get Harry a pint and nothing greater or stronger than that. It was becoming increasingly cramped as they re-entered the dressing room and the band looked decidedly queasy as male body parts began to be oiled and preened in front of them.

Harry took hold of his saxophone case and held on for comfort. God, he could murder another drink and he could murder it now, not in two hours' time. The pint they had got him didn't touch the sides. Nevertheless, he was fascinated by the images of male perfection surrounding him in the dressing room. There was, he recalled, a clarinet player in Frankie Longford's band who went in for that sort of thing, other men, but that was the full extent of his exposure to it. Harry was very sanguine about it. Frankie had been a first rate clarinet player and wasn't shy of standing his round and that was good enough for him. He licked his lips as the desire for a livener before they went on stage surfaced again. That was when he needed it the most, just before he set foot on stage, to get the creative juices flowing, but he could see that Kyle wasn't going to let him off the leash too early and it was clear that more than one drink was verboten. One drink wasn't a drink at all, you needed to top up constantly if it was going to register. Then again, if he was going to win Louise back there would obviously have to be some small sacrifices. Perhaps this was a blessing in disguise, but God it hurt.

"Remember the deal?"

Harry was shaken out of his study. How could he forget? Kyle had repeated it every ten minutes on the way there.

"There's a half bottle of scotch in the van for you as soon as we come off tonight."

"Can't we have a little on appro now?"

Fortunately at that precise moment Bobby appeared, clearly on edge. The lights in the concert room had dimmed... it was "show time".

"Right, best kick off or they're going to get restless. On you get and don't take anything they do personally. Oh! And warn the bunch from the WRVS about fire extinguishers. Tell them any more bloody antics like last month and they'll be barred again."

★

For Dainty the day had been a non-stop assault on her credit cards pausing only for food and drink when her feet screamed for rest. There had been some concessions to austerity; she had rejected eighty per cent of the things she had tried on, well almost eighty, certainly fifty per cent plus. Now, however, she was ready to call it a day and get the bus home, late night shopping or no late night shopping. It had gone eight o'clock and most shops were already closing up. At first she tried to put a spring in her weary step but somewhere between the bus stop and her conscience the little voice that had been nagging in her head took over. The day spent trying to drown out its refrain with retail and consumer durables hadn't worked at all. Why should she be so beholden to the vows that he had cast aside so lightly for nothing more than a shag with her best friend? Back it came... "for richer for poorer, in sickness and in

239

health"… in bed with her and in bed with her Bridesmaid! Bastard. If she got to the bus stop but missed the bus then she'd be almost on top of the place with nowhere else to go. It wasn't like it would kill her and she'd never bottled anything else before in her life. There was no rush now, it didn't matter how long it took.

She had worked out the best way to balance her purchases. It was actually two bags in one hand and four bags in the other because the boots and shoes weighed more than the tops and skirts. She could tell how much she had bought by the heavier sound of her stilettos on the floor as they echoed up and down the corridors. These places were so vast these days and utterly obsessed by cleanliness. She had only been in five minutes and she'd already had to clean her hands half a dozen times. The place she wanted, she'd been informed by a staff nurse, was ward forty-six opposite and down a bit from the maternity ward, which was ironic in the circumstances. The heavy bags were starting to carve grooves into her fingers as the maternity ward loomed up; she gave it a wistful look and considered popping in, briefly, but thought better of it. She was only thirty-one… there would be time yet to be a bona fide in-patient but the sight and sound of the place was intoxicating. As promised, a bit further up on the right, ward forty-six and not before time. She approached the reception.

"I'm here to visit Mr Fuller, I'm his wife. And I know it's late but I only recently heard he was in here and I'm not going home till I've seen him."

Chapter 28

"We'll start off as surreptitiously as possible while we size this lot up, then we'll take it from there."

Kyle led the band gingerly on to the stage, fear rising in his throat. He wanted to be more inspiring to his troops but he was more concerned about not starting a riot. They had barely managed to get in place before the grief started.

"Get em off," came a cry from the back as a ripple of laughter ran through the crowd.

"God in heaven no, put them back on." This was followed by somewhat derisory, laughter.

Now he understood "Lambs to the slaughter." Raspberries and cat calls followed freely in the wake of this slight. He checked the band again before he counted in the first number. Andy and Harry seemed unphased by the audience's responses but Ludo and Barry were looking uneasier by the minute. There was nothing for it but to abandon the set list and think on his feet. He guessed his best option was the fastest and most furious numbers he could think of with as short a gap in-between them as was humanly possible. He could see the sweat rising on Andy's forehead as he got into his stride but for once Barry was putting him in the shade. Still the calls came.

"Hoy Mick Jagger's dad, got no songs by people still alive?"

"Try doing stuff they've heard off the telly, adverts and stuff, you know the one for the perfume where she's eating chocolate in the bath." Ludo's suggestion wasn't a bad one but the next batch of tunes were as curtly dismissed as the rest. Harry seemed oblivious…

it was clear, once he was playing he wasn't easily put off his stride.

Kyle closed his eyes and tried to imagine the cat calls were exclamations of excitement and encouragement… it was a big ask. As he opened his eyes at the end of "Giant Steps" he saw Harry wink at one of the girls in the front row. My God, the mad old sod was actually enjoying this. Still they ploughed on, neither side willing to give way.

Half way through he started to pray, as the announcement was made that the buffet was available. Hopefully they were all too hungry to use the food as projectiles. He got his wish as the girls set about the buffet with relish, accompanied by even more drinking. By the end of the first set he was as sweaty as the rest of the band. As the curtains closed behind them, Bobby shot through the drapes to the stage, yelling over the din behind as he went.

"Well done, you're alive… they liked you."

Kyle peeped through the curtains. He was keen to see if it was everybody the audience had it in for or just the band. Bobby mopped his balding brow as he took his place in the centre of the 'arena'. He could almost see the outsized Comperes' heart pounding through his shirt. The buffet, within minutes, looked like it had been hit by a plague of locusts and, with the food gone, the girls were soon restless again.

Bobby held on to the microphone stand with both hands. Even at a distance you could see his hand shaking. The audience, it was evident, could smell fear and Kyle was glued to the spectacle despite himself.

"Steady on, girls… you'll get your meat in good time. So are you enjoying yourselves?"

This elicited yet more raspberries and catcalls as well as one spirited request for him to "Show us your tackle, big Bob."

Bobby stared at the ceiling, eyes half closed as if in prayer as he went into his act.

"Now tell me girls, do you know why a woman's never been sent to the moon before?"

In a millisecond silence filled the room.

"Because it doesn't need tidying up yet."

A darker silence descended, Kyle knew that this was the worst thing that could happen. If they just ignored you, then you could say your piece and slope off, but this was the kind of stillness you got before the guillotine lopped your head off. Despite this, he couldn't stop watching the spectacle. Bobby kept his eyes firmly fixed on the damp patch on the ceiling, looking for divine inspiration.

"So why do men break wind more often than women? Because women can't keep their gobs shut long enough to build up the required pressure."

"Sexist bastard." yelled one of the younger girls. With one hand vice-like on the microphone stand and the other trying to get the sweat out of his eyes, Bobby, ever the determined pro, ploughed on.

"I was out shopping the other day when I saw six women beating up my Mother-in-law. As I stood there and watched, our neighbour said, "Well, aren't you going to help?" I replied, "No... six of them should be enough."

One girl laughed heartily which echoed maniacally around the otherwise deathly sombre hall before she wisely cut it short and the silence of the sisterhood was imposed again. Bobby mopped his head nervously looking for traces of blood. There were a flood of cat-calls now and the odd stray sausage roll lobbed his way as he desperately made a bid to get on the right side of the girls. It was painfully evident he was a drowning man.

"You know, girls, there's a funny man lives next door to me."

The line hung in the air like a condemned game bird for a split second.

"Why the fuck didn't you bring him with you." came the inevitable response.

This got the biggest laugh of night and it was clear he was done for. Kyle laughed despite himself... it was no joke though... the band had to go on and follow this at the end of the evening. Christ!

The whole crowd knew they had triumphed and that Bobby's performance was over. There was no come-back from a crack like that. He started his 'walk of shame' with as much dignity as he could muster even before the audience, as one, had started to chant "off, off, off". Kyle realised that the least he could do now was effect a swift return to the dressing room so Bobby didn't realise he had been party to it all.

Try as he might, Kyle couldn't ignore the increasing noise of the audience that permeated the dressing room's thin walls. The chant for Bobbie's removal had been overtaken by a thunderous call for "Linford" which finally shifted in to a demand for "Lunchbox". Kyle took in the scene around him in the shabby dressing room. For the strippers it seemed like this was all in a day's work; the band were less sanguine about the situation. There was a wall-shuddering cheer as the P.A. cranked out Abba's Gimmie, Gimmie, Gimmie (A Man after Midnight.) The man in question, Kyle assumed, must be Mr Lunchbox and there and then he made a mental note to kill Sid Chase at the first opportunity.

★

Dainty didn't fancy going through the repeat humiliation of looking like the World's worst wife just because she hadn't been at her scumbag ex's bedside since the poor dear had got his comeuppance at the hands of her former best friend. But if that's what it took... then the deception was inevitable but on top of that there was a whole hoo-ha about the visiting hours anyway. The Ward Sister had had to be tracked down in order to give her "exceptional permission in the circumstances." She could feel the opprobrium of the staff nurse as her eyes focused on the numerous shopping bags she had with her. Honestly, give some people a uniform and all of a sudden they were the head of a right wing military coup. In her defence, as she had walked through the hospitals corridors, she did admit to a small twinge of guilt at the genuine mishaps she had wished upon her ex-husband since his betrayal. It was a funny situation. If she came across her bridesmaid now she wasn't sure whether she'd shake her hand or slap her face. However, she was now being noble, coming here to cheer him up. She was sure that if the nurses had known the true situation they would recognise that she was the aggrieved party. But she would still keep the full facts to herself. She had some dignity... her mother had instilled that in her from day one.

She would probably come in again at least once or twice till he was back on his feet, which would allow him time to remember how fabulous she was. Then he would never see her again and serve him right.

According to the staff nurse, the bitch of a bridesmaid, her former best friend, had walked away with barely a scratch. When was she going to get hers? She had ruined a good... OK, an alright marriage, and now she had nearly killed the groom by driving like an idiot, in all probability. After more washing of hands, which entailed endless putting down and picking up of her bags, the nurse handed her a gown. The girl didn't look old enough to have a paper-round, let alone have peoples' lives in her hands. Once she had successfully navigated the less than flattering garment, she was led down a deathly silent corridor to a room marked 'Intensive Care'. The rigmarole around something as simple as visiting your Ex in hospital was starting to unnerve her... and then she saw him stretched out on the bed. Michael Anthony Fuller, aged thirty-five, compliance recruitment consultant, of Alderney Drive Leechmere, Sunderland. It was not what she had expected and it was not a sight for which she was prepared.

★

"I could do that, getting me kit off, easiest gig in the world," said Andy, who seemed completely unphased by the night's activity.

The remaining strippers looked him up and down.

"On a night like tonight, love, the floor's all yours. Mind, a word to the wise if they turn on you, you're on your own."

It was clear from the tone of Gloria's voice that he bore the scars that came with the job. Andy looked at the floor and mumbled incomprehensibly.

"No. I didn't think so," Gloria said, his voice a combination of bitterness and satisfaction.

Before Abba had managed to get through their second chorus, Linford staggered into the dressing room. He had been mobbed by the girls and looked like he had been in a bear fight.

"It would appear our ladies are a little feisty this evening." drawled Brokeback Duncan, without bothering to take his eyes from the mirror as he touched up his make-up.

Kyle could see that they had experienced this sort of reaction before and very little seemed to phase them. Their audience were just girls letting their hair down on their big night out and most of the injuries they sustained would be minor but it made "The Happy Man" seem a tranquil artistic haven by comparison.

"This is how a boy gets through a medical degree in the 21st century," winced Linford, shaking his head as he examined the scratches on his body. He reached into his holdall, pulled out a tube of anti-septic cream and patched himself up as best he could, with Brokeback Duncan taking care of the places he couldn't reach. Even in this situation Kyle could appreciate how the strippers pulled together so the show would go on, much as he had to do with the band, although it was something of a relief not to have to apply anything to any part of Barry, or any of the rest of them for that matter. Once Linford was patched up he sat wearily on one of the plastic-backed seats before turning to Kyle.

"They take no prisoners that mob. I'd hang on to your crotchets when you go back on boys. You better get out there, Dunc."

At this point Kyle was convinced that he could hear Barry above the din, sobbing from behind the toilet door. Nothing in Barry's life before this point had prepared him for being in the same room as a bunch of naked men. Before 'Dunc' left for the stage he turned to Kyle and asked him to pass the elastic band which was placed on the table beside him. It seemed a simple enough request which he was happy to comply with. There was a slight snap as 'Dunc' applied the band to his 'working tool'. Kyle, who was not use to seeing stationary applied to people's genitals, looked suitably stunned, contemplating the fingers which he had used to pass the item over with a degree of disgust.

"Makes it look its best" said 'Dunc.' "See!"

To Kyle's horror he did.

Chapter 29

The waiters glided around them as if on casters, as more and more expensive food and drink was delivered to their table. Charlotte felt more than content to do the eating, leaving Ethan free to do the vast majority of the talking.

"Seriously, you should practice in the states. Those guys get to print money for fun. The first party sues the second party, and the second party counter sues the first. Swear to God somewhere in America there's someone suing himself... twice. You can't lose."

"Or win?"

The bottle of Chassagne-Montrachet had eventually worked its magic and Charlotte felt like a girl again as Ethan continued.

"I've pretty much grown up around the law. Dad's firm was already a big player in NYC when I left Stanford, although these days he's more of a business man than a working lawyer. The thing is if I'd just sailed into my family's firm it would have put a lot of backs up, so here I am out in the world earning my spurs."

"Surely there's got to be something in between doing your thing at the Supreme Court and Peterson partners... besides the Atlantic."

"Well... and this is not for repeating but... we own you."

"Sorry... you what?"

"Well, it involved one consortium acquiring another ad infinitum but ultimately Peterson's recently became a branch of Kayblat Holdings, a conglomerate in which my family has a substantial, although not majority, shareholding. We cast our eyes over a bunch of places and this was part of a medium sized enterprise that filled in some corporate gaps for us. Somebody owns you and we own them. It's the usual minefield, we once made a move on a small company and after we unravelled the paperwork it turned out we already owned it."

"That's… that's… there are no words for what that is."

"Byzantine is a start but that doesn't go nearly close enough. Anyway, Petersons is small enough and out of the way and nobody knows my dirty secret, which at the minute is just how we'd like to keep it. The future of litigation is in celebrity and business law, especially in Europe. A little covertly gained inside knowledge of PR over the water is, the family reckons, a smart move for our portfolio."

"So when the boss gives you a hard time… technically you own her and she hasn't the foggiest?"

"Lovely as that sounds it's over egging the pudding a little. A firm which is part owned by my family has a majority stake in a number of PR firms around the globe, of which Peterson Partners is one. Sorry if that's not such sharp copy but that's the real truth of it."

"And you're never tempted to pull rank?"

"And blow the whole deal? That would be quite a crass stunt."

"I know, but just once?"

"There is no "just once", it's like a bee sting, you do it once and it's over."

"That is officially the coolest thing I've ever heard."

"You've led a sheltered life. Not a word though, promise."

★

Back in the dressing room Gloria turned her attention to Andy again.

"I suppose you must have powerful arms then, being a drummer?"

Kyle could see where this was going, Andy remained blissfully unaware.

"Actually, it's more about your wrists."

"Strong wrists?" purred Gloria "Let me see them."

Andy, whilst savvy at the workings of the female heart, was less sure of himself with Gloria. Once the penny dropped Kyle knew he was witnessing a rare thing, Andy embarrassed and confused in a matter of 'romance'. Women he could handle but six foot plus male strippers were clearly light years beyond his comfort zone.

"Where's Harry?" said Ludo. A bolt of terror ran down Kyle's spine as it dawned on him that in his enjoyment he had taken his eye off the ball.

"You can relax" said Andy, keen to discuss something else. "He's gone to get a reed for his sax from the van… said he'd split one."

"You gave him your key?" Kyle could feel the sweat, cold on his skin.

"Sure I did, it's not like he's going to drive it away is it?"

Within seconds Kyle was headed out to the wasteland behind the club where the van was parked; his one chance was to get to the van before Harry got his hands on the bottle of scotch. There was no sign of him by the vehicle as he began to search frantically for the whisky bottle. He wasn't aided in his endeavour by the pitch black of his surroundings. The van's interior light hadn't worked since the "Happy Man" debacle… then again even when it had it was so dim it only succeeded in making the place look darker still.

Perhaps Harry hadn't found the bottle, perhaps Harry hadn't even got there yet, perhaps he had actually split a reed, perhaps bears had secretly devised their own advanced water based sanitation system. He rummaged around blindly until, with a sick thud in his guts, he found the drained bottle minus the cap under the back seat. He was just taking in the full implication of his discovery when his attention was drawn to the ominous sound of wild saxophone coming from back inside the club.

*

Darkness had fallen and a few other guests had come in to enjoy the ambience and the good food. Charlotte had devoured enough to satisfy herself. She could relax. This was what life should be like.

"I'm not sure if I'd be up to defending class actions by multi-national corporations." she said, once the last of her main course had disappeared. "I'd feel happier engaged in getting a decent settlement for some worn out, underpaid, school dinner lady."

Ethan held his hands up in mock horror.

"Only the English factor guilt into their career structure. You hate your billionaires, we love ours."

"I won't be talked down to by someone from the Colonies." Charlotte countered, as she jabbed at him playfully with an unused fork.

"You're forgetting I've seen the way you English conduct yourselves in public and the debauchery it entails… how is Dainty by the way?"

"She rang me just as I was leaving. She's engaging in an intensive course of retail therapy."

★

Running as fast as he could Kyle re-entered the concert room to be greeted by the traumatizing sight of Harry, alone on stage, in nothing more than his underpants and socks playing saxophone like a man possessed. It was clear that the rest of the terrified band didn't know quite what to do.

"He's gone a bit New Year's Eve," offered Ludo, as Kyle caught up with them in the wings.

The audience, however, were having a ball as a chant of "Birdseye, Birdseye, Birdseye." began to ring out through the concert room due to Harry's passing resemblance to the fish finger touting Sea Captain.

As Harry's solo reached a crescendo he was, without warning, suddenly lofted into the air on the more than broad shoulders of Linford. Without missing a beat Harry segued into "The Stripper" by David Rose, like it was the most natural thing in the world to do.

Kyle surveyed the mayhem aghast. Where did they go from here? There would be no fancy gigs in the future now, not once word got out. No London audition, no recording session, no reconciliation… it was over… there was only one course of action that could save them.

In a flash Kyle was down to his underpants and marshalling the remaining band members, who had been rooted to the spot since Harry's singular entrance. He'd come this far they weren't going to go down without a fight. He tried to remember the motto of the SAS but it proved beyond him as he pushed the rest of the semi-naked band towards the stage and Harry.

"We've got a job to do, lads. Let's really make them dance."

Grabbing his sax he picked up "The Stripper" theme as Linford lowered Harry to the floor. After the initial shock the audience reacted like it was the best thing they'd ever seen in their lives. Before long he could see across the entire width and breadth of the club an outbreak of girls from eighteen to eighty gyrating against each other. Resembling nothing so much as 'Happy Hour' at a pole dancers' Christmas party. The song built to a second climax as he got Harry into a sonic duel, facing him as they traded solos sans clothing. Harry, even in this state, dazzled but Kyle knew that he was, possibly for the first time, at least making a match of it.

Before he could reflect on holding his own with Harry, a large pair of woman's pants landed over the bell of his sax. Harry, eyes closed, was oblivious as Kyle desperately tried to remove them. Then another pair of pants hit him square in the face as the cheers grew deafening.

They followed "The Stripper" with a rousing "When the saints go marching in". Kyle knew now, instinctively, which songs would work. A conga formed during "March of the Mods", containing most of the girls. It left the building only to snake back in minutes later with a number of traffic cones and what looked like a couple of dozen bags of chips on board. Kyle turned around, at the song's conclusion, to catch the rest of the real strippers doing their bit by working up a sweat with a dance routine effortlessly in keeping with the music. Gloria stood close to Andy and, when the music allowed, blew him kisses. Andy concentrated on his drums very, very hard.

The show was rounded off with an encore, the girls, arm in arm, singing "The White Cliffs of Dover" with the strippers forming a passable male voice choir at the side of the stage. Even Bobby was admitted back into the fold to conduct proceedings.

"We didn't even have to call the cops this time… result!" Bobby said at the denouement, smiling as he made his way off stage, mopping his brow.

★

The lights had been turned down low and candles had been lit on each table. Charlotte moved her chair beside Ethan's as he flicked through the photographs on his iPhone. She could still taste the clafoutis and cherries which, to her own surprise, had won out over the chocolate ganache. It had been truly delicious and she had demolished it… you weren't meant to demolish anything on a date if you were a girl. You were meant to pick at your food wistfully. Well, this wasn't a proper date and she wasn't going to pay a small fortune just to manoeuvre clafoutis with black cherries round her plate before it was taken away by a waiter, never to be seen again. She made a vow to return alone at a later date and order the ganache for all three courses and have done with it. Ethan, meanwhile, scrolled through the pictures unaware of her inner dessert demons.

"Here it is. This is home, well, my favourite home."

"You have more than one?"

Ethan nodded.

"But you're not going to tell me how many because it's embarrassing, right?"

He nodded again.

"Not that we were short beforehand but my dad bought it after he represented a major fast food outlet in a libel case in 2005."

"A major fast food outlet? Aren't they the bad guys?"

"Well the Judge ultimately described them as being prone to consistent lapses of moral judgement."

"So they're... "

"The bad guys, OK hands up. You win, 'Your Honour'".

★

Kyle sat on the stage and savoured his pint. He could relax. For once in his life he had snatched victory from the jaws of defeat and it felt good. He savoured the beer all the more as it had come courtesy of Bobby. He tried to make sense of what they had just experienced but ultimately he thought it was best not to analyse it too far. Whatever they had done, it had worked. Andy, meanwhile, stuck very close to Kyle, unable to contemplate being the object of affection of a six foot six skinhead with a girl's name.

With the show over the punters joined an orderly queue at the back of the concert room. Both the audience and venue looked like a bomb had hit it. Some of the girls were being supported by their more sober sisters as the night's celebration finally began to catch up with them. His attention was drawn to the top of a queue where two of the barmaids were dispensing what looked like large sponge cakes complete with icing, one each from several large boxes, as the girls tottered their way into the night, most of them still singing.

"Fantastic lads, fantastic" said the Bobby as a grin broke out across his face a mile wide. "Your finale is a bit full on, isn't it?"

Kyle had prepared exactly what he wanted to say.

"Well, to be honest it's how we end most of our gigs, apart from the weddings. Mr Chase, our Agent, insists on it."

"By, you musicians are a funny breed. Still, I knew you wouldn't let me down. Are you free next month?" Bobby had clearly been taken in by every word he had been told.

"I'll need to check my diary." Kyle knew better than to just accept a gig. Let the Compere think that his diary was full to bursting. He flicked through his phone, looking at an imaginary planner.

"I'm sure we could sort you something out, a hundred quid a man and you can pick the songs, a hundred and twenty and you can sing some of them."

If this was a way to keep a roof over his head and get enough cash to record in "Trinity Heights" with Harry, then that's what they'd have to do. As the strippers departed into the night Gloria caught Andy's eye and gave him a wink Andy busied himself with moving some cases and didn't return the kind gesture, despite encouragement from almost everyone in the band.

As the last of the girls left the building Kyle's curiosity finally got the better of him as he turned to Bobby.

"What's with the cakes?"

The Compare looked sanguine for a moment.

"Second Thursday in the month for three and a half years they've been coming here, letting their hair down, having a night like bears in a bun factory and then going home and telling their hubbies they've been at a cookery class. Deadlier than the male? You bet your bloody life they are. Now, next month, can you do some other stuff... you know... the classics... 'Blue Suede Shoes', 'Hound Dog', 'Simply the Best'?

Chapter 30

The lights were low and her coffee felt cold in her grasp… stone cold. She couldn't remember when she had got here or even how, but she knew she had been in the small café for some time. It was pitch black outside and there was little in the way of traffic on the main road. From the look of the décor it was a French bistro with lots of raffia furniture and pictures of the old country on the walls. The place was devoid of customers and, if she was honest, she couldn't remember if anyone had ever been in. From the noises coming from the kitchen it was clear that the café's owners were looking to close. She felt down at her side… there was nothing there, nothing at all, all those new clothes gone! She hadn't said a word… couldn't say a word, she'd just dropped the bags and left. She thought it would have been plaster casts and bandages, not him unconscious and hooked up to lots of machines looking more dead than alive.

"I'm sorry."

Dainty looked up. The man was in his early sixties, overweight and no more French than her but there was an avuncular smile behind the overgrown beard. She followed his gaze to the clock on the wall.

"I'm sorry, but we're looking to lock up now."

Oh God! If that genuinely was the time then she'd missed the last metro. As she came to she realised he had come to talk to her because the rest of the staff were too frightened. Why? The kind of thing she'd been through happened to people every day; everyday all over the world… it was nothing special. She was just dealing with a sudden shock in the best way she could.

"I'm sorry I've had some bad news... have I been here very long?"

The man smiled and clasped his hands around a tea cloth like it was a set of rosary beads as he spoke.

"Whatever it is that's troubling you, it will seem easier after a night's sleep. Shall I call you a taxi?"

"No thank you. I'm fine, you've been kind enough already."

She could get a cab herself or better still she could walk, now that she didn't have the tiresome bags to cope with. She stepped out into the empty street, not a soul anywhere to be seen and she was glad of it.

★

The 'Irish coffee' which was Charlotte's one concession to the 'hard stuff' rounded the meal off. She didn't want Ethan thinking she had a problem, but surely an 'Irish coffee' didn't count. It always felt like she was being covered by a warm duvet at the first sip and she genuinely felt happy and content for the first time in ages. There wasn't anything in the world she couldn't accomplish, now that she was free.

"Don't you believe in synchronicity?"

She had to confess that she did and that it's was a pretty good offer. She could easily picture herself in Manhattan. It felt right, like she had been born to live there. Although she had to admit to herself that this was partly fuelled by having watched Paul Newman, yet again, in *The Verdict*. It might have been set in Boston but it was close enough to NYC and a million miles away from the oppressed dinner ladies of Sunderland.

"I'm finishing my contract with "Peterson Partners" next month and I'm headed back to the States, where I can prepare the way for you. You can follow me over in the New Year. You'd work for Dad and in return he'd put you through college. He needs someone smart and female; they're pretty serious about quotas over there.

You get to start off with one of the biggest law firms in the City. We get the hot, new English legal student."

"Hot" as in capable?"

"Absolutely."

"I'm finding it difficult to come up with objections."

"I should think so. There's a whole world of rich experiences out there to take advantage of?"

As he said this he shot her the kind of look that had led to overpopulation the World over. She had better be careful. She hadn't even kissed him yet. A waiter arrived at the table and handed him the bill.

"He called you by your name. Do you eat here regularly?"

"Sure, or I have them deliver sometimes. Most places in the world, but particularly in the States, having money oils the wheels and makes your life run that bit more smoothly.

"Shall we just split this?" she said and she very much meant it.

"I'm sure you can pay me back in time" he said, as he settled up.

★

Kyle wallowed in the upbeat feeling around him as the van navigated its lonely way back up the A19. Another successful gig, another offer in the pipeline and a residency at that. Things had definitely picked up. He was really getting fired up about the idea of recording with Harry. By the time they had a few more gigs under their belts they would be in top shape for it. They would go into "Trinity Heights" recording studio, hidden in the outskirts of Newcastle in Denton Burn and the nearest thing to heaven he had ever experienced. They would create something there to show the faint hearts what they were capable of and put Harry back on the map into the bargain. Perhaps in fifty years' time someone would be paying over the odds for a copy of that recording on EBay. OK, so Harry had lapsed a little, they could all plead guilty to that at one time or another. They'd managed to get away with it and he had been truly apologetic afterwards. Next time he would get the whole band to keep an eye on him… God, that was the London gig… a wedding anniversary and hardly likely to be a booze free affair. Well, it was too late to back out now and he felt a little more battle hardened than before. He'd definitely earned his spurs with the last few gigs and he knew it. Whatever shenanigans Harry had in store for them they were going to London where they would, hopefully, both make their mark!

Harry liked being in the van, he liked the atmosphere amongst the band, he liked the smell of sweat and diesel, he liked the romance of going round the country and sparkling for the people and then disappearing to do it all over again somewhere else. He took a swig from his beer and smiled to himself. The talk turned to Louise and their colourful past and even their future. These boys had given him a new lease of life. They might not be the best players in the world but they weren't bad and the sax player was shaping up at a rate of bloody knots. He'd have to start digging in himself if he didn't want to be surpassed.

"I'm meeting with Carol's parents tomorrow." They had just crossed the border into County Durham and Ludo sounded serious for once. Harry shook his head and handed him a beer.

"God, I really ballsed things up when I met Louise's folks in the sixties" he ruminated.

"I was getting on famously with them both, her Mum was all hugs and home cooking and her Dad had played the bugle in the "Band of the Black Watch" so we had something going there already. We'd stuffed our faces, three courses, and her old man starts breaking out his twelve year old malt. I thought 'I'm in here'. The food I got in the Nick was a darn sight better than the usual fare I knocked up for myself so when I said that the meal had reminded me of the grub that we'd had in prison I meant it as a compliment but somehow it all went a bit frosty after that.

★

Dainty turned the key in the door. It was a relief to find no one home. At first she didn't bother to put on any lights or take her coat

259

off. She had to keep reminding herself that she'd done nothing wrong, that all the stuff in her head didn't count. If she'd wanted to cause him physical harm she'd have done it long ago. She had just been letting off some steam and she was entitled to do that. He had behaved badly; really badly. Nobody could deny that. Nobody could blame her for the things she had thought and said. God what was she going to tell her mother. Her mother had doted on him and had welcomed him into her extended family with open arms once she'd let her guard down. Her mum had been angrier at his betrayal than her own daughter.

Dainty knew it was the most stupid things she could do but she still went and unearthed the few mementos she had kept from her fateful wedding day, locked away for posterity and never to be looked at again. By the low wattage of her bedside lamp, drink in hand, she went through the keep-sakes from their first meeting to their last across a solicitor's desk. A picture from her eighteenth birthday party, a time when they had both been naïve and in love. A receipt from their first stay in a hotel where, in a drunken fug, they had managed to destroy the three condoms they thought were more than enough to see them leave their virginities behind them and a half empty bottle of his aftershave whose scent even now transported her to a time when they had meant everything to each other. Eventually this, as she always knew it would, kick-started the tears she should have shed months earlier.

★

The journey had seemed much shorter tonight as they began the process of dropping off the various band members. Kyle didn't know how he'd managed to get through the gig, but he had and he was shattered. It was no good worrying about how Harry would behave on the gig if he didn't manage to get him there. It would take some degree of planning. He had done gigs in London where he'd driven down and played two sets before immediately driving back. He doubted he could physically handle that anymore, let alone Harry.

They had a couple of weeks to sort it out and hopefully get another rehearsal, or two, in beforehand so they'd be in peak condition. He hadn't heard from Jacqui Drinkwater but something in his bones told him she was going to be there. Harry had opened up a door for him and he was charging straight through it and nothing or no one was going to stop him anymore.

Eventually they crossed the River Wear and turned off the A19 before heading for Harry's bed-sit. The van pulled up at the dilapidated flats as various ne'er-do-wells went about their business under the cover of darkness. Before he took his leave, sax in hand, he leant in through the open van window and handed Kyle the scrap of paper with Louise's number on it.

"Can you hang on to this? My phone doesn't work and I'd only lose it, keep it safe somewhere. You know, tonight, just a bit… it felt like the old times. You're alright, you lot." Looking truly happy, he kissed Kyle's hand as he made his way into his shabby dwelling. It grieved Kyle that a man of Harry's talents lived in such squalid poverty. But he had the bit between his teeth now and he was going to put Harry back on top come hell or high water.

The van continued on its way. Even it seemed to be behaving itself of late.

"I never thought I'd say this" Andy said, as he prepared to take his leave, "but I'm getting fond of the old duffer."

"Not so much of the 'old'," said Barry.

"Got to admit he knows that horn inside out," Andy offered as they pulled away.

Kyle put the van into fifth gear with a smile. He hadn't thought about Charlotte for almost an hour now, which was something of an achievement.

Chapter 31

It was a grey, cold Saturday morning. Kyle gently stirred a second spoon of sugar into his tea as he contemplated his lot. The "bowling ball" still lurked there but as long as he stayed busy he could cope. He was getting use to lugging it around. The club where they had played the previous week had booked the band for the "Ladies nights" for the rest of the following year at £120 a man and a very favourable review of the "Black Rabbit" gig had appeared on the "Be-bop Spoken Here" website. Admittedly it was back of a fag packet stuff but he reckoned if he could take 10% of every gig they did for the next few months he could pay for the recording session… as long as he didn't have to pay his rent or eat. There was nothing for it, he would have to push harder for some peripatetic work. For the first time in his life he was going to have to do some hustling. His lofty plans were suddenly interrupted by his phone which had become located, for reasons he could no longer remember, in a pile of clean laundry. He didn't recognise the number but as he answered it he recognised the voice.

"Hello, is that Kyle Johnson?"

"It is."

"You left me a message regarding a vacancy in my band, my name's Jacqui Drinkwater."

"Right… OK… sorry, yes. I rambled on a bit, I got a bit overwhelmed."

"You made me laugh; my dad said Harry Crabb always made him laugh. I'm still using a few Deps. I haven't found quite the right person to fill the job; this gig's the thirteenth of December right? In an ideal world I'll be there, I might even bring dad; he'd love to see Harry again. But if the worst comes to the worst I'll send someone from the band along. Anyway, tell me a little about yourself... "

Having Jacqui Drinkwater on the other end of the phone and taking him seriously as a musician was intoxicating. He'd always imagined that it would have unnerved him, but if anything, now that the prospect had reared its head, he rather relished the notion of performing for her, or even her and her Dad... Jazz Royalty!

At the phone call's conclusion he was fizzing with energy. He made a start on clearing up the rest of the house... anything was possible now. Within an hour parts of it looked like a reasonable human being lived there if you squinted. You couldn't eat your dinner off the floor yet but it was at least possible to eat it from the kitchen table. Whatever else he did, he mustn't dwell on the notion that, had he done all of this sooner, he might not have lost the one person who truly mattered to him. There was too much water under the bridge to get back in contact with Charlotte now. She was the person he most wanted to tell about the phone call and his audition. But now? Now, it would it just look like a desperate attempt to win her back. He'd finally done what she had begged him to do and yet she was the last person in the world he could tell.

★

For a few days Dainty had said nothing to anyone and spent most of the time trawling through the memories of her marriage to see if she could find any way of blaming herself, swinging dementedly between self-recrimination and anger. Charlotte was busy with plans for a possible move to the US, which hadn't improved Dainty's mood any and their paths barely crossed. The more time passed, the harder Dainty found it to broach the subject, especially as Charlotte seemed to be so taken with the idea of working abroad. Her closest friend leaving her, just when she needed her most. Charlotte had never met Michael and if all she had to go on was Dainty's own description of him then she'd probably think the world no worse a place for his accident. Now, though, she could see her flatmate knew something was up. If she didn't come clean soon Charlotte would start blaming their living arrangements for her low mood, which was about as far away from the truth as was humanly possible. She wouldn't let it stop Charlotte going to America. Bringing her and Ethan together had been her big success. She would drive Charlotte to the airport herself if she had to… gun in hand. Eventually she steeled herself to raise it over breakfast on Saturday when they hadn't got to dash out to work. She entered the kitchen to find Charlotte engrossed in the prospectus for an American university. Holding on to a chair for added support, she began.

"You know I've been a little uptight of late and I want you to know that it's nothing you've done… really, nothing. The thing is… it's him… my Ex… Michael. There was an accident… his car… she was driving… there's not much that's left of who he was."

She could see from Charlotte's face that she wasn't sure at first what kind of response to give.

But as ever her reaction was perfect. There were no words she just held on to her until she felt she could cope with the world again. Quite what her mother's response would be to her standing by her man was another matter.

★

Kyle was in the process of drying the last plate of the washing up and trying to get the tune of "The Stripper" out of his head where it had been lodged for the past week, when there was a knock at the door. He opened it to find two uniformed Police officers, a man and a woman.

"Sorry to bother you Sir. I'm looking for a Mr Johnson, Kyle Johnson."

"Yes that's me. There isn't anything the matter is there? If there is, at a wild guess it involves a Mr Crabb… am I right?"

None of Harry's brushes with the law were what you would call serious and at Harry's age he was pretty sure it would be a slap on the wrist or at worst having to pay a fine. Nothing was going to stop the London gig happening now even if that meant paying bail and, anyway, these days you could rack up a dozen cautions before they incarcerated you.

"Yes Sir, it is about Mr Crabb. Do you mind if we come in. This is PC. Fortnum, I'm PC. Mason."

"You're kidding."

"Yes, it's an unfortunate pairing."

"I suppose you've heard all the jokes."

"Pretty much, Sir... if I could just... "

Kyle couldn't resist a gag at their expense.

"Well I don't want to 'hamper' your investigation, that sort of thing."

"Yes, Sir... if we might... "

The other police officer, a girl in her late twenties, was beginning to look a little uncomfortable.

"Truncheon meat past its sell buy date, sorry! Yes... yes, I'm done now, sorry... about Harry?"

"Sir, do you know a Harold Arthur Crabb of 17a Crimea house, Harrington Sunderland?"

"Yes. I do. What's he done?"

"I'm sorry to have to tell you this, Sir. I'm afraid Mr Crabb is dead. He was found in his flat late last night. We were tipped off anonymously, possibly by an intruder. The neighbours weren't too forthcoming. Yours was the only contact address we could find at his home... "

"What happened?" It was his own voice but he wasn't conscious of speaking. He couldn't remember if he was sitting down already or if he had just sat down.

"The Coroner has yet to confirm the cause of death. I shouldn't say anything but between ourselves there was no sign of any suspicious circumstances or of anyone else involved at the scene. Were you a friend or a relative?"

He desperately wanted to say they were blood brothers but he knew that wasn't what the officer meant.

"… I have a number for his ex-wife."

★

Dainty had walked her feet off, by now she must have busted the limit of her credit cards ten times over. She walked purposefully to her next port of call. She was pleased with her purchases, everyone had given her the sort of life affirming tingle that simply had to be good for you. She didn't know why, just that in this case in particular it wasn't something she could do without due care and attention. If that meant it came at top dollar then she would worry about it later. She wanted the stuff; she worked damn hard all week, so she was having it. She put down the bags and worried about sizes, if anything wasn't right or didn't fit it could go back. There wasn't much she was good at but she was good at this. She lugged her purchases onto the bus, yes she could walk the short distance but dammit she was shattered. Within fifteen minutes she was walking back through the sterilised portals towards ward forty six. She knew she could forget about the items she had abandoned on her first visit, hanging by now in all probability, in some junior staff nurse's wardrobe. It could count as her donation to the "Big Society" although size fourteen was as big as she was willing to admit to.

But, as she'd told Charlotte when she had come clean to the reason for her black mood, "I know he didn't exactly make the running for 'husband of the year' but I did love him once and we did say, before God, till death do us part, so I'm going to do what I can for him." She hadn't meant her voice to break at the time but it did.

"Can you tell me, has anyone else visited since the accident?" The staff nurse looked up and smiled wearily.

"Well, obviously I'm not here all the time but I've been on the day shift since he came in and as far as I know it's only been you…

oh, and a bunch of half a dozen lads with sports bags in tow, who came in about three days ago… they didn't say much, didn't stay long.

She washed her hands for the umpteenth time before the rigmarole of putting on the gown; it hadn't got any more fetching in the interim. He was still the only one in the intensive care ward, which she was thankful for. They could have some privacy there.

"Tough luck, I'm back." There was, to no great surprise, no response.

At first, chatting to him seemed a little odd, forced. After the split she had been determined to be sitting pretty, on top the next time they met, but this wasn't the kind of victory she had envisioned. Sitting by his side, she dabbed at his mouth with a small damp sponge.

"I'm not getting much of a reaction… can he hear me?"

The busy nurse was non-committal and soon gone with, "You can't expect miracles, this isn't Holby City," as her parting shot.

"There, that's a little better… I should have read the small print… "For better or for worse and where's that "Horizontal Harpy" now, now that you need her? Making big spending plans for your compensation money, that's where. Come on, we can try some of these on now and I can take them back if necessary."

She delved into her bags and produced the expensive pyjamas, dressing gowns and even a cashmere cardigan. She'd forgotten about the various tubes and wires that covered his body, perhaps the nurses could try the stuff on him when she was gone, but she wanted him to look his best and for people to know that someone, out there, still cared for him. Most of his family had long since moved to Spain and hadn't even turned up for their wedding.

She chatted to him about the weather, applying for Charlotte's job, her credit card bill, Charlotte again and her break-up with Kyle. Anything really, just to make some sort of connection. As she sat there, she was thinking that he hadn't been a bad lot all told, just a weak one… there had been some good times before the pain.

"It's a good job somebody loves you. I'll pop in at the weekend so you'd better come up with some ideas about where you're taking me on holiday. I'm game for almost anything but I'd put a skiing holiday fairly well down the list. I have no sense of balance."

As he walked into the room Dainty caught her breath. She knew in an instant that this was the man who was going to tell her what had happened and more importantly what the future held. He was old and his dress was reassuringly eccentric, a pair of spectacles hung on a chain around his neck and she could see the remains of "the soup of the day" still on his tie, which annoyed her a little after all the trouble she had taken to be completely bacteria free.

"Hello, I'm Mr Porterfield. Now, I don't know how much they've told you. I'm afraid the poor fellow has suffered an extra-dural haematoma as a result of a traumatic brain injury... a swelling caused by a bit of a knock to his noggin. I'd like to tell you that there's going to be some sort of improvement in his situation but whilst anything is possible I wouldn't get your hopes up too much."

Dainty's mind was a blur. She didn't know anything about brain injuries. What was she meant to say in the circumstances?

"Is he in any sort of pain?"

"Almost certainly not... he's probably not aware of anything much. Still, don't let that stop you... because we're never really sure about what's going on inside. This is still very early days and there could be an improvement at any time in the next couple of years but I wouldn't plan your life around it happening. Sorry I can't be more helpful."

"No. Thank you. I'm sure you're right."

"The one thing I can guarantee you is that there's no pain."

She shook his hand as he left. It was easy to see how people began to see surgeons as Gods even though this one couldn't do much more than tell her the game was up and it was all over. She stayed for a little while after and updated him on the football, Sunderland had beaten Newcastle and if he could hear her she was sure that that, more than anything else in the world, would cheer him up... silly boy.

As she got up to leave she took a framed photograph from her bag and after giving it a wipe placed it on the drawers by his bed. The picture was one from their wedding day which, with the aid of some glue and scissors, she had managed to patch up quite well. She kissed him on the cheek and quietly left the room.

★

Kyle stared at the ceiling above him trying to get his head around the day's events. That would teach him a lesson… it had been the first time since his split with Charlotte that he hadn't awoken to a feeling of heavy dread, a feeling that had now returned tenfold. One thing he knew for sure, he had to get hold of Louise before the police did. She mustn't hear it from them. It would soften the blow a little, coming from him. To think that it had taken so much time and energy getting the courage up to ring Jacqui Drinkwater, which seemed like small potatoes compared to what he had to do now. The last phone call he had made to Louise had brought her and her Ex-husband together, now he had to tell her that Harry was dead. He'd brought them together for his own ends and all it was going to cause was pain and misery for all concerned. He pulled out his mobile and flicked through to Louise's number. He knew from experience that putting it off would only make the task increasingly hard. The phone began to ring… what would he say? The one thing he knew for sure was he couldn't just leave a message.

"Hello, Mrs Campbell… Louise… its Kyle… Kyle Johnson."

"Well, well, the young apprentice himself. To what do I owe the pleasure? The bastard's not after a sub already is he?"

She gave a short laugh as she said it, but when he didn't join in he could hear the apprehension in her voice.

"It's not good is it… how bad?"

"I'm so, so, sorry" was as much as it took for the penny to drop. "Was it quick?"

There seemed no point in saying anything other than it had been and hoping that that in time the facts would bear him out. There were no tears from the other end but he could tell it was a struggle.

"I hope you don't mind, I gave the police your number."

"No of course not… we're going to have to do right by him now."

"I want to pay… for the funeral." Kyle didn't know where his offer had come from only that it had and that it was right. He owed Harry and Louise.

There was a long pause.

"You realise we're talking upwards of £4,000 here?"

Kyle swallowed hard; with the best will in the world there was no way he could afford even a tenth of that. While he was still coming to terms with the figure, Louise spoke.

"Don't worry, I know from painful experience the financial wherewithal of jazz musicians. I might be able to take out a loan through my union but you're going to have to help me with the practical stuff, what with me stuck here in Edinburgh. I was his and he was mine and this is the last chance I have to do anything for him and I'll not see him go without, not now."

Kyle lay stationary on his bed for some time after the call, he wasn't sure how long but it was starting to get dark. Eventually he pulled out his phone and flicked through to Charlotte's number. She'd never actually met Harry so it wasn't much of an excuse but he wanted her, needed her, by his side and the sooner the better. By the time night had fallen completely the phone was back in his pocket, unused. This was about him and Harry and he was going to have to handle it himself.

Chapter 32

Charlotte looked at the chaos covering the room that she had called home for the past month and then returned to filling in the F1 Visa form. It would be months before going to America was finalised but, according to Ethan, visas could take forever. She wasn't keen on paper work and certainly not the sort that was this obtrusive but it was, she realised, a necessary evil. She had procrastinated enough, now she was determined not to walk away from it until it was done. How quickly your life could change. It had only been a fortnight since her first date with Ethan and here she was preparing to travel to the other side of the World for a new career. Before she left she would have to do something really nice for Dainty, who had been a brick of late despite having her own trials. As she worked her way through the questionnaire, delving as it did into her medical history and finances, she realised Ethan had been right. Once you had money, or someone with money behind you, life in general got a lot easier and a lot more promising. She had never truly realised her financial advantages as a child. Perhaps in retrospect, she had needed her time with Kyle to realise what it was like to be relatively poor. She certainly knew, as she listed Ethan's father as her sponsor, that it was unlikely that anyone would give her a hard time at immigration, not if they wanted to keep their job. He was a smart and powerful man who always got what he wanted and she was only too glad to have him batting on her side.

It was only when she reached the question "How long do you intend to stay in the U.S" that she faltered. But she couldn't dawdle over it too long, she was meeting Ethan for a drink and she didn't want to be late again. Eventually she sealed the last of the two letters that would determine her future, one to the U.S. Immigration service and one to Columbia University in New York State. She had done it; her life was moving on, she was one rung up the ladder she had desperately wanted to climb for so long. It was something of a blessing not to have time to think too deeply about what these missives would set running. She would just pull over at the first letterbox she saw and set the thing in motion.

Leaving Dainty's flat she looked wistfully at her old Ford Fiesta, which was looking more and more like a veteran from a stock car race. There were some things she would miss when she left the UK for her bright new world but you really had to be a sad sap to feel guilty about abandoning an inanimate object, even a loyal one.

★

"I'm not at my desk right now but please leave a message after the beep, unless you're George Clooney and if it is you, George, leave me alone. For the last time, it's over."

There were a few bars of Patsy Cline singing "Your Cheating Heart" before the beep. In the days that had followed Kyle's first call, he had got used to hearing Louise's answer-phone message. They rang each other daily as they planned the funeral and pieced together the missing gaps in Harry's existence. This time Louise picked up before the song kicked in.

"In the absence of any other family, I've assumed responsibility as Harry's next of kin. I'm just having to go by my gut instinct at the minute and the things he told me when we were still… "

He instinctively understood that it was easier for Louise not to say the word out loud, that if she didn't say "When we were still married." then she could pretend they had never been and that was easier to bear.

Life felt strange in the week after Harry's death; events came thick and fast whilst the individual hours still managed to drag like time in a dentist's waiting room. He was astonished at the instruments of state that swung into action in the aftermath of a death. Doctors, coroners, pathologists, had his Mother had to cope with all this when his Father died? He was nine years old... what use would he have been.

His conscience pricked him then. Tomorrow, without fail, he would ring his mum.

"He didn't have a doctor? Why would the silly bastard not have himself a doctor?"

This one he could answer for Louise, Harry had let it slip during the drink they had before the Norham gig.

"He was afraid of being found by the tax man. They caught up with him sometime in the late nineties when he was still in Hackney and they claimed he owed all manner of back taxes from his years of success, probably money that other people had trousered for the most part. That was why he moved back up to Sunderland and went incognito."

"But a doctor wouldn't tell the tax man where he was."

"I know that and you know that but Harry... ?"

"The body is with the coroner, there'll have to be an autopsy but they all but told me it was his heart... it always was big and flawed." Louise sighed.

Kyle could hear the sadness in her voice but he couldn't stay on the phone.

"I'm going to have to leave you shortly. The Vicar is coming round... not something that I ever thought I'd hear myself say."

There was that laugh of Louise's again as he said it. They were doing alright between them, buoying each other up so they could do what had to be done.

"Probably just as well. I've got someone due to discuss about getting a loan. I'll let you know how it goes."

He wished he could help financially but his own situation was still pretty dire. The London gig was going to pay quite well but could they still play it in the circumstances?

"And don't forget Harry's favourite song. If the Vicar gives you any earache about it I'll talk to him… I don't think you'll have any trouble though. When are you due to meet him?"

"Any minute."

"Shouldn't you be off then?"

"No, his mother lives two streets away so he said it was as easy to pop round here if I wanted."

"Well, take care of yourself and chin up… with Harry not here you're going to have to blow that horn of yours just that bit harder."

How would he have managed without Louise?

He looked around the flat. It wasn't quite as tidy as he had hoped but in the circumstances he was sure the Vicar would overlook it. He'd prepared some sandwiches, he wanted everything to be welcoming, they had some pretty serious stuff to navigate. His hopes and schemes for the future had disappeared in an instant and now here he was organising a funeral. He tried to content himself with the notion that out of nowhere he'd had the privilege of meeting Harry Crabb and that no matter how brief their friendship, it'd had a lasting effect on him.

There was no doubt that Harry counted as family now. The last funeral that had affected him this deeply was his fathers but he hadn't even been allowed to attend, his mum had considered him too young to go at nine years old… she was probably right.

The band had all offered to help in whatever way necessary including the cost, even Andy. All that remained now was to wait for the Vicar's arrival to discuss the arrangements. Kyle gave the working surfaces in the kitchen one last wipe… it would probably count against him at St. Peter's gate if he gave botulism to one of God's representatives on earth.

★

Charlotte got to the wine bar with seconds to spare. At least that's what she had planned; the truth of it was that a puncture had ruined everything. All done up with somewhere to go and now a very flat car tyre to change. She was, from experience, very adept at changing wheels and at least, she thought, as she got to grips with the problem, it wasn't raining. It would have been easier in daylight but no... the absence of rain was the big plus. She'd changed too many tyres for Kyle's bloody band not to know that a downpour was the killer. In any other circumstance it would have been quite therapeutic. She would have been driving away within fifteen minutes although she had to spend an extra ten turning down offers of help from men. Was that a good thing or not? She wasn't sure. Would they have stopped to help her if she'd been in her sixties? She decided on this occasion to give the weaker Sex the benefit of the doubt. She looked at herself in the car's mirror before she pulled away, bitterly regretting her decision to wear a white blouse but what the hell, it could have been worse, she'd rung Ethan so there was no real harm done.

Ethan ordered them both a drink as she took the stool next to his in the swish new wine bar that was still getting over the festivities of its opening night. He eyed her top disapprovingly.

"You want to change that?"

"Sure, but thirteen miles from home? I don't think it's really worth it."

"You still haven't got it yet, have you? The reason you have money is to employ people to make these problems go away." He took out his IPhone.

"I can get my PA to deliver something to you here in forty-five minutes, an hour tops."

"Your PA? You're kidding me?"

"No, at the moment it looks as though I'm on a date with a car mechanic. If we give her your keys she could let herself in... "

For a second they contemplated each other silently.

"I'm thinking that's a no then?" he said at last.

Charlotte took a deep breath.

"Is it really that important? It's a little oil and dirt."

His expression made her look around at her immaculately attired companions in the fashion-conscious bar. She did stick out like a sore thumb.

★

Kyle ushered the Vicar into the flat. He liked him on sight for no other reason than he reminded him of Noel from "The Black Rabbit"... well-scrubbed, urbane and in his early sixties. The moment they shook hands Kyle knew he could relax. Tea was brewed and sandwiches taken. They discussed hymns, the reading and the order of service. No flowers, they had decided but donations to Al-Anon.

The vicar was waxing lyrical. "You know, I met Mr Crabb when I lived in London. He held court in "The Coach and Horses" in Soho. He ran with a very interesting crowd, some marvellous gigs in all manner of dives. I played a little myself so obviously I was in thrall to him and his various outfits."

That the Vicar knew anything about jazz was a plus, that he had known Harry personally was a big comfort. His worry had been that the funeral would be an impersonal affair and not what he wanted or more importantly what Harry deserved, which was a celebration of his life and art. He couldn't put him back on top anymore but he could let the people, or at least some of the people, know that Harry wasn't just some old wino "has been" who died alone in a decrepit flat.

"I was wondering, have you considered playing some music during the service, perhaps one of Harry's tunes."

"You mean actually play it live?" It was a wonderful idea. Over a second pot of Earl Grey they sorted through the details. He had been unsure how to broach the subject but the Reverent Heavysides took the notion of the congregation singing "Devil May Care" in his stride. He would say a few words and then the band would play. Obviously it would have to be one of Harry's tunes. The Vicar had referred to them as Harry's band. Kyle liked that, it felt like something had been handed on, passed down.

It was all settled and so much easier than he had imagined… it made him understand, perhaps for the first time, that death, even of outstanding jazz musicians was a natural thing. It was all set for the 13th of December which gave him five days to pull everything together. It was only when he saw the details down in black and white that he clicked why the date had caused him so much unease. The London gig, December 13th, the wedding anniversary of Sir John Lindhope. Kyle's head had been so full of Harry and the funeral that he hadn't thought ahead. They couldn't do the London gig now, not the day of Harry's funeral and anyway what would be the point when the person it was all about was dead and gone.

An hour later he informed Sid Chase that due to circumstances beyond their control there would be no performance in London. To his surprise Sid sounded mortified, said he would inform Sir John and told him he would be coming to the funeral. He couldn't decide whether this was a good thing or whether Harry would be turning in his grave as Sid headed north in an attempt to crowbar a last 17.5 % out of him. Then there was Jacqui Drinkwater to phone. Again, it was a difficult phone call to make but it seemed less daunting to talk to Jacqui Drinkwater than before. Like a lot of singers she knew how to put people at their ease.

"My dad will be really upset. We've just accepted a gig together, out of the country, otherwise we'd both be there but I'm sure the place will be heaving. I'm so sorry. The stories he's told me about what the pair of them got up to in the sixties were mind-boggling. I wish I'd had the opportunity to meet him. We seem a pretty tame bunch today by comparison. Are you bearing up ok?"

It didn't seem right to talk about the vacancy in her band. Harry had appeared in his life and seemed like a means to an end but when it actually came down to it his friendship with Harry was more important than the music itself. He understood that now in a way he probably hadn't before. The one time he'd stepped up to the plate and this had happened. Still his tribulations were slight compared to the pain that Louise would be going through. Whatever else he did he would have to make sure that there wasn't just him and Louise at the funeral.

★

Charlotte stared at her drink and made a mental note that she wouldn't wash the blouse; no she would hang it up as it was and would make a point of wearing it, oil and all, the next time she was out with Ethan, even if the place had "Michelin stars" coming out of its arse like a Roman candle. She was going to drive herself home, which had seemed the wise thing to do at the time but now she longed for the escape that too many cocktails would bring. As the night had worn on, the canned music in the wine bar had grown ever more intrusive and annoying.

"Sure, Dad has some misgivings about representing multinationals but ultimately everybody has a price on their heads. Anyone who thinks otherwise is a sap and deserves everything they get, which is most likely to be nothing... well nothing of any value."

"Everybody?"

"Absolutely. Some prices come in higher than others but ultimately, everybody can be bought. Case in point, Dad got me off a misdemeanour charge after a rowdy night at a bar in my youth by greasing the right palms. The state-appointed guy didn't know what had hit him. I was walking before the ink was dry on the charge sheet. If you have access to the best contacts money can buy, you can get away with murder, whether you're a regular guy with a healthy bank balance or a major corporation.

"Have you ever done anything just because you believed in it?"

"Sure! I played college football and I did get an offer to go pro but I can tell you that's a pretty tough life. They start you off cleaning some other guy's boots and you're washed up by the time you're in your thirties. When Dad offered me a place in the family firm I didn't have to think twice. Keep your eye on the gossip pages in your daily newspaper. That's where the big money legal cases are going to be appearing from now on. Your insane divorce laws mean that there are a lot of rich guys willing to pay upfront to protect their wealth and a lot of women who will pay to get their hands on some of it. That's where you and I come in."

"This has got to be something of a backwater for you. Why not London or somewhere like that?"

"Never show your hand unless you're forced too. Being here, I get to learn what's going on without anyone being any the wiser. Then we launch a bid for an established firm in the Capital that's seen better days, we take their clients and get a foothold in London and the UK and off we jolly well go, as you say. Come on, I'll get you another drink."

"Isn't it my shout?"

"Save the money for putting down a payment on a decent car… actually, strike that… wait till you're in the States, we have a family friend who has a dealership. We'll get you a steal."

★

"I suppose, in retrospect, calling them 'blood sucking parasites' wasn't my wisest move. There was no shortage of people willing to stump up but, Jesus, they wanted their pound of flesh back and then some. I would have been paying it off from beyond my own grave."

Kyle put down his cuppa, his mind racing as he pressed the phone closer to his ear. Louise clearly wasn't going to take this knock back in trying to raise the cash for the funeral lying down. She was still emoting.

"Ultimately we can just have the damn thing and I'll work out how to pay for it afterwards."

"I'm not sure about that?" Kyle's heart was sinking "Can't we get some help from the social."

"I'm not having my ex-husband buried a pauper and I doubt

very much whether the bunch of chinless millionaires that run the country now would be sticking their hands very deeply in their tailcoat pockets for his sake anyway. If push comes to shove I can go to my brother. I haven't spoken to the bastard in three years but I dare say I could crow-bar a few grand out of him if I lay on a few tears."

"I wish I could do more."

"Son, you're doing all you can and I know how much that would have meant to Harry." As the call ended, this, in turn, meant a great deal to Kyle.

Chapter 33

Did they have sweet and sour pork in the US? They probably claimed to have invented it, Charlotte thought, as she stuck her spoon into the intoxicating gloop. The imagined threat of its non-availability across the water was a good enough excuse to pig out on a take-away with Dainty at their flat while she had the chance. The food she had eaten the previous night at the wine bar had been so insubstantial as to leave her hungrier at the end of her meal that she had been at the start. As far as she could see, girls in the US were either clinically obese or anorexic enhanced catwalk models.

"You know that you've been trying to get me to accept some rent money?" Dainty said as Charlotte devoured her last spoonful.

"And you put me off and say you'll sort something out later."

"And I put you off and say we'll sort something out later... well I've thought of a way for you to repay me."

"Go on."

"I want to hire you... I want to hire you as a lawyer, solicitor whatever."

Charlotte put down her spoon.

"It'll be a long while before I qualify but... "

"Don't worry, we've got a while before we need to get down to the nitty gritty. I want you to make sure that when Michael gets his compensation it's spent on him and not that scheming cow of an ex-bridesmaid of mine. It'll be a long while before anyone is waving a cheque book about... say you'll do it... be like Jennifer Brown."

"Sorry?"

"Jennifer Brown, the Brief from "Modern Law, the crusading one with the heart of gold and Tourette's."

"I won't have to swear and twitch, will I?"

"No. All you have to do is put the frighteners on "Little Ms Yo-Yo Knickers" before she tries to make off with the loot."

"Well, I guess I owe you."

"Consider yourself hired for your first job… I can help you. It'll give us an excuse to meet up when you leave work.

"Have you forgotten I'm moving to the US?"

"We can do it by internet and web-cam and stuff."

"Actually a letter from a big American firm of lawyers would probably be enough in itself. It would certainly put the fear of God in me."

There would be somewhere in Chinatown that sold sweet and sour pork. New York must have a Chinatown, probably a huge one with bigger portions of sweet and sour pork then anyone could be expected to consume in one sitting. You could bet your life on it.

★

In the days that followed the meeting with the Vicar, Kyle got little in the way of sleep. On the second night he awoke in a cold sweat after barely half an hour dozing. Then it struck him, the thought that had been lying dormant in his head since Harry's heart attack, 'What had happened to 'Baby'? The police had been tipped off anonymously about the body… they must have been in Harry's flat, which wouldn't have been like breaking into "Fort Knox" at the best of times. News of a sudden death would be round an area like that in no time at all. If that was the case then 'Baby' was already long gone to pay for some skanky drug deal or booze… the irony of which wasn't lost on him. He lay back down and tried to close his eyes but the events of the past month swirled round his head. He knew there would be no peace or rest at all until he had been to Harry's to at least attempt to find his sax. He gave sleep one last try to prove it to himself but all he could see was an image of 'Baby' alone and unloved there in the dilapidated bed-sit.

After several deep breaths in the darkness he turned the radio on and caught the news on the World Service. Students had clashed with Police again in London. It was just as well he had got his degree when he had. Jessica Linley, a law student who had been crowned Miss England in September 2010 told the press that she wouldn't be able to afford to go to university if the tuition fees were increased. Perhaps it was for the best that he and Charlotte had split up; paying off five figure sums wouldn't trouble her, not now that he was out of the way, and she could return to the bosom of her family. He sat up. It was just gone two AM. Stumbling across the bedroom in the semi darkness of his bedside light, he took out a black sweater and pulled on a pair of black trousers from the floor. If he was going to break into somewhere he might as well look the part. Ludo had the van for a job so there was nothing for it but to walk the four miles to Harry's bed-sit.

As he made his way into the chill night Kyle began to wonder if Harry's place counted as a crime scene. The coroner's inquest and the post-mortem were already over and anyway he didn't care. He hadn't killed Harry so they could hardly pin that on him. The truth was clear to anyone that had known him; it was Harry who had killed Harry. Not so much murder as manslaughter. As he progressed towards the roughest part of town he found himself being suspicious of every passing stranger. A few drunk revellers on foot, some singing from a take-away shop, taxis ferrying people back to their homes, it all seemed to pose a threat, now that he was about to cross a legal line, all in aid of an old lump of brass with holes in it.

What would his mother say if she knew he was sneaking out in the middle of the night to break into a flat that was decidedly on the wrong side of town? She would kill him and that was only for starters. Harry's death had made him realise that you had a responsibility to people, or at least a responsibility to the people who cared about you. His mum had sacrificed too much bringing him up to let him throw his life away for nothing. The problem was that it wasn't nothing. 'Baby' had been important to Harry and now was to him. He would look for her but he'd be ultra-careful and if anything looked at all dodgy then he'd back off and give up.

'Be careful, our Kyle' his mother used to say. Now he knew why. He'd been nine when his dad died and she'd brought him up alone after that. There hadn't been a lot in the way of money. His dad had been a merchant seaman and she'd given up her cleaning job when she fell pregnant. The one thing she was determined on, more than anything else, was that her only child would have his chance. He smiled; he could bet that jazz musician wasn't on her list but if that's what he'd wanted that was what he'd be. She'd remarried when he was twenty-two, and moved to Liverpool. He really should ring her more often.

He was getting closer to Harry's now and the risk of trouble was increasing exponentially. He imagined some police officer having to break it to his mum that her only son had been found dead whilst trying to retrieve a saxophone called 'Baby' from a squalid, deserted flat. Still, Stuart would calm her down. He was alright, his step-dad, Stuart. He'd been down to see them a few times and he was pleased that his mum had made a new life for herself. They were worth ten of Charlotte's parents, that was for sure.

The nearer to his destination he got, the greater the activity there seemed to be and the younger its participants. There seemed to be little in the way of any police presence, perhaps they had all been drafted down to London and were busy kettling the life out of students somewhere. On arrival at Harry's he hesitated, his heart pounding in his ears. He watched and waited in the shadows as a few dubious looking characters made their way in and out of the building. Eventually he screwed up his courage and headed for the locked main door. There was nothing he could do but wait for someone to leave. This was a vulnerable spot and it was without a doubt the longest five minutes of his life. Eventually two girls who couldn't have been more than fifteen exited the flats. What in the name of God were they doing leaving any building at three in the morning? He put this notion to the back of his mind as he took the offer of the open door. One of the girls, who had enough eyebrow piercings to look as though she intended installing a curtain rail, eyed him suspiciously. He was a stranger around here, he knew it and she knew it. She whispered to her friend and they laughed conspiratorially as they set off into the blackness.

Having gained access he navigated the numerous flights of stairs as quickly as he could, motoring past the doors with overly loud music coming out of them. The mission was to get in, scout about and then get out, job done, conscience clear. He was pretty certain "Baby" would be long gone but at least this way he would know for sure. The door to Harry's bedsit was locked although, from the look of it, someone else had forced the door beforehand. He pushed against it with increasing pressure… it wasn't going to give. Wasn't there something about using a credit card he'd seen on a television programme? Pointless notion really, he didn't have a credit card and in the circumstances he was hardly going to be able to apply and receive one in the next ten minutes. He was still pondering his predicament as two large bikers, helmets in hand walked towards him. He thought it best to look like he was leaving somewhere, rather than trying to get in, as he made to retrace his steps. Just as he came level with them the stockier of the two turned to him.

"She's long gone, man. You're going to have to get yer jump elsewhere."

He could guess easily enough what they thought he was hanging around for. As the men went their way and entered another flat he breathed a sigh of relief but this left him no closer to gaining access to Harry's. He was just about to give it up when a commotion broke out below him. Someone was having a domestic and from the sound of it, it was no holds barred. The increasingly frequent sound of smashing crockery was a testament to the full blooded nature of the dispute. This was, he realised, his best chance. He could take a run at Harry's door and the noise and force would probably be lost in the continuing pagga below him. He took three deep breaths and charged at the door. This first attempt almost put his shoulder out and deposited him on the ground but the second time the door's lock gave way and left him sprawled in the dark flat. He took a few minutes to recover. Whatever he had done to his shoulder, it was going to be as stiff as hell the following day. As long as it sorted itself out in time for the funeral he'd be happy.

From his prone position he could see little from the street lights that shone through the window. He should have brought a torch but really was anyone going to notice if he put a light on, would the lights necessarily work even if he did put them on? Once he had recovered enough he got to his feet and as a precautionary measure attempted to draw the curtains… 'curtain' as it turned out and it only covered half the window. After some fumbling around the walls he found the switch. The lights did work. He could hear his heart pounding through to his ears now. Could you get concussion from a blow to the shoulder? The fight downstairs had ceased and all was deathly quiet. The problem was it was difficult to tell if the place had been ransacked, it looked pretty much the same as the last time he had seen it. There was some police ephemera around, some tape marking out where they had found Harry and some powder he assumed was for fingerprinting but anyone could have tampered with 'the crime scene' if they'd been minded to. It didn't seem as though anything had gone. Kyle sifted through some of the remnants of Harry's life but there was little there of any worth save for the odd rare UK jazz album.

Despite going over the place twice, much as he'd expected there was no sign of 'Baby. There was however, on top of the dusty defunct television set, the picture of Harry and Louise on their wedding day. The photo had clearly had a bit of a polish and someone, presumably Harry, had replaced the broken glass in the frame. Harry had been motivated enough to take it to be repaired. At the end of his days the only two things he had left intact were his wedding photograph and 'Baby', who was now nowhere to be seen. He picked up the photograph. If nothing else he could give it to Louise and it might give her some comfort.

At some point during his second trawl through the room, the fight between the young couple in the flat below kicked off again. Someone was clearly hitting someone else and it sounded like the crockery that had survived the first altercation was being co-opted for the second. It also sounded like both parties were giving as good as they got. He thought about his arguments with Charlotte. They seemed laughably tame by comparison, so much so that he realised that he had actually missed their confrontations... just a bit.

Before he could exit with the lone photograph he saw, beneath the table, a dead mouse next to an antique looking 'chocolate orange' which the tiny rodent had clearly had a go at devouring. He couldn't explain why but, on the spur of the moment, he grabbed a scrap of newspaper and scooped the mouse up. He would bury it somewhere nicer than this hellhole. The tears, which were many, didn't come until he was miles away and on safer ground.

Chapter 34

Kyle didn't bother with bed when he got home. Dawn had already broken. He would try scouring the second hand shops of Sunderland and Newcastle but, deep down, he knew that finding "Baby" was a lost cause. All he could do was hope that she had ended up in the hands of someone who was serious about their music, someone who would take care of her the way Harry had. He patted down the earth on the patch of land outside his flat's main window and then said a short prayer. He felt a bit silly. What would he say if anyone saw him burying a mouse? Actually, on reflection, he was now old enough to do what he damn well pleased and anyone who didn't understand him could get bent. This was, he concluded, a very Harry-like notion.

He washed the dirt from his hands before donning his coat for a visit to 'The Skinners Arms.' He desperately wanted a good showing at the funeral, Harry had his drinking buddies but whether or not they knew of his death he couldn't be sure. He'd already experienced missing the funeral of musicians he'd worked with because he'd heard the news of their death third or fourth hand. He had rung the national press but it hadn't generated anything in the way of coverage; the death of some minor pop star in a drink fuelled car accident had severely dented the chances of getting any kind of obituary worth reading for a genuine talent. If he went to 'The Skinners' later on he could alert some of Harry's old cohorts, those lost souls who Harry would have communed with for years on a daily basis, without ever knowing much about their personal lives. He felt a pang of guilt that he had waited until it was too late before going to what was really one of Harry's favourite haunts. If the man had a natural habitat The Skinners was it.

★

The flat was a sea of bras, tights and other various assorted items of feminine attire. The sudden demise of the washing machine had stymied them with having to wring out their clothes to dry where they could. She would get Dainty a new machine as a moving out present, although she was going to have to watch the pennies if everything was going to go to plan. But if she shopped around then she'd be sure to come up with something, she couldn't leave Dainty's flat looking like a Chinese laundry. The one thing she hadn't regretted spending money on was re-directing her mail. It wasn't cheap but the thought of having to go back to Kyle's flat every few days filled her with dread. She poured herself a cup of tea and began opening her post. A prospectus from Sunderland Faculty of Business and Law had come through, all bright and shiny. It might not be New York City but by God that didn't seem to be stopping them any. How much her life had changed since she had put that letter in the post. The chance to swap stotty cake in Sunderland for pastrami on rye in "The Big Apple" had dropped into her lap. Life could be funny like that, you never knew when the Ford Fiesta of life was going to come across a major detour.

★

It was lunchtime as he walked in to 'The Skinners' and the place was practically deserted. The barman wiped his hands on his apron before pouring him a beer and returning to his Racing Post. It had been a while since he'd had had a beer and he was determined to enjoy at least a part of it before he addressed the real reason for his visit to the pub.

He broke the news at the start of his second pint. "I thought as much" said the barman with a frown. "He'd gone AWOL a few times before but only when the bones of his arse were practically showing through. Other than that he was like clockwork... you'd have to be Kyle then, am I right? They shook hands as the barman poured his own pint and introduced himself.

There was a steady flow of free drink as they talked but not so much that it got in the way of business. The Barman had a small notepad in his apron pocket and a stub of a pencil he took from a drawer.

"I think we can sort something out. I'm sure there'd be a gang of lads willing to step up as pall bearers. There's Bob and Terry, Mr Sinclair, the Bewleys. Actually, forget Mr Sinclair he comes in at around six foot eight. Anyway, rest assured, it won't be a problem.

★

Charlotte was contemplating a second cup of tea when her mobile went. She could tell, from the breathing at the other end, that Dainty was excited about something.

"Have you heard?"

"Go on."

She could barely get the words out fast enough.

"The bastards are downsizing us; five full time posts are for the chop. I told you this would happen, bastards, bastards, bastards. I said, didn't I? I said when we got taken over. They're going to bring in someone from the new 'parent company' and... God... bastards."

Charlotte took a deep breath. "I'll put in a word for you... you're the only one there who has a handle on that place, they lose you and the whole thing will fall apart."

As she put down the phone Charlotte didn't know quite what to feel, trepidation for her friend or relief at having made plans to get out before the shit truly hit the fan. She could have a word with Ethan. He'd make sure that Dainty would be alright. Then again, if she did that some other poor sod was going to get their marching orders. Every year more and more takeovers were putting the squeeze on ordinary people, getting them to do ten per cent more for ten per cent less, all so a few greedy bastards at the top could gold plate their second swimming pool. An uneasy thought that the person at the top of this particular pile was the man she was proposing to work for hit her hard but she quelled it.

★

It was later now but "The Skinners" wasn't the kind of place to get going until other places were thinking of calling it a day. Kyle's visit had been a much more pleasant experience than he had feared, Dave O Driscoll proving himself a more than generous host. There was only one thing that still nagged at his head as he readied himself to leave.

"They're not likely to get pissed and drop the coffin are they?" Kyle was still determined that nothing would go wrong at the funeral.

"I wouldn't concern yourself, I'm quite sure that they'll show Harry the respect he deserves and anyway, would the great man himself not think it fitting if he ended up on the floor on account of the drink, even if it wasn't his own. Relax! It'll be fine… you do realise he held you in high regard?"

With a smile he was almost out of the door when the Barman called him back. "You know, that explains the saxophone horn."

Kyle stopped in his tracks.

"He couldn't bear to be apart from the thing, especially for this length of time."

"You know where his sax is?"

"Yes, he was usually glued to it, never left it at his digs if he wasn't there… took it home with him most nights, unless he was in a really sorry state. So, yes, I was a little surprised when he asked me to keep it by for him. He said if he didn't come in to collect it then you would pick it up. He mentioned something… I didn't quite understand it… something about if you came to collect it then you were good and ready."

Kyle rocked back on his heels. He'd read how a shock could turn your legs to jelly but he'd always considered that poetic licence. Now, sure enough, he knew the truth of it.

"He also said if I ever saw you drunk like him two nights in a row... then I was to kick your arse from one end of Argyle Street to the other."

Dave went into the back room and retrieved the cased saxophone and handed it over.

"You take it now and do it justice for the man."

That evening Kyle phoned his mother. He told her about Harry and their gigs together but not about Charlotte, that could wait.

"I love you, mam." He knew as he rang off that he'd told her before, but this time he knew that he meant it.

★

For once they turned their back on glitz and glamour and opted for the pub around the corner from Dainty's flat. It was quiet and homely and perfect for what felt, more than they would have wished, like a wake. Charlotte felt a degree of guilt to be getting out just in time, especially seeing what the thought of becoming unemployed did to Dainty. They spent the night drowning their sorrows. Charlotte knew there would be at least a few more nights out before she left the country for good but the threat to Peterson partners hung over their heads like a bad smell.

Dainty, as ever, was in favour of direct action involving Molotov cocktails and baseball bats but it just left Charlotte feeling depressed. Dainty remained incandescent.

"I didn't get any say when we were bought out by some faceless, bloodsucking multinational giant. A hundred years on and we're still being bought and sold like property... bastards, bastards."

"There's always the nuclear option, set up your own PR company."

"It's not me really; I'm smart enough to know that you've got to be a real workaholic to get that sort of thing off the ground."

"You could always come with me, just think of it… the two of us together."

"If this had happened a month ago I would have bitten your hand off, but now? I have to stay, even if it's just till I see the lay of the land."

"Michael?"

"Yes, Michael. In sickness and in health… Yadder! Yadder! Yadder! You know the rest."

"But you're not even married anymore."

"I know but that's still not an excuse to behave as badly as he did. I'm not daft. He's never going to be anything like he was and I'm certainly not going to throw myself away on what's left of him. But if I can make a life here and keep an eye on him into the bargain I'll just find it easier to sleep at night. From the look of him it might not be that long a vigil. Anyway we need to change the subject, what about you and lover boy?"

"Who?"

"Don't play dumb with me, the tall guy, drives a flash red car… Well… is it on?"

"Were spending some time together and it's OK."

"Talk about getting blood from a stone. It's… OK? You're going half-way around the world with him and it's OK?"

"I'm going half-way around the world and he happens to be there."

"Well that's quite some coincidence and when you get there, is it on then?"

"When I get there we shall see."

"Christ, don't tease him as much as you're teasing me. I need more vodka."

Charlotte was keen to get off this subject and fast and vodka offered an easy escape route for both of them. She also needed a stiff drink to stop her dwelling on her suspicion that Ethan had been sent into Peterson's with the express intent of sizing the place up for asset stripping.

Chapter 35

In the days that followed finding 'Baby', the planning of the service came together although the amount of work involved came as a surprise to Kyle. Having got to bed at four AM on the day of the funeral, he had set the alarm on both his mobile phone and two alarm clocks. Louise was staying overnight at 'The Skinners' to keep an eye on all concerned. He rose early, bathed, made some final phone calls… Ludo, the vicar, Dave O Driscoll, Ludo again. He was determined that everything would go as smoothly as possible and that the funeral would be a great tribute to Harry. His hair was still wet as he pressed the mobile to his ear and spoke to Louise for the first time that morning.

"How are you bearing up?" He tried to sound as positive as he could in the circumstances. There was a long pause before Louise spoke.

"I'm OK, as long as I keep busy. It's not as if I've been depending on the 'Old Sod' for anything in recent years. Just like Harry to be absent when there's work to be done. Everything's organised for the buffet in the church hall after the crematorium."

"You know I'm just at the end of the phone if you need me. I'll keep it switched on right up until the moment I go into the church."

"No, Kyle, I'll be fine. I'm all sorted. I'm just inspecting the troops."

"The Skinners bar flies?"

"The very same and they've scrubbed up quite well. Lord in heaven, you should have seen the clip of them before I started. But don't worry. Everything is going to be OK."

By ten o clock he was dressed in his best suit. It had seen better days and it was a little shiny in places but he'd had it dry cleaned and all in all he thought he looked pretty good. As he steadied himself on a chair to put on his shoes he realised, for the first time since his gigs as a teenager, that he was shaking like a leaf. After a brief word with himself and a shot of Harry playing "Cherokee" he made for the door but before he could leave his eyes settled on the previous days post. Other than bills and junk mail he received little in the way of daily post, especially since Charlotte had left. Louise, as the official next of kin, had received most of the details regarding the funeral arrangements. It was with a degree of apprehension that he opened the large official looking envelope with a London postmark. He glanced at the elegant font that headed the notepaper "Whitney, Pratt and Malone". Then his eyes scanned the page.

Dear Mr Johnson, Our client, Sir John Lindhope, informs us that you had agreed a contract with him to perform with your jazz quintet on the 13th December 2011 at the Swan public house, Haringey, North London on the occasion of his wedding anniversary. We now understand that, due to circumstances beyond your control, you have broken the said contract.

Our client was looking forward to the performance not least because he wished to conclude an important and somewhat overdue business transaction. During our clients wedding in December1961 a jazz quintet was hired for the sum of £20. Due to circumstances beyond our clients control, i.e. the breakdown of his motor vehicle which necessitated the hiring of another on the way to the wedding, he was unable to pay the band leader, Mr Crabb, the full amount for the band's exemplary performance. Furthermore, it was brought to our client's attention a short time later that Mr Crabb, as band leader and a man of his word, had paid his band members in full, resulting in him being unable to take any payment for the performance himself. In the light of this information our client considers it only good and proper business practice to contribute to Mr Crabb's estate a sum which reflects what he considers Mr Crabb was owed, accounting for inflation and his inconvenience. Please find enclosed a cheque for the sum of £4,568.

Yours faithfully,

Wesley Malone

★

Charlotte gazed at the alarm clock with bleary eyes. Lovely as her bed was, she had a duty to perform and one that couldn't be put off. As she ran the bath she mulled over the previous day's bombshell. Once the previous night's drink had worn off a wave of guilt had hit her. Even through the fog of the alcohol she could tell that Dainty was covering up more pain than she cared to let on. Charlotte didn't like being in a position where she had to lie to her best friend. She positively hated being in such a position. But Ethan, the boy that Dainty admired so much, had sworn her to secrecy and dropping him in it wouldn't do anyone's prospects any good, not least her own. If her own suspicions were right, Dainty would feel terribly betrayed by Ethan and the poor girl had already had enough betrayal in her life. A fresh wave of guilt hit her as she thought about deceiving a friend to advance her own career prospects. She could be there if Dainty needed a shoulder to cry on... at least she'd be there until she had to leave for the States.

★

Kyle had studied every inch of stonework at the entrance to St Dunstan's, having got there hours early in case of any problems.

The weather conditions were what his Dad would have called "dreek" It felt as if the whole world had come out in mourning for Harry as the continuous drizzle coated everything around him. He looked at his watch nervously before starting down the lane from the church. He wanted to help the band, time was pressing but there was no band to help yet. Louise had suggested he travel to the church with her but he knew that he really needed to be on hand from the off, for whatever problems reared their ugly heads at the church. A few mourners began to turn up and although some looked vaguely familiar only two stood out from the small ensemble, the two gents from the gig at the "The Fatted Ox." He knew one of them was called Albert but try as he might he couldn't recall the other. He thought it best to leave them to their own devices. The other one was looking rather grumpy. Besides, he was so tense he could barely speak. It wasn't difficult to guess why one of the gentlemen looked so forlorn. His original investment of fifteen shillings in Harry Crab in 1967 had increased more than six-fold thanks to a recent purchase of two double whiskeys and there was no retrieving it now.

A few more familiar mourners began to appear, some nodding to Kyle as he waited ever more nervously for the band. He checked his phone… nothing. And then a group came around the corner. It was easy enough to spot Harry's drinking companions, men of a certain age heavy with the knowledge that their own 'last orders' might only be one or two rounds away. He checked his watch again.

The mourners were starting to turn up in numbers now, which was a comfort. People were smiling warmly at him, which was touching enough to briefly stop him panicking. The band were now thirty minutes late. He'd give them another ring, they simply couldn't let him down on this one. Obviously something had gone wrong. He decided to move off consecrated ground to allow himself to apply a little more invective to his query. However, the signal was as weak as he was feeling. His fury would have to wait.

He arrived back to see the mourners, not yet inside, fall silent as the cortege turned into the street before making its slow way up to the church. Drizzle continued to fall from the overcast skies. Louise got out of the only car behind the hearse. Clearly this was something she had wanted to face alone or perhaps, more grimly, after Harry there hadn't been anyone else that close to her. They really had been each other's soul mates. For a second he thought about Charlotte but he knew that if he was to have any chance of getting through to the end of the day then all such memories would have to be cast aside. In the absence of anyone else it seemed natural, after a hug, to take Louise by the arm as they progressed to the front of the church. He would wait for a quiet moment in the church before telling her that their financial worries over the funeral were over.

The Vicar gave him a reassuring nod as the last mourners filed into the Church. It was strange how the donning of a dog collar had turned him from a nice bloke he'd had a chat with into a dignitary with an important legal function.

"My Father's house has many rooms, if it were not so I would have told you. I go to prepare a place for you… "

The words drifted over him as he checked his watch. Everything else was just as it should be, the bloody band were the only missing piece of the jigsaw. The pall bearers had clearly had a day off the drink and had benefited from Louise's once over. They were, to a man, turned out like an army regiment on parade for the Queen.

He tried to settle himself by taking in his surroundings. The stained glass, the dusty sandstone, the dark wooden pews, the well-thumbed hymn books none of it made the place look like the natural habitat of the likes of Harry A. Crabb. The December chill in the air cut into his bones. How would he be able to play with no band, his fingers numb with cold and a shoulder that still felt calcified due to the door of Harry's bed-sit?

Soothing organ music was playing unobtrusively as the last mourner took his place. If the organist could manage to perform then he could too. Sitting next to Louise at the front of the church, saxophone at his feet, he realised that it didn't matter, that all he could do now was his best for Harry... that was enough. That said, if he had his way, if the band did show up, there would be another three bodies to bury.

Louise looked every inch the glamorous widow but smaller than he remembered her. She had clearly decided that if this was the last time she would see Harry then she was going to look her very best for him. His nervous scanning of his watch had now gravitated into checking the entrance of the church every five seconds but instead of the band, who he was expecting to arrive, it was Charlotte, who he was not.

She scouted around the congregation before his embarrassed half-wave led her to his row, taking a seat on the other side of him with as little fuss as she could manage. He had no idea how or why she was there but he was pitifully grateful that she was. She'd changed her hair and she now had a look that reminded him of their first dates. The bowling ball in his guts, which had been put to one side from necessity, bounced around causing havoc like never before. She gave his hand a sympathetic squeeze. It was all too much.

The congregation fell silent as the Vicar began to grapple with the task of summing up Harry's life in a few short minutes.

"When I was first asked to perform this service today I was quite genuinely honoured, but also in a very real sense saddened at the death of one of the legendary figures of British jazz. Harold Arthur Crabb was born in Sunderland in 1940. His first encounter with music was at Hendon Junior Mixed School and involved a recorder, which after he had exhausted its potential as a pea-shooter he discovered, to his delight, could be used to play the hit of the day "Sentimental Journey."

An encounter with the works of Charlie Parker inspired his devotion to the saxophone and after a part time job in a pawn shop in Sunderland he was able to buy his own saxophone at thirteen. After a little experimentation he formed his first band "Harold

Crabb's Hot Six". Turning professional at seventeen and moving to London at nineteen, where he soon established a fiery reputation. Indeed, I have several personal recollections of Harry in the clubs of Soho in the Sixties and he was quite a force of nature I can tell you."

Kyle hugged his saxophone case. He couldn't help but see the anxious look he got from the pulpit. Damn the band! The Vicar ran through Harry's illustrious early career with its plaudits and prizes. Again he glanced over. All Kyle could do was give a fretful shrug. It was clear that the first instance of improvisation at this "Jazz Funeral" was going to have to come from the Cleric himself as he elongated his sermon to cover the delay. He took it on like a true pro.

"I first met Harry Crabb in Spinnetti's in Great Portland Street more than forty years ago when I was a much thinner prospect than I am now. I had just experienced him playing some truly wonderful music and after plucking up my courage I approached him and told him of my own rather lame attempts to master a woodwind instrument. He couldn't have been more hospitable and as well as encouraging me in my musical endeavours, once he learned about my ecclesiastical studies at Sion College, he assured me that within forty-eight hours he could provide me with three copies of the Bible personally signed by the author that were in the possession of a close associate of his he referred to as 'Gideon from Hackney Wick'. All that was necessary for me to secure the said items was to advance him the price of two double whiskeys. Though I somewhat doubted the authenticity of the works in question I still found it remarkably easy to succumb to his request."

There was some polite laughter at this, it was clear that the Vicar was one of their own.

"Where the hell are they?" asked Kyle, sotto voce.

"The bibles?"

"No, the band." Charlotte covered her mouth to hide her smile.

"I'm sure they'll turn up." she said and squeezed his hand again.

It was the most reassuring thing that had ever happened to him. And then he heard the sound of the van as someone, probably Ludo, coaxed it through the last part of the journey. It wasn't difficult to imagine steam pouring out from beneath the bonnet, Ludo giving it the 'Last Rites', Barry calculating his share of the petrol and Andy trying to remove the lipstick from his collar, to say nothing of several more earthy stains. Before Kyle could breathe a sigh of relief the band entered the church like men possessed. Each one immaculately dressed, they conveyed the gear through the church like the SAS on manoeuvres. Despite their best efforts, the more quiet and low key they tried to be the louder and more noticeable they became. Kyle looked towards the Vicar, a look of pained relief passing between them.

"If you would care to stand, we will now sing "Devil May Care"… Due to an oversight in "Hymns Ancient and Modern" I've had Mr Harper print it out on a separate sheet."

Kyle relaxed a little and smiled to himself. The organist had clearly never seen or heard "Devil May Care" until that very moment, which lent it a satanic air that the original never possessed but which he was sure Harry would have approved of. The musicians and fans in the congregation proceeded to sing at the tops of their voices.

No one cares for me
I'm happy as I can be
I learn to love and to live
Devil may care.

No cares and woes
Whatever comes later goes
That's how I'll take and I'll give
Devil may care.

When the day is through, I suffer no regrets

I know that he who frets, loses the night
For only a fool, thinks he can hold back the dawn
He was wise to, never tries to revise what's past and gone.

Live love today, love come tomorrow or May
Don't even stop for a sigh, it doesn't help if you cry
That's how I live and I'll die
Devil may care.

As the song progressed the band quietly and efficiently assembled the equipment before they regrouped as Andy gave them the once over to make sure they were presentable. Even Barry allowed himself to be licked into shape before their official appearance before the congregation.

With the song over and the band ready the Vicar looked towards Louise. A quick shake of the head was all that was needed, she couldn't speak and was visibly only just holding it together.

The Vicar continued.

"He had two brushes with Royalty first in 'The Royal Variety Performance of 1966' where he played "Sentimental Journey" for Queen Elizabeth II and again as the personal guest of Her Majesty at Pentonville Prison London in 1971 following a late spot of what might be best described as bodysnatching. Now anyone who ever met Harry would know that jazz was meat and drink to him… well, meat certainly."

A nod from the Vicar was all it took. Taking "Baby" out of its case Kyle moved towards the font as the rest of the band took their places in as reverent a way as they could manage.

"Now, as it says in Chronicles 5:13. 'It came to pass, as the trumpeters and singers were as one, to make one sound to be heard in praising and thanking the Lord; and when they lifted up their voice with trumpets and cymbals and instruments of music, praising the Lord, saying, For he is good; for his mercy endureth for ever'.

I like to think of Harry's music enduring for ever, Harry the man might not be here with us now in this, the physical world, but these days it isn't difficult with all this new technology around to have a little bit of Harry readily to hand, so in truth he's never far away from us. Mr Johnson… "

Kyle held "Baby" nervously. It took a while to get use to a different saxophone, weeks, even month's sometimes, but he knew that he hadn't any option but to play Harry's sax at this, the end. It was quite simply the right thing to do. He'd had a little time with it and he was just going to have to trust to fate. As he looked out at the sizable congregation it began to feel good in his hands, solid and weighty. It would be alright. As he glanced up his eye caught one of the stained glass windows. It showed an angel blowing an elongated trumpet. If Harry had made it to God's right hand, and it was a big if, it would be nice to think of him getting another outfit together.

They were ready to go, sweating and panting perhaps but ready. A smile and a wink from Ludo brought Kyle back to the matter at hand. He moved slowly towards the rest of the band the echo of his footsteps emphasising the hush. Turning to face them he nodded. They were a battle hardened outfit now and ready to perform at their best. Facing the congregation he shut his eyes before he put the horn to his lips but before any sound could issue forth a ring tone shattered the atmosphere as a mobile phone went off. Not for the first time that day he was considering the physical retribution he was going to meet out to the phone's owner at the end of the service before he realised with a chill that it was his phone screeching into the cold air of the building. His phone, in his saxophone case right by Charlotte. Watching intently, Charlotte saw the anguish in Kyle's face and realised at once what she had to do. She grasped the phone and silenced it.

The urgency of this task didn't prevent her from seeing the caller ID, it was the singer Jacqui Drinkwater and it didn't take a genius to work out that whatever else he had done with himself since he had left he had made some sort of contact with her. If only he could have done that when she had been with him, but it was no use contemplating what might have been. Now suddenly someone was talking. It was Ludo.

"That was Harry… he says he wants royalties for all this and in cash, none of that cheque bollocks."

The tension lifted and once the laughter had died down Kyle seriously considered kissing his bass player in front of the entire congregation.

"This" he said as order was restored "is a tune by Harold Arthur Crabb, the best tenor sax player this country has ever produced. Harry, you taught me more than you could possibly imagine and what's more, the boys in the band, we still love you madly."

As the first few bars of "All I ask" reverberated around the church he caught sight of Louise. She had, up to that point, managed to control her grief but now finally succumbed as the tears coursed down her cheeks unchecked.

The band were in full flow and the music was easy and heartfelt. Nothing could stop him now, all that mattered was that they, Harry's band, did justice to him.

The modern hymn to love by Harold Arthur Crabb reverberated around the church as Kyle poured himself into the sax. The whole thing was effortless and the best eulogy they could have provided. After the song's end he said a short prayer of his own prior to the Vicar's final words and the congregation slowly filing out into the Churchyard, where they met with considerably improved weather.

It was over and they had managed it. The band, the Vicar, Louise, Charlotte, Dave O' Driscoll and the Barflies, they had all pulled together and given Harry the send-off he deserved.

Chapter 36

The ending of the drizzle raised Kyle's spirits a little as he mingled with the other mourners. True, Sid Chase hadn't turned up but it didn't come as much of a shock. Probably in the Bahamas' unable to tear himself away from his money, 'his money' being the loot he had syphoned off from Harry and a thousand other innocents like him. But it hadn't exactly spoilt 'the party'. Today was a day for being thankful for what you had and what you had managed to achieve.

"I liked you on that... trombone."

There was a time when Kyle would have gone to great lengths to correct the man in front of him. But the fact that his fellow mourner had enjoyed the music was enough for him these days. He looked four-square into the man's face, his oyster eyes betraying the same forlorn story that Harry's had.

"He told us you were good, he normally didn't have a good word to say about any musician under sixty, or even fifty if it was approaching time at the bar. And if there was anything resembling pop music on in the pub he used to call it "The theme tune to the cretin's club." But he liked you, said you had the calling, deep down inside."

The man patted his heart as he said this, giving a little wheeze at the effort it took. Only one of the mourners seemed not to know anyone else, a dapper gentleman who looked like he wasn't far off his nineties. Kyle went up to him and introduced himself and the man shook his hand warmly.

"Thank you, I liked your band, I liked them very much."

"You can't go wrong with one of Harry's tunes."

"Sorry, you'll have to speak up… I'm a little deaf… he came back a few times, you know, and I gave him a few bob when I could… came back for our twenty-fifth of course, but by then it was all rock and roll but he still got them up and working on the classics. It was a sad day when he left us; still you're not allowed to hang on to them once they've served their sentence, mores the pity."

The man laughed before steadying himself on his walking stick and continuing. "He brightened up the whole place."

Slowly it dawned on Kyle that the man in front of him was someone from the prison where Harry had done his time.

"I was in charge the night he accused the guitarists from E Wing of murdering "Mack the Knife"… almost caused a full scale riot."

The man began to laugh again and Kyle saw his chance to introduce him to the other mourners. It wasn't out of the bounds of possibility that there were other 'old lags' in attendance. But the 'Governor' seemed a genial enough fellow to get on with just about anybody… very Harry.

Eventually he managed to free himself from the pack and made his way over to Louise, who had been waving off what seemed like the oldest mourner there. Partially sighted and frail, he had clearly made a big effort to be there. Kyle helped to get the elderly gent into a taxi before he addressed Louise.

"Are you OK?"

"I'm fine now, now it's all over, I truly am." She sighed and looked a little wistfully at the church.

"For almost thirteen years I've wondered where Harry was… I was always going to get in touch with him when the dust had settled, in a week, a month, as soon as life got less complicated and I had some spare time. Now, I'll never get to slug it out with the obstinate bastard again. What I wouldn't give to have a real go at him now."

She hugged Kyle and he readily gave in to it.

"The music in the church said everything that was best about Harry. Thank you."

"I'm sorry I dredged all this up for you."

"No, no… I can't deny that it's brought me low… look at me. I haven't cried this much since Rangers lost seven one in the Scottish League Cup. I was only six years old and my dad and my three brothers were already sobbing before I started to blub. But this… "

She tried to smile, but he could see it wasn't easy.

"Kyle you have to understand that this was all for the good, it was how it was meant to be. If you hadn't brought us together before the old devil walked out on us then I really would have been damned. We got to see each other and make our peace, just the two of us and just in time. I couldn't bear to think of how I would feel now if we hadn't done that."

She hugged him again and gave way a little in a way that reminded him of his mother after his own father had passed away all those years ago. They parted with a promise that they would meet up together soon and that she would come to their next gig. No words were necessary when he handed over the photograph from their wedding day in the restored frame and the letter from Sir John Lindhope with the cheque for £4,568 inside. He would tell her another time how he had come by the picture and how, in his last days, Harry had repaired it.

Charlotte sat alone in the church. Despite not knowing Harry Crabb, it had been an emotional event, even before her own affairs of the heart were dragged into it. Churches, she reckoned, were probably best left as just that, rather than being turned into fancy restaurants. She had wanted to leave, needed to leave, but she wanted to wait for the right moment before going. She had done her duty and she was glad of it. She wasn't sure if she believed in God but she said a short prayer for them all before she left and walked out into the fresh air. There were still a lot of mourners milling around chatting and organising travel arrangements for the crematorium. It was through the elderly throng that she saw him come towards her. Not to be outdone she met him half way on shaky legs. She didn't know whether to kiss him or shake hands and they ended up like two snooker players after a close fought match. Now that the drama of the funeral was over it was awkward and she knew they were on dodgy ground again.

"You heard about Harry then? I hadn't expected to see you. I was going to call but… "

"Andy rang and told me. He thought you might need a bit of moral support in the circumstances. You don't mind that I came?"

"No, no… far from it."

"How are things?" "Good, good, fine, things are fine. Well apart from… you know… obviously… "

"That's nice; that it's OK… apart from… was it sudden?"

"From what I've been able to piece together from the Police and Dave, the landlord of his local, he'd spent the night busking and singing, had a drink, went home, sat down to the sandwiches Dave had given him and died."

"I suppose there are worse ways to go."

Kyle looked at her, suddenly afraid of what he might say if his emotions ran away with him. He was relieved when she spoke.

"I heard about your debauched gig in Teesside. The Ladies Night". Carly from our HR department was there. Said it was unbelievable, she's talked of nothing else… you won't be doing the London gig then?"

"It was scheduled for today… but there was no real point to it any more, not once Harry was… I couldn't have gone down there without him. We were his family in the end. I couldn't take off to London on the day of his last hurrah, it wouldn't have seemed right."

He fell silent for a moment and then concluded.

"I was about to say life's like that but I suppose what I mean is death's like that. Just when it seemed Harry's life was on an upturn he goes and checks out."

Charlotte smiled warmly as she spoke.

"The week he died he'd been playing at the top of his form with an audience of a thousand appreciative randy women chanting his name. Two months earlier he might have just died alone and forgotten in his flat."

"I see you haven't lost your ability to see the best in any given situation."

"You know me. I'm an uptown, up-tempo woman… "

He smiled at the memory from their shared past, a time when they had drunk themselves silly after a student ball gig in Durham University before dancing to the cheesiest disco music imaginable.

"Andy reckons he can get me some work with his agency. You know promotions and stuff."

"OK, but no big shoes and no red noses."

"Who told you?"

"Andy himself. He tried it on with Dainty last week and I finally recognised the woeful chat up lines."

He could handle this, they were beginning to adjust to their new situation, they were getting on OK. But he didn't want it to end; he was looking for something, anything to prolong their conversation. "If there's anything you need… from the flat I mean, I could help you or make myself scarce or whatever."

The moment the words left his mouth he regretted them.

"Oh! Right… yes… OK… well, whenever you want."

"I mean, not right away. Not unless you want to get it sorted now… really, whenever suits you."

"Yes. Whatever, if you want. I could do it now. Get it over and done with."

She could see what he was doing. At some point she was going to have to tell him she was leaving for America but not now. This was not the time.

He had that slightly bemused look that she recognised from their first few dates as he gave her a peck on the cheek. She realised now that she wanted the pain of this to be over for both their sakes and as quickly as possible. He was still speaking.

"You've still got your keys, haven't you?" She nodded a little sadly.

"Yes. I'll leave them on the coffee table, shall I, when I've finished?"

This was it, if one of them didn't say something now there was no turning back. But she knew she hadn't got the stomach to stay any longer and she was adamant she wasn't going to cry in front of him. Before anything else could happen, Ludo's head popped up from behind the stricken van.

"She's a goner that's for sure. I've got you a lift to the Crematorium but you'll have to come now."

The spell around them broken, Kyle headed towards his band mate, turning towards Charlotte a last time.

"I'm going to have to get off to the crematorium and then there's a buffet in the Church Hall afterwards. Are you going… ?"

Charlotte shook her head.

"I have a lot to do."

She didn't want to lie, she did have a lot to do but this wasn't the time to tell Kyle that she was preparing to up sticks and locate across the other side of the Atlantic. He had coped with the funeral far better than she imagined but there was no need to add to his burdens now. She had wanted to support him for as long as she could for the day but the lead weight she had carried in her guts since they split had been doing summersaults since the night before. She'd done what she'd could and got through the service. She'd managed to stand by him this one last time. It came and went, the lead weight, and she pretty much had a handle on it but when she was face to face with him its presence was unbearable. With a quick wave to the band she was back in the red Ford Fiesta that looked like it belonged to the same ancient tribe as their van.

Chapter 37

Something resembling sunshine was threatening to appear as Charlotte headed towards Kyle's flat. She had contemplated going straight back to Dainty's. The funeral had left her feeling drained, but ultimately she realised the best policy was to strike while the iron was hot. If she didn't get her possessions now it was only going to get progressively more painful and embarrassing. She also needed to be considering storage before she embarked to the States.

As she drove towards the flat she remembered the first time she had taken the route and how appalled she had been by the chaos that Kyle called home, despite the fact that he claimed to have "tidied it up a bit". It had smelt heavily of air freshener and she couldn't decide whether she was touched that he had bothered or appalled that he had needed to.

She was still reminiscing as she turned up his street and saw a small, highly animated figure on the doorstep of the flat. She pulled up, a little unsure as to whom he was or why he was there. He looked slight, couldn't have been any more than eleven, twelve at most, wearing clothes that suggested there was an older brother somewhere along the line. What was not debatable was his overwhelming excitement. She had never seen anyone quite so possessed of joy. He leapt up and down, laughing one minute, singing breathlessly the next as she searched for the keys in her handbag. He held a slip of paper in his right hand which, in between waving, he held out in full view as she stepped out of the car.

This, she eventually realised, must be Craig. She considered the diminutive scrap in front of her, freckled and thin, squinting through glasses held together with electrical tape. It wasn't so easy to think of his lessons as a drain on their resources when he was standing, blinking at the light, in front of her. She bit her lip; she was going to have to at least be polite.

"Is he in, is he in. I've been four times today already. That's eleven thousand, two hundred and thirty-two steps."

"Are you Craig?" He nodded frantically.

"Kyle's working away with the band." Something told her instinctively that any mention of funerals was probably not a wise move.

"I got it. I got it. I passed… I passed… I passed my exam."

Was that what this was all about? It wasn't exactly a cure for cancer he'd found. Still at least there was one person around that day who was excessively happy.

"Well done, you. Why don't you come inside? Would you like something to drink, orange juice, coke?" She didn't know what else to do. It was starting to rain again and he hadn't got anything with him resembling a coat yet he seemed completely oblivious to the December chill.

Within a minute Craig was in the kitchen, practically inhaling a large drink of orange squash. The kitchen wasn't perfect but it was a damn sight more habitable than the last time she had seen it.

"Are you his wife?"

"No, not exactly."

"Do you live here? How old are you? I'm thirteen. My Nan has one of them." He pointed at the toaster. "He's the best isn't he? I mean on the saxophone." He started to make an approximation of a saxophone sound with his thumb in his mouth. "Are you his girlfriend? You're pretty but not as pretty as Miss Hartley. I like Kyle, he's the best. My last saxophone teacher didn't like me."

"Oh!"

"Smelly Mrs Langford doesn't either. She kept putting in bad reports on me."

As he spoke he looked around the room and began to pick things up at random, examining them at close quarters.

"Are you hungry Craig? When did you last eat?" The least she could do was send him away with a full belly. After a perplexing question and answer session it was agreed that she would make him a sandwich, no butter, marge, cheese or coleslaw but otherwise anything. It was as she rooted around in Kyle's under-stocked fridge that it finally hit her. She realised what had been nagging away at her since she had left Ethan in the wine bar. It might possibly be true, as had been proclaimed, that "We're all in this together" but that was only in as much as the emperor would be in the Coliseum as the lions picked off the Christians. Dainty was probably smart and savvy enough to hang on to her job but a lot of the others would be finding themselves on the outside of the machinery that these days seemed only to exist to siphon money up to those at the very top. Ethan might believe that everything had a price on its head Peterson Partners and himself included but what she had failed to state in any meaningful way in the wine bar was that she did know of at least one person who was immune to the mighty Dollar and the Pound Sterling, and the Euro, and the Yen and just about every other currency for that matter. He might be maddeningly stubborn, self-obsessed and economically illiterate but whatever else you could say about Kyle, he couldn't be bought.

Craig was by now bouncing up and down, arms firmly by his side as he tried to touch the ceiling with the top of his forehead.

"Kyle's my friend. There's Kyle... my Mam... Doctor Jacobs... and Little Tess. Are you going to get married, I could play the saxophone and Kyle could have a rest. Dr Jacobs says I'm clamorous. Do you play top trumps? Miss Hartley was married but her husband ran away. She was at school and she cried... Kyle's the best isn't he?"

Epilogue

Kyle surveyed the Church Hall and loosened his tie. For the first time that day he could relax. A lot of the mourners had stayed on but he and Louise had prepared for that. Now that he had given her the cheque from Sir John they could be a little more relaxed about giving Harry the send-off he merited. The Bar Flies, who had looked so haunted in the church, were now in a more jovial spirit and bursts of raucous laughter permeated the general din. Andy had used his contacts to get the booze cheap and the current Mrs Valentine was manning the tea and coffee as the band worked their way round the mourners making pleasantries. He was proud of them now. True, they weren't the greatest musicians on the planet but they were a damn sight more ship-shape than they had been before they had met Harry. They all were. Everything seemed to be running fine without him and now his overwhelming urge was to get away, even if it was just for a while. Missing the gig for Jacqui Drinkwater, Harry's death and seeing Charlotte look so breathtaking had all been a bit too much to cope with in one go.

At least he could address the problem of the van's engine. Ludo had managed to pick up a "Haynes manual for Transit Vans" on EBay and after a quick root through the vehicle's general detritus he found it, wedged between the spare wheel and a decaying meat pie. A quick flick through the index and he was in business, although it looked mind bogglingly complex. His good jacket was off in an instant before he rolled up his sleeves and went into battle. Over the course of the next hour he struggled with the engine aided by occasional visits from the band bearing food and drink. He was guts-deep in the engine and straining to get to the fan belt as he became aware of another presence close by. He wondered if it was too much to hope that it was someone with a comprehensive knowledge of the Essex V4 two litre petrol-engine when he heard her voice.

"I'll give you a clue. I always checked the thrust bearings first."

Before he could answer or even turn around two arms snaked around his middle in the familiar embrace that was Charlie. The touch was warm and reassuring although his first instinct was that he mustn't cry.

Charlotte felt him breathe deeply under her embrace and she allowed her head to rest against his back. Try as she might, she had been unable to forget that mixture of soap and marmite that was Kyle's natural aroma as she had lain awake at night, alone on Dainty's camp bed. There was also a hint of the aftershave she had bought him two Christmases earlier, which he had rationed to using on special occasions. But that wasn't the thing that caught her attention; there was something different now, a new note in this make-up. At least new to Kyle. She had come across it before in her youth but she couldn't quite place it, not now, not on him. But she knew instinctively that it made her feel blissful. It was only when she caught full sight of his face that it all fell into place, that mixture of elbow grease, citronella and spindle oil that came from a can of Three-In-One which had followed in the wake of everywhere that Mr Sykes had gone.

Kyle eventually straightened up and twisted around to speak.

"I must admit it is proving a bit tricky."

"I could help. I do have some experience."

"We could be here for some time."

"I'm not planning on going anywhere."

He wrinkled his nose, obviously he couldn't use his hands; they were covered in gunk and she was wearing a white blouse so he used his arms to hug her as best he could, inadvertently smearing her face with the oil in the process. They kissed and it was good but his mind was racing. The van was going to have to last them. Apart from anything else he had three schools to get round now as a peripatetic teacher. The pay was pretty good and it still left him time for gigs and practicing. He kissed her again before he spoke.

"Probably best I get the hang of this. We can't have you turning up in court everyday with your wig covered in sump."